The Dead Walk

"Observe."

He held one palm over the other
and spoke an incantation.

An image appeared, and into it he projected
the memory of what his brief contact
with the Astral Plane had revealed:

A glimpse into a future in which the warriors
of Sshamath fought, died, then rose to fight again—
against their former comrades.

Wave upon wave of undead,
spreading through the Underdark,
overwhelming all like a rushing tide,
feeding and growing with each new army
sent against it.

As the vision unfolded, a single word
pealed like a bell:

Defeat.

The New York Times
Best-selling Author

THE
LADY PENITENT

Book I
Sacrifice of the Widow

Book II
Storm of the Dead

Book III
Ascendancy of the Last
June 2008

FORGOTTEN REALMS

LISA SMEDMAN

STORM
OF THE
DEAD

THE
LADY PENITENT

BOOK
II

Wizards
OF THE COAST

The Lady Penitent, Book II

STORM OF THE DEAD

©2007 Wizards of the Coast, Inc.

Cover art by Wes Benscoter

First Printing: September 2007

9 8 7 6 5 4 3 2 1

ISBN: 978-0-7869-4701-0
620-20133740-001-EN

U.S., CANADA,
ASIA, PACIFIC, & LATIN AMERICA
Wizards of the Coast, Inc.
P.O. Box 707
Renton, WA 98057-0707
+1-800-324-6496

EUROPEAN HEADQUARTERS
Hasbro UK Ltd
Caswell Way
Newport, Gwent NP9 0YH
GREAT BRITAIN
Save this address for your records.

Visit our web site at www.wizards.com

Also by Lisa Smedman

HOUSE OF SERPENTS

Book I
Venom's Taste

Book II
Viper's Kiss

Book III
Vanity's Brood

R.A. SALVATORE'S
WAR OF THE SPIDER QUEEN

Book IV
Extinction

SEMBIA:
GATEWAY TO THE REALMS

The Halls of Stormweather

Heirs of Prophecy

PRELUDE

The *sava* board hung in a space between the planes, a bridge between the realms of two rival goddesses.

On one side was Lolth's realm—the Demonweb Pits—a blasted ruin of blackened rock, over-shadowed by a dark sky the color of a bruise. Eight pinpoints of ruddy light shone down with a fitful glow, turning blood-red the spiderwebs that drifted on the wind. Souls drifted with them, their agonized screams and howls rending the air.

On the other side was Eilistraee's realm, a forest dappled with light and shadow. Thick branches screened the moon, the only source of illumination. It hung in the sky, unmoving, a blade-straight line bisecting its face. Half illuminated, half in shadow—like the moonstone fruits that hung from the branches below.

Songs drifted through the woods on which the half-moon shone: a multitude of duets. High, female voices paired with mid-range male voices. Yet some of the male voices had an edge. They sounded strained, pain-choked, as though forced to sing in a higher range than they were accustomed to. Other male voices droned in low bass, obstinately repeating the same phrase over and over: a melodic background at odds with the rest of the music.

Eilistraee's realm had once been a place of perfect harmony. It had grown larger, made stronger by a recent influx of souls. Yet that potency was the product of an uneasy compromise.

The goddess, too, had changed. Eilistraee stood naked, her ankle-length hair the only covering for her velvet-black skin. Her hair had once been uniformly silver-white but was streaked with black. Her twin swords floated in the air, one at each hip. One still shone silver bright, but the other had turned the color of obsidian. Across the lower half of the goddess's face was a faint shadow, a trophy of her recent victory: Vhaeraun's mask.

As Eilistraee waited for her opponent to move one of her *sava* pieces, a hint of red glinted in her otherwise moon-white eyes.

Lolth, seated on her black iron throne and currently wearing her drow form, smiled at the flash of irritation in her daughter's eyes. Instead of making the move she'd been contemplating, Lolth lifted a hand and watched, idly, as a spider spun a web between her splayed fingers. Other spiders scurried across her dark skin or nested in her long, tangled hair. One of these nests erupted like a boil as she dallied, releasing a cloud of tiny red spiders into the air. They drifted away on the wind, hair-thin strands of web trailing in their wake.

When the web between her fingers was complete, Lolth flicked the spider away and licked its spinnings from her fingers, savoring both the stickiness and her opponent's rising irritation.

"Patience, daughter." Her chiding voice reverberated with the echoes of her other seven aspects. "Patience. Just look where your brother's rash actions brought him to."

Lolth gestured. A window opened onto the Astral Plane. In the distance of that silver void, moldering fragments drifted: the body of a god, sliced to pieces by Eilistraee's swords. A fragment that might have been the head groaned faintly, then stilled.

Lolth feigned sadness as she stared at the corpse. "No redemption for him. Not now."

Eilistraee's jaw clenched. Beneath the shadow of her brother's mask, her lips were a thin line. But she would give her mother no satisfaction.

"Sacrifices are sometimes necessary," she said. "Vhaeraun gave me no choice."

Lolth waved her hand again, and the window closed. She stared across the *sava* board at Eilistraee, one eyebrow mockingly raised. "You're getting more like him, every day," she taunted. "Too 'clever' for your own good. It won't be long, now, before you make a similar mistake."

That said, she casually leaned forward and picked up one of her Priestess pieces. The piece—shaped like a drow female, but with a bestial face and eight spider legs protruding from its chest—cringed under her touch. Lolth moved it next to another of her pieces, one that had remained motionless for millennia—a piece that had not been moved, in fact, since the game began. That piece, a massive Warrior with bat wings and horns, blazed to life as Lolth's retreating hand brushed against it. Lurid orange flames danced over its black body and its wings unfolded with audible creaks.

"Not yet, my love," Lolth whispered, her breath heavy with spider musk. "Not yet."

The demonic Warrior piece stilled. Its wings folded back against its body. The flames turned a dull red, then vanished.

Eilistraee, studying the board, spotted a path along its web-shaped lines that would allow her to capture the piece that had just stirred. She could do it with one of her Priestess pieces. Taking out Lolth's Warrior would involve several preparatory moves, some of them risky feints, but ultimately the Priestess piece could move into a position where it could strike the Warrior from behind.

As Eilistraee made the first of those moves, a ripple formed at the place where her domain met Lolth's. Both goddesses started and looked up from their game. Eilistraee's perfect nose crinkled at the scent that seeped from the ripple as it solidified into a dark crack—a sickly sweet odor, laden with millennia of dust and ash—the scent of death.

A voice whispered from the crack between the domains. It had the sound of something produced by vocal cords long since gone tight and dry. "You play . . . without me?"

A burst of cackling laughter followed. It danced at the edge of madness, then was gone.

Eilistraee's and Lolth's eyes met across the board.

"Kiaransalee," Eilistraee whispered.

Lolth cocked her head in the direction of the disturbance and raised one eyebrow. "Shall we let her join our game?"

Eilistraee gave careful thought to the question. Kiaransalee, goddess of vengeance and queen of the undead, hated Lolth as much as Eilistraee pitied her. The once-mortal necromancer queen had, after her ascension to demigod status, joined Lolth's assault on Arvandor, but her fealty to the Spider Queen was fitful and forced. Since Lolth's assumption of Moander's hegemony of rot, death, and decay, Kiaransalee had smoldered with jealousy—and had lashed out in anger more than once against her former ally. If Kiaransalee entered the game, Lolth would have to watch her back.

"On whose side would you play?" Eilistraee asked.

"Neither side," Kiaransalee croaked. Another cackle of laughter burst from the gap between realms: a dry sound, like bones rattling in a cup. "I'll play against both of you at once."

Eilistraee nodded. She'd expected this. Kiaransalee knew that Eilistraee and Lolth would never unite their forces. And her hatred of both of them ran deep. Eilistraee felt certain it would be a three-way game to the bitter end.

Lolth swept a hand over the board and its hundreds of thousands of pieces, and spoke to Kiaransalee. "What use have you for the drow, banshee? Have you suddenly developed a taste for the living?" She scoffed. "I thought you preferred to line your bed with the husks of the soulless. After all . . . who else would have you?"

Inarticulate rage boiled out of the crack between realms. Abruptly, it switched to wild, mocking laughter. "*Spider* Queen," it burbled. "Who else would have *you*, but insects?"

Lolth reclined lazily on her throne. "You betray your ignorance, banshee," she retorted. "Spiders are not insects. They are creatures unto themselves. Arachnids."

A pause, then, " 'Arachnids' they may be, but they squish just as messily as insects."

Fury blazed in Lolth's coal-red eyes. "You wouldn't dare," she hissed.

"I just did," Kiaransalee gloated. "Squish. Squish squish." A babble of taunting laughter followed. "Aren't you sorry now, for yanking my domain into yours?"

Eilistraee interrupted the tirade. "Let her play."

Lolth looked up sharply. Her eyes bored into Eilistraee's for several moments. Then her gaze drifted to the *sava* board. She pretended to look at it idly, but Eilistraee could tell that Lolth was studying the pattern of pieces intently. The Spider Queen wasn't stupid. She would know what Eilistraee hoped: that Kiaransalee's chaotic moves would provide a screen for Eilistraee's own, more careful maneuvers.

Lolth smiled. A spider the size of a bead of sweat crawled across her upper lip, then disappeared into the crack between her parted teeth. "Yes, indeed," she breathed. "Why not?"

"With Ao as witness," Eilistraee added. "And under the same terms that we agreed to. A contest to the death. Winner take all."

Kiaransalee's voice issued from the crack between realms. "To the death," she chortled.

The crack widened, revealing the goddess and her realm.

Kiaransalee was horrible to look at, gruesome as any mortal lich. Her coal-dark skin stretched tight over a near-skeletal face, and her hair was lusterless as bleached bone. The rotted silks that hung from her wasted body had faded to gray, mottled with mold. A multitude of silver rings hung loose on her bony fingers. She sat cross-legged on a slab of marble: a tombstone whose inscription had been obscured by moss. A field studded with other gravestones stretched behind it, under an ice-white sky.

Kiaransalee pulled a maggot from her flesh and shaped its soft, dough-like mass into a Mother piece, giving it the form she wore when appearing before her worshipers: that of a beautiful drow female. As it darkened to black, she placed it on the *sava* board, then swept an arm in a scythe-like motion. A host of lesser pieces appeared in the crook of her arm: skeletal Slaves, slavering ghoul Warriors, lich-like Wizards, and Priestess pieces in black robes with hooded cowls. These she sprinkled across the board, letting them fall like a scattering of ashes over an open grave.

"My move!" she cried. Leaping from her tombstone, she shoved two pieces forward at once, neatly flanking the Priestess piece Eilistraee had planned to use, leaving it with only one avenue of escape: one that would force it to move against the Warrior sooner than Eilistraee had planned.

Eilistraee turned her eyes to the space above the *sava* board. "You permit this?" she raged.

Ao was silent.

Lolth laughed. "She is playing against both of us at once, daughter. Two moves seems only fair."

Eilistraee's mask hid the thin line of her lips.

Lolth leaned forward. "My turn, now." Deliberately, savoring Eilistraee's growing unease, she picked up the demonic Warrior piece. She held it up for Eilistraee to see, then slid it in front of the Priestess, cutting off her line of escape.

Eilistraee fumed. If her Priestess piece went down, a host of other pieces would follow. Lolth's Warrior, once again animate and blazing with unholy glee, was poised to cut a swath right through them.

Was there no move she could make to prevent this?

Her gaze fell on a piece that stood well outside her House. Half off the board, it appeared to have been taken out of play. But in truth, it had not yet been removed. If her opponents made the moves she expected, the path between it and one of Kiaransalee's most important pieces would soon be clear.

Several of Eilistraee's own pieces would have to be sacrificed along the way. But if it worked, the result would be worth it.

She moved a Priestess forward—a piece that wore Vhaeraun's mask. It was a less than perfect move, one that would probably be easily countered. But it would buy her time. If she were lucky, it would serve as a distraction for the move she planned to make—the one that would end this game.

CHAPTER 1

The Month of Alturiak
The Year of the Bent Blade (1376 DR)

W here are you going?"

At the sound of the voice, Q'arlynd froze. The words had come from a distance, carried on the wind. They held a note of alarm, even panic. Warily, he looked around but saw nothing. The moon was a mere sliver, but it provided ample light for his drow eyes. The moor stretched flat in all directions. The low jumbles of stone that dotted it—the ruins of ancient Talthalaran—offered little concealment, except to someone lying prone. The shifting mists were another matter. Even with summer approaching, they rose from the ground every night.

"Where are you going?"

There it was again, but from a slightly different direction. It sounded like the same voice: high and squeaky, not recognizably female or male, with a strange gulp between each word. Like the words were hic-cupped out.

Q'arlynd reached into his belt pouch and drew out a pinch of gum arabic. As he rolled it between his fingers, he spoke the words of a spell. His body shimmered and vanished. He teleported away from the spot where he'd stood, materializing a good hundred paces from the foundation of the ruined tower he'd just searched.

"Stand and fight, you coward!" the voice gulped.

"I will," Q'arlynd breathed, unfastening the ties on his wand sheath. "If you just show yourself."

The wind shifted, wafting a foul odor from the direction of the voice.

"Stand and . . ."

The voice came closer.

"Coward!"

Closer still.

"Stand and fight, you. Fight you."

Almost there . . .

"Coward!"

There! It wasn't a drow, but a surface creature—one Q'arlynd had never seen before. Fast as a hunting lizard, it hurtled out of the mist toward him. It was enormous, its torso almost twice as long as Q'arlynd was tall. It had four legs that ended in hooves, a body covered with short brown hair, and a tufted tail that lashed behind it as it charged. Its wedge-shaped head had triangular, erect ears, and eyes that glowed a dull red. Drool streamed from its panting mouth. Despite Q'arlynd's invisibility, the creature charged straight for him. Into the wind. It must have picked up his scent.

Q'arlynd leaped into the air and was borne upward by his House insignia. Its magic would hold him above the monster while he blasted it from a safe distance.

The creature was fast, with powerful legs. It sprang after Q'arlynd with a leap that would have made a hunting spider envious. By scent alone it found him; jagged teeth clamped onto the hem of Q'arlynd's cloak. The creature hung for a moment, eyes blazing, dragging Q'arlynd down with it. Then the cloak tore, sending Q'arlynd tumbling upward. The creature fell to the ground, a now-visible chunk of the cloak in its teeth.

It spat the material out, then circled below Q'arlynd, nostrils flaring as it tried to pinpoint his scent. Q'arlynd wondered how it could smell anything over its own stench. The monster stank like a catch of blindfish left to rot.

He drew a fur-wrapped rod of glass from his pouch and aimed it at the creature. As magical energy crackled to life at its tip in a haze of purple sparks, the creature halted, cocked its head to the side, and gulped out more words.

"Where? Are you? Eldrinn?"

Q'arlynd completed his spell. Lightning streaked into the creature and blasted it. The beast staggered and twisted its head back to stare at the blackened, oozing wound in its flank. Then it glanced up at Q'arlynd, who was no longer invisible. Though staggering on its feet, it still snarled.

"Take a good look," Q'arlynd said as he sighted along the rod a second time. "It'll be your last."

A second streak of lightning smashed the creature onto its side. It quivered for a moment, legs stiff and trembling, then collapsed.

Still levitating, Q'arlynd reached into his pouch for a piece of leather stiffened with beeswax. Touching it to his chest, he cloaked himself in invisible armor. Only then did he drift to the ground. He stood, braced and ready, half expecting another of the creatures to come hurtling at him out of the mist, but all was quiet. At last he walked to the fallen creature and nudged it with his boot. It was dead.

Q'arlynd tucked the glass rod back in his pouch and ran a hand through his shoulder-length white hair, combing it back from his forehead. When he'd passed this way three months ago with the priestesses of Eilistraee, neither Leliana or Rowaan had mentioned creatures like it. They'd warned that the High Moor was home to orcs and hobgoblins, as well as the occasional troll, but they hadn't said anything about four-legged predators that could talk.

Though perhaps "talk" wasn't the word for it, exactly. The creature had uttered the same phrases over and over, sometimes in fragments, as if repeating something it had heard. Q'arlynd suspected it was imitating the panicked voice of someone shouting for a companion who, it would seem, had left that individual behind to become the creature's next meal.

Q'arlynd decided to see if his guess was correct. He drew his dagger and sliced open the monster's belly. He had to pinch his nose shut as he worked—whatever the creature was, its flesh oozed an oil that *stank*. A moment later, his guess was confirmed. A severed foot spilled out of the creature's stomach with the rest of its recent meal. Not yet fully digested, the foot had skin as black as Q'arlynd's own.

The creature *had* eaten a drow, and not too long ago. Someone else had been out on the moor that night.

One of Eilistraee's priestesses, en route to the Misty Forest with a petitioner? The foot offered no answers: it might have belonged to a male or a female. Q'arlynd hoped it wasn't Rowaan or Leliana who'd been eaten—that it hadn't been one of them who had been calling for the missing Eldrinn. Q'arlynd hadn't seen them since his impulsive departure from the Promenade. He'd spent all of his time on the High Moor since then, searching—aside from brief teleportations away to raid surface towns for supplies.

He glanced back at the foundation he'd been inspecting for the past three nights. It was identical to the ruined foundation he'd seen during his trip across the moor with Rowaan and Leliana three months ago. Like that other ruin, this one was also the base of a wizard's tower; it had the same arcane symbol on the floor. Q'arlynd had decided that it must have once been a teleportation circle. The amber that had filled the grooves in the floor had been destroyed millennia ago, when the killing storms had been unleashed on ancient Miyeritar, turning it into the blasted wasteland that was the High Moor.

Q'arlynd sighed. Two months of searching through the ruins of Talthalaran for even so much as a magical trinket, but without success. He'd searched the first ruined tower thoroughly, working outward from its foundation in a careful spiral, but found nothing. No secret passages leading below to hidden treasure troves of ancient wizards. This second tower, on what had been the outskirts of the city, had looked just as promising but was proving equally unfruitful.

He reminded himself that it had taken Malvag nearly a *century* to find the scroll that had opened a gate between two rival gods' realms. Yet Q'arlynd couldn't help but believe he'd come full circle. He'd learned much—that a male could seize power on his own terms, rather than by standing in the shadow of a powerful female—but where had that gotten him? Scavenging in the ruins, just as he'd been doing before he left Ched Nasad. The difference, of course, was that now he scavenged for himself, and not for a noble House that regarded him as little better than a common lackey. At first, this sense of independence had sustained him, but the end result was the same. Though he might be able to keep everything he found, the sum total of what he'd found, so far, was nothing.

Q'arlynd had, of course, known full well that there would be little left to pick from the bones of the ancient city; it had not only been blasted flat by the Dark Disaster, but had lain in ruins for more than eleven thousand years. Yet he'd been hopeful—and vain enough to think that only he had spotted the symbols in the ruined towers' foundations which marked them as belonging to wizards. He realized that others would have been drawn to that spot, too. Come to think of it, the foot he'd just found might have belonged to a fellow wizard, a rival in the scavenging game.

There was one sliver of hope. Eldrinn, whoever he—or she—might be, had probably run off, judging by the words the surface creature had mimicked. But the body of Eldrinn's companion, minus its foot, likely still lay on the moor. If that companion had unearthed anything and been abandoned in a hurry by Eldrinn, those spoils might still be with the body.

Q'arlynd wiped his dagger clean and sheathed it. He didn't have much skill at tracking, especially up on the surface, but the dead creature's feet were cloven, like those of a demon—sharp enough to leave a recognizable pattern.

He followed the creature's trail. In places where grass grew it had left a swath of crushed stems. In other spots, it had knocked stones loose from the crumbling foundations. The drifting mist caused Q'arlynd to lose the trail once or twice, but he persevered and eventually spotted what he'd been looking for: a drow's body, missing the lower portion of one leg. It was a male. The stomach had been chewed open and intestines were strewn across the ground. Flies droned into the air at Q'arlynd's approach, buzzing about in lazy circles, then settled again.

The dead drow was large for a male—nearly as tall and well muscled as a female. He wore an adamantine chain mail shirt—the creature had dragged it away from the stomach to feed—and a simple bowl-shaped helmet. The white hair that splayed out from it was crusted with blood. The back of the helm was gone, snipped neatly away. So too was a large part of the scalp beneath. The monster had bitten right through the metal, perhaps knocking the male down before he could use the sword that lay on the ground near his feet. He'd managed to fire his wristbow, though: the bolt had torn a furrow in the ground, a few paces away.

Q'arlynd shook his head. The fellow should have spent more time aiming and less time shouting after his companion.

He passed his hands over the body and whispered an incantation. A weak aura sprang into being around the *piwafwi*, a stronger one around the sword. Both items were of drow manufacture.

Q'arlynd rummaged through the dead male's pack. It contained nothing of interest. Just a half-eaten loaf of spore-bread, a flask of wine, and the usual gear a House soldier carried: whetstone, spare boots, extra gut for his wristbow, and a vial of sleep-poison for the bolts. The male's clothes were of a plain cut, and he wore no insignia: a commoner, then, despite the magical sword.

Q'arlynd's stomach growled, reminding him that he'd gone the night without eating. He'd tried hunting after his latest batch of supplies ran out, but the few birds and rodents he'd managed to blast with his magical missiles had been bony and unappetizing. Right then, even sporebread looked good.

He ate the loaf, washing it down with wine. When he finished, he circled the area, looking for the tracks of the companion who'd fled. The ground was a confusion of mashed grass. It looked as though the pair had camped there for a day or two. Footprints led off in several directions—and back again. Nothing was immediately obvious as a trail someone might have had made while fleeing.

Q'arlynd sighed. " 'Where are you,' indeed?" he repeated. It was possible, he supposed, that the dead male's companion had used magic to escape. Or that he'd bolted down a hole into the Underdark.

If there was an entrance to the Underdark nearby, it was well hidden—possibly concealed by magic. Q'arlynd had an answer for that. He pulled out his quartz crystal and held it up to his eyes. He turned slowly, searching the nearby ground. Anything magically hidden would . . .

Wait a moment. What was that, off in the distance? It looked like another drow. Another male, judging by the figure's height and build. He was standing several hundred paces away, leaning on a staff and staring at the ground.

Q'arlynd lowered the crystal. The figure vanished. He raised the crystal again, and saw that the hitherto invisible male still stood there. Staring at the ground. Not moving.

Paralyzed, perhaps?

No, not paralyzed. The male began walking in a slow circle, head down, as if searching for something on the ground.

Q'arlynd stared at him. "Lost something else besides your nerve, did you?"

Whatever the male was so intent on finding, it must have been valuable enough to warrant his full attention. He never even glanced in Q'arlynd's direction, even though Q'arlynd was plainly visible; all of his attention was focused on the ground.

Q'arlynd smiled and rendered himself invisible as well. When the male halted again, Q'arlynd teleported to a spot a few paces to his rear. The grass rustled slightly as Q'arlynd's feet touched ground. If the other male heard it, he gave no sign. He resumed walking, head down, staring at the ground, the tip of his staff dragging behind him. Q'arlynd studied him through his crystal.

Eldrinn—if that's who it was—couldn't have been more than three or four decades old. A mere boy. He wore an ornately embroidered *piwafwi* over pale gray trousers and a shirt that shimmered like spider silk. His waist-length, chalk-white hair was gathered in a silver clip at the small of his back. His skin was a lighter shade than usual; he probably wasn't pure drow. Q'arlynd could see a smudge of something black on the boy's high forehead that glistened like axle grease.

Q'arlynd's quiet divination revealed several magical items. The boy's staff glowed, as did his *piwafwi*, his boots, his hair clip, and the ring that must have been sustaining his invisibility.

By the look of him, the boy was a noble. Probably the son of a wealthy House, one with plenty of coin to purchase expensive magical items. That staff, for example, had a potent aura that spiraled up then down the length of pale wood, alternately filling, then draining from the tiny hourglass-shaped diamond suspended between the forked top of the staff. Q'arlynd fairly itched to get his hands on the thing. A staff with that level of magical potency must be worth at least a hundred thousand gold pieces. Two hundred thousand, even. A fortune, in one hand.

When the boy completed his circuit and turned in Q'arlynd's direction, Q'arlynd let his invisibility drop. When the other male spotted him, Q'arlynd would bow and offer the services of a simple spell that might prove useful in the search. If that didn't work, well . . . the glass rod was concealed in his hand, ready for use.

Eldrinn, however, paid Q'arlynd no heed. There seemed to be something wrong with him. His eyes looked flat, lifeless. His mouth hung slack; spittle dribbled from one corner. He stumbled slightly, then stopped and shook his head like a surface elf who had spent too long in Reverie. Then he began walking again, plodding along, still staring at the ground.

Every few steps, he mumbled. Q'arlynd could just barely make out the words.

"Bag," the boy slurred. "Mus' geddid bag.'"

Q'arlynd had no idea what it meant, but he was certain of one thing, the fellow posed no threat. If startled, he wasn't in any condition to blast Q'arlynd with a spell.

Q'arlynd dispelled the invisibility that cloaked the other male. Then he lowered his crystal and said in a soft voice, "Eldrinn?"

The boy blinked. He briefly lifted dull eyes to Q'arlynd, then dropped them again and resumed his shuffling. He brushed past as if Q'arlynd wasn't there.

The boy looked like the victim of a feeblemind spell—something only a cleric's prayers or a magical wish could cure. Q'arlynd had neither at his disposal just then.

Q'arlynd stroked his chin and watched the other male tromp circles in the grass. The boy wore an amulet around his neck. Q'arlynd walked beside the boy and lifted the adamantine disc from his chest, curious to see if it bore a House glyph. It didn't. There was, however, an arcane symbol on it that Q'arlynd immediately recognized: "Divination."

Q'arlynd let the amulet fall back against the boy's chest. He understood, now, the lack of an insignia on the dead soldier. The boy—and the soldier who had accompanied him there—were from Sshamath, a city ruled by a conclave of wizards rather than the matrons of noble Houses. The amulet was the College equivalent of a House insignia in a city where House names were seldom used.

Q'arlynd shook his head, not quite believing the coincidence. Sshamath was the city where he hoped to make his new home. Maybe—and this was a disturbing thought—his finding Eldrinn had been more than mere coincidence. Had one of the gods arranged this meeting? Q'arlynd couldn't think of a single deity who might take an interest in him, however. He'd failed to attract the attention of Mystra's Chosen and had betrayed instead of aided Eilistraee—though that *had* led to the death of Vhaeraun. And yet . . .

Something on the ground caught Q'arlynd's eye. A crystal, winking at him in the moonlight. It was about half the length of his little finger. Hexagonal in cross section, it tapered to a point at each end. Pale blue at one end, it darkened along its length to blue-green. The crystal had fallen into tall grass; but for the moonlight glinting on it, Q'arlynd never would have spotted it.

He waited until the other wizard had walked past the crystal, then cast a divination. The crystal shone with an aura that was almost blinding—a magical radiance that made even the staff's aura seem dim in comparison. Q'arlynd whistled softly as he realized what the crystal must be. A *kiira*. A lorestone. He wet his lips nervously. The gods only knew what ancient spells it might contain.

The lorestone had to be what the boy was looking for. It had probably been the cause of his mental affliction. A damp black smudge on the side of the crystal matched the one on the boy's forehead.

Q'arlynd levitated the crystal into his pouch and tied the pouch shut. He wasn't about to touch the crystal with his bare hands—not after what it had, in all likelihood, done to the boy.

His prize secure, Q'arlynd drew his dagger and halted the boy by grasping his shoulder. Then he touched the point of his dagger to Eldrinn's chest. One quick push to drive the dagger home, and the staff, the *piwafwi*, and all the other magical items would be his. Yet for some reason, Q'arlynd couldn't bring himself to do it. Perhaps because Eldrinn's eyes looked so trusting—they reminded Q'arlynd of the look his younger brother had given him, just before Q'arlynd betrayed him.

Q'arlynd lowered his dagger and sighed. Just a short time on the surface, and he was going soft. That's what keeping company with Eilistraee's priestesses did to a male. Made him soft.

But perhaps it was just as well, he told himself. Killing the boy could have brought unwelcome consequences. Though Eldrinn was young, and likely just a novice, someone from his College might come looking for him. If evidence was found of his murder . . . well, a master of divination would quickly uncover the drow who'd done the deed.

Q'arlynd sheathed his dagger and let the boy trudge in a circle again. As Eldrinn passed him on his circuit, Q'arlynd reached out and plucked the staff from his hands. The boy let it go without protest. Easy as that.

Resting the staff against his shoulder, Q'arlynd waited for Eldrinn to circle back again. He'd remove those magical items, one by one, then leave the boy for the creatures of the High Moor to finish off, he thought. But then he realized that idea, too, had its drawbacks. Monsters didn't carry off magical items; they left them scattered about next to the kill. Any master of divination worthy of the title would take one look at the ravaged body and immediately search for the missing items. Especially for something as powerful as the boy's staff.

Q'arlynd let his hand fall. No, there was only one thing to be done. Teleport Eldrinn back to Sshamath, his magical items unpilfered.

Except, of course, for the *kiira*. It was a safe bet that Eldrinn hadn't reported finding it to his superiors at the College of Divination. If he had, other wizards would have shown up to claim it. It was likely, therefore, that only Eldrinn knew about the *kiira*. If whatever afflicted him proved too powerful to dispel, the lorestone would be Q'arlynd's. He could return to the High Moor and "find" it at his leisure.

And if Eldrinn did recover, and guessed that Q'arlynd had pocketed the *kiira*, perhaps a deal could be struck. Q'arlynd could agree to hand the lorestone over in return for a share of whatever knowledge it held.

He smiled. After two months of fruitless searching, not one but two prizes had dropped into his lap. A *kiira*—and a mind-damaged wizard, ripe for rescue, whose return to Sshamath might just warrant a reward.

For the time being, he would tuck the *kiira* away in a place where it would be impossible to find: in a certain cavern with no natural entrances or exits, completely lined with darkstone crystals that would block all scrying and detection attempts. Only three drow, besides Q'arlynd, had known of the cavern's existence. Two were dead—their bodies had been lying on the cavern's floor when Q'arlynd had briefly returned to it a month ago. The third was unlikely to ever visit it again.

Q'arlynd teleported to the cavern, deposited his prize amid the darkstone crystals, then returned to the High Moor. The journey took only a few moments. Eldrinn still stood where Q'arlynd had left him, staring vacantly at the ground. He leaned forward, as if about to trudge in circles again, but Q'arlynd caught his arm, stopping him.

He turned his thoughts to Sshamath. He'd visited the city only once before—on a trading mission, decades ago—yet he still had a clear memory of its main point of entry: the cavern at the top of the Z'orr'bauth Pillar. He let this fill his mind. Then, his hand gripping Eldrinn's shoulder, he teleported them both to it.

❧ ❧ ❧ ❧ ❧

The Month of Tarsakh
The Year of the Bent Blade (1376 DR)

Kâras waved a hand to catch the eye of the bet runner. "Three gold on the derro."

The bet runner, a lanky slave with ice-white hair and eyes that darted about like a hunting lizard's, sprinted up the stairs of the arena to the top row of seats. He took Kâras's coin and passed him a token.

The female seated next to Kâras laughed. "That derro won't last a minute against the quaggoth. Just look at the size of her!" She caught the bet runner's arm and wrenched him to her side. "Seven gold on the quaggoth."

The boy took her coin, wincing slightly at her grip on his arm.

"The females don't always win," Kâras said, idly stroking his chin. "The derro may appear weaker, but appearances can be deceiving."

His comment prompted a derisive snort from the female. She was secure in her finery and status—a priestess of Lolth, judging by the whip that hung from her belt. The bet runner, however, took Kâras's meaning. He coughed into his hand, then wiped his fingers across his mouth. Secretly returning the sign of the mask. His other hand moved at his side. *Directly across from you. Top row. Three this side of the pillar.*

Kâras gave the slightest of nods. The boy darted away to take another bet.

As the stone benches filled with spectators, Kâras sized up the male he'd been sent to kill. The fellow was slender-boned and delicate looking, but clearly used to taking care of himself, judging by his confident expression. He sat with his back against the wall, on the top bench. Every few moments he glanced around, alert for threats. His *piwafwi* hid his forearms, but Kâras spotted the head of a wristbow bolt peeking out from the edge of the cloth.

Kâras had been told his target's name: Valdar. Aside from that, he knew little. Only that the fellow was a former priest of Vhaeraun, just as Kâras was. The target wasn't wearing his mask; that would have been suicide, there in Guallidurth. Perhaps he'd given up the faith altogether after Vhaeraun's death. More than one Nightshadow had done that, rather than bow to the Masked Lord's conqueror.

Kâras, however, was more practical than that.

Rather than moving into position at once, he feigned interest in the upcoming match. The quaggoth was, as the female sitting beside him had just noted, an enormous creature, one and a half times the height of a drow, as broad as one of the World Above's bears. The white-furred creature was indeed female, though it was hard to tell with all that fur. She had disdainfully cast aside the club they'd given her and was flexing her hooked claws and roaring, working herself up into a killing rage.

The derro on the opposite side of the circular ring was less than half the quaggoth's height. His coarse white hair fell in a tangle across his pale blue face, hiding his blind eyes. He would be relying upon sound and smell alone to tell him where his opponent was. He gripped a dagger in each fist. The blades appeared clean, but Kâras had learned they were coated with greenblood oil, rendered invisible by a spell.

When it came to laying odds, Kâras would take small and sneaky over brute force any day.

The crowd thickened. Most of the spectators crowded the first few rows, seats so close to the arena that their occupants were sometimes hit with a hot spray of blood.

As the bet runner moved into place, climbing the stairs toward the spot where the target sat, Kâras rose to his feet, shouting out a last-moment bet. "Three gold!" He waved his arm, as if trying to catch the bet runner's eye.

The bet runner ignored him.

Kâras clambered down the stairs, unfastening the coin purse at his hip. "Three more gold on the derro!" he shouted again. He continued calling and waving as he climbed the stairs on the other side of the arena.

Before he could reach the bet runner, the gong sounded, signaling the start of the combat.

"Out of the way!" a spectator cried. "I can't see."

Kâras continued up the steps to the bet runner. The boy had positioned himself next to Kâras's target, as was the custom when each fight began, with his back against the wall so as not to block the view.

"Didn't you hear me, boy?" Kâras shouted. "I wanted to place a bet."

The bet runner cringed. "Sorry, Master! Too late. The fight's already—"

Kâras cuffed him, splitting his lip.

The boy was good. He glared back at Kâras as if he wanted to kill him, and cringed when Kâras raised his hand a second time. Seemingly cowed, he slunk away.

Kâras glanced back at the combat, sighed heavily, then squeezed onto the bench next to Valdar.

His target glanced at him, his unusual pink eyes flicking briefly to Kâras's wrist-crossbow and dagger and lingering a moment longer on the scars that gave Kâras's left eye a perpetual squint. If Valdar survived, he'd remember Kâras. Survival was unlikely, however.

Kâras turned his attention to the fight. In the arena below, the quaggoth leaped forward with a roar. Despite her size, she was swift as a jumping spider. The derro deftly sidestepped and slashed, but missed. The quaggoth spun and raked the derro's shoulder with its claws, drawing first blood.

The crowd shouted its approval.

Kâras snorted. "Hah. Perhaps it's just as well I didn't get to place that bet."

His target didn't comment.

The derro feinted with his left, stabbed with his right.

The second dagger almost scored a hit, parting the fur at the quaggoth's hip.

The female sitting on the other side of Valdar leaped to her feet and shook her fist. "Kill him!" she screamed.

The quaggoth slammed a paw into the derro's back, sending the little male stumbling. The derro turned it into a somersault and sprang back to his feet. He shouted something at the quaggoth—a shout laden with magic that sent the quaggoth reeling. Before she could recover, the derro raced in and stabbed her in the thigh. Bright red blood stained her fur. She staggered, blinked stupidly at the wound. Then she fell.

The crowd roared.

"Ha!" Kâras cried. "I wish I *had* placed that bet. I knew the derro would win. But at least I've made a little profit, this match." He folded his arms and leaned back, as if pleased with himself.

Now was the moment. Before the noise of the crowd ebbed, he whispered a terse prayer that would freeze his target in place. He abruptly leaned sideways, jostling Valdar. The dagger concealed by his folded arm stabbed into Valdar's side.

The point grated against something—fine-woven mail, by the feel of it—turning what should have been a fatal thrust into a bruising punch.

To Kâras's surprise, Valdar moved. Before Kâras could react, Valdar grasped his arm and "spoke" a command with his fingers: *Come.* Kâras suddenly felt an urge to follow the other male wherever he might lead. Before he could shake off the magical compulsion, his target moved his fingers in a silent prayer.

The arena disappeared.

Off-balance from the sudden absence of the bench, Kâras nearly fell. Rather than leaping away—a move the other male would have anticipated—Kâras hurled himself forward, knocking the other male off-balance. Then he sprang back, nearly twisting a foot on the uneven floor in the process. He glanced around, saw that they had teleported to a crystal-lined cavern. As the other male sprang to his feet, Kâras shifted his dagger. Valdar refused to be distracted by it. His arm flew up and his wristbow twanged. The bolt tore past Kâras's head and cracked against the wall behind him. Kâras answered it with a thrown dagger. It should have spitted Valdar in the throat, but Valdar dodged it easily.

Kâras drew his second dagger. Valdar likewise drew steel. Kâras leaped forward. Thrust.

His target dodged aside. Valdar slashed, but Kâras barked out a one-word prayer. A shield of magical energy caught the blade and turned it aside.

The two males circled each other warily, each realizing he was evenly matched.

"Kill me and you'll be trapped here," Valdar said. His free hand flicked to the side. "Like them."

Kâras didn't need to look. He'd already noted the two drow corpses that lay nearby: one bled out from slit wrists, the other bone-thin from starvation. Each wore a black mask.

He continued to circle Valdar—a motion that allowed him to take in all of the cavern without shifting his attention from his opponent. Valdar just might be telling the truth: the cavern had no visible exits. And Kâras couldn't teleport.

"You're a Nightshadow," Valdar said. A statement, rather than a question. He'd obviously recognized Kâras's prayer.

Kâras watched his opponent closely. When Valdar lunged, he twisted aside. Kâras slashed, but the other male also danced nimbly away.

"Do you know who I am?" Valdar asked.

"I was told you must die. Who you are is not my concern."

"I'm a Nightshadow, like yourself. But not just any cleric. I'm the one who opened the gate between Vhaeraun's and Eilistraee's domains." Valdar gestured at the darkstones that lined the cavern. "This is where it was done."

Kâras couldn't help but reply. "If that's true, you're a traitor," he spat.

"Not at all. I merely did as Vhaeraun commanded." He nodded at the dagger in Kâras's fist and made a *tsk* noise. "And *this* is the reward I get."

"You did as Eilistraee commanded," Kâras corrected. "But that doesn't matter any more. I serve her, now."

"It was a priestess who ordered my assassination?" Valdar asked. His surprise seemed genuine. "But I thought . . ."

Kâras lunged. His target parried. The daggers clashed, and both males sprang away. Kâras circled, watching for another opening.

Valdar gave Kâras a scornful look. "You allow females to order you about? What kind of Nightshadow *are* you?"

Kâras felt his jaw muscles tighten. "One who now pays homage to the Masked Lady."

"The Masked Lord, you mean. It was Vhaeraun who killed Eilistraee. The priestesses are lying when they say it was the other way around."

Kâras couldn't let that pass without comment. "Then why is it you're not attacking me with your prayers? I'll tell you why; because Eilistraee won't grant you the spells to harm me." He nodded at the other male's dagger. "You're left with only one weapon: steel."

Valdar smiled. "In that regard, I'd say we're evenly matched. But now that we've taken each other's measure, I'd rather speak to you than stab you. And why?" He lowered his dagger slightly. "Because Vhaeraun still has need of you."

Kâras refused to be taken in by so obvious a feint.

"I assure you," Valdar continued, his dagger still lowered. "I'm telling the truth. Eilistraee is dead. Vhaeraun *lives*."

Bitterness welled in Kâras. "Then why have our most potent spells been stripped from us? Why is it that Eilistraee's priestesses have all the power, while we've lost ours?" He could hear the ache in his own voice. He was giving too much away, but he didn't care. "Why must I dance and sing instead of meditating in shadow and silence?"

Valdar nodded, as if in sympathy. "I know exactly how you feel. That first month, after I opened the gate, guilt nearly consumed me. Then I saw the shadows behind the light."

Both still held their weapons, but for the moment, they exchanged only stares. Valdar spoke first. "The priestesses are teaching that it was Eilistraee who entered Vhaeraun's domain, aren't they?"

Kâras said nothing.

"They lie. I was *here*. I saw what happened. Vhaeraun leaped through the gate to attack Eilistraee."

"Suppose you're right. What does it matter? He was still slain."

Valdar shook his head. "Tell me this. Have you attempted an augury these past four months?"

Kâras gave a terse nod.

"Was it answered?"

Kâras spoke guardedly. "Yes."

"Did the one who answered wear a mask?"

"Of course. A trophy of her victory."

"And the face—what you could see of it? Female or male?"

"Neither. And both. Just like the voice. But the priestesses have an answer for that, too. It is part of the balance. Vhaeraun allowed himself to be killed so the two deities could merge."

Valdar raised an eyebrow. "And you believe that?"

"Not . . . entirely."

"Look closely, next time you attempt an augury. Look into the eyes of this 'Eilistraee.' See if they are entirely moonstone blue—or if they contain a flash of some other color."

Kâras lowered his dagger slightly. "You've seen this?"

"Yes."

Kâras thought about that. He shook his head. "That proves nothing. Eilistraee took on aspects of Vhaeraun when she killed him."

"Did she? Or did Vhaeraun take on aspects of Eilistraee?"

Kâras waved his dagger. "We're arguing in circles. And none of it matters. It's Eilistraee's priestesses who are in charge now, not us."

"Are they? Or is it Vhaeraun who's the true power behind the throne?" Valdar held his free hand across his mouth. "What better mask to hide behind, than the illusion of defeat?" He lowered his hand again. "I've thought long on this—asked myself the very questions you're asking now. Then I realized that feigning his own death and giving the priestesses the illusion of control was all part of the Masked Lord's plan. Just as we infiltrate the settlements of the Night Above in the guise of surface elves, Vhaeraun has infiltrated Eilistraee's realm. Our clerics are within her shrines, constantly testing the limits of her priestess's control with scores of tiny acts of defiance. Soon, we'll be inside the Promenade itself. When the time comes, Vhaeraun will throw off his disguise, and those who have maintained his faith will take her strongholds from within."

It sounded good—too good. Kâras couldn't allow himself to be seduced by it. "And what if you're wrong?" he countered. "What if it's Eilistraee's priestesses who are eroding our faith from within?" He gave a bitter laugh. "We're already nine-tenths defeated. Better to claim what power you can within the new order than to cling to false hope."

"It is *not* a false hope!" Valdar snapped, his pink eyes blazing. "Nobody *saw* Vhaeraun die. Not even me—and I was *here*, staring through the gate as it opened. Think about it. Vhaeraun has tricked Eilistraee's faithful into joining our fight. He's using her shrines as a stepping stone. A staging ground for the eventual overthrow of Lolth and her matriarchies. Then the natural order *will* be restored. We Nightshadows will return to the Underdark, and males will rule." He paused to catch his breath. "Vhaeraun's plan is a brilliant one, in every detail. What more perfect treachery can there be than to feign one's own death and infiltrate the very body of one's enemy? It's the perfect disguise."

Kâras had been listening intently. But the time for talking was almost at an end. In another moment, he'd finish it—kill his target, and probably take a fatal wound himself. If he survived, he might very well wind up trapped in this cavern, eventually dying of starvation. He was resigned to that. But before he pressed home his attack, there was one last question he had to ask.

"It all sounds plausible," he said. "But what proof can you offer that it's true?"

Valdar's eyes gleamed. "The order to kill me came from a priestess. And that priestess—whoever she is—takes *her* orders from her deity. Do you honestly believe *Eilistraee* would condone an assassination of one of her own? Or does that strike you as being more like an order that Vhaeraun would give?"

"Why would he order you killed? If, as you say, you only did as he commanded."

Valdar's eyes bored into his. "As a trial. He knew it would bring you face to face with me, and test your faith."

Kâras's body was still, but his thoughts churned. He searched for a counter argument, but couldn't find one. Nor did he want to. Something was breaking in him—breaking open. The brittle shell he'd encased his anguish in, these past four months.

"There's a way to test whether what I say is true," Valdar said softly. "Return to the female who gave you the order. Tell her I've been slain. See if divine retribution follows." He leaned forward, lowering his voice. "Or if reward follows, instead."

Without waiting to hear what Kâras would say next, he sheathed his dagger.

For several moments, Kâras remained motionless. Then he nodded to himself. "I think I'll do just that. If you're wrong, I can always kill you another day." Slowly, he slid his own dagger back into its sheath.

CHAPTER 2

Halisstra cringed on the floor, watching Lolth. The goddess was in her spider form, her body a glossy black, her eyes a burning crimson. She dangled upside down from the ceiling of the web-choked room, slowly spinning in place.

Halisstra kept her head bowed—she didn't dare look fully upon the goddess. As she watched, the hourglass-shaped pattern on the underside of Lolth's abdomen shrank as her body contracted. A crack appeared beside each of Lolth's fang-tipped jaws. With a sharp cracking sound it enlarged until the skin peeled back from her face.

The goddess shuddered. She contracted still more, tearing the rest of her head free from its hard coating of chitin. Then the cracks spread to the abdomen, releasing her. Lolth tumbled onto the cold iron floor, leaving her molted skin behind. The empty husk, still dangling from its strand of web, twisted above her.

As she stood, Lolth assumed her hybrid form, sprouting a drow head. Her spider body was enormous.Though Halisstra stood twice the height of a drow, she could have walked upright between the goddess's spider legs with room to spare. The new skin on that body, all wrinkled and soft, glistened with the fluids that had loosened the old skin. As the abdomen pulsed, drawing breath, the skin smoothed and hardened to glossy black.

The goddess twisted her head back and forth to work out kinks in her neck and flicked damp hair out of her eyes. Her face was the epitome of beauty: velvet-smooth skin, delicately pointed ears, arched white eyebrows and kiss-pout lips.

Danifae's face. The visage the goddess had worn since consuming her chosen one.

Lolth's pale gray eyes shone with malice. "Battle-captive. I hunger. Attend me."

Halisstra crept forward, trying not to reveal the loathing she felt, and prostrated herself before the goddess. Lolth moved over her, claws clicking like sword points against the cold black iron of the floor. Her cheeks bulged as two palps emerged from them. These probed Halisstra's bare back, parting the matted hair that covered it. Lolth vomited.

As the digestive juices struck her back, Halisstra gasped. There was a moment of warmth—then pain comparable to being scalded. The pain bored deeper, down into the flesh of her back. She could feel her flesh dissolving, sloughing away from her ribs and backbone. Could smell the reek of bile and hear Lolth taking the half-digested flesh up in great, greedy slurps.

Halisstra collapsed, the sudden weight of her body snapping two of the eight tiny legs that protruded from her chest. Yet the pain of cracking chitin was nothing compared to the raw, open mess that was her back. She lay, barely conscious, the jaws protruding from her cheeks gnashing weakly as Lolth loomed over her, eating her fill.

Halisstra had once been a drow, heir to the throne of House Melarn of Ched Nasad. Now she was the Lady Penitent. Doomed to suffer forever at the hands of the female she had formerly commanded. Danifae had once been Halisstra's battle-captive, but now she was Lolth's chosen one. No longer a drow, she had become part of the Spider Queen.

The slurping noises stopped. Lolth laughed—a gloating sound that was all Danifae. Halisstra felt herself gathered up off the floor by arms—drow arms—and cradled against a woman's chest. Lolth had assumed drow form. Despite the disparity in their sizes, she rocked Halisstra back and forth like an infant, one hand caressing the half-dissolved flesh of Halisstra's back as it slowly regenerated. Then she kissed Halisstra—a long, brutal kiss. The kind a matron would force on a House boy.

Halisstra tore her mouth away and retched.

Lolth stood, dumping her to the floor. "Weakling," she spat.

Halisstra hung her head. Even after nearly five years, the word still stung.

Lolth strode in a circle around the room, her arms extended. Webs stuck to her skin, covering the body that had once been Danifae's in a layer of overlapping white filaments. With a snap of her fingers, she summoned tiny red spiders. These scurried back and forth, weaving the webs into a long white gown. When they were done, the spiders dangled from the hem and cuffs in a living fringe.

Huddled on the floor, Halisstra watched the goddess out of the corner of her eye, not daring to say what she was thinking. Before her fall from grace, Lolth had been the Weaver of Destiny. The goddess needed the help of arachnids to construct so much as a simple garment. Everything Lolth touched turned into a tangled mess; every web Halisstra had seen her spin had been lopsided and asymmetrical. As skewed in their design as the restless and confused mind of the Queen of Spiders herself.

Halisstra felt the prickle of flesh knitting back together as her muscles grew into place, and the stretch of new skin spreading across her back. When she was strong enough, she rose to her feet and waited for the goddess to speak.

"Do you know why I summoned you to my chamber, Halisstra?"

"To feed?"

The goddess laughed. "More than that. Guess again."

Halisstra felt her pulse quicken. It had been almost two years, by her rough reckoning, since Lolth had sealed her inside a cell, deep within her iron fortress. In all that time, she had removed Halisstra from the cell perhaps a dozen times, in order to feed. What new torment did the goddess have in mind this time?

"You've taken me out because . . ." Halisstra paused, searching for the most unlikely of answers—something that would amuse the goddess. ". . . because you've decided to set me free?"

Lolth spun and clapped her hands together. "Exactly!" she cried. "I'm sending you away from the Demonweb Pits."

Halisstra prostrated herself, hiding the thrill of anticipation she felt. "How am I to serve you, Mistress?"

"Serve *me?*" Lolth tossed her head. "Think again, mortal."

Halisstra hesitated, uncertain of the goddess's meaning. During the time she'd done penitence to the queen of the Demonweb Pits, she had come to know Lolth as well as any mortal could. Even so, she had no idea which twisted path Lolth's mind was walking now. Anything, however, would be better than being locked away—practically forgotten—in a cell.

That imprisonment, the goddess had explained, had been Halisstra's punishment for helping to kill Selvetarm, the demigod who had been Lolth's champion. He had been slain—in the Demonweb Pits—by a priestess of Eilistraee, the Darksong Knight Cavatina. When all had seemed lost,

Halisstra handed Cavatina the sword that made Selvetarm's death possible.

Halisstra had expected to be commended by Lolth for her "cunning" in aiding the Darksong Knight. The Spider Queen had *intended* for her champion to be slain; that's what she'd wanted all along. She'd gloated about Selvetarm's death afterward—spoken with glee about how his priests had thrown down their temples and scuttled back to her, like flies to a web.

Then she'd imprisoned Halisstra.

"Where are you sending me, Mistress?" Halisstra asked.

Lolth laughed, her lips emitting a gout of spiders. Then she waved a hand. The iron-walled room disappeared.

Halisstra found herself standing next to Lolth on a featureless, wind-blasted plain illuminated by a pale yellow sun. She tasted salt on her lips and squinted against the wind-borne grit that stung like shards of glass. The wind whipped her hair around, flicking it against her face. It tore at Lolth's web-garment, swiftly pulling it to pieces that streamed away on the wind.

One of these brushed against a mound of salt, its sticky filaments pulling a little of the salt away. A heartbeat later, the entire pile collapsed as something crouched under it suddenly rose. Enormous bat wings flicked open, and a shaggy head shook off the dust that obscured the face. Massive horns protruded straight out from the creature's head in the place where ears would normally be. His muzzle, when it opened in a lazy yawn, revealed row upon row of jagged teeth.

A balor.

The demon cleared his wide, flat nose in a violent exhalation that sent a gout of flame out of each nostril, and spat a gob of sticky black tar onto the salt-encrusted ground. He folded his wings over his shoulders and lazily scratched his blood-red chest as he stared at the Spider Queen.

The wind died. A palpable tension filled the stillness.

"Lolth," the demon said. "At last." Each word released a puff of oily black smoke.

The demon had a sword strapped to his back; his flame-shaped blade glowed white-hot. Smoke curled lazily from the place where the weapon touched a strip of black hair that ran down the demon's back, hair that curled around his buttocks to his groin. Within this dark tangle was something bulbous and red.

"After so many centuries, have you at last come to play?" the balor hissed.

Halisstra felt fingers lock in her hair.

"No," Lolth said, her voice a lazy purr. "But this one has." She shoved Halisstra forward.

Halisstra gasped as she realized what was happening. Lolth didn't have a new mission in mind for her. She was discarding Halisstra like a toy she'd grown bored of playing with. "Mistress, no!" Halisstra gasped. "I can still serve you. Pl—"

Lolth's harsh laughter cut her off. "The Lady Penitent," she mocked. "*Pleading?* You should know better than that by now."

"Mistress," Halisstra whimpered, "let me prove myself. I'll do anything."

"Of course you will," Lolth said, her voice as smooth as freshly spun silk. "We both already know that, don't we?"

The demon moved closer, his clawed feet crunching against the salt-encrusted ground. He pointed a finger at Halisstra, then dropped his hand. Compelled, she fell to her knees. With the demon so close, she realized that he was not much taller than she was; had they stood side by side, their eyes would almost be level. Yet the raw power he exuded was nearly as great as Lolth's own.

Involuntary tears squeezed from Halisstra's eyes and trickled down her face, carrying the taste of salt to her lips.

Lolth laughed at Halisstra's discomfort. A snap of her fingers brought a strand of web tumbling from the sky. She seized it with one hand, then turned back to the demon.

"I'll call for your services soon, Wendonai," the goddess told him. "Until then, I'm sure you can find a way to amuse yourself." She nodded at Halisstra. Then she scurried up the strand of web and was gone.

The demon loomed over Halisstra. This close, she could smell the stench of scorched hair and the oily tang of his breath. He lowered his nose until it almost touched the top of her head, and inhaled deeply.

He jerked back. "You're not—" He halted, as if suddenly reconsidering what he'd been about to say. He forced her prone, then craned his head back. "Lolth!"

No response came from the empty sky.

"Lolth!"

Unable to contain her curiosity, Halisstra peered up at the demon. He was upset about something. Her scent? Had it revealed the fact that she had once been a priestess of Eilistraee? That she served Lolth under duress? Whatever Halisstra lacked, it made the demon furious. As his agitation grew, the wind rose.

The blowing grit crusted her nostrils when she breathed. It filled the air with glittering salt dust, obscuring the landscape once more. Small drifts formed against the demon's feet as he raged at the sky, still shouting Lolth's name. Halisstra rose to her hands and knees, but the demon didn't seem to notice. Encouraged, she began to creep away. Depending upon which layer of the Abyss they were in, she might be able to locate a portal back to the Prime Material Plane. Once there, she could prove to Lolth that she was no weakling, that she was worthy of—

A clawed foot crashed down onto her head, slamming her to the ground.

"Drow!" he roared. "There will be no escape. I am your *master!*"

Halisstra tasted blood; the demon had split her lip. "Yes, Master," she gasped.

The wind stilled.

"That's better," the demon said, shifting his foot from her head. He squatted beside her. "I'll strike you a bargain. You want your freedom, and I want someone to play with. Someone more . . . agreeable to my tastes." He reached out and hooked a finger under Halisstra's chin, spearing her flesh on the point of his claw. "Think carefully. Is there anyone who might trade positions with you to save your wretched hide?"

The rush of relief left Halisstra lightheaded. "There's someone who . . . owes me a great favor."

"Her name?"

"Cavatina."

"Cavatina." The demon rolled the name around in his mouth as if sucking on something sweet. "What is she to you? Lover? Kin?"

Relief flooded Halisstra. She'd gambled that the demon hadn't heard of Cavatina—he'd been buried under salt for "centuries," after all. It looked as though her gamble might pay off. Cavatina was a Darksong Knight, a hunter of demons. A slayer of demigods. She'd make short work of the balor. One swing of the Crescent Blade, and Lolth's pet demon would be dead.

That would make the Spider Queen sorry for tossing Halisstra to him.

Halisstra shook her head in answer to the demon's question, but the motion drove the claw deeper into her flesh, making her wince. "Cavatina is neither lover, nor kin. She's a priestess of Eilistraee. I saved her life, once. I'm certain she would feel compelled to do the same for me."

The demon smiled, revealing jagged teeth. "Perfect."

He removed his claw from under her chin. He straightened, grabbed the claw with his other hand, and yanked. The claw came free in a burst of dark, tarry blood. Taking Halisstra's left hand, he pressed the claw against her palm. It stung like hot wax as it was forced into her flesh. When it was done, only a dark, rough callus remained.

"When you find Cavatina, touch her with this hand, and call my name," the demon instructed. "Do you understand?"

Halisstra rubbed her palm, already regretting what she'd just promised. The spot on her palm ached with a fierce heat. "I understand."

The demon swept Halisstra up as if her body were as light as a web and stared into her eyes. "Go. Find Cavatina." Then he raised her above his head and hurled her into the air.

The sky split open in a flaming crack, and a shrieking wind carried Halisstra away.

Cavatina ran through the woods, heedless of the scratches the branches left on her bare skin. Off to her left she could hear the beaters crashing swords against shields, moving steadily through the forest. Most of the priestesses would be ahead of them, swords poised to skewer whatever monsters the lay worshipers flushed out, but Cavatina preferred to hunt alone.

She'd stripped off even her boots for the High Hunt; she wore only her holy symbol. The dull-bladed ceremonial silver dagger bounced against her chest as she ran. She'd also left most of her magical items behind, trusting to the goddess's blessings to protect her. She carried only her magical hunting horn, slung over her shoulder on a strap, and her sword.

The sword sang as Cavatina ran, its silvered blade vibrating in the warm night air like the reed of a woodwind instrument. Gripping the hilt tightly in her right hand, Cavatina felt the weapon's anticipation. It was one of twenty-four sacred weapons identical to Lady Qilué's own blade—forged, according to the sacred hymns, by Eilistraee herself from a solidified moonbeam. The pommel was set with a translucent white moonstone that glowed faintly with a tinge of blue whenever the moon struck it. Half of the moonstone, however, had turned black—dark as the half of the moon that lay in shadow on this night of the autumn equinox.

Dark as a Nightshadow's heart.

Cavatina didn't want to think about that. Running alone through the moonlit woods, it was easy to pretend that the changes that began in the winter of that fateful Year of Risen Elfkin hadn't happened. That Eilistraee's worship was as it had always been. That the goddess herself was unchanged, more than a year and a half after assuming Vhaeraun's worshipers as her own.

Cavatina leaped across a fallen log as gracefully as a deer. She was tall, with a body narrow as a sword blade, her muscles honed by a lifetime of dancing and fighting. Her skin, black as a moonless night, contrasted with her long, ivory-colored hair. Normally, she wore her hair bound in a braid or bun so it wouldn't fall across her face and distract her while she fought, but tonight she'd left it loose. Tonight she let herself run wild, open to whatever the Shilmista Forest threw at her. She prayed whatever monster Eilistraee caused to cross her path would be a challenging one. Something worthy of the singing sword, and the Darksong Knight who held it.

She heard the blare of a hunting horn. Another of the priestesses had spotted something. A voice sang out through the night, calling for the others to join her. The cacophony of banging shields fell away; the beaters had done their work and were no longer needed.

Cavatina ignored the exhortations to join in the kill. She ran until the voices and horns faded in the distance. She plunged down a slope and found a shallow stream that sparkled with reflected moonlight. On impulse she followed it, her bare feet dancing lightly from stone to stone. At first, the stream wound through verdant forest, but as Cavatina followed it downhill, the vegetation on either side grew increasingly sparse. She clambered over a dead tree that had fallen across the stream—a tree whose trunk had been eaten away on one side. Other trees on both sides of the stream showed similar gouges. Their bark hung in tattered strips. Some had been stripped of their branches, leaving only skeletal trunks that were dark against the moonlit sky.

Something had been feeding on the vegetation there. Something big.

Cavatina slowed, her senses alert. She was panting heavily from her run, but the singing sword was steady in her hand. It, too, fell silent as if listening. The only sound came from the stream that flowed past Cavatina's ankles, chilling her bare feet.

A faint splash came from the bank to her left. A tiny head broke the surface a moment later: a small black creature with a pointed muzzle and rounded ears, its bare pink tail lashing behind it as it swam. A rat.

Swift as a striking hawk, Cavatina jabbed her sword down, skewering it. The creature squeaked as the sword point thrust it under water, a peculiar noise that almost sounded like a cry. When Cavatina lifted her sword again, the rat was dead. She flicked it from her blade, into the dead foliage at the side of the stream.

Something else moved on her right—a second rat. It emerged from the stream and scurried uphill through the shadows that had given the forest its Elvish name. Cavatina saw the disturbance it made through the scatter of dead sticks and leaves as it climbed the bank, but made no move to follow it. She was already sorry she'd sullied a singing sword with the blood of vermin.

She held the tip of the blade in the stream, letting the water wash it clean, and asked, "Is that the best you can send me, Eilistraee? A *rat?*"

This hunt was already a disappointment.

She walked on, following the stream. After several dozen paces, she noted movement to her left. The hillside shifted. She whirled to face it just as a tree toppled across the stream with a splash.

A creature erupted from the earth: an enormous beetle the size of a cabin, with mandibles as big as stag antlers and a curved claw at the end of each of its six legs. Chunks of soil slid off its gleaming black carapace as it reared up; it must have been hiding just below the surface. It stared at Cavatina, its dimpled red eyes gleaming faintly in the moonlight.

She smiled and raised her sword. Ready.

The beetle sprang.

Cavatina thrust her sword at its thorax. The blade sliced through chitin and cut deep into flesh. The sword sang a joyous peal as bright orange blood rushed from the wound. Then the mandibles scissored shut, their jagged points gouging into Cavatina's sides. The beetle reared up to bring its front two legs into play, yanking her into the air.

Shuddering with pain, blood flowing down her sides, Cavatina gasped out a prayer. A circle of blinding white appeared on her palm, and streaked from it to strike the beetle's head. Suddenly weakened, it sagged backward and let Cavatina fall to the ground.

Cavatina lurched to her feet, the singing sword still in her hand. It sang a soothing melody as she slapped her free hand to her blood-slippery side and prayed. Eilistraee's moonlight sparkled brightly against Cavatina's skin as healing energy flowed into her, closing her wounds.

The beetle struggled to rise on trembling legs. Before it could recover, Cavatina danced in close and slashed. With a blow like an axe striking a heavy tree limb, she severed one of the mandibles. The beetle stabbed a leg down at her but Cavatina twisted aside just in time. The claw thudded into the fallen tree instead. The beetle yanked free, tossing the trunk aside like a stick. The log tumbled down the bank toward the stream, branches snapping from it.

Though weakened, the beetle was still very much alive. Cavatina might hack at it all night and still not kill it—the beetle was that large. The hunting horn that hung from her shoulder was capable of taking the beetle down, but its blare would be heard throughout the forest. It would draw the other priestesses like moths. Cavatina wanted to make this kill on her own, with sword and spell, as was proper for the High Hunt.

The beetle lunged, snapping at her with its remaining mandible. Alerted by her sword's warning peal, Cavatina leaped to the side, avoiding all but a grazing blow. She retaliated with a prayer that summoned a whirling circle of magical energy, pale and sparkling as a moon halo. It coalesced into individual blades of flashing silver and blue-black steel, each as sharp as a freshly honed dagger. With a twist of her hand, Cavatina hurled the whirring circle of magical blades at the monster's head. Whipping her hand around in an ever-tightening spiral, she closed the circle. It tightened in a deadly noose that sent bits of black chitin flying in all directions. Even as it closed, Cavatina raced forward and plunged the singing sword into the beetle's thorax.

As it died, the beetle let out an angry whir. Then its stiffened front wings sprang open. The whirring noise intensified, drowning out the muffled singing of Cavatina's sword, buried to the hilt in the beetle's thorax. Something whizzed past Cavatina's head: a winged, wormlike creature half the length of her forearm. Then another, until the air was thick with flying creatures.

Cavatina yanked her sword free and jumped back as the beetle collapsed. The air was filled with dozens of the flying creatures: the beetle's young, launching themselves from beneath the hard exoskeleton that formed the front wings. Like wasps spilling from a smashed nest they buzzed through the air, forcing Cavatina to dodge and weave. She slashed right and left with her singing sword, slicing several of them in two, but the rest rose up through the trees and escaped.

"Eilistraee!" she cried. "Smite them!"

Whipping her hand forward, she clawed magic from the moon and hurled it at the departing swarm. Moonlight flared, illuminating the trees around her in a wide circle. Wings shriveled and larval bodies imploded under the sheer weight of the goddess's magic. What remained thudded to the ground like soggy hail. A handful of the brood, however—perhaps half a dozen insects—whirred away into the night.

When each landed, it would carve out a home for itself in the forest. There, it would feed, and grow. And if it was female, produce yet another brood.

Cavatina swore softly. She hadn't purged vermin from the forest this night. She'd just spread it around a little, like a demon sowing taint.

The sword in her hand sang a victory paean, but Cavatina didn't share its zeal. She'd killed a brood beetle—quite an accomplishment for a priestess hunting alone—but the rush of exultation that should have accompanied her kill hadn't come.

Part of the reason, she realized, was that nothing could ever live up to slaying a demigod. Any kill paled in comparison to the fierce joy she'd felt in the moment that her sword had severed Selvetarm's neck.

Her eyes narrowed. Not *her* sword. Not any longer. The Crescent Blade was Qilué's now.

She shoved the jealousy aside but couldn't shake off her melancholy. There had been streaks of darkness in the moon bolt she'd used to weaken the beetle, and black blades among the silver in the magical circle of steel. Reminders, each of them, of how much had changed.

Cavatina didn't want things to change. The sound of male voices singing the Evensong hymn was just *wrong*. So was the energy they added to the sacred dance. It was supposed to end in a shout of joy and the clash of swords, not in couples slinking off into the darkness to sheathe swords of a different kind.

She shook her head. She wasn't foolish enough to try to pretend that nothing had changed. Nor was she about to go to the other extreme and give up her faith entirely, as many of Vhaeraun's clerics—and a handful of Eilistraee's priestesses—had done. But that didn't mean she had to embrace the changes enthusiastically. Some rituals, at least, could be performed in solitude.

She nudged the severed mandible with the point of her sword. It was a trophy of the night's kill, one she normally would have carried back to the shrine. She decided to leave it there. To be burned, together with the rest of the brood beetle's body.

She trudged back down the bank, stepping over bits of shattered chitin and earth that had been torn up by the beetle's emergence from the ground. Kneeling beside the stream, she washed her blade clean, splashed water on her skin, and washed off the sticky beetle blood. Then she stood and waved the sword back and forth, drying it. The singing sword let out a low, contented hum, as if pleased with the night's work. It, at least, drew no distinction between degrees of victory.

Balancing the blade on her shoulder, savoring the feel of the silvered metal against her skin, Cavatina walked back the way she had come. For her, the High Hunt was over this night. Eilistraee had caused her to cross paths with a monster, and Cavatina had slain it. That the brood beetle had been about to release a swarm of young was something Cavatina could not have known, she told herself. Perhaps the goddess had been trying to remind her of something: that even the tiniest fragment of evil could beget more evil. That evil had to be eradicated at its root, *before* it could spread. That—

As she passed the spot where she'd seen the rats, a movement at the top of the bank caught her eye. A drow male stood there, silhouetted by the motes of light that trailed behind the moon on its passage through the evening sky. And not just any drow, but one of the recent converts who'd been invited to take part in the hunt this night.

Like her, he was naked, and his thin, muscular body gleamed with sweat from his run. A square of black cloth covered much of his face. His holy symbol. Vhaeraun's mask.

The mask that Eilistraee herself wore as a trophy of her kill.

Cavatina's eyes narrowed. Bad enough, having Nightshadows involved in the High Hunt. Worse luck still, that one had crossed her path. She glared up at him.

The male glanced down at something on the ground, then crouched and spoke in a voice just low enough that Cavatina couldn't make out what he was saying over the gurgle of the stream. He nodded, then pulled a ring off his finger and held it out. A small black rat—identical to the one Cavatina had killed a short time ago—rose up on its hind legs and plucked the ring from his fingers. The rat turned the ring with its forefeet, sniffed it, and slipped the ring onto one foreleg as if it were an armband. Then it scurried away.

As the male rose from his crouch, Cavatina strode up the hill. She knew full well what the male was doing: talking to the creatures of the forest, no doubt asking them where a suitably impressive monster might be found. One that would "prove" his worth as a hunter. But that wasn't how it was supposed to work. Participants in the High Hunt weren't meant to sneak up on their prey and stab it in the back. They were supposed to take down whatever monsters Eilistraee chose for them. Kill them using only their swords—not with the hand-crossbow that Cavatina could see strapped to the back of the male's left forearm. Nor were they supposed to wear magical protections, like the amulet that hung from a chain around his neck.

"What do you think you're doing?" Cavatina demanded.

The male whirled and raised his short sword. For a moment, Cavatina thought he would attack. She slapped it aside with the singing sword; the blades clanged together.

The male's eyes blazed with anger. "Dark Lady." His voice sounded surprisingly even, given his expression. "You startled me."

His accent hinted that he was fresh out of the Underdark, but surely he recognized her. Any moment now, he would whisper her name in awe or fold in a subservient bow. He did neither. Cavatina found herself getting even more annoyed by the way his amber-orange eyes refused to so much as blink under her challenge. "You're supposed to be killing vermin, not conversing with them."

His eyes narrowed slightly. "The rat."

"The rat," she agreed.

"A moon rat," he added. "A creature that *gains* intelligence as the moon waxes."

The unspoken jibe rang loudly in Cavatina's ears. Her singing sword hummed a warning as she readied it. "Are you looking for a fight?"

The male stared up at her. That close, she could see the scar tissue on the left side of his face. Most of it was hidden by his mask, but what showed of the old wound gave his left eye an ugly pucker. "No need to look," he said in a level voice. He nodded at something behind her. "One's already found me."

Cavatina danced back, wary of trickery, and glanced around. A few paces distant, a figure stood in the forest, its body shrouded in an enveloping black robe. Though a hood hid its face, Cavatina could see hands as black as her own. A silver ring gleamed on each finger, marking the figure as one of Kiaransalee's priestesses.

"By all that dances," Cavatina whispered under her breath. "A Crone."

The male touched his mask. "Shield me, Masked Lady."

A haze of darkness blurred his outline—darkness shot through with sparkles of moonlight.

Cavatina sang her own protective prayer. Moonlight glowed briefly on her skin as it took hold—moonlight marred by motes of black. Then she hurled a spell. A ray of moon-chilled light sprang from her hand, striking the evil priestess in the chest.

Instead of retreating, the Crone flung up one ring-encrusted hand. Without so much as a glance in Cavatina's direction she addressed the Nightshadow. "You!" she screamed, pointing a finger at him. "Assassin!"

The cleric cringed, raising one hand to shield his eyes. His other arm swung up in a gesture that mirrored the Crone's and his hand-crossbow thrummed. A bolt streaked through the air, burying itself in the Crone's throat. The priestess clawed at the black fletches and made a strangled sound, but did not fall. Her cowl fell back, revealing a face with sunken cheeks and hollow, staring eyes. Her bone-white hair was matted and filthy. She yanked the bolt out of her throat.

"That . . . won't work, Kâras," she croaked, flinging the bolt aside. "Not . . . this time."

The breeze carried the stench of death to Cavatina's nostrils. She grabbed the silver dagger that hung around her neck. She wrenched its chain over her head and thrust Eilistraee's symbol in the direction of the undead Crone.

"By Eilistraee's holy light," she shouted. "Return to the grave from which you came!"

Cavatina had her sword ready. Should the undead priestess merely turn away, instead of being destroyed utterly, she would slice the creature in half. The blade sang a high-pitched peal. Eager. Ready.

But the Crone neither crumpled nor turned. She strode toward the Nightshadow, a dry, half-strangled chuckle rasping out of the hole in her throat.

The male didn't move. He stood stock still, his arm not quite high enough to shield his eyes.

Paralyzed.

Cavatina blinked. What *was* this thing? Even something as powerful as a lich should have hesitated at the sight of her holy symbol.

Cavatina leaped forward, her weapon raised. The undead priestess turned toward her and sang a single, mournful note. Low as a shaum, it reverberated through Cavatina's mind.

Suddenly, Cavatina's mother was before her. Her long white hair whipped around her head as she spun with a dancer's grace. She flung up an arm to meet Cavatina's descending sword. Only at the last moment was Cavatina able to wrench the sword aside to avoid severing her mother's arm.

The singing sword shrilled a warning. The shrill, urgent note penetrated Cavatina's consciousness, shredding the veil that had clouded her mind. The illusion of her mother was replaced by the reality: a desiccated corpse that had been given a hideous semblance of life. White nubs of bone protruded through the tips of those grasping fingers. The cloak hung loose on bony shoulders.

One hand lashed out. Bony fingers brushed Cavatina's shoulder. A wound appeared there, as if a dagger had sliced it open. Not deep, but it stung.

"This is not . . . your affair," the Crone croaked. Its voice was stronger, and Cavatina could see that the wound the crossbow bolt had torn in its throat had already knitted together.

Cavatina blinked, surprised at the Crone's complete disdain. She raised her sword and swung—a powerful two-handed blow. The singing sword gave a peal of glee as it descended.

In that same instant, the Nightshadow moved. He lashed out with his own sword in an upward diagonal blow. Their two blades clanged together, throwing both Cavatina and the Nightshadow off balance. The Crone ducked aside, unwounded.

"Out of the way!" the Nightshadow shouted.

The Crone lunged, slapping at him with a bare, bony hand. Only by twisting violently aside was the Nightshadow able to avoid being disemboweled. He gasped as the fingers brushed across his hip and buttocks, opening a deep wound.

While the Crone's back was turned, Cavatina leaped and swung. This time, her sword connected. It bit deep into the Crone's neck, cutting through the tough, dry skin and severing the spine. The headless body folded, then fell.

The Nightshadow stared at it, his panting breaths fluttering his mask. One hand clutching his wound, he gasped out a prayer. Slowly, the bleeding stopped.

Cavatina waited, keeping an eye on the body of the Crone, making sure it wasn't going to rise again.

Instead of thanking her, the Nightshadow spat out a curse. "Next time, keep out of the way."

Cavatina stiffened. She couldn't believe what she'd heard. "And let her kill you?"

"She nearly did, thanks to you."

Cavatina's face grew hot. "You were paralyzed," she said. "Helpless."

"I faked it. To draw her in close."

He was lying, of course. It was only to be expected from a Nightshadow. Cavatina was already sorry she'd stepped in. But then she gave herself time to think about it, and realized the unlikelihood of the paralysis wearing off precisely at the moment the Crone came in close enough to kill with a sword blow. Maybe he *wasn't* lying.

"My apologies," she said at last. "If it happens again, I'll wait until I'm absolutely *certain* you really do need my help, before jumping in." She shrugged. "Of course, next time you might not be faking the paralysis."

The male met and held her eye in a flat, level stare. Then he turned his attention to the corpse. "It has to be burned," he said. "Before it knits itself back together again."

The head rocked back and forth, as if struggling to do just that. The Nightshadow rolled it away from the body with his sword. Without another word to Cavatina, he began gathering dried wood and placing it atop the dead torso.

"What—" Cavatina stopped herself before asking the question. As a Darksong Knight, her training had focused on hunting demons, and only to a lesser degree on the undead. She was loath to reveal her ignorance by asking about the creature. She nodded at the severed head. "She knew your name: Kâras."

He nodded.

"Why?"

"I was one of her consorts. Briefly."

"Until you learned who she served?"

"Until I killed her."

"Ah," Cavatina said, suddenly understanding. "She's a revenant."

"Yes."

That made sense. The Crones' thirst for vengeance was unquenchable. Their goddess dictated that any slight, no matter how small, must be avenged. A fatal bolt in the back from the crossbow of a consort would rank right at the top of the list. Kiaransalee herself must have lifted it from the grave.

Cavatina used her sword to flick the robe away from what remained of the Crone's feet. They were mere stubs, the toes and front of each foot long since worn away. "Looks like she walked a long way."

Kâras nodded. "All the way from Maerimydra."

Cavatina looked up. "Were you there—in Maerimydra? When it fell to Kiaransalee's cultists?"

"Yes. And before that, when the army of Kurgoth Hellspawn overran the cavern."

Cavatina stared at Kâras with a fresh respect. Whatever else he might be, he was a survivor. Kurgoth's army of goblins, bugbears, and ogres had laid waste to the Underdark city of Maerimydra during Lolth's Silence. According to the stories, its streets had been filled with thousands of corpses after the army had sacked it. A bountiful harvest for the Crones who'd ruled what remained of the city afterward.

"Did you see Kurgoth yourself?"

"No, shadows be praised."

"That's . . . fortunate," Cavatina said. A lie—she would have loved to have crossed swords with a fire giant who was reputed to be half fiend. She supposed, however, there had been plenty of other adversaries wandering the streets of Maerimydra after the city's fall. She wondered if the Crone they'd just battled was the only one of Kiaransalee's worshipers Kâras had killed.

She glanced around at the moonlit forest. "Do you expect more of them? More revenants?"

"No." He dumped more wood on the corpse. "The moon rat only mentioned this one." Over his shoulder, he added, "Do you know a prayer that can raise fire?"

"No."

He sighed then unfastened the straps that held the crossbow to his forearm and detached the bow from the rest of the mechanism. Then he reached for a stick.

Cavatina sheathed her sword and watched Kâras twist the bowstring around the stick. He carved a hole in a dried scrap of wood and set one end of the stick in it, and added some dried moss. Then, holding the top of the stick loosely, he sawed the bow back and forth, twirling the stick rapidly in place. Eventually the base of it smoldered. A moment later, tiny flames crackled through the dried moss. Kâras blew them to life, gradually adding tinder. Soon, he had a fire.

The flames licked at the undead priestess's robe, charring it. Then the body itself burst into flame. It burned rapidly and with great heat, melting away like a candle. Kâras rolled the head into the fire. A smell like burning leather filled the air.

Cavatina moved closer to Kâras as the Crone's head was consumed. The Nightshadow stared at it without emotion as the flames danced across its desiccated flesh. She wondered if the Crone had been beautiful when still alive—whether Kâras had loved the woman, once. Then she remembered that they did things differently in the Underdark. Females simply "took" males when they wanted them. If it had been like that, little wonder Kâras betrayed no emotion.

Cavatina was curious to hear how the undead hordes of Kiaransalee had been driven from the city, and even more interested in hearing about Kurgoth Hellspawn. She turned to ask Kâras about the city's fall and recapture.

He was gone.

CHAPTER 3

The Month of Marpenoth
The Year of the Haunting (1377 DR)

Q'arlynd stood beside the workbench where his scrolls
and spell ingredients were laid out. He watched
as the duergar metal crafter slid a long-handled
crucible into the darkfire furnace. Sweat beaded
the metal crafter's bald head and trickled down his
temples into the steel-gray stubble on his cheeks
and chin. With flat black eyes, he stared at the
darkfire that licked the underside of the ceramic
dish. So still did he stand that his body might have
been carved from gray stone. His thick-fingered
hands were dotted with teardrop-sized patches of
white where splashes of molten metal had burned
them, yet they gripped the handle with the confidence of a soldier holding a pike.

The magical darkfire burned with great heat,
but no light. The flames flickering inside the

furnace were black as dancing shadows. Coal-dark smoke poured out of a chimney atop the furnace and twisted up through the hollowed-out stalagmite that was Darbleth's workshop. The top of the stalagmite had been lopped off to release the smoke. Once, which rose toward the ceiling of the cave above, blending there with the outpourings of dozens of other forges and furnaces. It spiraled lazily above, eventually disappearing into a one-way portal at the center of the cavern that conveyed it to the surface realm.

When the copper in the crucible collapsed into a glowing puddle, Darbleth pulled the bowl from the furnace and swung it around in front of Q'arlynd. The wizard picked up a scroll and held his free hand over the dish, low enough to feel the heat rising from the molten metal. As he read from the parchment, he crossed each finger over the one next to it, then uncrossed them again, from forefinger to little finger and back again. Then he clenched his hand, as if grasping the haze of heat that rippled above the dish.

As Q'arlynd opened his hand, sparks of violet light erupted from his palm and spun off into the air. Startled, he jerked his hand back. There it was again: another of the manifestations that had been perplexing the sages at the College of Divination. For the past two cycles, any time anyone in the city cast a divination spell, bright sparkles of faerie fire appeared on his hands or lips—something that could be annoyingly inconvenient when secrecy was the aim. It didn't seem to matter how weak or powerful the divination spell, how skilled the caster, or even what method of spellcasting was being attempted. Wizard, sorcerer, bard, or cleric, the result was always the same, as long as the caster was drow: an involuntary glimmer of faerie fire. And it was getting worse. Two cycles ago, it had been a faint, barely noticeable glimmer; now it came as bright, crackling sparks.

No one had any idea why—least of all, Master Seldszar, head of the College of Divination.

A bit of an embarrassment, that. Especially when it was Seldszar's College that had been charged with finding a solution to the problem.

So far, the best theory his sages had come up with was that the effect was linked with the sun. They noted that all drow, down to the youngest, most unschooled boy, had the innate ability to evoke faerie fire and use it to clothe either their own bodies or whatever objects they pointed at in heatless, sparkling radiance. Everyone knew that this ability was tied to the passage of the sun through the skies of the surface realms—drow could only invoke faerie fire once per cycle—and so the sages speculated that something must be affecting the sun. Increasing its intensity, perhaps, to the point where faerie fire was invoked whether a drow willed it or not.

As to why involuntary manifestations occurred during the casting of divination spells, the sages opined that the practice of the divinatory arts made spellcasters especially sensitive to the passage of time. All that was required was a little mental discipline, they said, and the involuntary manifestations of faerie fire would end. Then all would be well again.

Nobody was buying that explanation. Especially when reports from the surface realms indicated that the sun appeared exactly as it always had.

But now was not the time to dwell upon this problem. Q'arlynd had a spell to complete. He repeated the pattern five more times, then let his hand fall.

The copper was cooling and crusting over. Q'arlynd nodded, and Darbleth moved the crucible back into the furnace.

They waited.

Q'arlynd was making six magical rings, one for himself and five for the wizards and sorcerers who would be the foundation of his school—four of whom he'd already chosen.

That "school" was still in its formative stages. Still based in Eldrinn's residence and under the patronage of the College of Divination, it was a long way from being ready to stand on its own. But one day it would do just that, and Master Seldszar would nominate it for official recognition as one of the city's Colleges. That would elevate Q'arlynd to a master's title, and a position on the Conclave. With that secured, he would build his College of Ancient Arcana into the greatest school the city of Sshamath had ever seen. Bound together by their rings, Q'arlynd and the five mages who served as his apprentices would wield magic undreamed of—magic equal in power to the spell that had opened a temporary gate between the domains of Vhaeraun and Eilistraee, nearly two years ago.

Arselu'tel'quess—high magic. Something said to be impossible for the drow.

Something Q'arlynd knew from experience *was* possible.

Opening the gate had opened Q'arlynd's eyes to the power that drow wizards might wield, if only they could pool their arcane talents and set their hearts and minds jointly on a casting—something they *would* be able to do with the rings he was creating. The rings would enable those mages who would form the core of his College to open their minds to each other. They would be able to listen in on each other's innermost thoughts—and to Q'arlynd's, if he so chose—but only if they opened their own minds to scrutiny at the same time. It would be difficult for them, at first, but in time they would learn to do something that drow found almost impossible: trust one another.

Of course, all this would come to pass only if Q'arlynd succeeded in prying the secrets of high magic out of the *kiira* he'd found. That was something he hadn't accomplished yet, despite a year and a half of trying.

The thought made him grind his teeth.

The copper was molten again. Darbleth removed it from the furnace and held it ready for the second spell.

Q'arlynd picked up a small glass vial and unstoppered it. Wisps of yellowish-red smoke rose from the acid it held. Carefully, he tipped the vial over the dish, letting five drops fall. He set the bottle aside on the workbench and picked up a bowl of bluish-gray powder. He dropped five pinches of this into the mix. Then he picked up the second of the four spell scrolls and an eagle feather, and touched the latter to the molten metal. The feather instantly burst into flame, but Q'arlynd forced the quill into the copper, stirring it as he read from the scroll. The vivid motes of faerie fire danced briefly across his knuckles. Q'arlynd ignored them and continued his casting.

The second spell would allow him to extend his mental reach through any of the five lesser rings at will and instantly see what its wearer was up to. It would also allow him to see the wearer's surroundings—clearly enough that he could teleport to that place, if he chose to.

The wearers of the lesser rings, of course, would expect to scry him in return. For that reason, he added a pinch of ground jade. If Q'arlynd chose, he could let the other wizards scry him. If, however, he was doing something he'd rather they not see, his ring would create a false image of his choosing.

The copper was cooling again, so Darbleth returned it to the furnace.

They waited.

Darbleth once more removed the crucible, and Q'arlynd picked up his third scroll. The first two parchments had held divination magic. This one was different. The spell it contained would cause the five lesser rings to exert a subtle influence on their wearers, making them loath to remove them. As he read the enchantment, Q'arlynd dropped a pinch of crushed pearl into the molten copper, followed by a sticky, fingernail-sized fragment of honeycomb.

The fourth scroll held the final spell—an enchantment that Q'arlynd would use only if absolutely necessary. As he read from it, he dropped five needle-thin slivers of iron into the crucible, one by one.

This done, he leaned over the crucible and let a strand of his shoulder-length hair touch the molten copper. The smell of scorched hair joined the reek of burned feather as he bound himself to the metal, ensuring that he would remain master of the six rings. He rose, and pinched off the singed bits of hair.

"I'm done," he told Darbleth. "Proceed with the casting."

The duergar, his expression as somber as ever, returned the crucible to the furnace and watched the copper melt. Then he took it to his centrifuge. He poured the copper into a ceramic flask at one end of the centrifuge's central arm, and yanked out the pin that held the arm in place. A powerful spring snapped the arm into motion, driving the molten metal into the plaster mold. The arm spun for a time, gradually slowed, then stopped.

Darbleth removed the mold. While they waited for the metal inside it to cool, Q'arlynd listened to the sounds that entered the workshop through the stalagmite's open roof. He heard the dull roar of other darkfire furnaces and forges, the muffled clank of hammers on anvils, the murmur of voices and the hiss of water-quenched metal. The sounds might have come from a duergar city; indeed, many of those who worked in the Darkfire Pillars were of that race. Few of the drow liked the duergar—the antipathy between the two ran deep—but they grudgingly admitted duergar were the best metal crafters in the Underdark.

Q'arlynd wanted nothing but the best, in every detail of the college he hoped to create. Fortunately, Master Seldszar's coin pouch proved deep enough to provide it.

When the metal was at last cool, Darbleth broke open the mold. Inside was the casting: five rings, linked by sprues to the master ring like fingers and thumb to a palm. He sawed the sprues off and filed the rings smooth. He gave each ring a final polish, then handed the lot to Q'arlynd. He finished by carefully sweeping the copper dust from his saw and his workbench onto a sheaf of parchment, added the sprues from the casting, then folded the parchment around them. This, too, he handed to Q'arlynd.

Later, Q'arlynd would negate any residual magic the waste metal held and dispose of it, lest anyone else use it to subvert the rings.

Q'arlynd paid the duergar his fee—coin that Q'arlynd's patron had provided without even asking what it was for—and left the workshop. Weaving between the workshops of the Darkfire Pillars, he made his way back to the city's main cavern.

Sshamath was smaller than Ched Nasad had been, but no less beautiful. Its main cavern was wide, rather than deep, and was dominated by Z'orr'bauth, a pillar of stone as thick, from one side to the other, as four blocks of a surface city. Sparkling with decorative faerie fire that shaded from blue-green to violet, it was connected to the cavern's lesser columns via a series of arched bridges. Across these flowed a steady stream of traffic: drow on foot or in palanquins borne by massive ogres or minotaurs, soldiers of the city guard, and diminutive goblin slaves. Wizards flew between the buildings, seated cross-legged on driftdiscs. A wide ramp spiraled around Z'orr'bauth itself, leading from the cavern floor up to a hole in the ceiling, the city's main entrance.

Hanging from the ceiling between Z'orr'bauth and the spot where Q'arlynd walked was the Stonestave, a stalactite that had been stoneshaped to resemble a wizard's staff. Seat of the city's government, it contained the chamber where the Conclave met.

One day, Q'arlynd would stand in that chamber as a master. First, however, he had to crack the *kiira's* secrets. And for that, he needed a test subject.

He made his way to the Dark Weavings Bazaar, a cluster of slender stalagmites that had been turned into shops and inns. It was also home to the slave market. Anywhere else, a slave market would include dozens of holding pens and auction blocks, but in Sshamath, where magic was prolific, the entire market was contained in one building. It lay near the bazaar's center, a blocky edifice of cut stone. Its walls were blank, save for a massive glyph, carved in relief on each side, that sent out a silent magical compulsion for passersby to make their lives easier by buying a slave. Or better yet, two slaves.

As he approached the building, Q'arlynd noticed two white-robed wizards from the College of Necromancy huddled together and talking in low voices, as if plotting something. Curious, he decided to eavesdrop on their discussion. It probably wasn't anything important, but one never knew what scrap of information might prove valuable.

He whispered a quick divination and flicked a finger in their direction, and their whispers became clear. ". . . a priestess of Eilistraee," one of them said, nodding in the direction of the slave house. "She's—"

The other necromancer made a furtive hand sign. The speaker abruptly fell silent and glanced in Q'arlynd's direction. Q'arlynd was puzzled—but only for a moment. Looking down, he saw violet sparks dancing around the finger he'd used to direct his spell. He curled his hand into a fist, cursing softly.

No matter. He'd heard enough. He strode briskly past the pair, toward the slave house. Out of the corner of his eye, he saw one of the necromancers hurry up the street. The other lingered outside the slave house, watching the entrance.

Q'arlynd stepped into a display room lined with shelves holding hundreds of hollowed-out chunks of clearstone, each of a size that would fit neatly in a cupped hand. Each clearstone contained a slave, temporarily reduced in size and bound inside the stone. Some sat on the floor of their clearstones, shoulders slumped in resignation. Others raged and pounded on the walls of their prisons with fists or feet, or butted with their horns, making tiny tinking noises. A few of them had their mouths open as if shouting, but since none of the slaves needed to breathe while magically bound, no sounds were escaping their mouths. Nor did they need to eat or drink, ensuring that they wouldn't foul the inside of the containers.

About a dozen customers eyed the merchandise. Q'arlynd immediately picked out the priestess by her posture. She stood with her back to him, staring intently at a chunk of clearstone on the shelf in front of her, her body rigid with disapproval.

Q'arlynd wondered what she was doing there.

Eilistraee's faithful opposed slavery, and often put themselves at risk to set slaves free. If that was what this priestess was plotting, she wasn't being very sly about it. She wasn't wearing her armor or carrying a hunting horn, and her holy symbol was tucked inside her shirt, with only the silver chain around her neck showing, but her body language all but shouted her faith to anyone familiar with Eilistraee's creed.

Q'arlynd sidled up behind her and glanced at the clearstone she stared at. In Sshamath, only "primitive" races could be kept as slaves, but Eilistraee's faith included a number of worshipers of the lesser races. Perhaps one of them had been captured and put up for sale. That would explain the priestess's lack of discretion.

The clearstone, however, held only a goblin: a scrawny little yellow-skinned creature that stared dully out through the clearstone like a mace-hammered lizard. Goblins were vicious, self-centered little beasts that scavenged in packs; it was doubtful they understood what a deity was, let alone were capable of worshiping one.

The priestess, Q'arlynd decided, must be in Sshamath for some other reason.

He cleared his throat. "Greetings, Lady."

As the priestess turned, he briefly touched his forefingers and thumbs together—in front of his body, where the other customers wouldn't see his gesture—to form the sign of Eilistraee's moon.

The priestess's eyes widened slightly. Then a hint of suspicion clouded them. "Who took your sword oath, and where?"

"Lady Karizra, at the shrine in the Misty Forest." Q'arlynd turned his right palm up, revealing the tiny, crescent-shaped scar the sword had left in his hand.

The priestess smiled, satisfied. She tipped her head in the direction of the shelves. "Slaves," she said in a low voice, the corners of her mouth curling in disapproval.

Q'arlynd gave a somber nod. He sighed, as though he agreed with her but was powerless to change such an institution. "What brings you to Sshamath, Lady? Can I be of assistance?"

"Not unless you can persuade the Conclave to hear me today, instead of keeping me waiting,"

Q'arlynd smiled. She was there to speak to the Conclave, was she? "Do they know who you represent?" He stared pointedly at the chain around her neck.

"I told the Speaker I had been sent by the Promenade," she said. Her gaze drifted to the door. Her eyes hardened as a priestess of Lolth was carried in on a palanquin borne by two minotaurs. "I didn't think it wise, however, to let who I am be generally known."

"Good idea," Q'arlynd agreed. Meanwhile, his mind was brimming with curiosity. Eilistraee's priestesses normally came below ground only to woo new converts and lead them to the surface—something that was normally done in secret. He wondered what might compel a priestess to announce herself to the rulers of an Underdark city. He decided to find out.

"The Conclave can be slow as a millstone, at times," he told her. "Here in the Underdark, we don't have night and day to remind us of the passage of time. Things tend to seem less . . . urgent than they might."

"So I've noticed."

"Would you like some company while you wait for your petition to be heard?"

She nodded. "I *could* use the company of someone who's more in tune with the customs of the World Above. The parts of Sshamath I've seen so far aren't exactly to my taste."

Q'arlynd smiled. The net had been cast. Time to haul in the blindfish.

He took stock. The priestess was far from beautiful. Acne had left her skin porous as limestone. Her braided hair was a dirty mushroom-white and lacking in luster. She was probably double Q'arlynd's age, well into her second century of life. Still, her body was firmly muscled, and her breasts generously endowed—her one redeeming feature. Q'arlynd let his eyes linger on them and smiled.

"I'd be delighted to give you a taste of Sshamath that's more to your liking," he murmured. "Lady . . . ?"

The color of her broad cheeks deepened in a blush as she noticed where he was staring. "Miverra."

"Lady Miverra," Q'arlynd repeated, as if savoring the taste of the name. He ran a hand through his hair and gave her his best "take-me" look.

Her blush deepened.

Q'arlynd gave a mental sigh. Miverra was from the Surface Realms, all right. She expected Q'arlynd to take the lead in this little dance.

So be it.

He bowed. "I'm Q'arlynd."

She showed no sign of recognizing his name. A pity, since this was one instance where he might have capitalized on it. Yet in many ways it was a relief. A handful of Nightshadows still skulked about Sshamath, despite the wave of assassinations that had left the halls of the Tower of the Masked Mage awash in blood. Those assassinations, part of a coup by Nightshadows who had shifted their allegiance to Shar, had taken out the few who insisted on worshiping what remained of Vhaeraun: that strange blend of deities they called the "Masked Lady." There weren't many of the latter left, but Q'arlynd didn't want them learning of his role in

Vhaeraun's death. Even one dagger in the back would be too many.

Fortunately, Q'arlynd's part in Vhaeraun's downfall had been overshadowed by Selvetarm's death at the hands of a mortal. Bards had composed a score of odes to the Darksong Knight who had slain a demigod, but not a single stanza had been written about the conjuring of a gate between Vhaeraun's and Eilistraee's domains.

Miverra glanced at the adamantine amulet that hung against Q'arlynd's chest. "You're with the College of Divination?"

"Currently, yes, but I'm in the process of founding my own school. One day, my School of Ancient Arcana will be recognized as a College in its own right." He gave a rueful look, and added, "Assuming, that is, the Conclave ever finds the time to listen to my petition."

A lie, that. When Q'arlynd did eventually appear before the Conclave, it would be with the backing of a master.

Miverra nodded in obvious sympathy.

Over her shoulder, Q'arlynd saw the proprietor of the slave house making his way across the display room toward them. Klizik's double chin wobbled as he walked. He held up a clearstone and waved to catch Q'arlynd's eye. "Something new has just come in," he called out. "A chitine. Would you like to—"

Not now, Q'arlynd signed. At his side, where Miverra wouldn't notice.

Klizik halted, uncertain.

Fortunately, a customer chose that moment to half-drop a clearstone on a shelf with a loud clunk. Q'arlynd glanced sharply in his direction. When Miverra turned as well, Q'arlynd signed at Klizik a second time. *Set it aside. I'll buy it later.*

A calculating look flickered—briefly—across Klizik's face. He realized Q'arlynd was up to something. The price of the chitine had probably just gone up.

Q'arlynd picked up the clearstone Miverra had been staring at and snapped his fingers at Klizik, as if he'd only just noticed the merchant. "How much for this one?"

As Klizik told him the price, Miverra frowned. "You own slaves?"

Q'arlynd winked at her. "Only for as long as it takes to teleport outside the city and set them free," he whispered back.

Her expression immediately softened.

The price Klizik had just quoted was inflated, but Q'arlynd didn't bother haggling. He fished coins out of his pouch, handed them over, and took the goblin.

"How many have you freed?" Miverra whispered.

"I couldn't begin to count them," Q'arlynd said breezily. She showed no signs of faerie fire, so it was probably safe to lie. "Why, only yesterday, I purchased two grimlocks."

"You teleported them outside the city?"

"Of course. Otherwise they'd be recaptured."

"Far from the city?"

There was a purpose behind her question, but Q'arlynd couldn't discern it. "Far enough." He tucked the clearstone under his arm and turned toward the door. "Let's go somewhere a little less public, shall we?" he suggested. "Somewhere we can . . . talk."

He noted the shiver of anticipation that passed through her and the slight dilation of her pupils. The priestess was pathetically easy to read.

Rather boring, really. He just hoped whatever information he gleaned would be worth it.

As they neared the door, Q'arlynd touched Miverra's arm, slowing her. "There's a wizard outside who's spying on you."

Miverra nodded. "I noticed him earlier. White robes—a necromancer."

Q'arlynd's opinion of her went up a notch. Miverra wasn't quite as naive as she seemed.

"Should I be concerned? Is he a threat?"

"Personally, I wouldn't want Master Tsabrak taking an interest in me."

"Why not?"

Q'arlynd lowered his voice, as if revealing a confidence. In fact, Master Tsabrak's predilection was an open secret among the higher-ranking wizards of Sshamath's other colleges. Even Eldrinn had heard of it. "He's a vampire."

Miverra's eyes widened slightly. She really was too easy to read.

"Will it cause problems for you to be seen with me?" she asked.

Q'arlynd shrugged, then gave her a coy smile. "Even if it does, I'm sure it will be worth it."

She nodded. "Then play along with me. When we step outside, pretend to say goodbye. Be sure to bow."

They exited the slave house, and Q'arlynd did as instructed. "A pleasure to meet you, Lady," he said, bowing. "May your stay in Sshamath be a pleasant one."

Miverra echoed his farewell and bowed, one hand briefly touching her chest—and her holy symbol. Then she straightened and strode away. The necromancer hesitated, glanced between Q'arlynd and the departing Miverra, and followed her into the crowd.

A moment later, Miverra's body shimmered back into view beside Q'arlynd. None of the people streaming by took any notice; they were used to wizards teleporting back and forth across the city.

"Well played," Q'arlynd said, "but I thought Eilistraee's faithful preferred a more direct approach when dealing with threats."

Miverra shrugged. Her eyes were almost level with his; she wasn't much taller than he was. "Things have changed. The goddess offers us a wider range of choices now."

"Let's leave before the necromancer realizes he's been tricked and comes back."

They moved deeper into the labyrinthine streets of the Dark Weavings bazaar, winding their way through the crowds that thronged it. As they walked, Miverra sang a song under her breath. She lightly touched first her own lips and ears then Q'arlynd's. As she did, the noise of the street suddenly fell away. Yet when she spoke he heard every word she said.

"Tell me about the other Masters of the Conclave. Is there anyone else I should be wary of?"

Q'arlynd laughed. "Just approach them as you would a council of matron mothers." At her puzzled look, he added, "With the utmost deference—and the utmost caution."

She nodded.

As they passed a building that sparkled with lavender faerie fire, Q'arlynd noticed Miverra's eyes following the light as it swirled up and down the hollowed-out columns. She probably didn't see many buildings like that on the surface.

"Let me offer these cautions, which may prove useful when you at last get to appear before the Conclave," Q'arlynd continued. "The College of Enchantment is in charge of Sshamath's slave market, so dealing with Master Malaggar may prove . . . problematic for you. And Master Felyndiira is as slippery as an oiled lizard; with an illusionist, you can't ever *really* trust what you're hearing or seeing. Master Urlryn is said to have poisoned his way to the top, while Master Masoj is said to prefer entombing his rivals deep in the earth. That is, supposedly, how he assumed his position at the College of Abjuration." He paused, as if thinking. "Of the ten masters who make up the Conclave, there's only one I'd recommend you trust: Seldszar Elpragh."

"Master of the College of Divination." She glanced pointedly at his amulet. "The college to which you belong, coincidentally enough."

"That's true. But I'm only trying to be helpful. You and I do, after all, share the same faith."

They passed a fungusmonger's stand, and the merchant held up an orange sporeball and cut a sliver from it, imploring them to take a bite. Miverra ignored him. Her attention, Q'arlynd saw, was focused on a bridge that spanned two buildings up ahead. A bridge that, like the column she'd just admired, sparkled with faerie fire.

Her expression was anything but one of admiration. In fact, she looked deeply troubled.

He suddenly realized a possible reason for her visit. "The faerie fire—is it affecting your priestesses too?"

She hesitated, not answering.

"Is that why you came to Sshamath? To learn what's causing the problem? Why . . . that's the very thing our college's sages have been studying."

She spoke slowly, as if thinking aloud. "Perhaps it *would* be better if I spoke to the master of your college, instead of appearing before the Conclave as a whole."

"I'm sure Master Seldszar will want to speak to you," Q'arlynd told her. "In fact, I think I can convince him to hear you this very 'day.' " He lifted a hand. "Shall I teleport us to the College of Divination at once?"

Miverra touched his arm and moved in close. "Isn't there something you're forgetting?"

"What's that?"

She nodded at the clearstone in his hands. "The goblin. Shouldn't you set it free first?"

Q'arlynd almost laughed. He'd forgotten about the slave entirely. "Of course. Wait here; I'll only be a moment."

He intended to teleport to the slave house, return the goblin, and ask for credit toward the purchase of the chitine. But as he glanced down at the goblin it reminded him—just for a moment—of someone. A svirfneblin he'd once owned. The goblin stared up at him with dull eyes, its naked body a mass of bruises. No doubt some child had played with the clearstone, shaking it to see what would happen to its contents.

Flinderspeld had looked just as bad, the day Q'arlynd had seen him standing on the auction block.

Q'arlynd sighed, then teleported to a cavern well beyond the city. It took him two tries—his maudlin mood must have interfered with his concentration—but when it eventually worked he was precisely on target.

He laid the clearstone on the cavern floor, dispelled its magic, and stepped back as it shattered. The goblin instantly assumed its full size. It staggered to its feet and stared at him, lips pulled back in a grimace that revealed a mouth of jagged teeth. If Q'arlynd got too close, the creature would no doubt bite him. Goblins were that stupid; they didn't understand what wizards could do to them.

"Go on," he told it, making shooing motions. "Run along now. You're free."

The goblin's head puckered in a frown that pulled its ears closer to its beady eyes. "Free?" it squeaked.

"Yes, free," Q'arlynd repeated, already regretting this. He flicked a finger and spoke a one-word spell that hurled a pebble at the creature. "Go!"

The goblin cringed.

Muttering at its stupidity, Q'arlynd teleported back to the city.

After he was gone, faerie fire puddled on the floor where he'd been standing, bathing the cavern in a pale violet light.

The goblin sniffed at the glow. Then it scurried away.

CHAPTER 4

Cavatina touched her fingers and thumbs together to form Eilistraee's sacred moon, and bowed. "Lady Qilué. You sent for me?"

"Cavatina. My thanks. For coming so quickly."

The high priestess levitated near the ceiling of the Hall of Swords, a large chamber in the Promenade where the Protectors of the Song honed their skills. She was naked, her ankle-length silver hair whirling like a wind-blown skirt around her as she spun in place. Motes of moonfire filled the air around her, shining with the many colors of the changing moon: blue-white, dusky yellow-orange, and harvest red reflected by the curved blade of the sword she danced with. The Crescent Blade.

Cavatina felt a pang of longing for the weapon. Her right hand clenched as she remembered its perfect heft, and how its leather-wrapped hilt had warmed in her palm.

"I have a mission for you. One that will require . . . your renown." The high priestess continued to dance as she spoke, her breathing rapid. Yet her voice betrayed no hint of weariness. Qilué had been performing the dance of attunement without pause for nine days and nine nights, according to the priestess who had greeted Cavatina upon her arrival at the Promenade. Yet the silver fire that flowed within her sustained her body. Aside from a sheen of sweat, the high priestess looked as strong as if she had only just begun her dance.

Qilué spun with the sword balanced atop her head, the midpoint of the blade lying flat against her silver tresses. A toss of her head sent it spinning into the air. She "caught" it on one arm, spun the weapon in a fast blur around her arm from wrist to elbow, then flicked it to her other arm and repeated the motion. A thrust of that arm sent it spinning into the air; it sailed toward the ceiling, slowed, then fell.

Cavatina gasped as the weapon whistled down, point first, at Qilué's upturned face. The high priestess twisted aside at the last moment and caught the hilt between her bare feet. A kick transferred the sword back into her hand.

"I am assembling a force," Qilué said as she shadow fenced with the weapon, "and sending it north. You will lead it. Six Protectors . . ."

The sword flashed in a high arc. Qilué caught it, point-first, between finger and thumb, and flipped the hilt into her hand.

". . . and six Nightshadows."

Cavatina's nostrils flared. "Nightshadows," she muttered.

"Do not denigrate them," Qilué admonished. "They are weapons. Finely honed. Eilistraee has embraced them. So must you."

Cavatina lowered her eyes. "My apologies, Lady Qilué."

She hadn't intended her comment to be heard. She knew she was being honored. The mission must be an important one if Protectors were being sent. The singing swords they carried left the temple only in times of dire need. Like the time, nearly two years ago, when Cavatina had been sent into the Demonweb Pits to recover the Crescent Blade, armed with the singing sword that now hung at her hip.

"Our objective?" she asked.

"The time has come." Qilué set the Crescent Blade spinning around her wrist. "To take on a foe. One that is equal. To Selvetarm." She stared down at Cavatina through the blur of the whirling blade. "Kiaransalee."

Cavatina drew in a sharp breath. Excitement flooded her body, making her giddy. "Am I to slay the Goddess of Death?"

"No. Throwing down her temple . . ." Qilué transferred the whirring blade to her other wrist. ". . . should be sufficient."

"Her temple," Cavatina echoed, unable to keep the disappointment from her voice.

Qilué tossed the Crescent Blade into the air. "Surrounded by an army of undead. Hundreds. Perhaps thousands."

Cavatina's eyes widened as she realized what the destination must be. "The Acropolis?"

"Yes."

"Why such a small force? Six Protectors is hardly enough to—"

"And six Nightshadows. An even dozen. Of our best."

Cavatina took a deep breath. "That's small, for a crusade."

"Not a crusade." Qilué caught the sword, held it above her in both hands, and spun from it as if dangling from a twisting rope. "An assassination. Hence . . ." She spun faster, until the curved blade described a blurred oval in the air. ". . . the Nightshadows."

"An assassination?" The word felt as wrong in Cavatina's mouth as a lump of sickstone. It suggested poison, a garrote around the throat. She preferred to meet her foes honorably. Face to face, with blade in hand.

"Think of it as a hunt," Qilué said. She slapped one arm to her side and halted, letting the Crescent Blade spiral down her upraised arm. "You are to kill the head priestess. Cut off the head," she said, as the weapon whirled past her face, ". . . and the temple will fall."

The weapon spun around her neck. Her hand slapped against the hilt, jerking the sword to a halt. The edge of the curved blade rested against her throat, unsettlingly reminiscent of a scythe poised against a stalk of wheat.

Even more disturbing was the thin line of blood that trickled down Qilué's wrist.

That shouldn't have happened.

Cavatina knew that first-hand; her mother had been a sword dancer. Jetel Xarann had prided herself on never—not once—being cut by the blades she danced with. Qilué was far more skilled, the high priestess of her faith. Yet she seemed not to have noticed an error that could have cost her a hand.

Now that the Crescent Blade had been stilled, Cavatina could see the spot where its two halves had been fused together again, and the silvered inscription that was interrupted at that place: "Be your heart filled with light and your cause be true, I shall n— fail you."

The Crescent Blade nearly *had* failed Cavatina. Only with Halisstra's help had she been able to prevail against Selvetarm. Now she wondered: when the time came for Qilué to wield it against Lolth, who would come to *her* aid?

". . . depart two nights from now, when the moon rises." Qilué was saying. "Our new battlemistress will tell you everything you need to know."

Cavatina was startled to realize that the high priestess had dismissed her. Qilué continued to dance, her eyes staring into the distance and her head cocked slightly, as though she were listening to a faint voice: the sword, whispering to her. Cavatina yearned to hear it too.

Qilué glanced sharply down at Cavatina. "Is something wrong?"

"Nothing," Cavatina said quickly. "Two nights from now, at moonrise. I'll be ready."

Master Seldszar sat cross-legged on a raised stone platform, cushioned by his meditation mat. At least two dozen crystal spheres no larger than pebbles orbited his head. Most were clear and contained a miniaturized image of a person or place the Master of Divination monitored, but one, Q'arlynd knew, could detect falsehoods spoken in the master's presence.

Even though Master Seldszar listened to Miverra speak, his glance kept drifting back to the crystals. Pale green faerie fire burst from his forehead and drifted toward them, fading just before it touched the spheres.

The master's eyes were pale yellow; rumor had it he'd had them replaced, decades ago, with the eyes of an eagle. His hair, too, tended toward yellow. It matched his *piwafwi*, which was embroidered, in black, with numerous eyes: the symbol of his college. The garment was magical, and the direction in which each embroidered eye seemed to be looking constantly shifted.

Q'arlynd stood to one side of the master's platform. Miverra was in front of it, her eyes barely level with its top. If she was intimidated by the master, she showed no sign.

"I understand, Master Seldszar, that the spellcasters of Sshamath are experiencing a strange manifestation whenever they attempt a divination spell. Our priestesses have also noticed peculiar things, whenever they sing a hymn of divination."

"Faerie fire," Q'arlynd added. "Just like our wizards. You see why I thought you should hear what Lady Miverra had to say."

Miverra turned to him. "Not quite, Q'arlynd. The faerie fire effect seems to be peculiar to Sshamath."

Q'arlynd fought to hide his startle. "But you said—"

"I did not." Her lips quirked slightly. "You made that assumption. But what I have to impart here today is equally worthy of Master Seldszar's time."

Master Seldszar shot a glance at Q'arlynd, then returned his attention to the spheres. "Go on," he told the priestess.

"Something is heightening the *Faerzress* that surround the vast majority of our Underdark communities. In areas adjacent to a *Faerzress*, it's become increasingly difficult to perform any acts of divination over the past little while, as well as to—"

"Teleport?" Q'arlynd interjected, suddenly realizing what her earlier question about setting the grimlocks free had really been about.

"Yes. But strangely enough, only for drow. All other races seem unaffected. The *Faerzress* still hamper them, but only to the degree that they always have."

"By 'drow,' you include half-drow?" Master Seldszar asked.

Q'arlynd nodded to himself; Seldszar was obviously thinking of his son.

"Half-drow, as well."

"You said 'over the past little while,'" Master Seldszar observed. "I take it this has been going on elsewhere for some time?"

"The first reports of the effect came in from far to the northeast a tenday ago, just after High Harvestide," Miverra said. "From the region south of the Moonsea, where our priestesses have labored, these past few years, to bring the survivors from Maerimydra up into the light."

Q'arlynd recognized the name. Maermydra was a drow city that, like Ched Nasad, had been invaded and destroyed during Lolth's Silence. He'd heard that what little of it remained was home to hordes of undead. Even fewer had survived there than in Ched Nasad.

Master Seldszar's arms were crossed, and the hand that was hidden under the sleeve of his *piwafwi* flicked a question at Q'arlynd: *Moon-sea? Surface?*

Q'arlynd turned to Miverra. "Forgive my ignorance, Lady Miverra, but is the Moonsea part of the Surface Realms?"

She nodded. "It lies directly above the Moondeep Sea, its Underdark counterpart in the Deep Wastes."

"Ah," Q'arlynd said.

"We believe that region contains the source of the problem," Miverra continued.

"Interesting," Master Seldszar commented.

The master's tone was carefully neutral, but Q'arlynd felt certain Seldszar was experiencing a rush of relief. When the manifestations had begun, Master Seldszar had concluded the faerie fire was a plot to discredit his college. He'd been obsessing about which of the other masters was scheming against him. He must have been glad to hear the problem was originating from somewhere . . . else. Somewhere outside Sshamath.

Miverra stared up at him. "The Acropolis of Thanatos—Kiaransalee's largest temple—lies under the Galena Mountains, just northeast of the Moondeep. That could be coincidence, but personally, I don't think so. We believe the Crones are behind whatever is affecting the *Faerzress*. We'll know soon enough if our guess is right."

"You've sent out spies?"

She hesitated. "We prefer to call them 'scouts.' An advance party. We'll be sending the best the Promenade has."

"I'm surprised that something so far away affects us here," Q'arlynd observed. "The Moondeep Sea is a long way from Sshamath. More than three hundred leagues."

"The effect is spreading," Miverra said. "It only just reached this far. And it's getting worse. Up around the Moondeep, it's grown very strong. Sing a divination hymn there—even a simple chant to reveal the presence of a magical aura—and it's not just more difficult than usual. Nothing happens at all. The same is true of scryings, spells of location, distance viewings, thought detection—any form of magic that imparts wisdom or extends the senses. They're all impossible."

Q'arlynd suddenly realized the implication. "Are you telling us it's going to get that bad here?"

"Yes. Every *Faerzress* we've monitored over the past few days has grown steadily brighter and larger. There's no *Faerzress* surrounding Sshamath, but that unwanted faerie fire that accompanies your castings may be part of the same effect. What you've seen so far is only the start. When it gets as bad here as it is in the Deep Wastes, you'll be blinded by faerie fire every time you attempt a divination."

Master Seldszar's attention was wholly upon Miverra. The tiny crystal balls zipped past his face unheeded. "How much time do we have?"

"At the rate it's growing . . . another tenday, give or take a day or two."

Q'arlynd's pulse raced. If it got as bad in Sshamath as Miverra had just described—if divination became impossible—the college he'd attached himself to would collapse. When it fell, he'd have neither funding for his experiments, nor a master to nominate his school. Q'arlynd would never become a master of a formally recognized college, never become a member of the Conclave. All his hard work would be for nothing.

Unless, he reminded himself, his school was somehow recognized as a college *before* that happened. As a separate entity, the College of Ancient Arcana would no longer be dependent upon anyone.

Q'arlynd's mind raced as he weighed the odds of that happening. It would certainly be possible, within the next tenday, to manipulate Master Seldszar into nominating the School of Ancient Arcana for acceptance as a college, but there would be strings attached. If the school was elevated to college status, Q'arlynd was likely to wind up a master in name only, with Seldszar the real power behind the throne. Seldszar might even try to seize control directly. His son Eldrinn was one of Q'arlynd's apprentices, after all, and "accidents" could always be arranged.

No, Q'arlynd would have to petition the Conclave on his own, without the benefit of a formal nomination. Just getting the masters to convene would require a miracle—especially if it were to happen within the next tenday. There were dozens of schools in Sshamath, all vying to be elevated to the status of the city's eleventh officially recognized college. Q'arlynd would first have to secure an audience with the Conclave—a difficult enough task, as Miverra could attest—and convince the masters that a school that most of them had never even heard of was worthy of elevation to college status. In order to do that, he'd have to do something *really* impressive. Demonstrate the capability to wield high magic, for example. Or something close enough to it that their eyes would widen. And the only way he was going to do that was by cracking the secrets of the *kiira*. Immediately.

Miverra was still talking. ". . . and that's why we're hoping that Sshamath will lend us its aid."

Master Seldszar had composed himself. His voice was stone-steady as he responded. "What do you propose?"

"We'd like you to share with us whatever you learn. The faerie fire effect is unique to Sshamath; there must be a reason for that. We'd like to know what that reason is. We're also seeking a contribution to any military campaign we might mount against Kiaransalee's temple, should our advance party prove unable to deal with the problem."

Q'arlynd found his voice. "An army would never reach the temple in time for a military campaign to benefit us. The Dark Wastes are leagues away. From what you've just described, teleportation to that region is already impossible."

"That's true. But we have other means of reaching the area: a portal." She stared up at Master Seldszar. "If it comes to a military campaign against the Acropolis, do you think you'll be able to convince the Conclave to join us?"

Q'arlynd waited as expectantly as Miverra for the master's reply. He could guess what must be going through Seldszar's mind. Though Q'arlynd had lived in Sshamath for only a short time, he knew how the pieces would line up. All of the colleges would be affected by the loss of divination magic, but their wizards relied on it to a lesser degree. If they needed a divination, they could always find a human wizard to cast one for them. The spells they specialized in would be unaffected; the crisis would leave them largely untouched. They might, in fact, be just as happy to see the College of Divination fall. Power sliced nine ways, instead of ten, would give each a larger piece of the pie that was Sshamath.

What's more, the other Masters would be loath to participate in a campaign that might cost them a number of the city's soldiers and battle mages. Lolth's temple in Sshamath was small, but since the upheaval that had thinned the ranks of Vhaeraun's clergy, the Spider Queen's priestesses controlled most of the healing magic. A crusade led by their hated rivals would be the last thing they would agree to. And without healing magic, any expeditionary force's losses would be unacceptably high.

Yet there might yet be a way to salvage things.

"Master, might I confer with you about something?" Q'arlynd asked.

Miverra shot him a glance. Q'arlynd gave her his best "trust me" look.

Master Seldszar gestured toward the door. "Please step outside for a moment, Lady Miverra."

The priestess straightened her shoulders indignantly. A moment later, however, she bowed. "I'll await your reply." She strode out of the room.

When she was gone, Q'arlynd took a deep breath. "Master, forgive my brashness, but I know a thing or two about Eilistraee's priestesses. My sister was one of them, after all. I understand how they think. Much of what they do is based on *trust*," he said, using the surface elves' word for the term that had, in High Drowic, no true equivalent. "If we tell Miverra a little of the truth, give her a hint of the complexity of what she's asking, we'll convince her that a small force is all that could possibly be mustered."

The master stared down at Q'arlynd. "Go on."

"The Conclave hasn't heard Miverra's petition yet. The other masters will know that a priestess of Eilistraee wished to speak to them, but not why. If she can be convinced to leave quietly with a small force of wizards drawn entirely from our college, we could secretly participate in the scouting expedition. Judging by the way she worded it, her 'advance party' hasn't departed yet. If the source of the problem does indeed turn out to be Kiaransalee's temple, and if its spread can be halted or even reversed by our wizards, then you, Master, could claim credit for 'solving' the problem. No one from the Conclave need know about the crisis our college is facing—or that we participated in an expedition headed by Eilistraee's priestesses. And if the other Masters do find out, well. . . ." Q'arlynd shrugged. "It's always been my experience that asking permission after the fact is easier."

Master Seldszar's eyes closed. His lips worked silently as he gestured. Motes of pale green faerie fire sparkled momentarily on his closed eyelids. For a moment, his face was gray and taut. But when his eyes opened again, they held a look of resolve. "We will do as you suggest. Send a small force of wizards. *Not* an army."

Q'arlynd frowned slightly. Who'd said anything about an army? Nevertheless, he was pleased. Once again, he'd proved his worth. The problem would be dealt with—and he could get back to his experiments.

He inclined his head toward the door. "Shall I call Miverra back in?"

Master Seldszar's eyebrows rose. "'Miverra?' Not, 'Lady Miverra?'"

Q'arlynd swallowed. He resisted the urge to close his fingers over the scar in his palm that marked him as having taken Eilistraee's sword oath. "I—"

"Just as well. She *trusts* you. That should prove useful."

"'Useful?'" Q'arlynd had a bad feeling about this.

The master's eyes flicked back to his crystal balls. "You'll be going, of course. On the expedition."

No! Q'arlynd silently moaned. *I can't! Not now!*

His mouth felt dry. If the priestess's scouting expedition failed and the College of Divination fell, he would lose valuable time. Time that might be used to unlock the secrets of the *kiira* and learn spells that would impress the Conclave. But he could hardly tell Master Seldszar that.

The master's eyes flicked down to Q'arlynd. "Is there a problem?"

"No. Of course not. It's just . . ." Q'arlynd hesitated. Master Seldszar had overlooked the glaringly obvious, yet how was Q'arlynd to word his reply without giving insult?

Q'arlynd chose his words carefully. "Perhaps I'm missing something. I would have thought that the party would consist of our non-drow wizards. Humans, surface elves—diviners whose magic won't be compromised by the augmented *Faerzress*."

Master Seldszar smiled. "Obviously, it will have to include them. But there is, as you pointed out, this little matter of 'trust.' Will non-drow truly care about solving our problem when they aren't affected by it personally? Should divination become impossible for drow, the talents of non-drow diviners will become immensely valuable. They may secretly be hoping that our college falls. They're the only possibly candidates for this mission, but who will keep an eye on them? Who can I *'trust'?* The choice is obvious: Eldrinn. He'll be in charge of the party—and you'll be there to back him up. The majority of your spells, as I recall, are non-divinatory and will be unaffected by *Faerzress* energy. Correct?"

"It is as you say, Master Seldszar," Q'arlynd admitted grudgingly.

Seldszar returned his attention to his crystal balls. "Call Lady Miverra back in and convey my decision to her. As soon as our mages are assembled, they'll depart with her, whenever she's ready to go."

As Cavatina strode into the Cavern of Song, all eyes turned toward her. After nearly two years of this, she should have gotten blasé about the admiring looks, yet they still filled her with a rush of pride. Her chin lifted and her shoulders squared. A smile played about her lips as her fellow priestesses either inclined their heads to her or bowed deeply, their marks of respect indicating how recently they'd left the customs of the Underdark behind. Their voices swelled, filling the cavern with a joyous sound.

Like the other priestesses, Cavatina was naked, save for her sword belt and the holy symbol that hung about her neck. She drew her sword and pointed it at the spot on the floor where Eilistraee's shimmering moonfire was brightest, marking the current location of the moon in the world beyond the Promenade. As she sang, she watched colorful waves of moonfire flow across the floor like ripples on a pond. They washed over the two dozen or so priestesses gathered there, and bathed in radiance the statue that dominated the cavern, a monument to the temple's founder and its high priestess.

The statue showed a youthful Qilué as she was imagined to have stood at the moment she defeated Ghaunadaur's avatar, her singing sword raised above her head in triumphant salute to the goddess. In fact, Qilué had collapsed immediately after that battle, spent and near death after Eilistraee used her body as a conduit for Mystra's silver fire.

Elsewhere in the Promenade, stone carvers were hard at work on a similar statue, this one commemorating the slaying of Selvetarm. When complete, it would be erected in the cavern that housed the Protectors' living quarters. It would show Cavatina, Crescent Blade in hand, delivering the blow that had severed the demigod's neck.

With Qilué's permission—and Cavatina was still working on achieving this—the statue would also depict Halisstra, one arm raised, her hand extended from having just passed Cavatina the sword. Halisstra would be carved as she had been before Lolth transformed her: as a drow female. It would be a slight untruth, but no one would be the wiser. Only Cavatina and Qilué had seen the horrible monster Halisstra had become.

Halisstra had disappeared after Selvetarm fell, and even Qilué had been unable to scry her. Cavatina had returned to the Demonweb Pits to search for Halisstra but had found no trace of the former priestess. Cavatina had battled her way past yochlols and questioned lesser demons at the point of her singing sword, but the paths they sent her on led only to the creeping horrors that thrived in Lolth's domain. Halisstra was just . . . gone. At last acknowledging that, Cavatina had allowed the Darkwatch portal to be sealed.

She sang a soft prayer, imploring Eilistraee to embrace Halisstra's dark soul, should it ever find its way to the goddess's side. Then she joined the others in the sacred hymn.

As always happened when Cavatina visited the Promenade, priestesses found an excuse to join whatever activity she was participating in. Moonrise—the time when most performed the Evensong devotion—was still some time away. Yet novices and higher-ranking priestesses alike were already slipping into the Cavern of Song in ones and twos. Cavatina nodded at each as she entered—but when a Nightshadow slid into the room, furtive as an assassin on the prowl, the hymn she sang died on her lips.

Though the Nightshadow was naked—he'd observed that doctrine, at least—his face was hidden behind his mask. The blade he carried wasn't a sword but an assassin's hollow-bladed dagger. He took up a place near the entrance—his back against the wall—and pointed his dagger at the spot where Eilistraee's moonfire bloomed. Then he began to sing.

As he did, streaks of darkfire threaded their way into Eilistraee's sacred light.

Throughout the cavern, eyes widened and voices faltered. Not once in the twenty-two years since the temple's founding had a male participated in the sacred hymn within the Cavern of Song. Despite the admission of Vhaeraun's clerics to Eilistraee's faith, this tradition still held. Males could pass through the cavern—they had to in order to get from one wing of the Promenade to the next—but the Cavern of Song was the one place in all of Eilistraee's many shrines that the old observances were retained.

But that long tradition had been broken.

Cavatina was appalled by the impudence of the male. The Nightshadows had been given another cavern elsewhere in the Promenade as a place where they might worship according to their traditions. The male should have gone there and honored the goddess in his own peculiar way, shrouded in darkness and silence.

Cavatina realized that the only voice in the cavern was the Nightshadow's. The females had fallen silent. He alone sustained the hymn that had continued, unbroken, since the temple's founding.

Cavatina swallowed—her mouth was suddenly very dry—and immediately began to sing. Her voice battled the Nightshadow's as each attempted to drag the other into a range more suited to the singer's gender. All at once, the other priestesses resumed the hymn, forcing the male to either find the harmony or falter.

Satisfied the song would be sustained without her assistance, Cavatina sheathed her sword and made her way across the cavern to the place where the Nightshadow stood. Aware that all eyes were upon her, she spoke with her hands as she approached him, so that all could "hear" her.

Males do not sing here, she signed with blunt, forceful movements of her fingers. *The Cavern of Song is for priestesses only.*

The Nightshadow continued to sing. His eyes slid toward her. They crinkled in a smile, puckering the scar next to his left eye.

Suddenly, Cavatina recognized him: the Nightshadow who had helped her battle the revenant in the Shilmista Forest. "Kâras!" she said aloud. "What—?"

His free hand answered the question she'd yet to complete. *Lady Qilué summoned me to the Promenade. I'll be joining your expedition.*

"Then you're under my command," Cavatina said aloud. "And my first order is this: leave the Cavern of Song. At once."

Kâras stopped singing in mid-stanza and lowered his dagger. He stared up at her, toying with the weapon as if testing its balance. "I'm not under your command," he said slowly. "I'm to lead the Nightshadows. *Ask* me to leave the Cavern of Song, and I will. But I won't take orders from you. I am a Black Moon, equivalent in rank to a Darksong Knight—the rank you still hold, Lady Cavatina."

Cavatina stared down at him, her eyes blazing. How dare he? She'd see about this. "Qilué," she said firmly.

A moment later the high priestess answered, mind to mind. *Yes, Cavatina?*

A male has entered the Cavern of Song, Cavatina thought back at her. *The Nightshadow Kâras. He—*

I sent him to find you, Qilué answered before Cavatina could finish. *He has a wealth of knowledge of Kiaransalee's cult. Listen to what he has to offer; you will need it.*

Cavatina's jaw clenched. Back in the forest, after Kâras had disappeared into the night, she'd chafed at missing an opportunity to hear more about Maerimydra. She should have been more careful about what she wished for. *I'll listen to him, but I don't want him on the expedition. He's . . . ill-suited to taking orders. He thinks he's to command the Nightshadows; he's actually got it into his head that he's to join this expedition as my equal.*

He is your equal, Qilué thought back. *Female and male, moonlight and darkness, sword and stealth—working hand in hand to return the drow to the World Above, just as the goddess has decreed.*

Cavatina winced. Before Eilistraee subsumed Vharaun's worshipers, Qilué would have said "up into the light," not, "to the World Above." Cavatina resisted the urge to rub her temples. The thought of what the goddess had become pained her.

You and Kâras must work together, Qilué continued.

Cavatina's jaw clenched. *If that is your command, Lady Qilué,* she answered, *I will obey it.*

It is.

The fact remains that males are not permitted to sing in the Cavern of Song, Cavatina shot back, still glaring at Kâras.

That, too, is something that must change. I will remedy it at once.

Cavatina was furious—but she was smart enough to know she needed to salvage the situation, and quickly. She spoke to Kâras in sign. *I have spoken to Lady Qilué. You may sing with us. Stay or leave the cavern, as you please.*

A moment later, several other priestesses cocked their heads slightly, listening. Cavatina heard the proclamation herself. Qilué told the faithful that Vhaeraun's former clerics—those who had embraced their god in his new aspect of the Masked Lady—were welcome to join the holy chorus in the Cavern of Song.

Kâras slid his dagger back into its forearm sheath and inclined his head. Slightly. "I look forward to working with you on our expedition to the Acropolis, Lady Cavatina."

Cavatina's eyes narrowed. Two could play at this match. "As do I," she parried, her voice cold as steel, "with you."

CHAPTER 5

Q'arlynd watched as the slaves manacled the chitine to the experimentation chamber's wall. Though the chitine wore the slave ring, it had a strong mind, highly resistant to enchantments. That might allow it to last a little longer than the other subjects, but strength of will made it difficult to handle; it kept shaking off Q'arlynd's mental control.

The chitine was thin and barely as tall as Q'arlynd's shoulder. In contrast, the gray-skinned grimlock slaves were taller than humans and powerfully muscled. Yet even they had a hard time forcing the chitine's fourth arm into a manacle. The chitine's oily skin made it difficult to grapple. Wrenching its arm free, it sank the hook in its palm into the shoulder of the larger grimlock, tearing a bloody gash. The grimlock yelped and slammed a fist into the chitine's face, knocking its head back against the wall. The chitine sagged at the knees and slowly shook its head, its multifaceted eyes unfocused.

Q'arlynd clenched his fist around his master ring. "No more of that!" he snapped at the grimlocks. "I need it awake and undamaged."

He forced the chitine to stand upright, and held its body still while the grimlocks completed their task. They were sightless creatures with only vestigial eyes. Though they couldn't see Q'arlynd standing with his arms folded, they could hear his impatient foot tap and smell his irritation. Q'arlynd knew this would be his last chance to experiment on the *kiira* before being sent away.

The chitine at last secure, the grimlocks turned and bowed to their master. Each cocked an oversized ear in his direction, awaiting his command. Blood dribbled down the injured one's arm and puddled on the floor.

"Go to the kitchen," Q'arlynd ordered. "Have the cook wash out that wound and bind it. Then eat; there's fresh meat for both of you."

The grimlocks broke into wide grins. They bobbed their heads and hurried from the room, heads tipping this way and that as they listened for the sounds of their footsteps echoing back off the walls.

Eldrinn sat in a corner of the room, watching, his spell-book lying open across his lap. Despite its ornately tooled leather cover and pages edged with gold, it held only a hand-ful of minor spells. Eldrinn's clothes were equally decorative. He wore an embroidered purple *piwafwi* over a white shirt and trousers that helped make his brownish skin seem darker than it was. His waist-length hair was neatly combed straight back from his high forehead and was bound in a silver clip that rested against the small of his back.

He shook his head. "Wash and bind the wound? You're coddling those grimlocks. That wound will heal by itself."

Q'arlynd gestured at their captive. "Look at the chitine's

hands; they're filthy. The wound could fester. No sense in wasting a good slave."

Eldrinn closed his spellbook and laid it on the table beside him, next to a wooden box. "There's plenty more where they came from."

"Slaves are expensive."

"So what? We can afford a dozen of them."

Q'arlynd sighed. The younger wizard had an intuitive grasp of magic that was well beyond his training and years, but what he knew about handling slaves wouldn't have filled a bunghole. Loyalty had to be built, one brick at a time. It couldn't be beaten into a slave. Whippings only produced fear and resentment—and a smoldering desire for revenge. Something Q'arlynd had learned early in life, as a boy in House Melarn.

Eldrinn, however, had grown up in Sshamath, the pampered and indulged son of the master of the city's College of Divination. The closest he'd ever come to anything resembling a matron mother's wrath was when he'd been teleported home by Q'arlynd a year and a half ago, mind-damaged and dragging behind him the powerful staff he'd "borrowed" from the master's private study.

Seldszar Elpragh had paid for the expensive spell that had cured his son, then raged at the boy for going off, with only one soldier accompanying him, to indulge in "pointless poking about" in the ruins of the High Moor. He'd cut off Eldrinn's stipend for a month—no real punishment. His son, he later admitted to Q'arlynd, was more valuable than any staff.

Q'arlynd had to agree, but for different reasons. Eldrinn not only had access to Master Seldszar's deep coin purse, but also a residence of his own that was perfect for secluded experimentation. And his thirst for arcane knowledge and the power that came with it equaled Q'arlynd's own. The boy acknowledged Q'arlynd as his superior in the Art and was keen to make good on the debt that he owed the older wizard for his rescue. He was almost pathetically grateful to Q'arlynd for being invited to participate in the experiments on the *kiira* Q'arlynd had "found" on the High Moor. Best of all, he had absolutely no recollection of ever having possessed the stone himself. All memories of his trip to the High Moor had been wiped from his mind, except for the odd muddled flash.

Which was precisely why Q'arlynd had encouraged the boy to participate in his experiments on the *kiira*, and why he kept Eldrinn by his side as much as possible. If Eldrinn suddenly remembered something about his expedition to the High Moor, Q'arlynd wanted to be the first to hear about it.

All he had to put up with in return were Eldrinn's incessant comments on how he should discipline the slaves.

Q'arlynd walked over to the chitine and grabbed the creature by the hair. It opened its eyes and strained at its manacles, hissing. Baring its teeth and clicking its curved mandibles, it attempted, futilely, to bite Q'arlynd's arm.

Q'arlynd examined the back of the creature's head. "No real damage done." He released the hair and stepped back.

"You should have whipped the grimlocks, just the same. Both of them."

Q'arlynd ignored the younger male's comment. He didn't want to get caught up in another lengthy debate. Too much rested on this experiment. "What about the others? Are they on their way?"

Eldrinn closed his eyes and toyed with the copper ring Q'arlynd had given him. Faerie fire danced across his closed eyelids as he used the ring to view the others from afar. "Piri's driftdisc is just passing the Web. Zarifar and Baltak are en route from the Quillspires; they should be right behind him."

"Good."

Eldrinn opened his eyes. "Could Alexa—?"

"No."

"But she's one of the most promising apprentices the College of Conjuration has. She created a sigil that—"

"We've been through this before," Q'arlynd said. "No." He knew why the boy wanted him to invite the female wizard to join their fledgling school: he was her consort. Which was exactly the reason Q'arlynd didn't want her. He didn't need her bedding any of the others, stirring up petty jealousies.

Eldrinn pouted but didn't protest further.

Q'arlynd tapped his foot impatiently. As they waited for the others, he performed an exploratory thrust into the mind of the chitine, ignoring the faerie fire that sparked from his temples as he did so. The chitine's mind was difficult to penetrate—and brutal to remain in, once he was inside.

Hate you, the creature raged back at him. *Kill you, filthy drows. Hook open stomach, spill your feces. Kill—*

Enough. Satisfied that he would be able to retain contact, Q'arlynd withdrew.

He stared at the creature, wondering why the wizards of Ched Nasad had ever bothered to create such a loathsome race. When Q'arlynd was a novice, chitines had been plentiful; the breeding pits of the Conservatory had been full of them. The masters used to set dozens free each year, to provide sport for the hunt. But now that Ched Nasad lay in ruins, chitines weren't being bred any more. And those that had escaped were hunting drow.

The chitine was a living reminder of Ched Nasad's former prowess at magic. As for Q'arlynd's former home, it had fallen during Lolth's Silence. Literally fallen to pieces, leaving only a rubble-choked cavern where a city of thirty thousand drow had once stood. The survivors were doing what they could to resurrect the city from the rubble, but even if they rebuilt everything from the rudest slave hovel to the grandest noble House, it would never be the same.

Q'arlynd's House—House Melarn—was gone for good.

The college he was creating would fill that void, but unless today's experiment succeeded, Q'arlynd's dream might never come to fruition.

The hiss of a driftdisc halting in the hallway announced Piri's arrival.

Piri entered the experimentation chamber with a quick sideways step, his back against the wall. His eyes darted around the room, as if searching for hidden threats. No matter how safe the venue, Piri always seemed overly cautious. How much of this was his own nature and how much was the result of the quasit demon he'd bonded with was hard to say.

The demon's skin had replaced Piri's own, giving his face and hands an oily, greenish tinge. The bonding made Piri quicker and tougher, and resistant to both fire and ice, but it gave his eyes—already too close together above a beakish nose—an unsettling glint. His hair, cut close, stood up in white tufts that would eventually fuse into spikes.

Piri claimed to have complete mastery over the demon he'd bonded with—quasits were among the lowliest of demonic creatures—but Q'arlynd wondered if the wizard wasn't already regretting the bonding. Piri had been all too quick to abandon the College of Mages for Q'arlynd's as-yet unproven school.

Perhaps Piri hadn't been welcome at his former college, despite his skill in piecing together arcane texts. Q'arlynd, however, recognized his worth. From imperfect copies of the original spell, Piri had cobbled together a Ritual of Bonding—and made it work. That was proof enough of his skill.

Piri nodded without speaking at Q'arlynd and Eldrinn: two quick jerks of his head. Sparkles of purple crackled at his temples. Q'arlynd felt the brush of the other mage's mind. To show he held no threats, he permitted Piri a quick glimpse of his surface thoughts.

Eldrinn stiffened and clenched the hand that wore the copper ring. He locked eyes with Piri, and faerie fire sparkled on both male's foreheads: dark purple from Piri's; blue-green from Eldrinn's.

"Satisfied?" Eldrinn asked.

Relaxing only slightly, Piri retreated to a spot at the back of the chamber and folded his arms.

A moment later, Zarifar and Baltak arrived.

Zarifar was tall and thin, with tightly kinked hair—a rarity among the drow. It surrounded his head in a white fuzz that he never combed; tufts of it stood out like bits of coiled wire. Perpetually dreamy and unfocused, he bumped into the doorjamb as he entered the room, and blinked as though he'd just noticed where he was. When greeted, he nodded and mumbled a vague hello.

Q'arlynd didn't need to dip into Zarifar's mind to know what it would be filled with: intricate geometric designs, expressed in complex mathematical formulae that made Q'arlynd feel as simpleminded as a goblin struggling with the grammatical complexities of High Drowic.

Zarifar was a brilliant geometer mage, no doubt about it. Yet he wandered through daily life like a child. He hadn't joined Q'arlynd's school on his own. He had to be led by the hand into it.

The wizard who had done that was as different from Zarifar as light from shadow. Baltak lived entirely for his body; the transmogrifist was continually sculpting it in an effort to attain the perfect form. He wore tight-fitting pants that hugged his muscular legs, and a shirt he left unbuttoned to show off the exquisitely honed muscles of his chest and abdomen. Currently his "hair" consisted of yellowish feathers, lying flat against his head and neck and sprouting from the points of his ears. His bare feet were wide and flat, with curved black claws on the toes that clicked against the stone floor as he walked—another hallmark of the owlbear that was currently his favorite creature to transform into.

Baltak strode into the room, his presence immediately filling it. He punched Piri lightly on the shoulder, ignored the withering glare he got in return, and flipped shut Eldrinn's spellbook. Fists on hips, he grinned at Q'arlynd with perfect white teeth. His deep voice boomed. "Well, looks like we're all here. Let's get this experiment rolling."

Q'arlynd pointed at a spot across the room from Eldrinn. "Stand over there, Baltak," he said. "You're blocking my view of the chitine."

"Whatever you say, Q'arlynd," Baltak answered with a half-chuckle. He snapped his fingers in front of Zarifar's nose, startling the geometer mage. "Come on, Zarifar. You heard him. Move!"

As the pair took their places, Eldrinn set his spellbook on the table beside him and rose from his seat. He closed the door and sealed it with a sprinkle of gold dust and a spoken word. The experimentation chamber had been magically screened to prevent scrying. Even so, Q'arlynd had taken additional precautions.

He gestured for Eldrinn to bring him the wooden box that lay on the table. With its crude decorations and sloppy construction, it looked like something an orc might have banged together. Yet only the correct combination of touches to its sides would open it. Inside it was the *kiira*, nested in a lining of ensorcelled chameleon skin. Any wizard scrying the box would perceive its contents to be a commonplace magical item that only the most unschooled novice would covet. Certainly unworthy of opening.

At Q'arlynd's touch, the puzzle box sprang open, revealing the *kiira*. He hid his smile at Eldrinn's slight intake of breath. The boy was always awed by the sight of the magical crystal, no matter how many times he saw it. Zarifar seemed oblivious to the magical treasure, but Baltak moved closer to stare down at the lorestone as if it were a delicious morsel waiting to be devoured. Piri kept his distance, eyeing the *kiira* with equal parts curiosity and caution.

Baltak reached for the *kiira*. Q'arlynd jerked the box aside. "Eldrinn will do it, this time."

Baltak's feathers lifted slightly from his scalp, but he otherwise hid his irritation well. "As you say," he rumbled.

Carefully, Eldrinn lifted the *kiira* from the box. Q'arlynd had never allowed him to touch the lorestone before; he'd been worried that it might trigger memories. But given their imminent departure, that was a risk Q'arlynd was willing to take. If the boy did remember something, it might even prove helpful.

He watched Eldrinn closely, but the boy's expression didn't change.

"Press it to the chitine's forehead," Q'arlynd instructed. "But not until my signal. I want to make certain I'm deep inside its mind before we begin."

Eldrinn nodded. He walked to the chitine and stood, the lorestone carefully cupped in his hands.

Q'arlynd raised his hand. "Link your minds with mine."

One by one, the other wizards activated their rings. Faerie fire sparked from their foreheads, the varied hues blending as they drifted through the room. Q'arlynd felt Baltak shoulder into his mind like a bear. A heartbeat later, Eldrinn stepped in. Piri lightly touched Q'arlynd's mind with his own, hesitated, then slid in partway. Zarifar drifted in last. His mind traced an imaginary pattern between the bodies of the five wizards, a complex spiral of overlapping ovals.

Q'arlynd closed his eyes and thrust his awareness deep into the chitine's mind. For several moments, the creature's rage held him at bay. Then he pushed past it. Viewed through its multifaceted eyes, Q'arlynd and the other wizards appeared as looming giants—a multitude of them.

Q'arlynd flicked his raised hand: the word *now* in silent speech.

Through the chitine's eyes, he saw Eldrinn reach forward. He saw—and felt—the *kiira* briefly touch the chitine's forehead, but then the lorestone fell away. Q'arlynd's eyes opened just in time for him to see the precious crystal clatter to the floor. Eldrinn scrambled to recover it, a horrified expression on his face. Q'arlynd felt Piri tense and heard Baltak's derisive snort and his mental sneer—*fumblehands*—overlaid by the chitine's cackle of wild laughter.

Q'arlynd choked the laughter off by mentally slamming the creature's jaw shut. That, at least, he could control.

Eldrinn rose, the *kiira* in his hands. "It's not broken," he said in a relieved voice. He glanced at the chitine. "It's the greasy skin. The *kiira* wouldn't stick to the chitine's . . ." Suddenly, his eyes grew as distant as Zarifar's. "Grease," he said slowly. "On its head." One hand drifted up to touch his own forehead.

Q'arlynd broke his mental connection with the other wizards. He knew that look: Eldrinn was struggling to remember the events that had transpired on the High Moor. Q'arlynd let a hand drift behind his back, where the preliminary motions of his spell wouldn't be seen by the others.

"What is it, Eldrinn?" he asked softly.

An intense frown creased Eldrinn's forehead. "It's . . . I feel as if . . ." Then he gave a frustrated grimace. "I can't remember."

Q'arlynd watched him a moment more, decided the boy wasn't lying, and let his spell dissipate. He plucked the *kiira* from Eldrinn's hand and gestured at the chair in the corner. "Sit down, Eldrinn," he suggested. "You don't look well."

Eldrinn nodded. He sat down, picked up his spellbook, and began leafing through it, as if hoping to find the answer there.

Baltak frowned at Q'arlynd. "What just happened?"

"The feeblemind spell," Q'arlynd explained smoothly. He was embarrassing Eldrinn, but it couldn't be helped. The others needed an explanation. "Eldrinn sometimes has . . . relapses. I was worried it might impair our concentration, but he's over it, now. We'll start again."

Baltak glared at Eldrinn, who was refusing to look up from his spellbook. "Maybe Eldrinn shouldn't be—"

Q'arlynd pressed the *kiira* into Baltak's hands. "Your hands are steadier. You do it."

Baltak grinned. He strode over to the chitine, pulled a cloth from his pocket, and used it to wipe away the oily film that covered the creature's forehead. "Problem solved," he said, tossing the cloth aside. He held up the *kiira*. "Let's do it."

"On my signal," Q'arlynd reminded them, lifting his hand. He waited while the others linked minds with him, and forced his way into the chitine's thoughts once more. At his signal, Baltak pressed the crystal to the creature's forehead—hard enough to hurt it—and stepped back.

A rush of images tumbled into Q'arlynd's mind, and through it, into the minds of the four wizards linked with him. The towers of a surface city. A brown-skinned face. A portion of a complex hand gesture. A stone door. A series of pages that flew through the chitine's mind as if they were blown by a howling storm, faster and fasterandfasterand . . .

Intense pain flared in Q'arlynd's temples as he was forcibly ejected from the chitine's mind. In the same instant he heard the clatter of chains. The chitine hung from its manacles, dead. A thin gray powder trickled out of its nostrils and drifted to the floor: the contents of its skull, instantly seared to ash.

Baltak shook his head. "Mother's blood. That *hurt*."

Eldrinn blinked rapidly, spellbook forgotten in his lap. Zarifar shivered. Piri pressed his back tightly to the wall and whispered a protective spell.

Q'arlynd's jaw clenched in frustration. The chitine was dead—just like the last test subject. He strode over to it and yanked the slave ring from its limp finger.

"Well?" he asked the others. "Did any of you manage to read those pages?"

Eldrinn and Piri shook their heads.

Baltak shrugged. "They went by too fast for me."

Zarifar fluttered his hands as if trying to recapture the pattern he'd seen. "Like . . . cave moths. Left . . . right . . ."

Eldrinn repeated the gesture they'd just seen, crossing the middle two fingers of his right hand and whipping his extended thumb in a tight circle. Q'arlynd watched expectantly. The boy had read a number of arcane texts, perhaps he recognized the spell it belonged to.

"Well?"

Eldrinn's hand fell. "Sorry. I've no idea what it means."

Q'arlynd gave a tight, frustrated nod.

"Those towers . . . were they in Talthalaran?" Baltak asked.

"They might have been," Q'arlynd said. "But that's not going to help us much. The city was blasted down to its foundations."

"Maybe we should search the ruins," Baltak said. "Perhaps there's another *kiira* in—"

"There isn't," Q'arlynd snapped. "But you're welcome to go look for yourself, if you like."

That shut Baltak up.

"That door," Zarifar said. "There were . . ." His voice trailed off. As usual, he didn't complete his thought. His forefinger traced a line through the air. "Patterns."

Q'arlynd sighed in frustration. This wasn't getting them anywhere.

"The door . . ." Eldrinn said softly. "I . . ."

Q'arlynd turned. The distant look was back in Eldrinn's eyes again. "Did you recognize it, Eldrinn? Have you seen it before?"

Eldrinn's eyes cleared. He jumped out of his chair and paced across the room. "I wish I knew!" As he passed the chitine, he halted and wrinkled his nose. "What's that smell?"

"Death," Q'arlynd answered. The chitine had voided its bowels when it died, and the room stank. He felt sorry for the creature, vicious little brute though it was. He reminded himself of the necessity of its sacrifice. At least the death he'd given it had been swift—quicker than it would have suffered at the hands of hunters or one of Lolth's priestesses.

"What's next?" Baltak asked. "Buy another slave and try again?"

Q'arlynd shook his head. "That will have to wait. Eldrinn and I will be departing soon. We'll be away for . . . a while."

Eldrinn nodded. "Father's orders. A trade mission to Sschindylryn, on behalf of the college."

Baltak nodded at the *kiira*. "But that's staying here, right? The rest of us can carry on, while you're gone."

"No," Q'arlynd replied. "In the College of Ancient Arcana, we work together. Or not at all."

Baltak shrugged but his eyes clung greedily to the *kiira*. "Fine. We wait until you get back."

Q'arlynd felt frustration build inside him. We can't wait! he wanted to shout. By then it might be too late! Yet he could hardly tell the others that. Only Eldrinn knew the extent of the looming crisis. He and Q'arlynd had been careful to keep it from the others, even when they were linked mind to mind. The boy wasn't stupid; if word got out that the College of Divination was teetering on the brink, someone just might be willing to give it an extra nudge.

Eldrinn stared at the dead chitine. "We're wasting our time with these lesser races. We need to try it on a *drow* instead."

"Good idea!" Baltak cried. "What about a battle-captive—someone no one really cares about?"

"What about the body?" Piri whispered from the back of the room. He pointed at Zarifar, who had wandered over to the chitine and was busy scuffing the toe of his boot through the ash at the chitine's feet, drawing in it. "Anyone who sees the corpse is going to wonder which spell burned its brains out so precisely."

"We'll disintegrate the body," Baltak said. "Or use quicklime."

"You're overlooking something," Q'arlynd said. "If the experiment succeeded, the battle-captive would learn the contents of the *kiira* at the same time we did—including, perhaps, a spell that might allow him to escape." He stared at the others. "We don't want to share our lorestone with anyone else just yet, do we?"

"I suppose you're right," Baltak grudgingly admitted.

"You completely missed my point," Eldrinn said.

Q'arlynd turned to him.

"I wasn't talking about battle-captives—I was talking about me. *I* could wear the *kiira*."

Q'arlynd's response was immediate. "No."

"It won't kill me. I know it. I have a . . . *feeling* about it. It's almost like . . ." Eldrinn stared at the lorestone. "A divination, or . . . something."

"Feeling or not," Q'arlynd said, "my answer is still no. It's too risky."

Eldrinn stood, fists on hips. "Why won't you let me try it, Q'arlynd? Are you worried that Father will find out?"

Q'arlynd nearly laughed. Eldrinn had, unwittingly, put his finger precisely on the problem. Q'arlynd already knew the lorestone wouldn't kill the boy. He had a pretty clear picture of what must have happened, that night on the High Moor. Eldrinn had run off when the monster had attacked the soldier he'd taken along as a bodyguard. Knowing that his own spells were too limited to deal with the monster, Eldrinn must have turned in desperation to the *kiira* and been unable to handle it. For some reason the lorestone hadn't blasted his brain to ash—Q'arlynd was still trying to figure that part out—but it had left the boy a feeblewit.

If Eldrinn tried the *kiira* a second time and was once again reduced to a drooling shell, Q'arlynd would be forced to explain how it had happened. Master Seldszar wasn't stupid; he'd guess that something other than the "magical predators" of the High Moor had scrambled the boy's mind, the first time around. He'd leave no mind unsifted until he found out what had really happened. The moment he learned of the *kiira* he'd claim it for his college, justifying its seizure as compensation for the coin it had cost him to cure the boy. Not once, but twice. And the foundation stone upon which Q'arlynd hoped to build his school would be gone.

"Well," Eldrinn prompted. "Is it Father you're worried about?"

Q'arlynd sighed. "Father" was a term he'd never get used to. It was a word borrowed from the surface elves; the drow of Ched Nasad never had a use for it. Descent was, and always had been, through the female line. The idea of a consort claiming children as his own was ludicrous.

"My answer is still no," Q'arlynd said. He pointed at the dead chitine. "I won't let you be reduced to that."

"I won't be," Eldrinn protested. "I've got an idea. A *foolproof* idea." Grinning, he pulled the silver clip from his hair and held it up for the others to see. "This is a contingency clip," he told them.

"What's that?" Baltak asked.

Eldrinn smiled. "Something our college's crafters created. It holds whatever spell is cast into it until a condition of the caster's choosing comes to pass, then releases it. The spell has to be one that affects the caster directly, and it can only be a lesser dweomer, but the spell I have in mind is perfect. I got the idea from the chitine."

"Go on," Q'arlynd said, intrigued despite himself.

"I'll cast a tightly targeted spell into the clip and make the actions of the *kiira* the contingency. The instant the lorestone tries to kill me, grease will appear on my forehead. The crystal won't be able to stick. It will slide off—just like it did from the chitine."

Q'arlynd nodded to himself. So that was what had happened. Now he understood the greasy smudge he'd seen on Eldrinn's forehead when he'd found the boy on the High Moor. It explained why Eldrinn had survived his first attempt to use the lorestone. A bit sad, really, that the boy could never be told this.

He realized that Eldrinn was still waiting for his reply. "Using the contingency clip is a clever idea . . ."

Eldrinn grinned.

". . . but I won't allow you to risk yourself."

The grin disappeared. "It will work," Eldrinn said fervently. "I *know* it."

Q'arlynd stared down at the *kiira*. "I'm sure it will."

Zarifar was still playing with the ash, but Baltak and Piri watched Q'arlynd intently.

"It's Eldrinn's life," Baltak rumbled. "If he wants to—"

"No," Q'arlynd said. The words slipped out of his mouth before he could stop them. "I'll do it."

Eldrinn's mouth opened in surprise.

"Your contingency clip," Q'arlynd asked him. "It's something any wizard can use, right?"

Eldrinn was about to lie—Q'arlynd could see it in his eye—but then reluctantly nodded. "As long as you're wearing it, yes."

"Even if it's you who casts the spell into the clip?"

Another grudging nod.

"Good," Q'arlynd said. "Do it, but make the contingency that will trigger the spell a little broader. Instead of something that will 'kill' me, word it so that anything that might 'damage' me will trigger the spell. Is that clear?"

Eldrinn nodded.

In another moment, all was ready. The contingency clip had been ensorcelled and clipped to Q'arlynd's hair. The *kiira* was in his hands. All that remained was to press it to his forehead.

Q'arlynd hesitated. Did he dare?

Of course he did. He must. It would be just like free-falling from a ledge. Whatever happened, the contingency clip would pull him up in time. Already his blood pounded in anticipation of the mental jump.

He motioned Eldrinn and the others away from the chair, then sat down. Slowly, he lifted the *kiira* to eye level. All of the others stared at him, even Zarifar. "Link with me," he told them.

They did.

Q'arlynd paused to give a mental nod to the others. Baltak stood braced and steady on his wide feet, Zarifar closed his eyes and once again imagined a pattern drawn between them. Piri hovered near the door, seemingly ready to bolt through it. Eldrinn nodded vigorously, as if to assure Q'arlynd that it was, really, all right.

Wherever the *kiira* took Q'arlynd, they were ready to come along.

"Wish me luck." Q'arlynd pressed the kiira to his forehead.

Eldrinn's eyes sparkled. "Good—"

Q'arlynd shivered. Cold. He felt cold. His legs trembled.

He put out a hand to steady himself and touched stone. He glanced up and saw that he was standing in front of a massive stone door. The carvings on it looked familiar, but he couldn't quite figure out why. He knew he'd seen the door somewhere before, but . . .

Where in the Abyss *was* he?

Below ground, somewhere in the Underdark. Somewhere he didn't recognize at all. A corridor stretched away behind him, its walls illuminated with the faintest shimmer of *Faerzress*, and dead-ended at the door. There was a musty smell in the air, and dust on the floor. And footprints—a lot of footprints. And tools. Picks, pry bars, and—Q'arlynd jumped back in alarm when he saw it—a stonefire bomb, like the ones that had laid waste to Ched Nasad. The bomb was spent, though, its magical fire long since spilled. There was a deep, charred hole in the stone just to the right of the door. Q'arlynd peered into it and saw that the door was thicker than the hole the stonefire had burned.

The puzzle of why someone would do that only briefly took his mind off the central question of where he was and how he'd gotten there. The last thing he could remember was talking to Eldrinn and the others he'd invited to join his school. They'd been standing in Eldrinn's residence in Sshamath, in the experimentation chamber, waiting for the two grimlock slaves to manacle a chitine to the wall so they could perform an experiment with the . . .

Q'arlynd stared up at the ceiling, searching for the word.

It floated just beyond his grasp. Something small, and pointed, and . . .

It was gone again.

Eldrinn. Whatever the experiment was, it had something to do with him.

Q'arlynd closed his eyes and tried to think. His thoughts kept circling back to when he'd found the boy wandering on the High Moor in the ruins of ancient Talthalaran. Eldrinn had been struck with a feeblemind spell, and couldn't remember anything about . . . something.

Q'arlynd felt his face pale. Had the same thing happened to him?

Words came to him then. A sentence that rattled in his head like a pebble in an empty cup. He said it aloud. "Must get it back."

He frowned. Must get *what* back? And to where?

He turned to the door. Twice as high as he was tall, it was carved with an unusual design: elves and dragons, standing side by side and holding scrolls, as if they were casting spells. A single word, written in archaic High Drowic, arched above the design. It looked like a name: "Kraanfhaor."

The door had no handle or hinges. More properly, it was a slab of stone. Yet Q'arlynd somehow *knew* it was a door. He touched its surface with his knuckles and spoke a simple, one-word spell: *"Obsul!"*

Nothing happened. Oddly, that was just what he'd expected.

A voice echoed down the corridor behind him, startling him. "Q'arlynd!"

Eldrinn's voice. He obviously knew Q'arlynd was there. Maybe he'd know why.

Q'arlynd heard footsteps hurrying toward him.

"Q'arlynd, are you there?" asked a different male voice.

He turned and saw Eldrinn running up the corridor, followed by Baltak and Zarifar. Piri was farther back, making his way along the corridor with caution. Alexa, the female

Eldrinn was consort to, was also with them. She was about Eldrinn's age, with bangs cut in a severe line across her forehead, and a wide mouth. She wore a leather apron smudged with yellow sulfur and streaks of red ochre. It looked as though she'd just stepped from a magical laboratory. She halted just behind the others and stood with her hands on her hips.

"Well, boys," she said in a voice that was husky from inhaling the smoke of her experiments. "You've found him. Can I get back to my potions, now?"

"In a moment, Alexa," Eldrinn said. He stared at the door, an odd look on his face. "It's the same one we saw," he whispered.

The others nodded.

Eldrinn tore his eyes away from the door and stepped closer to Q'arlynd. "Are you all right?"

Q'arlynd opened his mouth. Closed it. Opened it again. "I really have no idea." He glanced down at himself. His body, at least, looked normal enough. Am I? he wondered.

Baltak stepped between them. "Why'd you teleport away?"

Q'arlynd simply stared at him. So that was how he got there. By teleporting.

Calm. He had to stay calm.

Piri sidled up to them. "You said something." He stared at the door, but his eyes kept sliding toward Q'arlynd's forehead. " 'I've got to put it back,' you said. Then you vanished."

Alexa stepped closer. "Put what back?"

Eldrinn caught Q'arlynd's eye; he looked worried. "Sorry," the boy muttered. "Everyone insisted on coming. We needed a teleportation circle to get us all here, and the nearest one was in the College of Conjuration. We needed Alexa's help to activate it—even so, it took three tries to get it to work. I wasn't trying to force your hand by bringing her. Honest."

"I see," Q'arlynd said. He didn't, though. He understood that Eldrinn was worried about him getting angry, and that

Alexa shouldn't be there. But why—and just where *there* was—remained a mystery.

Baltak circled Q'arlynd, eyeing him intently. He stopped in front of Q'arlynd and stared at his forehead, as if he were trying to bore a hole with his eyes and see inside it. Sparkles of faerie fire erupted from Baltak's own forehead. Q'arlynd felt Baltak's awareness push into his mind.

"What are you *doing*?" he asked, shoving the transmogrifist out.

"Where is it?" Baltak demanded.

"Where is what?"

"The *kiira*."

Alexa's eyes widened. "He's got a *kiira*?"

"Not any more," Baltak said.

Q'arlynd felt a chill run through him. Something was wrong. Very wrong. His stomach felt as though it were flopping like a landed blindfish.

"A *kiira*," he whispered. So that was what had done this to him. He'd obviously been foolish enough to try wearing a lorestone. Why?

Then he remembered Miverra's warning. In a tenday, perhaps even sooner, divination spells would become impossible and the College of Divination would fall. Q'arlynd needed his school to be recognized as a college before then. In order for that to happen, the experiments with the—with the *kiira*, he realized—had to be speeded up. The spells inside the—the *kiira*—had to be recovered, mastered, and . . .

A flash of memory came back: his hands, holding a lorestone.

By all the gods. He *had* put a *kiira* on his head.

He must have been crazy.

Alexa stepped closer and ran a hand over the carving on the door. "What *is* this place?" she asked. She craned her head to look up at the inscription. "Kraanfhaor. What's that? An ancient House name?"

"Not a House," Piri said softly. "A college."

Q'arlynd ran a hand through his hair. His fingers were trembling. He had no idea what Piri was talking about—but admitting that would make him seem a fool in front of the others. He assumed the tone of a master grilling a student. "Tell the others what you know about it, Piri."

"I read about this place in a text written by the surface elves. The entry was a short one. It said only that 'Kraanfhaor's Door' was supposedly the entrance to an ancient college of the same name, one that dated back millennia, to an age before the Descent. It added that dozens of adventurers have tried to open the door, and dozens have failed." Piri shrugged. "That's all there was, but I think we can guess the rest." His glance slid sideways to Q'arlynd. "This is where you found the *kiira*, isn't it?"

"Abyss take me," Baltak blurted. "We're in the ruins of Talthalaran?"

"Yes," Q'arlynd said, his mind racing. "Talthalaran."

That sounded right, somehow. It helped Q'arlynd—a little— to know where he was: somewhere under the High Moor. In Talthalaran. But how could he have teleported there? During his months spent searching that ruined city, he'd found one or two subterranean chambers that had survived the Dark Disaster, but none that looked like this. He was *certain* he'd never seen this place before. Except, perhaps, for the door . . .

He glanced at it again. No, he was wrong. He definitely hadn't seen it before.

Then how had he teleported there?

A terrible realization came to him then: he *must* have seen it before. Perhaps even been there before. The *kiira* had torn a hole in his memory, ripping chunks of it away like a hand clawing apart a fragile web.

Eldrinn stared at the door. "You know something? I have the oddest feeling. That I've stood here once before. In front of Kraanfhaor's Door."

Q'arlynd was instantly wary, though he didn't understand why.

"I remember . . ." Eldrinn tipped his head and closed his eyes slightly. "The moor. Someone shouting at me. Something in my hands." He began to lift his hands to his forehead, then abruptly halted. His eyes sprang open and he glared at Q'arlynd. "I had the *kiira*, didn't I? When you found me on the High Moor. I tried it, and it feebleminded me, and I forgot all about it. And now the same thing's happened to you. Except that you weren't feebleminded, because you knew how to word the contingency."

"That's . . . possible," Q'arlynd admitted.

Eldrinn's eyes narrowed. "You *lied* to me," he said in a tight, quiet voice. "You didn't find the *kiira*. I did. And you took it from me."

Nervous sweat trickled down Q'arlynd's back. The boy had accused him, and the others were all staring. If Q'arlynd didn't come up with something quickly, everything would fall apart. The relationship he'd built with Eldrinn and the other three mages he'd selected as apprentices—not to mention the steady source of coin the boy's father provided—all teetered on the brink of ruin. Yet what could he say?

Then it came to him. Drawing himself up, he spoke imperiously, like a matron mother addressing a boy. "You're alive, Eldrinn," he said sternly. "Any other drow would have slain you—or left you to fend for yourself on the High Moor, fodder for the monsters that prowl there. I, however, not only saved you, but invited to share with you whatever knowledge the *kiira* held. And where is your gratitude?"

The other mages were staring at Eldrinn. The *sava* board had been turned. The boy winced. He opened his mouth, closed it, then muttered a grudging apology. "Sorry, Q'arlynd."

Q'arlynd acknowledged it with a nod, then turned to the others. "Did any of you see me put the *kiira* back?"

"You must have," Baltak said. "It's gone."

"Yes, but did you *see* me?"

"Not directly," Eldrinn said, finding his voice again. "But only a few moments elapsed between the time you teleported away and my scrying; you probably teleported straight here. When I saw you in the font, you were standing with your palm pressed to the door, as if you'd just pushed it shut."

"So you're not *certain* I opened the door," Q'arlynd said. "Perhaps the *kiira* is still on me, or somewhere nearby. Search me."

"All right." Eldrinn pulled a piece of forked twig from his pocket and whispered a quick incantation. He held the twig above Q'arlynd's head, then ran it down first the front of his body, then the back.

"You don't have it," he concluded. "And . . ." He turned in a circle. "It's not here. At least, not on this side of the door."

Q'arlynd's heart raced. "So I 'put it back,' did I?" He turned slowly toward Kraanfhaor's Door. If it turned out to be what he suspected, knowledge beyond his wildest dreams was his for the taking. "That's an odd choice of words—one which makes me wonder what this door opens onto. A library with dozens of ancient *kiira*? Hundreds? *Thousands?*" He paused for breath, barely able to restrain himself from laughing out loud in delight. If this door could be opened, it wouldn't matter if the College of Divination fell. Beyond the door was a treasure trove he could use to purchase all of the power and prestige any wizard could ever desire.

Assuming he was right about what lay behind it.

He glanced at the others and smiled as he saw parted lips and gleams in their eyes. Even Zarifar was paying attention. So was Alexa, but that couldn't be helped. Q'arlynd would have to invite her to join his college as his fifth apprentice, after all, to ensure her silence. Fortunately the ring was in his pocket. He might need it to test her potential loyalty.

"Instead of squabbling about who had the lorestone first," he suggested, "we should ask ourselves a more important question." He rapped a hand against the door. "How do we get this open again?"

Eldrinn nudged the empty stonefire bomb with a toe. "It's supposedly impossible."

"Wrong," Q'arlynd said. "I just opened it, didn't I? And if you had the *kiira* before me, Eldrinn, you must have gotten it from somewhere—perhaps by also opening the door. We just need to figure out how it's done."

He turned to the others. "Piri, I want you to study that text you read for other clues. Baltak, you can try assuming different shapes; perhaps the door is keyed to a particular race. Alexa can provide teleportation back and forth between Sshamath and here. Assuming, that is, she's willing to join our school and not tell anyone else about the door."

Alexa nodded briskly.

"And Zarifar can . . ." Q'arlynd paused. The geometer mage stared dreamily at a spot above Kraanfhaor's Door, idly tracing a pattern in the air with his finger. "Zarifar can study the door's . . . patterns. Or something. Eldrinn and I will be away for a time on the trade mission, but I'll be scrying you—frequently—to check on your progress."

That would, of course, be impossible where Q'arlynd was going—but they needn't know that.

He held up a finger in a gesture reminiscent of a lecturing master. "Remember this: if any of us does find the key, I want him to inform the others immediately. When the time comes to open the door, we're going to do it together."

Heads dutifully nodded.

Q'arlynd knew better than to trust them, however. They'd only worn their rings a short time, and they weren't used to working as a team yet. One or more of them would probably try opening the door on his own—or her own—while he and Eldrinn were gone. Q'arlynd doubted they would succeed, though. Eldrinn, he suspected, was the key.

And Q'arlynd intended to keep that key securely in his pocket.

CHAPTER 6

Urlryn Khalazza strode through the scriptorium door—*literally* strode through it, as if the heavy wooden door were a mere illusion. The scribe at the table closest to the door gave a start and lost control of his quill, but the others kept at their copywork, forefingers twitching as they magically directed quills that scribbled rapidly on parchment.

Seldszar glanced past the tiny spheres that circled his head, noting the door. For several moments, it held an outline of Urlryn, limned in crackling indigo. Then the faerie fire faded.

"Master Urlryn," he said. "Thank you for responding so swiftly to my invitation."

The master of the College of Conjuration and Summoning nodded. He was a large male, broad-shouldered for a drow, with a stomach that strained the ties of his vest, the visible result of his love of excessively rich, conjured feasts. His college insignia hung against his chest on a mithral chain: a golden goblet, ensorcelled to expand and fill with wine whenever he raised it to his wide lips. Though Urlryn's thinning hair and drooping jowls gave the impression of age and sloth, he was amply protected. Trotting at his side—invisible to the scribes but clear to Seldszar's eye—was a vicious phantasmal dog. It eyed Seldszar warily, lips twitching and hackles raised. At the slightest hint of a threat to its master, it would attack.

Urlryn halted in front of Seldszar and stared meaningfully at the faerie fire that sparked from the other master's forehead. "You wish to discuss our mutual problem?"

"Indeed I do." Seldszar spoke while staring at the spheres. Though the faerie fire posed irritating interruptions to his view of them, his observations continued. He'd shifted their focus to his own college and the mages therein. "I've learned something interesting about the . . . disruption."

Urlryn cleared his throat in warning and tipped his head at the nearest scribes.

"Indeed," Seldszar told him. "Pointed ears and private business." He hissed, releasing a spell. Heads thunked onto wooden tables as the scribes fell forward, unconscious. An inkwell clattered to the floor, leaving a splash of dark blue ink. The quills continued scribbling a moment more, then collapsed onto their parchments.

"Have your sages come up with any answers yet?" Urlryn asked.

Seldszar glanced briefly at the sphere that showed his college's most learned wizards arguing vociferously around a table. "No. But I recently received a visitor who claims to know who's causing this plague of faerie fire— though she was vague on the details. That visitor was a priestess of Eilistraee, from the Promenade. She blames Kiaransalee's cult. Something they are doing in a temple far to the northeast is augmenting *Faerzress* throughout the Underdark—including ours."

"I see."

For several moments, neither wizard spoke. The only sound came from a water clock that hung from the scriptorium's ceiling. Drops fell steadily from a tiny hole in the bottom of the cut-glass bowl into a pan below with dull, metallic thunks. The clock was a thing of the World Above, calibrated to mark the quarters of the day and night, so of little practical use in the Underdark—until then. Like the water sinking almost imperceptibly lower in the bowl, time was running out.

"I, too, received a visitor," Urlryn said at last. "A cleric of Vhaeraun, from Skullport. He told me much the same thing. Including the fact that the augmentation of the *Faerzress* seems to be affecting only drow."

Seldszar nodded, his attention still on his spheres. He'd offered the other master a morsel of information, and Urlryn had done as he'd anticipated. Gulped it down, then offered a tidbit of his own. It was the way the game was played.

Seldszar, of course, already knew of the "Nightshadow's" visit to Urlryn's college. When Miverra had departed from his college, Seldszar had locked one of his tiny crystal balls on her. Through it, he'd seen her alter her female body, reshaping it into the image of a male rogue. She'd then teleported into the heart of the College of Conjuration and Summoning—something that should have been impossible for a stranger. It had drawn Urlryn's attention at once. Questioned by him, she admitted to being a Nightshadow, then spun much the same story for Urlryn that she had for Seldszar.

Except that she'd told Urlryn it was Vhaeraun's clerics who needed the Conclave's aid.

It was almost as if she'd known of Urlryn's role in conveying the survivors of the slaughter in the Tower of the Masked Mage to safety—an act that had seemed out of character for Urlryn, unless one knew of the little "favor" the black-masked assassins had done for him, more than a dozen years ago. A favor involving poison.

"Did you believe the Nightshadow's story?" Seldszar asked.

Urlryn shrugged. "Possibly."

Noncommittal answers were typical of Urlryn. Yet the other master had obviously taken the visitor seriously. Like Seldszar, Urlryn had agreed to attach wizards from his college to the band of spies that would be snooping around Kiaransalee's temple. Even then, one of the spheres orbiting Seldszar's head showed Urlyn's three conjurers making their departure. Fortunately, it zipped past too swiftly for Urlryn to make out details of the scene it contained.

"Did you tell the Nightshadow anything about the *Faerzress?*" Seldszar asked. He waited for the answer— there was a slight chance that Urlryn had confounded his earlier scrying.

The other master shook his head. "No."

Seldszar saw his purple sphere speed past; its color hadn't changed. Urlryn might have shielded his mind against intrusion—every mage capable of it did so whenever they stepped within range of Seldszar's spells—but Urlryn couldn't do anything about the crystal. He wasn't lying. Their secret was safe.

And a strange secret it was. For centuries, it had been passed down from one master to the next. Seldszar wasn't privy to how this had been done in the College of Conjuration and Summoning, but he knew how it worked within his own college. More than two centuries ago, when the previous master of the College of Divination had died and Seldszar had been selected to sit in the master's chair, he'd had a dream. In it, the college's first master, Chal'dzar, had appeared in ghostly form to impart the tale of how their city came to be.

More than four thousand years ago, Chal'dzar, together with a powerful conjurer named Yithzin who specialized in teleportation, had worked a spell that forever altered the face of Sshamath. They'd wrenched loose the *Faerzress* that permeated the stone surrounding the city, forever flinging aside this impediment to their spells.

Or so they thought. For three centuries prior to their casting, more males than females had been born. After the *Faerzress* "disappeared," the city's rulers—at that time, priestesses of Lolth—noticed that males trained in spellcasting were developing augmented powers. If the uneven birthrates persisted, those individuals, combined, would one day wield power greater than Lolth's clergy. In a typically drow attempt to thwart the rebellion they were certain would come, the priestesses attempted a culling of those with arcane talent. Their attack quickly brought about the rebellion they'd tried to prevent in the first place. The noble Houses fell and the wizards stepped into power. The Conclave had ruled Sshamath ever since.

The ghostly Chal'dzar had imparted no details of the spell he and his partner had wrought, but he had speculated upon one point. That the *Faerzress*, instead of being shifted to another location in the Underdark, had found a new home in Sshamath: within the drow who inhabited the city. Were all of Sshamath's drow to suddenly depart the cavern, he surmised, the *Faerzress* would return to the stone from whence it came.

The centuries that followed provided ample evidence that Chal'dzar had guessed correctly. As the city's population rose, the percentage of those born with innate arcane talents gradually declined. The *Faerzress*, it seemed, spread itself thinner as it took up residence within all of the drow of Sshamath—both those born there and those only recently arrived in the city—until it bled out of them every time a drow cast a spell involving divination or any of the various modes of teleportation.

With a nod, Seldszar indicated the faerie fire that crackled between his forehead and the circling spheres. "Did the Nightshadow warn you that it's going to get worse?"

"Yes. Though it won't be as bad for us as it will be for you. Only about *half* of our spells will cease to function. We'll still have one leg to stand on—until someone shoves us over." Urlryn gave a sarcastic laugh. "I might be able to fool the other masters, for a time, by arranging for an 'incident' that will force a magical lockdown of the city, but Masoj will figure it out, in time."

"As will the rest of the Conclave," Seldszar said. He nodded at the sphere that showed the cluster of fine-spun stalagmites and stalactites that formed the temple of the Spider Queen, but it moved too quickly for Urlryn to peer into it. "And so will Lolth's priestesses. They may jump to the conclusion that *all* of the colleges are about to topple. It could be the Rebellion, all over again. In reverse, this time."

Urlryn conjured a silk handkerchief into his hand and wiped his forehead. Despite the cool, dry air of the scriptorium, he was sweating. A flick of his fingers, and the handkerchief vanished. "Do you think it *is* the Crones?"

"I don't need to think. I know. They are the cause of it."

Urlryn tilted his head slightly, something he did whenever he had second thoughts. "Should we inform the Conclave? Send an army?"

"No," Seldszar said. Forcibly. "That would be the wrong thing to do."

Urlryn nodded. "One of your premonitions?"

"Yes." Seldszar spoke more to himself than to Urlryn. "Absolutely the wrong thing to do. Observe." He held one palm over the other and spoke an incantation; after a moment, an image appeared between them. Into it, he projected the memory of what his brief contact with the Astral Plane had revealed: a glimpse into a future in which the warriors of Sshamath fought, died, then rose to fight again—against their former comrades. Wave upon wave of undead spread through the Underdark, overwhelming all like a rushing tide, feeding and growing with each new army sent against it. As the vision unfolded, a single word pealed like a bell: *Defeat . . . Defeat . . . Defeat.*

"Thus did the Observarium predict," Seldszar said, clapping his hands shut.

It was a moment before Urlryn spoke. "If we could find a way to reverse the spell that Yithzin and Chal'dzar cast and drive the *Faerzress* back into the stone, then perhaps—"

"I thought of that too, but it's no solution. It will conceal the problem but not make it go away. Inside us or inside the stone of Sshamath's cavern, the *Faerzress* will still negate our spells."

"Our colleges could relocate. Somewhere beyond the effect."

"To where? A city ruled by these?" Seldszar snatched one of his crystals out of the air, focused it on Lolth's temple in Menzoberranzan, and held it up for Urlryn to see. Inside the tiny sphere, a priestess moved through a temple nursery, her snake-headed whip driving a terrified gaggle of children ahead of her. One male slipped on his own blood, fell—and continued to be whipped, long after his small body had stopped twitching.

Urlryn's lip curled.

Seldszar flicked the sphere back into orbit. "Even if we chose to flee, it would only be a temporary measure. Our visitor said the effect would spread across all of Faerûn. Throughout the Underdark. There's nowhere to run to. Save for the World Above. And that's somewhere, I'm sure, neither you nor I would ever choose to live."

"There *must* be a way out of this," Urlryn said. "We just haven't seen it yet."

Seldszar glanced at his fellow master, eyes glittering. "I'd like to show you something. Indulge me, if you would. Transpose us."

The other master looked puzzled. "As you wish." He moved a few paces away from Seldszar, then held up his hand. "Ready?"

Seldszar nodded.

Urlryn stared at Seldszar's feet, then snapped his fingers. Instantly, the two swapped places. Urlryn stood next to the water clock, his body shimmering with faerie fire. Seldszar peered back at him through his own veil of pale-green sparkles.

"Again," Seldszar demanded.

With a whispered word, Urlryn magically swapped their positions a second time.

"Again."

By the third translocation, both mages were covered head to toe in glittering faerie fire. Urlryn, squinting, threw up his hands. "Enough! What does this prove?"

Seldszar held out his arms and turned in a slow circle. "What do you observe?"

Urlryn squinted against the glare of the faerie fire that surrounded him. He waved a hand in front of his face, as if trying to shoo away a gnat. "Not much, thanks to this."

"Yes, but note the color. Your faerie fire is a deep blue. Mine, a pale green."

"Signifying?"

"Indulge me a moment more. Summon faerie fire intentionally, this time. See if you can make it violet, instead."

Urlryn spoke a brief incantation and traced a finger through the air. The water inside the clock was suddenly illuminated from within by motes of indigo. A frown of concentration on his forehead, he shifted the hue to a lighter blue, then to green, then back to blue again and finally to a purplish shade.

"As I thought," Seldszar said. "You can consciously manifest faerie fire in any shade you wish, but the involuntary manifestations are limited to your habitual color."

Urlryn stared at Seldszar. " 'Habitual color.' That's a term I haven't heard before."

Seldszar smiled. "It's one I came up with a few years back. A little academic, but it will serve. Ask a drow to evoke faerie fire, and he'll habitually manifest a particular color.

The same color, I'll wager, that he's involuntarily manifesting now." He gestured at the unconscious mages. "Were we to wake one of them up and repeat the experiment I just performed, you'd see the same thing. The faerie fire he manifests when asked to cast a divination or to teleport will match whatever his habitual color is."

Seldszar snatched one of his crystals from the air. "Observe the mages of my college."

Urlryn moved closer and peered into the crystal. Within it, blue faerie fire crackled around the head of one wizard as he cast a spell, and green around the hands of another. Still other mages emitted lavender or purple hues when casting their divinations.

Seldszar tossed the sphere into orbit again. "There's a hypothesis I've been researching for some time. That *Faerzress* and faerie fire are one and the same thing. Hence, the odd spelling. 'Faerie' instead of 'fairy.' It wasn't originally 'faerie fire,' but '*Faerzress* fire.' "

Urlryn folded his arms. "You mean to tell me that every drow on Toril has *Faerzress* energy inside him? Not just those in Sshamath? Did Yithzin and Chal'dzar's spell extend that far?"

"I don't think so," Seldszar said. "But it looks as though every drow—spellcaster or not—can *channel* that energy. Act as a conduit for it. Our race is linked with it, somehow."

"That would explain why drow are the only ones affected by the augmentation of the *Faerzress*." Urlryn paced back and forth. "But why would Kiaransalee's cult—if they are indeed behind this—instigate something that would hamstring every drow on Toril? What purpose would that serve?"

"Who knows?" Seldszar shook his head. "From the little I've heard of Kiaransalee's worship, that goddess is even more crazed than Lolth. Perhaps this is Kiaransalee's version of the Silence."

"A 'web of silence,' " the other master said, quoting the ancient song. " 'And at its center, death.' " He looked up.

"So how does your deeper understanding of '*Faerzress* fire' help us?"

"It doesn't—unless we can find a way to break the link between drow and *Faerzress* energy."

"A difficult undertaking," Ulryn observed.

"Yes. One that may take months—even years. Time we don't have." Seldszar locked his eyes on the other master. "Which is why I asked you here today. I propose an alliance of our two colleges. Pooling our respective talents is our best hope at finding the answer before it's too late. You will share with me the fruits of whatever your sages might discover—and I will do the same, with you." He paused. "Well? Will you agree to it?"

"I will." Urlryn bowed, his stomach straining the front of his vest. "You have my word on it."

A quick glance at the discernment sphere—which had darkened, but only slightly—told Seldszar the other master was telling the truth, for the most part. He would cooperate. For now.

"I thank you for your time," Seldszar told Urlryn. "And your ear. It's comforting to know that another master shares my concerns."

"Q'arlynd, what a pleasant surprise," Qilué said. "I had wondered if I would see you again. Your departure from the Promenade a year and a half ago was somewhat . . . abrupt."

Q'arlynd, Eldrinn and the other two diviners bowed as the high priestesses entered the room. Qilué was just as imposing—and beautiful—as Q'arlynd remembered. "I apologize for that, Lady Qilué, but I had pressing business elsewhere," he said as he rose from his bow.

"You wound up in Sshamath, Miverra tells me."

"The city of wizards suits me, Lady. I've made my home there." This wouldn't be news to Qilué. She would have scried him after he left the Promenade. Several times since then, the back of his neck had prickled, telling him that someone was looking at him from afar. Of course, that could have been Master Seldszar.

"Miverra also told me you've founded a school of wizardry there. Are these your apprentices?"

Q'arlynd noted—without directly looking at Eldrinn—that the boy's shoulders tensed. The other two wizards Master Seldszar had chosen for this mission were listening closely; they would have already noted the time Q'arlynd and Eldrinn had been spending together, and would wonder if the son was planning to step out from his father's shadow.

Q'arlynd smiled. "Having a school recognized as a college is the dream of every wizard in Sshamath," he said smoothly. "As for my 'school,' it's little more than a salon. A gathering of friends of the master's young son, here." He spread his hands. "I teach them what I can."

Qilué's eyes locked on his. "Teleportation?"

"Among other things."

"You were very good at it, as I recall."

Q'arlynd tipped his head.

He wondered if the teleport he'd just performed had been a test, either of the Promenade's defenses or of the degree to which the increase in *Faerzress* energy was affecting Sshamath. Perhaps both. He supposed he'd passed. Despite the faerie fire that had erupted when he'd cast his spell, it had been a relatively easy jump. It helped that the room Miverra had shown him in her scrying was quite a distinctive chamber: circular, its walls ribbed with arched columns that met overhead, and with only the one exit. The floor was inlaid with thousands of chips of colored stone: a mosaic that showed drow females practicing swordplay.

Qilué turned to the wizards who had accompanied him. "I am Lady Qilué, high priestess of the Promenade, Chosen of Mystra. And these mages are . . . ?"

Q'arlynd gestured at their most senior member. "Khorl Krissellian, sorcerer and farseer."

Khorl was a sun elf with pale skin and off-white hair. As he stepped forward and returned Qilué's bow, his age-seamed face betrayed just a hint of haughtiness. He was nearly four centuries old and had lived the bulk of his life in Sshamath. Long enough to dress like a drow and be just as scheming, yet he still ranked drow one notch below the "true" elven race.

His greeting, slow and deep, was entirely cordial, however. "Lady Qilué, Chosen of Mystra. It is indeed an honor to meet the one about whom I have heard so many wondrous tales." The magical amulets on the fringes of his *piwafwi* tinkled as he rose.

Q'arlynd introduced the second mage. "Daffir the Prescient."

"Madam," Daffir said, bowing. He was a human from the south, his skin nearly as dark as a drow's. He was bald, whip-thin, and as tall as Qilué. Dark oval lenses hovered just in front of his eyes, hiding them. He leaned on the staff Eldrinn had been holding when Q'arlynd found him on the High Moor. The fact that another wizard had been allowed to carry it out of the city proved just how seriously Master Seldszar took their mission; the staff was one of his most treasured possessions. Next to his son, of course.

"A human and a sun elf," Qilué said. "Wise choices for where you're headed."

Q'arlynd nodded. "Our third member is Eldrinn Elpragh, also of the College of Divination."

Eldrinn bowed. "Will you lead the expedition, Lady Qilué?"

The high priestess shook her head. "I have pressing business that requires my presence here in the Promenade." As she spoke, her right hand drifted toward her hip to the place where a sword would normally hang, then halted as if she'd just realized she was unarmed. A curious gesture.

"I wanted to meet you all in person, and to thank you for

joining our expedition," Qilué continued. "Please come with me. I wish to speak to all of its members before you depart."

Q'arlynd and the others followed her through the door. She led them deeper into the building, which turned out to be a barracks. They passed several closed doors. The sound of voices raised in song filled the area—predominantly female voices, underscored by a handful of deeper male voices.

Eventually the corridor ended at massive double doors that opened onto a large, rectangular marshalling hall. Shields hung on the longer walls, while crossed swords were mounted above each doorway. The vaulted ceiling's carved central beam resembled a crescent moon resting on its points. Yet it wasn't the architecture that caught Q'arlynd's eye. Three drow stood at the center of the hall, glancing around as if they too had just arrived there.

Two were male, one female. One of them, Q'arlynd immediately recognized: Gilkriz, one of the senior wizards of Sshamath's College of Conjuration and Summoning. Beak-nosed, Gilkriz stood with arms folded, his ring-bedecked fingers restlessly drumming against his cloth-of-gold sleeves. A gold skullcap adorned his shaven head.

Q'arlynd tucked a hand under one arm, nudged Eldrinn with his elbow and spoke in sign with his hidden hand. *What's he doing here? And who are the other two?*

Eldrinn answered in kind. *Don't worry. Father warned me about this. They'll be working with us.*

Q'arlynd had to damp down his irritation. Eldrinn should have told him this before now.

Khorl glanced sidelong at Eldrinn, as if looking for a cue to hang his reaction on. Daffir only nodded to himself, as if he'd been expecting this.

Eldrinn squared his shoulders and strode to where the other wizards stood. "Gilkriz," he said with a polite nod. "Glad to see you here. Urlryn chose wisely." He turned to the others, nodding at each in turn. "Jyzrill. Mazeer. Good to have you along, also."

Q'arlynd hid his wince. The boy was trying to take charge but doing a less than convincing job of it. He was too young, his movements too uncertain.

Jyzrill, an unusually short male with a pointed chin and a deep scowl that would have been more in place on a dwarf, muttered a greeting. The other mage, Mazeer, stood with hands on hips, forearms bristling with wands that were shoved into a two specially designed bracers. Her voice was silky as she returned Eldrinn's greeting, but her eyes remained cold as steel.

Gilkriz ignored Eldrinn. He turned to the other diviners and smiled, revealing gold-capped teeth. "Khorl. Daffir. So glad you'll be helping out with this one." He turned to Q'arlynd. "And . . ."

Eldrinn answered before Q'arlynd could. "Q'arlynd Melarn, originally of Ched Nasad. A prominent battle mage from that city who joined our college more than a year ago—an addition which obviously escaped your notice."

Q'arlynd gave a slight nod—just enough to be polite.

"Ah yes," Gilkriz said. "I remember now. Isn't this the wizard who rescued you after your disastrous journey to the surface? The trip that left you a feeblewit?" His derisive chuckle was echoed by the slight twist of Jyzrill's and Mazeer's lips.

Eldrinn's nostrils flared. "I—"

"Say nothing, Eldrinn," Q'arlynd interrupted. "They're trying to learn now what their spies failed to uncover earlier. One of their wizards probably faces a similar problem, himself—and they don't know what to do about it."

Eldrinn had the good sense to smile knowingly.

Voices filled the space behind them. Q'arlynd glanced back at the double doors where Qilué still stood. Striding through them was a statuesque female Q'arlynd recognized at once: Cavatina, slayer of Selvetarm. Six females followed her: five drow and surprisingly, a halfling who wore the full vestments of Eilistraee's faith. The priestesses deferred to Cavatina with every gesture, their expressions filled with awe.

Mixed into the priestesses' ranks were an equal number of Nightshadows: six in all. Though the males walked with the priestesses, they conveyed the impression of being separate from them. They kept sneaking glances at Cavatina—their expressions wary rather than worshipful.

Q'arlynd was instantly on alert. He scanned the Nightshadows' faces, looking for signs that any had recognized him, but the glances they gave him were bland. They paid no more attention to him than they did to any of the other mages.

The thin, muscular male was obviously the Nightshadows' leader. He was dressed all in black. A mask covered much of his face. An old scar puckered his left eye. His long stride compelled Cavatina to speed up in order to keep ahead of him.

Q'arlynd gave a mental head shake. Just like the wizards, the clerics and priestesses were trying to one-up each other. Factions within factions.

He glanced at Qilué. As always, her expression was impassive. She watched the newcomers sort themselves out. Then she shut the double doors and strode to the front of the hall.

Aside from Cavatina—and Daffir, whose height made him tower above the drow males—Qilué was the tallest in the room. When she held her hands above her head, the murmurs fell away.

"A song of welcome," she ordered, "for the mages of Sshamath."

The females broke into song. The male clerics joined in a heartbeat later. They sang in low voices, as if unused to talking above a whisper. Their leader studied the wizards as he sang. He actually met their eyes—a rarity, for a Nightshadow.

When the song ended, Qilué nodded at Cavatina. "For most of you, the priestess who will lead this expedition needs no introduction. But those from Sshamath may not know her." She waved Cavatina forward. "The Darksong Knight Cavatina, slayer of Selvetarm."

Q'arlynd glanced at his fellow mages. Their lips parted slightly, their eyes widened. Only Khorl remained unmoved. Eldrinn stared like a smitten house boy until Q'arlynd nudged him.

Cavatina, poised as a statue, glanced down her nose at the group. Her eyes briefly lingered on Q'arlynd—she obviously recognized him—but she made no move to acknowledge him.

Qilué stepped back a pace. "Cavatina will tell you what lies ahead. May the Masked Lady bless you all and watch over you." That said, she vanished.

Q'arlynd was tempted to pull his crystal out of his pocket and sneak a glance through it to see if the high priestess had really teleported away—or if she lingered nearby, watching invisibly—but that was only idle curiosity. He studied Cavatina instead. He'd met her only briefly, nearly two years ago. He wanted to get a sense of what she'd be like as a leader.

The Darksong Knight was not one to waste time with formal greetings. "You all know our mission," she told them. "To halt whatever's augmenting the *Faerzress*. We believe the cause to lie within Kiaransalee's Acropolis. That's what has prompted our decision to attack it."

Q'arlynd's eyebrows rose. He caught Eldrinn's eye. *Attack?* he signed, down where no one else would see it.

Eldrinn gave a slight shrug.

Q'arlynd glanced at Gilkriz. The conjurer's eyebrows had drawn together slightly. Gilkriz was hiding it, for the most part, but he seemed as surprised by Cavatina's choice of words as Q'arlynd had been. He, too, must have been told it was merely a scouting mission.

"We leave tonight, as soon as Selûne has risen," Cavatina continued. "We'll be using the Moonspring Portal. Those of you who haven't used it before should note that it involves immersion in water. If you're carrying scrolls or equipment that will be harmed by a dunking, either find a way to protect them or leave them behind." She paused. "And if any of you can't swim, now's the time to say so. We'll be emerging into a lake. A *deep* lake."

"The Moondeep," said the Nightshadow that the others deferred to. He stepped forward a pace, shoulder to shoulder with Cavatina. "Northeast of the Moondeep Sea, in the Deep Wastes. Several leagues from our destination. Teleportation isn't possible where we're going, so be prepared for a long hike."

"Thank you, Kâras," Cavatina said, easing in front of him. "I'll take it from here."

She snapped her fingers, and a drift disc hissed into the room. The group parted, letting it pass through their ranks. It slid to a stop in front of Cavatina. She tugged on the edge of the shield-sized disc and turned it to the vertical. Q'arlynd saw that it was engraved with a map. With the point of her sword, Cavatina gestured at an irregularly shaped oval.

"The Acropolis of Thanatos lies here, in this cavern." Her sword point shifted to a larger circle on the opposite side of the map. "We'll be portalling in here, at the Moondeep Sea. From there, we'll enter a played-out duergar mine, several tunnels of which eventually lead to the cavern that houses the Acropolis. Those passages will be well guarded, but this one—" the sword traced a line that snaked away from the sea, but stopped before reaching the first cavern she'd pointed out— "won't be. It's on one of the lowest levels of the mine and partially flooded. At its end is an entrance the Crones don't yet know about. It only just opened up, due to a recent collapse. They haven't found it because it's below water." Her sword tapped the drift disc again with a faint clank. "That's our way in."

Kâras glanced at the map. "With respect, Lady Cavatina, there's something you're overlooking. We're a large group. Too large to hide easily, with members who aren't as skilled in stealth as Nightshadows. For this 'attack' to work, we need to hold the main force back and send in spies—and from more than one direction." His finger traced its own line across the map to the cavern of the Acropolis. "Enter the Crones' cavern not only by the route you just named, but also here, and here, and—"

"No." Cavatina's voice was firm. She tapped the map. "This will be the only unguarded route."

"My Nightshadows can slip past any guards."

"Once past them, they'll need the battle experience and singing swords of the Protectors. And the spells of the wizards. No, we stick together." She paused. "Qilué's orders."

Kâras bowed, but not before Q'arlynd spotted a flash of anger in his eyes.

Cavatina went on to describe the Acropolis itself. The temple, she told them, was situated on an island in the middle of a lake-filled cavern. A cavern immediately recognizable by the thousands of skulls spiked into its stone ceiling. The island had once been home to V'elddrinnsshar, a drow city that fell a century ago to plague—a remark that raised nervous murmurs in the assembled crowd. Cavatina assured them the plague was long gone. She reminded them that the ruined city was home to much more potent dangers: Kiaransalee's priestesses and their undead minions.

She touched what looked like a square wooden bead tied about her upper left arm. All of the priestesses and Nightshadows wore a similar bead. "These phylacteries will help my clerics and priestesses fight the undead." She turned to the wizards. "I assume you've made similar preparations?"

"Indeed we have, Lady," Gilkriz said, nodding down at one of the rings on his ever-drumming fingers. Beside him, Mazeer lifted one arm, drawing attention to the wands sheathed in her bracer. Jyzrill simply snorted, as if his scowl would be enough to wither undead where they stood.

"My staff will warn me," Daffir said.

"As will my trinkets," said Khorl.

"We're protected," said Eldrinn, indicating both Q'arlynd and himself.

Q'arlynd nodded in agreement. Master Seldszar had given the boy half a dozen potions; each would provide complete concealment from undead creatures—for a time. Three of these rested in Q'arlynd's pocket for "safekeeping."

"I hope so," Cavatina said. "If it comes to a battle, we won't just face mindless animated corpses. Many Crones embrace undeath themselves, or rise as revenants when slain, as Kâras can personally attest."

Kâras looked uncomfortable—a fact Q'arlynd noted with more than a little alarm. Cavatina had spilled something the Nightshadow hadn't wanted her to. She didn't know when to keep her mouth shut. At the first opportunity, Q'arlynd would have to speak to the Darksong Knight. He didn't want her mentioning his role in Vhaeraun's death. Not with six Nightshadows at his back.

Kâras cleared his throat. "I have indeed seen Crones rise as revenants. And as something more than revenants. I was in Maerimydra when it fell to the army of Kurgoth Hellspawn. In the aftermath of that battle, the traitors of House T'sarran seized control of the city in Kiaransalee's name. Among their ranks were spirits whose wailing scythed down dozens of mortals where they stood." He paused, then added grimly, "A small taste of what will await us at the Acropolis of Thanatos."

Once again, the hall filled with uneasy murmurs.

"We're prepared," Cavatina said confidently. She nodded at the halfling priestess.

The halfling—an odd-looking individual with copper-colored hair and skin stained black as a drow's—reached into her pouch and pulled out what resembled a ball of fired clay tufted with feathers. "Silence stones," she said in a voice that was surprisingly husky for such a small person. She patted a sling tucked into her belt in the place where a scabbard would normally hang, but her sword was strapped to her back.

Cavatina turned back to the group. "If others among you also have the ability to create magical silence, I suggest you review those spells before we leave. Next to the singing swords, they're our best defense."

Q'arlynd felt Eldrinn nudging his arm. He glanced at the boy and saw Eldrinn's quick question. *You?*

Q'arlynd shook his head slightly. *You?*

No.

Cavatina continued her briefing, warning them of the various forms of undead sure to populate the Acropolis. Q'arlynd listened attentively, eyes focused on the drift-disc map as he memorized all possible routes between the Moondeep and the Acropolis. Just in case.

"It's not just undead we have to watch out for," Kâras added. "I grew up in the Deep Wastes and know its dangers." He held up a hand and counted off fingers. "Purple worms, delvers, umber hulks . . ." He glanced around. "If any of you feels the tiniest vibration, I want to hear about it."

"Thank you, Kâras, for the warning," Cavatina said. She turned to the others. "Knowing what to avoid for in the Deep Wastes will be valuable."

"What to watch for, you mean," Kâras interjected. "If a fresh tunnel's been bored we might be able to make use of it. Shorten the distance."

"No," Cavatina said firmly. "We stick to the route we've chosen. We don't want to wander into any dead ends and get trapped."

"How do we know the route you've chosen won't be a trap?" Kâras protested. "If the Crones have found out about it—"

Cavatina's eyes smoldered. "They haven't."

Kâras frowned. "How did *you* learn of this route?"

"Through our allies in the Deep Wastes."

Khorl cleared his throat. "What allies would those be, Lady?"

Cavatina seemed relieved to answer someone else's question. "The svirfneblin."

Q'arlynd's eyes widened in surprise. For a fleeting instant, he wondered if his former slave might have wound up in the Deep Wastes. It had been a long time since Q'arlynd had last seen Flinderspeld, and over the past year and a half, he'd often wondered how the deep gnome was faring. But Silverymoon was a long way from the Moondeep. More than five hundred leagues.

Kâras's eyebrows rose. "Deep gnomes, helping drow?" He looked as if he wanted to laugh. "The svirfneblin hate us. They'll lead us into an ambush or hand us over to the Crones."

"No, they won't," Cavatina said. "The svirfneblin hate the Crones. And they don't hate all drow; they trust in Eilistraee's grace. They'll act as our guides on this expedition. They have already braved much to scout the way to the Acropolis. One of them drowned while tracing the route through the flooded cavern." Her eyes locked on Kâras. "Please remember that sacrifice, and treat the svirfneblin with respect when we meet them."

Kâras inclined his head. Slightly. "To each who contributes to our mission, I will give his fair due."

Judging by the expressions of the priestesses, Q'arlynd wasn't the only one to note the choice of gender.

Cavatina finished her briefing and asked for questions. There were several. Q'arlynd waited until most had been answered, lest he seem anxious. Then he cleared his throat and asked his question in an offhanded tone. "Lady, a question. Will our passage through the portal be a one-way trip?"

"No. Once we accomplish our mission, we'll use the portal to return. But bear in mind that it only functions between moonrise and moonset when the moon is magically 'reflected' on its surface."

Q'arlynd raised his hand again. "If we're unable to scry the surface, how will we know when the moon has risen?"

"The Moondeep is a magical sea," Cavatina answered. "When Selûne shines on the Moonsea above, its reflection also illuminates the waters of the Moondeep. Hence the name. But you don't have to worry. The priestesses will open the portal." She looked around. "Any other questions?"

There were a handful.

The overall plan was in place. Once inside the cavern that housed the Acropolis, they would make their way across the lake to infiltrate the temple, some under cover of invisibility, others by rendering themselves ethereal. Still others would use illusion to disguise themselves as undead.

"Once we're on the island, we will slay as many of Kiaransalee's priestesses as possible," Cavatina reminded them. "But our goal is to find out what's augmenting the *Faerzress*. The moment any of you discovers anything you even *think* might be significant, report your findings to Qilué. Just speak her name, and she will hear you. She'll relay your findings to the rest of us and guide us from there."

She shifted her attention to the wizards. "You will, of course, be tempted to report to the masters of your respective colleges first. That's only natural. But remember this. Your masters do not control the Moonspring Portal. We do. With teleportation blocked, it's the only way drow can access an area close to the Acropolis. If our expedition runs into trouble, it will be the Promenade coming to our aid." She paused. "I realize that vows mean little in the cities where many of you were born, but I give you my solemn word on this. Anything that is reported to Qilué will be passed on to your masters immediately. We all have a stake in this. Cooperation is the key."

The priestesses around her nodded. Q'arlynd dutifully bobbed his head while noting Gilkriz's faintly skeptical look. He also noted the way the other Nightshadows drew closer to Kâras, whose fingers made a quick gesture Q'arlynd couldn't read.

The priestesses broke into song again. Q'arlynd wished they'd just get going. Two days had passed since he met Miverra in Sshamath. In eight days more, perhaps less, divination magic would become impossible in Sshamath and the College of Divination would fall. And with it would go Q'arlynd's dreams of becoming one of Sshamath's masters.

For the time being, there was still a chance to stave off the looming crisis.

Assuming, he thought as he glanced around at the clearly visible factions, this group held together long enough.

CHAPTER 7

Halisstra hummed softly, using her *bae'qeshel* magic to conceal herself from sight. Slowly she descended on a thread of web toward the pair who walked below. The tree she lurked in was thick with leaves. Though they rustled slightly during her descent, the male and female below didn't seem to notice. The couple was in the throes of a heated argument, their raised voices obscuring the slight sounds from above.

"—why we need to keep up this pretense," the male said. " 'She' is no longer 'Lady' anything—just listen to her voice!"

"Eilistraee is still female," his companion insisted. "She assumed the mask—and the voice—as an encouragement for you to join her faith. You *chose* to acknowledge her as your patron deity. Now you must pay her the proper respect."

"I chose nothing," the male answered. "My hand was forced."

"You could have gone off with the others—the ones who think a portion of Vhaeraun is still alive, somewhere on the Astral Plane."

"He *is* alive. He lives inside Eilistraee."

"She killed him."

"Vhaeraun allowed his body to be stripped away so he might join with her. The resulting union is the Masked Lord and Lady of the Dance in one. *Either* title is equally appropriate. Your faith is a matriarchy no more."

"*Our* faith, for better or worse. We—"

The pair moved on. Halisstra landed gently on the trail they'd just passed along. Her glimpse of them through the moon-dappled branches had confirmed that both were drow. The male wore black leather armor and a soft black mask, and was armed with a wristbow on each forearm. The female wore mithral chainmail over her clothes and carried a sword and shield. An astonishing sight: a priestess of Eilistraee and a cleric of Vhaeraun, patrolling a stretch of the Forest of Shadows together. And doing a poor job of it.

Halisstra pointed at a branch ahead of the pair and off to one side in the forest. She sang a brief melody. The branch bent then sprang back. The pair gave a start, then leaped into action. The male signaled *flank left* and fell back along the trail, toward the spot where the invisible Halisstra crouched. As the female cautiously moved ahead, Halisstra whispered her song a second time, causing a rustling deeper in the woods. The female moved through the trees in pursuit of whatever she imagined was lurking at the side of the trail.

In another moment the pair would realize they'd been tricked—but a moment was all Halisstra needed.

The male had shrouded himself in darkness, but Halisstra's eyes penetrated his flimsy concealment. She sprang at him. He whirled and raised both fists, his wristbows thrumming. One of the bolts glanced harmlessly off Halisstra's hardened skin. The second punched into her torso just beneath her left breast. It stung—but the puncture immediately began to heal, pushing the bolt outward. The poison that coated it did nothing to slow her. Grabbing the cleric by his outstretched arms, she yanked him close and sank her fangs into his neck. Pain stiffened his body. His eyes rolled back in his head. Then he gave a soft grunt and sagged in her arms.

Halisstra, visible for the time being, examined his body. Her single bite had only rendered the cleric unconscious. She spun him, laying on a thin coating of web. Then, clutching the sticky body to her chest with her spider legs, she sprang into a nearby tree. Swift as a spider, she swarmed up its trunk and deposited the cleric in the crook of a branch.

A moment later, Eilistraee's priestess reappeared below. "Glorst?" she whispered. She glanced around, then squatted and touched something on the ground. Web glinted on her fingers as she rose. She touched the holy symbol that hung against her chest and glanced up.

Halisstra waved down at her, releasing a spray of hair-thin web.

The priestess sang a shrill note and grabbed a beam of moonlight that appeared over her head. She hurled it like a lance at Halisstra. The moonbeam plunged into Halisstra's stomach, droning through her vitals and leaving them feeling loose and watery. Bloody bile rose in her throat. Even as she choked it down she felt her damaged organs mending.

"Why do you attack me, priestess?" she gasped. "I've done nothing to you."

The priestess yanked a hunting horn from her belt and blew a strident plea for help. Halisstra knew no one would arrive in time. She'd deliberately chosen an ambush point on the outskirts of the shrine's territory.

The crossbow bolt had nearly worked its way free of Halisstra's ribs. She yanked it out and tossed it down. "Your companion tried to kill me," she told the priestess. "And yet . . ." She lifted the cleric's body and tossed it down. "I showed mercy."

The unconscious cleric tumbled through the branches, the sticky webbing that coated him slowing his descent. He landed with barely a thud on the forest floor.

The priestess frantically sang a protective hymn.

"Don't you know who I *am?*" Halisstra cried. "Why do you fear me?"

"Your tricks won't work on me, demon," the priestess shouted back. Though her sword was steady enough in her hand, her voice quavered. She bent to touch fingers lightly to her companion's throat.

The gesture told Halisstra everything she needed to know: the pair were more than fellow clerics. No one but a lust-addled fool would pause to check if her consort was alive. Halisstra had made the right decision in not killing the male outright.

"I came to beg your help," she told the priestess. "And instead of showing Eilistraee's mercy, you and your male try to *kill* me." She leaped to the ground, clutched herself as she landed, and pretended to stagger. She forced herself to vomit, filling the air with the tang of bilious blood.

To her credit, the priestess didn't flinch. Even though Halisstra loomed over her, she stepped between Halisstra and the paralyzed male.

"I mean you no harm," Halisstra continued. "I'm looking for Lady Cavatina. She promised to help me." She looked down at her misshapen hands. "I wasn't always a monster. I was a priestess, like yourself, until I was transformed by Lolth's foul magic."

Doubt showed for the first time in the priestess's eyes. "Who are you?"

"Halisstra Melarn."

"No," the priestess whispered—but the word held no conviction. She lowered her sword slightly. "By Eilistraee's silver tresses, is it true?"

Halisstra lifted a hand, hesitated, then held out fingers that were dark with blood from her wounds. "It's true," she sang.

Into those two brief words, she spun powerful magic. The priestess's expression softened. She sheathed her sword. "I'm so sorry," she said. "Had I known—"

Halisstra waved the apology away, spiderwebs drifting from her hand. "How *could* you have known? I was captured by yochlols and subjected to . . ." She lowered her voice to a hoarse whisper, ". . . unthinkable torments. For nearly two years, I languished in the Demonweb Pits before at last escaping."

The priestess frowned. "Two years? Lady Halisstra, it has been nearly *five* years since you set out for the Demonweb Pits with the Crescent Blade."

"And nearly two years ago that I escaped—and returned to the Demonweb Pits with Lady Cavatina, to slay Selvetarm."

"But . . ." The priestess's frown deepened. "It was Lady Cavatina who killed Selvetarm . . . wasn't it?"

"With my help."

"Then why do the odes say nothing of—"

"Aside from Lady Qilué, only Cavatina knew that I still lived. And Cavatina has a Darksong Knight's pride. She would hardly have admitted to letting Lolth's minions capture me a second time, would she? Better not to mention my involvement at all. To pretend that I had died years before, during Lolth's Silence."

At the word "died," the priestess glanced down at the male. The cleric didn't look good; his eyes had fully rolled back in his head and his skin was turning gray. Halisstra reached out and lifted the priestess's chin, forcing her to look away. "It's only a weak venom," she lied. "You have plenty of time to heal him. Plenty of time, still."

"Yes," the priestess repeated softly. "Plenty of time."

Her eyes reminded Halisstra of another priestess who'd succumbed to Halisstra's *bae'qeshel* magic, years ago. Seyll had stared just as trustingly into Halisstra's eyes a heart-beat before Halisstra plunged a sword into her. And yet Seyll had told Halisstra, as she lay dying, that no one was beyond redemption—not even Halisstra.

She'd been wrong.

This priestess had a wide mouth and creases at the sides of her eyes that could only have come from frequent laughter. The frown of confusion looked out of place on her forehead. The slight bulge of her stomach hinted she might be carrying a child.

Halisstra hated her.

"What's your name, priestess?"

"Shoshara."

"I need to find Cavatina, Shoshara. She's the only one who can lift the Spider Queen's curse. The priestesses at the Lake Sember shrine told me she came here for the High Hunt. Is she still in the Shilmista Forest?"

The priestess shook her head. "Lady Cavatina left a few days ago. Lady Qilué summoned her to the Promenade."

Halisstra's jaw clenched. "Which road is she traveling?"

"She isn't going by road. She used the portal. She'll be at the Promenade already."

Halisstra hissed angrily. This was an obstacle she hadn't counted on. Portal or no, she'd never get inside the Promenade—not with a demon's mark on her palm. Her fingers inadvertently tightened on the priestess's chin, and her claws pricked flesh. When Shoshara gasped, Halisstra released her and feigned contrition, curling her body into a submissive ball. "I'm sorry! I didn't mean to. Please don't hurt me again, Mistress."

The priestess rubbed her chin, then glanced at the faint smudge of blood on her fingers. "No real harm done," she said with a vague laugh. "Eilistraee's mercy is infinite." Her eyes strayed to the cleric. His mask lay flat against his mouth and nose; he no longer breathed.

Halisstra rose and caught the priestess's hands in hers. She turned Shoshara slightly, preventing her from looking at the corpse. "Shoshara, please. I can't enter the Promenade. Not looking like . . . this. You have to call Cavatina back to the Shilmista Forest."

"I'll send word to her. Tell her you're coming and—what's happened to you."

"No!" Halisstra cried. "Cavatina will feel immense guilt at having abandoned me. She'll refuse to come."

"Not Lady Cavatina. She has more honor than that."

"You don't know her. Not the way I do. You haven't seen what she's capable of. I . . ." Halisstra paused, trying to call tears to her eyes. It didn't work. "I have. Nearly two years ago, in the Demonweb Pits." She lowered her voice to a harsh whisper. "Abandoned."

That emotion, at least, was easy enough for Halisstra. All she had to do was think of Eilistraee's betrayal. The Lady of the Dance had indeed turned away from Halisstra, leaving her to face Lolth alone on that first journey to the Demonweb Pits during Lolth's Silence. No matter what excuses Qilué might give, that fact remained.

And just look what had come of it.

"But Lady Cavatina returned to the Demonweb Pits after slaying Selvetarm," the priestess exclaimed. "She must have gone there to search for you, before sealing the portal."

Halisstra widened her eyes in feigned shock. "*Cavatina* sealed the portal? I thought that was Lolth's doing!" She shook her head in mock disbelief. "So *that's* why my first escape attempt failed. Cavatina betrayed my faith in her." She glared. "Cavatina should apologize to me. She owes me at least that much."

The enchantment she'd placed on Shoshara was strong; Halisstra could see the pity in the other female's eyes—and the rising anger at Cavatina's "betrayal" of Halisstra. Shoshara believed Halisstra's story. Every word of it.

"You said you have the magic to contact Cavatina?" Halisstra asked.

Shoshara nodded, much to Halisstra's relief.

"With a sending song?"

Another nod.

"*Will* you call her back to the Shilmista? I want to hear from Cavatina's own lips that she didn't just abandon me. But please, make up some other reason for calling her back. Don't tell Cavatina I'm here. I want to see how she reacts when she sees me, and give her the chance to explain herself. If I'm wrong about her, I wouldn't want to embarrass her or . . . anger her."

Shoshara took a deep breath, then made her decision. "I'll do it."

The priestess sang a brief melody and stared off into the darkened woods, as if looking across a great distance. For several moments, she was silent. She frowned slightly, then nodded. "Lady Cavatina cannot come to the Shilmista. Not now. Lady Qilué is sending her away on an urgent mission. One that must preclude all else."

"Where?" Halisstra hissed. "Where is she being sent?"

Her outburst startled Shoshara. The priestess blinked. "I asked, but she wouldn't . . ." Her eyes strayed to the prone cleric. Then they widened. "Glorst!" she gasped. She gaped at Halisstra, eyes wide. "You—"

The charm had broken.

Halisstra lashed out, slapping the priestess's face so hard her fingers left a mark. "Die!" she shouted.

Without so much as a cry, Shoshara crumpled atop the body of her consort.

Halisstra stared down at them, her mouth twisted in a grimace of disgust. "Weak!" she spat at the priestess. "You're weak!" Her voice rose to a shriek. "Just look at *what you've done!*"

She yanked the priestess's body into her arms and bit it savagely on the face, throat, and arms. Again. And again. It was a bloody ruin when she at last threw the priestess down. Panting, she shook her head, clearing it. When her breathing slowed again, she bent and—very deliberately, this time—inflicted several bites on the already cooling body of the male.

She drew the priestess's sword and placed it where it might have fallen, had it tumbled from Shoshara's dead hand, and shrouded both bodies with web. Halisstra couldn't mimic a spider's digestive juices, but she could strew web about the bushes, as if it had been shot from above by spinnerets.

Halisstra was angry at herself—angry for not having first asked where the portal to the Promenade was. But she could hazard a guess. During her time at the Velarswood shrine, she'd observed priestesses, recently arrived from the Promenade, who were dripping wet. There had been a pool near that shrine, innocent looking, yet always heavily guarded from moonrise to moonset. She'd seen a similar pool in the Shilmista Forest.

She squinted through the branches at the night sky and smiled.

Eilistraee's moon would light the way to her prey.

Cavatina squinted as she swam upward through the ice-cold water. The surface of the lake, bright with the light of the full moon, rippled above. They'd portaled in deep; the surface was farther above her than she'd expected. Already her lungs strained from the lack of air. When she broke the surface, she gasped in a long, grateful breath.

Treading water, she twisted around. The Moondeep Sea glowed with moonlight—bright enough to illuminate the ceiling, nearly two hundred paces above.

A head broke the surface next to her: Kâras. His mask was plastered against his mouth; a shake of his head freed it. "You should have . . . warned us . . . the portal was . . . so deep," he gasped.

Cavatina thought the same thing—of Qilué.

"Watch for the others," she told Kâras. "If any don't make it, we'll have to revive them."

That said, she levitated. A quick glance around revealed no imminent threats. Aside from the disturbance caused by the portal, the Moondeep Sea was quiet and still. She'd been wrong about it being moonlight illuminating the ceiling. Everywhere she looked, the stone that made up the cavern was infused with a faint glow. It shimmered with a pale blue light that was almost white: the largest *Faerzress* she'd ever seen.

She counted heads as the Protectors and Nightshadows broke the surface, one by one. Some used prayers to stand upon the moonlit ripples, and others hovered just below the surface, breathing water, then rose and sprayed water from their nostrils in fine sheets.

Two of the wizards sputtered up without any visible magical aid: Q'arlynd and the young mage from the College of Divination. A short distance from them, the female conjurer rose to the surface in a swell of water, the cupped hands of an elemental she must have summoned. As it was subsumed into the lake, a whirlpool dimpled the surface directly below. The human wizard with the staff rose out of it, bone dry, and levitated beside her.

The other wizards used equally creative methods to exit the depths. One climbed out of the lake as if scaling an invisible ladder, while another rose to the surface sucking on a blue, blown-glass bottle that didn't look as if it could possibly contain enough air to sustain her. The wizard in the gold skullcap tossed a tiny wooden box away from himself as he broke the surface, and it unfolded into a small wooden boat. He climbed, dripping, into it, and with a flick of his hand magically set its oars to sculling.

Everyone was accounted for. Those who hadn't risen from the water by magical means were treading water. Cavatina glanced around to get her bearings, then pointed at the spot where they were to meet the svirfneblin: a tunnel, bored into the cavern, with a beachlike mound of rubble in the lake below. Fortunately, it wasn't too far away.

That tunnel, she signed to the others. *Make for it.*

With a mental command, she lowered herself until she hung horizontally above the lake. Then she "swam" forward, immersing only her hands. When she reached the base of the rockfall, she drew her singing sword and climbed the slope. Her boots let her spring lightly from one foothold to the next. Pausing at the top, she peered into the mine tunnel. It should have been gloomy, but instead, its walls were illuminated with the faint, flickering light of the *Faerzress*.

Nothing stirred inside the tunnel.

That didn't surprise her. The Acropolis was several leagues away, and the Moondeep Sea was remote and rarely visited. The Crones would position any guards closer to their own cavern. Nevertheless, as the first of the Protectors reached the spot where she stood, Cavatina pointed down the narrow tunnel. *Scout ahead,* she ordered in silent speech, *one thousand paces. Report each quarter count.* The priestess nodded and disappeared into the tunnel.

Cavatina ordered another Protector to remain at the bottom of the rockfall and keep watch over the lake. That priestess took up her position, singing sword in hand, as the others climbed or levitated to the spot where Cavatina stood.

Much to her irritation, Kâras set up his own guard at the bottom of the rockfall and ordered a Nightshadow into the tunnel. Cavatina caught the male's arm as he tried to pass her. "Wait," she whispered. "We'll have our first report in a moment."

The Nightshadow glanced back at Kâras.

"*I* give the commands," she hissed at the Nightshadow. "Not him."

"Yes, Lady," he murmured.

Kâras climbed up next to them. "Are we not following Qilué's orders? 'Stick together,' you quoted her as saying. Nar'bith is a master at stealth, silent as shadow. And two pairs of eyes are better than one."

Two more Nightshadows had just climbed up the rockfall behind Kâras, eyes watchful above their masks.

"Four eyes are better than two," Cavatina agreed. "But if you give orders that overlap mine, there will be unfortunate consequences." She nodded at the Nightshadow whose arm she still held. "This male, skewered on the Protector's sword. I must warn my priestess he's coming."

Kâras inclined his head. "Fair enough." His eyes remained unrepentant. "Warn her."

Cavatina's eyes narrowed. She knew he was trying, once again, to one-up her, to appear as if he was giving the orders, but she wasn't about to waste time sparring with him. She warned Halav with a sending then she released the Nightshadow.

He drifted away into the tunnel, his footsteps utterly silent. Kâras turned away and clambered back down to the water. He disappeared from Cavatina's view.

The rest of the Nightshadows, Protectors and wizards gathered around her at the mouth of the tunnel, their sodden clothing dribbling water. Some stared at the *Faerzress* but most had their attention on Cavatina.

"So far, so good," she told them, voice low. "We appear to have arrived undetected." As she spoke, she wondered where the deep gnomes were. They'd been told to return that night, as soon as the full moon appeared on the underground sea's surface. But the Promenade's battlemistress hadn't been clear on how the svirfneblin would arrive. Over the Moondeep, by boat? Or from the tunnels?

Several moments passed. The Protectors stood patiently, waiting for Cavatina's orders, but the mages and Nightshadows were getting restless.

Where *were* those svirfneblin?

A sending came from the priestess Cavatina had ordered into the tunnel. *I'm two hundred and fifty paces in,* Halav reported. *All clear so far.*

A moment later, Kâras climbed back to where Cavatina stood. "I've just found a svirfneblin in the water," he said in a low voice. "Dead."

"Show me."

She followed him down the rockfall, a handful of the others trailing behind her. As they approached, she spotted a ripple in the water, a few paces out on the Moondeep: a small animal, swimming. It looked like a rat. As if sensing her presence, the rat dived beneath the surface and vanished.

Kâras squatted beside the water. *There*, he signed, pointing to a water-filled crevice between the rocks.

Cavatina kneeled beside him. It was a deep gnome, all right, little bigger than a child, but with a stocky body that bulged with muscle. Cavatina reached into the water, gently pulled the body out, and set it on the rocks at her feet. The head was missing, and by the ragged look of the neck it had been yanked or chewed off. Whether that had happened before or after the deep gnome died was impossible to tell. There weren't any other visible wounds. The svirfneblin's clothing—plain leather trousers and a sleeveless shirt—was also undamaged. His feet were bare; perhaps he'd been swimming when he died.

"Eilistraee's mercy," she whispered.

The others crowded close, staring down at the corpse. Q'arlynd squatted next to it. He lifted a limp hand and studied it a moment, then let it fall.

Daffir passed a hand over the body, not quite touching it. His other hand tightened on his staff. "A bad omen."

Cavatina didn't need magic to tell her that.

"Is this our guide?" the female wizard asked.

Kâras stared grimly down at it. "Not anymore."

Another sending from Halav: *I'm five hundred paces in. No sign of the svirfneblin, aside from a prospector's pick. Looks like it was dropped here. No telling when.*

The svirfneblin's gray flesh had a waxy, bloated look. Despite its immersion in cold water, the body was starting to smell.

"If this is our guide, he arrived several days early." Cavatina stood and glanced at the reflection of Selûne and the scattering of Tears that trailed the moon's reflection as it slid slowly across the Moondeep. "We'll continue to wait. We'll give it until moonset."

"Waiting is a waste of time." Kâras said. "No guide's going to show. Not after what happened to this fellow."

"We don't know that," Cavatina said. "If we leave now, we'll have to guess which way to go once we've reached the limits of our map, which will mean an even greater waste of time." She nodded to the wizards. "That won't sit well with the masters of your colleges."

Several of the mages nodded.

The sun elf, however, shook his head. "I see no point in waiting," Khorl said. "When we reach the end of the mapped region, my magic will show us the way. Unlike the rest of you, I can still cast divinations, despite the *Faerzress* that surrounds us."

Cavatina shook her head firmly. "Kiaransalee's priestesses may be crazed, but they aren't fools. They'll have warded their cavern with protections similar to those of the Promenade. Your divinations may find the path—or they may not. In case they can't, we stick to the original plan. We wait."

She pointed at the corpse. "In the meantime, do any of you know what should be done? What the svirfneblin customs are when dealing with the dead? When our guide shows up, we don't want to offend him."

"I do," Q'arlynd said. "I had a . . . an ally, years ago, who was svirfneblin. He told me about the god the deep gnomes venerate—Callarduran Smoothhands, master of stone. When a deep gnome dies, it's appropriate for him to be 'returned to Smoothhands's embrace.'" Q'arlynd paused and stroked his chin. "With your permission, Lady Cavatina, I have a spell that can do just that."

Cavatina nodded. "Use it."

Another sending came from Halav. *Seven hundred and fifty paces in. Still clear.*

Q'arlynd motioned the others back. He reached into a pocket of his *piwafwi*, pulled out a pinch of something, and tossed it onto the stones beside the body. As he chanted, the rocks beneath the corpse slumped and became as soft as mud. Q'arlynd gently pushed the body into them, submerging it. That done, he washed the mud from his hands and spoke a second arcane word. The mud solidified, stone once more.

As they climbed back to the tunnel mouth, Cavatina leaned close to Q'arlynd. "Well done. Your friend would have been proud."

"My ally," Q'arlynd corrected.

"As you wish."

Those who had followed Cavatina down to the water returned to the tunnel's mouth. Once again they stood about. Waiting. Cavatina wondered if the svirfneblin would show. Perhaps the corpse Q'arlynd had just buried *had* been their guide.

The human diviner was leaning against his staff, watching. Suddenly he tensed. "Something's coming."

"What is it?" Cavatina asked, instantly alert.

"Something . . . big." Daffir turned and stared out across the underground sea.

"A boat?" one of the Protectors guessed.

"As big as a boat, but . . . not a boat. A . . . creature. Whatever it is, it means us ill."

Cavatina scanned the Moondeep, but the surface of the water was unbroken. Nothing moved on it—not even a rat. She glanced at Daffir but couldn't see his eyes behind those dark lenses.

The others drew weapons or readied spell components. The Nightshadows faded back into the tunnel.

"Where is it now, Daffir?" Cavatina demanded.

Daffir shook his head. "That, Lady, I cannot tell. Only where it . . . will be."

"We should move away from the water," the wizard in the gold skullcap said. "Up the tunnel."

"Agreed," Kâras said. "Before whatever killed the svirfneblin realizes we're here."

"No," Cavatina countered. "We stay here. Conceal ourselves and watch the lake." She did, however, call back the Protector and the Nightshadow who were down at the lake's edge. No sense taking chances.

Another sending came: *One thousand paces in.* With a

chuckle in her voice, Halav added. *Still nothing—except for a pair of boots, this time.*

Cavatina frowned. Boots? She glanced down at where the svirfneblin's body lay. *How large are they?*

Small. Child-sized.

The Nightshadow whom Kâras had sent down the tunnel reappeared and signaled that the way was clear.

"That's it," Kâras said. "We're going." His forefinger flicked a signal to the other Nightshadows. *Move out.*

"Hold it right there," Cavatina barked.

The Nightshadows hesitated. They glanced between Kâras and Cavatina.

She rounded on Kâras. "We're having this out, here and now," she said in a low voice. "Qilué put me in charge of this expedition, not you. Eilistraee deemed it should be so. Do you dare risk displeasing her by disobeying me?"

Without waiting for his answer, she turned to the others. "My priestess just found a pair of boots in the tunnel." She pointed down at the dead svirfneblin. "Gnome-sized boots. If they're his, maybe he was forced to run before he could put them on. Whatever killed him might still be lurking in the tunnel."

"You heard Daffir's prophecy," Kâras countered. "Whatever's going to attack us is out there. Submerged in the Moondeep."

"'Attack us?'" Cavatina echoed. She shook her head at Kâras. She was fed up with this. "Tell you what. I'll call my priestess back. You, personally, can take her place. That way, if something does rise out of the Moondeep, you'll be in a nice, safe place where nothing's going to—"

A faint wail came from deep in the tunnel: the sound of a singing sword in combat. The Protector's sending came a heartbeat later: *Undead! Huge! Its head alone blocks the—*

The sending cut off abruptly.

Fall back, Cavatina sent back at Halav. *We're coming.* She pointed briskly at the Protectors. "You, you, and you, follow me. The rest of you wait here. Whatever Daffir sensed isn't in the lake—it's in the tunnel. We'll draw it back here. Attack when it emerges."

To her surprise, Kâras nodded briskly. Gilkriz did the same. As Cavatina sprinted away down the tunnel, the three Protectors close on her heels, she glanced over her shoulder and saw some of the wizards levitating away from the opening of the tunnel and others vanishing. Daffir, however, remained in plain sight, leaning on his staff and nodding.

She kept running. The floor of the tunnel was flat. Cavatina and the priestesses made good speed. The sound of Halav's singing sword—and the howls of whatever she fought—grew louder. Then Halav was in sight.

The Protector battled furiously, her sword a melodic blur as she hacked at the thing that blocked the tunnel: an enormous head, large as a giant's. It crept along the tunnel on a tentacle-like nest of writhing veins, its enormous mouth opening and closing as it came. Other, smaller heads bulged out of its forehead and cheeks as it slithered along. These screamed or moaned piteously as they broke the skin, then fell silent as they sank back into it again.

Even from a distance, Cavatina felt the waves of fear pulsing off the thing. She raised her singing sword in front of her as she ran and felt it slice through the magical fear, sending it sloughing off to each side. Only a hundred paces remained; they were almost there.

Rearing up, the monstrosity pointed a tentacle at Halav. "Die," it croaked.

Halav stiffened. Her sword drooped in her hand, its singing fading to a moan. But Halav was strong and shielded by Eilistraee's blessings. Shaking off the creature's spell, she staggered back.

"Halav!" Cavatina cried. "We're right behind you. Fall back!"

Cavatina was close enough to get a good look at the smaller faces that bulged out of the monstrous head. One of them was gray-skinned and bald: a svirfneblin. She grabbed her holy symbol as she ran, intending to sing a prayer. "Fall back, Halav!" she shouted. "You're in the way."

Halav tried to back away, but a tentacle whipped out and coiled around her chest. It snapped taut, yanking her off her feet. It pulled the failing priestess head-first toward the gaping mouth. Teeth snapped shut, severing her neck.

"No!" Cavatina cried.

The tentacle flung the headless body aside. A heartbeat later, Halav's face bulged out of the monstrous head's cheek, screaming.

Cavatina shouted a prayer. A bolt of moonlight streaked from her hand like a thrown lance. It slammed into the enormous forehead in the same instant that two other magical attacks flew past her: a streak of holy fire and a sparkling sheen of positive energy that rippled down the tunnel like diamond dust carried by ripples on a pond. The enormous head rocked back on its tentacles as they struck.

That was it. Cavatina's chance. She leaped forward, sword raised—

A tentacle lashed out, slapping against her breastplate. A weak blow, not enough to halt her charge, but Cavatina felt a rush of pain. Her chest was warm and wet. Bloody. The thing had used magic to wound her, magic that had bypassed her armor.

She staggered back and gasped out a healing prayer. She expected the creature to follow her, to try to snatch her with a tentacle, yet it remained where it was. One of the smaller heads disappeared with a wet pop, like a boil bursting. The enormous mouth creaked open wide, as if taking a deep breath.

"Tash'kla!" Cavatina shouted. "Ward us!"

In the same instant the Protector behind Cavatina sang out her prayer, the undead head gave a ghastly wail. A chill swept through Cavatina, weakening her. Then the ward muted the sound. Cavatina and the three priestesses behind her remained standing, saved by Eilistraee's blessing.

She flung out an arm, pointing. "Get Halav's body out of here!" At the same time, she pressed home her attack.

A tentacle lashed out at her, and she sliced it off. The undead thing drew back, its smaller heads bulging then disappearing again, all of them howling and screaming. Cavatina thrust at the spot where Halav's face bulged—a mercy blow—but her sword point struck an invisible shield and skewed to the side. Momentarily unbalanced, she staggered and nearly fell. She quickly recovered, dancing out of range of yet another tentacle. Risking a glance behind her, she saw two of the Protectors lifting Halav's headless body and hurrying away. The halfling Brindell scooped up Halav's singing sword in one hand while whirling her sling. Before Cavatina could order her not to, she let fly one of her magical pellets.

Suddenly, Cavatina was fighting in utter silence. She could see the smaller heads screaming as they rose like boils, then sank away again into the morbid flesh. Her sword vibrated in her hands yet she couldn't hear the sharp smack of it hitting flesh or the sound of its singing.

Brindell had silenced the head, but she'd snared Cavatina, as well. Cavatina had been about to sing a prayer, but couldn't.

She danced backward, fighting with one hand. *By my side!* she signed with her free hand. *A fighting retreat.*

Together with the halfling she fell back, always just a few paces from the monstrous head, which came on in eerie silence. Halav had been right: it completely filled the tunnel. There was no way to squeeze past it, and there seemed precious little they could do to defeat it. Prayers that would have reduced a lesser undead creature to an inert mass of flesh had no effect, and the head could throw a magical shield in front of itself at will. It slithered relentlessly along on its tentacles, bearing down on the two retreating priestesses.

The magical silence that enveloped the head abruptly fell away. Its smaller heads shrieking in agony, the monster head slithered up the wall as though weightless. It seemed to be avoiding the floor of the tunnel. Why?

Cavatina glanced down. The floor was slippery from the water that had dribbled from their wet clothing when they ran into the tunnel. A tentacle brushed against it, then recoiled.

Cavatina smiled. Now she knew how to defeat the thing.

She twisted around and snapped out a sending to the female wizard. *Mazeer! Fill the tunnel with water. Now!*

A moment later, a sloshing rumble filled the corridor behind them. "Hold your breath!" Cavatina shouted at Brindell.

A wall of water slammed into them, sweeping both priestesses off their feet. Cavatina crashed into the monstrous head, barely managing to keep hold of her sword. Tentacles flailed at her arms, legs, torso. One wrapped around her and squeezed, driving the air from her lungs. Then it slipped away. The wall of flesh buckled and the cacophony of the smaller heads turned to a weak gurgling. Then the head broke apart. The water shoved Cavatina and Brindell forward, carrying them along in a wave of disintegrating flesh and sodden bone.

Cavatina clambered to her feet as the slimy water receded in a reeking wave. Brindell lay gasping on the floor, and Cavatina helped her to her feet. "Are you injured?"

Brindell shook her head. "I'm fine," she gasped. She bent to pick up the singing sword and her sling.

A moment later, feet splashed up the tunnel toward them. Kâras skidded to a halt in front of Cavatina and stared at the remains of the head. "What in the Abyss were you fighting?"

"A giant's head," Cavatina answered, still panting from the fight. "Raised from the dead and animated to move about on its own. The lakewater disintegrated it."

Two more Nightshadows hurried up the tunnel toward them. With a flick of his hand, Kâras sent them a few paces beyond the spot where they stood to keep watch. His eyes were thoughtful as he glanced down at the smear of putrid flesh on the floor.

"Looks like you guessed right about the boots," he conceded. "The thing Daffir warned us about was in the tunnel, after all. But how did you know water would—"

"Daffir's prophecy," Cavatina said. "He said he knew where it was 'going.' " She pointed back toward the main cavern. "To the Moondeep. In pieces." She shook her head. "No wonder he was so nonchalant when the rest of the group scattered. He foresaw victory."

Kâras nodded. He peered down the tunnel. "Was there just the one head?"

Cavatina was suddenly angry. " 'Just the one' was enough to kill Halav," she snapped.

Kâras looked contrite. "My apologies, Lady. I meant no disrespect."

Cavatina sighed. "Where is her body now?"

"I ordered Gilkriz to ready his magical boat and place her body in it, so she could be rowed back to the portal. I realized she would need to be returned to the Promenade. She'll need resurrection, since she's not . . . whole."

Cavatina nodded wearily. So soon into their mission, and already one of those under her command was dead. Halav would be resurrected and made whole again, Eilistraee willing, but that was a process that took time. Kâras was correct in his guess that the prayer couldn't be attempted there. Surprisingly, he'd anticipated the very order Cavatina had been about to give. He'd even done her the courtesy of waiting, so she might give the order herself. "Thank you, Kâras."

She considered her options, speaking aloud. "We're going to need the Protectors if we encounter more of these heads. We'll send one of your Nightshadows back with the body to the Promenade."

"That won't be possible."

"Why not?"

Kâras gave an elaborate shrug. "None of them knows the hymn that opens the portal."

Cavatina was startled. "They weren't taught it?"

"No. It's as if our voices weren't wanted."

"That's not true."

Kâras shrugged. "You could teach one of us the hymn of opening, of course, but by then the moon will have set—and the body's return will be delayed until tomorrow. If another of those heads shows up in the meantime. . . ." Kâras glanced over his shoulder—probably hiding the smirk in his eyes.

Cavatina clenched her teeth and stared past him. Kâras was right, Abyss take him. It would have to be a Protector who took Halav's body back.

The goodwill she'd been feeling earlier evaporated. Kâras was using Halav's death to tip the scales in his favor. With one of her Protectors slain and a second returned to the temple, only four Protectors would be left under Cavatina's command. As compared to six Nightshadows—including the openly rebellious Kâras. That imbalance would persist until tomorrow's moonrise, when whichever priestess accompanied Halav's body back to the Promenade was at last able to return. The group would probably be long gone from the Moondeep by then.

Without another word, she strode back to the main cavern and instructed the most junior of the Protectors to return to the temple with the body. That priestess looked angry at being ordered back, but immediately bowed. "Eilistraee's will be done, Lady."

The Protector climbed into Gilkriz's boat and sat down next to Halav's body. Gilkriz settled in beside her and spoke its command word. The paddles rose and fell of their own accord, swiftly carrying the boat out toward the shimmering crescent of moonlight at the middle of the lake.

Cavatina, meanwhile, signaled for the others to gather around her. "I've reached a decision," she told them. "That . . . thing . . . was obviously the Crones' work. They must be patrolling this far, so we have to expect more of the same. As soon as Gilkriz rows back, we're going to move away from here, without our guide. We'll see if Khorl can show us the way. But one of us will remain here, in case the guide shows up." She glanced around the group. "Who else of you, besides the Protectors, can sing a sending?"

The Nightshadows glanced at Kâras. He made no noticeable gesture, but a heartbeat later they all shook their heads. So did the wizards.

"None of you?" Cavatina asked. She found that hard to believe. It was more likely a matter of nobody wanting to be left behind on their own. Such cowardly behavior was to be expected of Nightshadows. In the wizards it was inexcusable.

"Q'arlynd," she said.

The wizard tensed.

"You're on good terms with the svirfneblin. You're the logical choice. You will stay."

He looked imploringly at her. "But I can't cast a sending. How will I—"

"Simply follow us. Catch up. You studied the map carefully; I'm sure you know the way." Anticipating his next protest, she added, "You need only wait here until the next moonrise. When Chizra returns, you'll have a sword at your side." As she spoke, she surreptitiously touched her holy symbol, weaving Eilistraee's magic into her words.

Q'arlynd cocked his head at the young wizard next to him. "With your permission, Lady Cavatina, I'd like Eldrinn to remain here as well. To watch with me, until Chizra's return."

The younger mage glanced sidelong at the other two diviners. "I can't, Q'arlynd. Father ordered me to—"

"Eldrinn comes with us, and you stay," Cavatina told Q'arlynd. "That's final."

She saw Q'arlynd's jaw tense, but he was quick to hide his anger. His face was expressionless as he bowed. "As you command, Lady Cavatina."

CHAPTER 8

Halisstra picked at the callus on her palm as she squatted on a ridge above the opening in the forest. At the center of the clearing, the dark waters of a pool reflected the stars above. Soon these pinpricks of light would be joined by the reflection of the rising moon. Then Halisstra would strike.

Two priestesses stood watch over the Shilmista Forest pool. Each wore chainmail and a mithral breastplate embossed with Eilistraee's moon and sword and had a hunting horn slung at her hip. One walked back and forth at the far side of the pool, her sword blade lightly resting on her shoulder. The other stood in a more formal guard position a few steps deeper into the forest, her two-handed sword held point-up in front of her as if ready for inspection. Both were drow, capable of seeing equally well in moonlight and shadow.

Though both watched the surrounding forest carefully, Halisstra observed something interesting. Neither paid much attention to the ridge where she hid. A quick *bae'qeshel* song revealed why: a third guard stood directly below Halisstra on the near side of the pool, cloaked in invisibility. He was clad all in black and wore Vhaeraun's mask. A brace of throwing daggers was strapped to his chest, and a hand crossbow was on one wrist.

Halisstra was twice the size of any one of the drow below and more powerful than the three of them combined. She could easily rend them with her claws or dispatch them with venomous bites. But she could not take down three at once, even with magic. One would certainly sound the alarm before they all died. To use the portal pool, Halisstra needed time to puzzle out its mysteries. She needed to kill all three guards swiftly and silently. But how?

She picked at her hand. The callus constantly burned, the pain secondary only to the throb of the punctures that Lolth's handmaidens had inflicted—punctures that would never heal. These were constant reminders of Halisstra's servitude to the goddess Lolth—and to Lolth's demonic minion.

"Wendonai," Halisstra breathed. Her lips twisted with the word. She hated the demon almost as much as she hated herself. She needed to deliver Cavatina to him. To free herself, and even more importantly, to prove herself to Lolth. The priestesses and cleric, below, were boulders that blocked that tunnel.

A warm breeze shivered through the leaves next to her, carrying with it a strange scent. None of the three below reacted to it, yet Halisstra's heightened senses detected it at once. A strange combination of sweetness and putridity, it smelled like perfume sprinkled on rotten meat. She'd smelled it once before, while roaming the Demonweb Pits.

She sniffed again to be sure.

Dread blossoms? Here, on Toril?

The breeze stilled.

"Wendonai," Halisstra whispered again—with a smile.

She crept away from the ridge and sprang into the tree-tops. Scuttling through them like a spider, leaving a trail of webs in her wake, she headed in the direction the scent had come from. It took her a while to locate its source, but eventually she spotted a dead moose. The massive creature lay on its side, legs thrust out stiffly. Lodged in its flesh were half a dozen dread blossoms. Their stalks pulsed as they extracted the last of the animal's blood. Gold and black pollen drifted out of the cup-shaped crimson flowers, dusting both the dead animal and the forest floor on which it lay.

Halisstra clambered down from the tree branch and squatted a few paces away from the carcass. The dread blossoms yanked their stems out of the dead animal. Chunks of flesh clung like dirt to the tendrils surrounding the lance-sharp point of each stalk. Swift as hummingbirds, the flowers twisted in mid-air, petals fluttering. Then they zipped to the spot where Halisstra waited.

They circled above her like swarming bees, loosing their pollen. It drifted down onto Halisstra's head, shoulders, and arms, fouling her web-sticky hair and clogging her nostrils. She breathed deep, savoring the nausea produced by the sickly sweet odor. The pollen tingled, and numbed her skin, but failed to paralyze her.

She threw her arms wide and froze, inviting attack. A dread blossom hummed away from the rest then reversed itself. It slammed into her stomach point-first with the force of a thrown lance. But instead of penetrating, the stalk splintered on her stone-hard skin. The dread blossom fell to the ground, limp.

Halisstra pouted. She'd hoped it would at least sting.

She loped away through the forest, the five remaining dread blossoms humming in her wake. They were mindless things, drawn by body heat and motion; the destruction of the first dread blossom was not something they had registered. They would keep trying to paralyze her until they ran out of pollen—or until they sensed another, easier target.

Halisstra led them back the way she had come. As she neared the ridge, she slowed to a walk. She stopped at the edge of the ridge and rendered herself invisible.

She smiled as first one dread blossom zipped away over the edge, then another. When the last of them vanished, she crept forward and peered down.

The dread blossoms circled just above the pool, dusting its surface with their pollen. The two priestesses stood below, already rendered motionless by the dread blossoms. One of them was pointing up, head thrown back and mouth open. The other was frozen in her on-guard position; she'd neither seen nor heard the dread blossoms coming. The Nightshadow, however, was nowhere to be seen. Halisstra repeated the *bae'qeshel* melody that had revealed him the first time, but saw no trace of him.

The dread blossoms plunged down in attack. One of them sank its tendril directly into the throat of the priestess whose head was upturned, and another slammed into the thigh of the second priestess. Halisstra watched the remaining three dread blossoms carefully. None of them veered from their course. All three sank into one or another of the priestesses and began feeding.

Halisstra sprang from the ridge, drifted down on a strand of spider silk, and landed beside the pool. She expected the Nightshadow to return at any moment, but no attack came. As she watched, first one of the priestesses toppled, then the other. The first landed with a splash in the pool. Blood trickled from the point in her throat where the dread blossom had attached itself, and a murky red stain rippled across the pool. Reflected pinpricks of light—the Tears of Selûne—danced in its wake.

Still no attack from the Nightshadow.

Satisfied he had fled, Halisstra bit her tongue and spat a gob of blood and spittle into the pond. She stirred it with her finger and sang softly. Webs trailed through the water from her fingers as she worked her magic.

"Cavatina," she breathed. "Show me Cavatina."

The water remained unchanged. The only thing Halisstra's fingers stirred up was mud.

Halisstra swore and yanked her fingers from the water. She had gambled that Cavatina would have journeyed on from the Promenade through its portal, which in turn was linked to this one. Halisstra's scrying should have shown the next link: Cavatina's destination. Yet nothing had been revealed.

Halisstra stared at the spreading ripples. Perhaps Cavatina had warded herself against magical intrusions. Or perhaps she held too much of Eilistraee's grace. Halisstra's hand ached after its immersion in the water, the callus on her palm was throbbing like—

Something slammed into the back of her neck, rocking her forward. Snarling, Halisstra clawed at her hair, yanking a shattered wristbow bolt from it. A second bolt plunged into her back, just below her left shoulder.

She whirled. The Nightshadow stood just a few paces away, next to one of the fallen priestesses. The dead female's hunting horn was in his hand. His eyes bulged as he saw Halisstra turn, the shattered wristbow bolt in her hand.

"Masked Lady, aid me!" he cried. "Slay the fiend!"

He thrust his free hand forward. A bolt of intertwined shadow and moonlight shot from his palm and struck Halisstra in the face. A blaze of white light filled one eye, a pall of darkness the other. Pain flared in her temples. Then Lolth's restorative magic asserted itself, and Halisstra could see again.

The Nightshadow was gone. A blare of noise came from close by in the woods: the hunting horn. A moment later, answering blares came from the direction of Eilistraee's shrine.

Halisstra snarled. She yearned to race through the woods after that Nightshadow and rip out his heart and squeeze it to bloody mush before it even stopped beating, but that would do little good. The damage was already done. A host of priestesses would be there in mere moments, intent on their hunt.

She smashed a fist into a nearby tree, splintering its bark. The tree groaned and fell across the pool, sending up a spray of water. Halisstra ground her teeth in frustration. She'd hoped the pool would lead her to Cavatina. A stupid idea. Now all she could do was flee or fight.

Pain pulsed through her palm—the demon's claw, shifting like a maggot under her skin. A word hissed into her ear like a trickle of hot sand. *Wait.*

Halisstra blinked in surprise. "Wendonai?"

A crack sounded nearby—a sharp sound, like rock splitting in a fire. A hot wind stirred the branches next to Halisstra. Grit tickled her skin and blew into her eyes.

"Wendonai," she said. With certainty, this time.

She tensed as something stepped out of the forest. It looked like a mummified drow, with skin that glinted in the moonlight as though it had been dusted with rock salt. Its eyes were an outgrowth of salt-crystal, their orbs replaced with jagged prisms. The thing clawed its way toward the pool, tearing at the vegetation that impeded it. Leaves withered and died on the branches it touched.

With jerking steps, the salt mummy moved past Halisstra and stumbled into the pool. When it was barely as deep as its ankles, its feet and lower limbs started to dissolve. Moaning, it collapsed to its knees and thrashed about in the water. Holes opened in its skin where the water splashed it, and pieces of its salt-impregnated flesh fell away.

The blare of horns drew nearer as the hunters closed in. The pool shrank as the salt mummy thrashed about in it. A crust of salt ringed the pool and the smell of brine filled the air. The plants that rimmed the pool withered.

Halisstra touched a hand to what remained of the water. This time, the callus in her palm didn't burn. Instead it drew in the water, lapping it up with the eagerness of a thirst-crazed dog.

Laughing, Halisstra stepped into the pool. The salt mummy was gone save for a rapidly dissolving lump that had been its head. Its jaw was still working; the callus in Halisstra's palm pulsed in time with its words. *Follow . . .*

She waded to the center of the pool. Near her feet, she spotted a faint sparkle of pale blue light that looked like faerie fire. She touched it with a foot and felt an emptiness, a hollow, waiting to swallow her. As the first of the priestesses of Eilistraee burst out of the woods, singing a spell that sent her sword dancing through the air, Halisstra sneered. A flick of her hand cast a web that tangled the sword in mid-flight.

Then she plunged headfirst into the reeking water, and into the portal that opened beneath her.

Q'arlynd stood in the tunnel as the rest of the group departed. No one had spared him so much as a backward glance—not even Eldrinn, though Q'arlynd could tell by the set of the boy's shoulders that he didn't like leaving his mentor behind.

When the last footfall faded, Q'arlynd waited for a thousand-count, then tried to follow. He managed no more than half a dozen steps before his body refused to move farther. Straining against the compulsion only made his stomach cramp. He doubled over and vomited on the floor. He pulled a handkerchief from his pocket and wiped his mouth clean.

He attempted to dispel the magic that compelled him to remain there, but without success. That was as he'd expected, but at least he'd tried.

"Abyss take those priestesses and their geas spells," he muttered.

He fumed at being forced to stay behind. He was the only one with a vested interest in keeping Eldrinn alive. If the boy was killed . . .

No. That didn't bear thinking about.

Q'arlynd wondered what his other apprentices were doing—how much progress, if any, they'd made in unlocking the door's secrets. He eyed the glowing wall beside him. Scrying was supposedly impossible in this place, but he wouldn't know that for certain until he tried. If the destination being scried was far enough from the source of the problem, the scrying just might work.

As a precaution—just in case any more of those enormous, undead heads came slithering along—he rendered himself invisible. He briefly considered which of his students to scry, then decided upon Baltak. The transmogrifist had been the most keen on the puzzle of Kraanfhaor's Door; likely he was still there, studying it. Or, knowing Baltak, trying to bash it down with brute magical force.

Q'arlynd concentrated on Baltak and activated his ring. The result was like staring full on into the sun. A flash of violet light filled his vision, sending him reeling. Blinking, blinded, he groped at the wall beside him for support. Slowly—too slowly—the tunnel around him came back into view again. The pale blue light that suffused its walls pulsed in time with the ache that filled his head.

"Mother's blood," he swore, rubbing his temples. "That *hurt.*"

He stared ruefully at the faintly glowing rock beside him. At least he'd learned one thing. It didn't matter where the subject was. If the caster was in the Deep Wastes, scrying was impossible. Even with a magical ring.

As long as the caster was drow, of course. Daffir hadn't had any problems with *his* divinations.

As Q'arlynd blinked away the residual spots from his eyes, he heard a faint sound, down by the Moondeep. He immediately flattened against the wall and checked to make sure his invisibility held. It did.

The noise came again: a faint scrabbling. Something climbed up the rockfall, toward the tunnel. Q'arlynd reached inside a pocket of his *piwafwi* for a tiny glass orb, then stopped himself. Blinding himself by casting a distant-seeing spell was the last thing he needed just then. Instead he readied a scrap of fur pierced by a shard of glass—components for a spell that would hurl lightning—then he steeled himself to confront whatever hideous undead monstrosity appeared next.

He nearly laughed when he saw the creature that had unnerved him so: a small black rat, its fur glistening wetly. It scurried into the tunnel where Q'arlynd hid, then jerked to a halt, whiskers twitching.

"What's there? What is it? Where is it?" the rat squeaked.

Q'arlynd's eyebrows rose in surprise. The rat was speaking High Drowic. Moving quietly, Q'arlynd pulled his quartz out of a pocket and peered through it, but the crystal clouded with violet faerie fire. Hoping that the creature in front of him was just as it seemed—a wet black rat—he lowered his crystal.

Just as Q'arlynd was debating whether to speak to it, the rat spoke again. "Kâras? Is it you?"

The rat moved closer to Q'arlynd, sniffed the ground beside his still-invisible feet, and gave a startled squeak. "Not him!" it said. "Not him! Not him!" It ran away down the tunnel, in the direction Eldrinn and the others had gone.

Interesting.

After the rat was gone, Q'arlynd listened for a time. The Moondeep lay in silence, its waters still against its shores. The only sounds were the occasional drip of water from the handful of stalactites that clung to the cavern's wide ceiling and a faint, crackling hiss, nearly imperceptible, from the *Faerzress* that infused the rock next to him.

He moved to the mouth of the tunnel and stared across the vast cavern that held the Moondeep Sea. The moon had set some time ago, its reflection vanishing from the dark surface of the water. Only a handful of the Tears of Selûne remained. One by one, those too vanished.

Q'arlynd was well and truly alone.

He stroked his chin. Cavatina had told him to wait there until moonrise. It had been couched as a suggestion, but her hand had brushed against her holy symbol as she spoke; that must have been when the geas was cast. If he *was* stuck there until the next moonrise, he might as well use the time wisely. A second experiment was in order. Qilué had, very pointedly, mentioned his skill at teleportation. Perhaps she hoped that he'd still be able to manage it, even there. That was certainly worth finding out.

He drew a deep breath—preparing himself, as he would for a freefall from one of Ched Nasad's ruined streets. He chose a spot just a few paces away, in the center of the tunnel. Concentrating on it, he spoke the words of his spell.

He slammed into a wall face-first. Pain flared in his nose—it felt like he'd broken it a second time—and warm blood slid from his nostrils. Bruised, embarrassed, he pushed himself roughly away from the wall. The *Faerzress* was, he noted, glowing more brightly than it had a moment before. A faint violet smudge had appeared on the pale blue, in the spot where his body had struck the wall. It looked, he thought wryly, like the dent his body would have made had it struck a soft patch of ground from a great height. He could even see the imprint of one outflung hand.

He watched as the violet glow slowly faded. A moment later, the *Faerzress* was back to its usual, pale-blue color.

Q'arlynd wiped his nose gingerly. That was enough experimentation for one night, he decided. He'd been lucky. His nose had indeed been re-broken, but at least the rest of his body was in one piece. He could have wound up a frayed, bloody mess after the teleportation mishap.

He sighed. It would be a long, tiresome wait for moonrise,

but with the first glint of moonlight on the underground sea, he'd be out of there.

He unfastened his belt and settled into a crosslegged position on the floor. He laid the belt across his knees and passed a hand over it, dispelling the magic that concealed the writing on the broad band of leather. His spells were written in a script so tiny it was almost impossible to read—he normally relied upon the crystal to magnify them—but the words were still crisp. The dunking in water hadn't blurred them.

Q'arlynd read, refreshing his spells. The night dragged on to its end. In the World Above, the sun rose, made its slow passage through the heavens, then set. The first of the evening stars sparkled against a purpling sky.

In the Underdark, in the tunnel where Q'arlynd waited, all was silent and dark—save for the *Faerzress* that shimmered across the rock next to him. Fortunately, no more undead came creeping or slithering along. The wait, though long, had been uneventful. Q'arlynd straightened as a thin wedge of light glinted on the water: one horn of the crescent moon, rising in the surface realms above.

"Come on," he said impatiently. "Come on." He paced back and forth to warm himself. The long wait had left a chill in his bones. "A little further. Just a little more . . ."

As Selûne shimmered fully into view on the Moondeep's surface, Q'arlynd heard a splash. A head broke the surface of the water some distance from shore—a head with sky-black skin and white hair. Probably the priestess who had returned to the temple with the body.

She twisted about, looking disoriented.

Q'arlynd stepped to the edge of the tumbled rock and waved. "Chizra!" he shouted. "I'm over . . ."

The words died in his throat as the swimmer turned toward him. That wasn't the priestess, or even a drow. It was too big, with strangely articulated arms and things protruding from its chest that churned the water like writhing snakes.

Q'arlynd stepped back into the corridor, rendering himself invisible the moment he was out of the creature's sight. Then he changed direction and ran forward. As the monster swam toward the tunnel with powerful strokes, he sprang from the lip of the rockfall into the air and activated his House insignia. His gamble paid off; the creature didn't look up. It didn't notice him levitating above.

Q'arlynd shielded himself and pulled out the components for a lightning bolt but held back on casting it. The thing in the water looked demonic, and he didn't want to draw its attention if he didn't have to.

Below him, the creature reached the shore and clambered up the rockfall toward the tunnel. Water streamed from its massive body as it paused at the tunnel mouth to look around and sniff the air. Now that the creature was out of the water, Q'arlynd could see it was female. She was twice the height of a drow, with matted white hair that hung in a tangle to her shoulders and back. The things protruding from her chest weren't snakes but spider legs.

Q'arlynd decided the creature must be a half-demon of some sort—perhaps some new form of draegloth. He was even more convinced when he got a good look at her face. It was the face of a drow female, yet twisted, like a clay sculpture that had been stretched and flattened while the clay was still wet. A hairy bulge protruded from each cheek, just under the eye. Fangs sprouted from these, scissoring together in front of an oversize mouth.

Q'arlynd frowned. The face looked familiar, somehow. As if he'd seen the creature somewhere before. He didn't mess around with demons—that was Piri's thing, not his—and yet . . .

The creature started to look up. Hurriedly, Q'arlynd cast a cantrip that caused a rock some distance down the tunnel to shift. At the faint noise, the she-demon whipped around, turning her attention to the tunnel. A malicious laugh gurgled from her throat. She stepped into the tunnel, turned back to face the cavern again, and flung out both hands. Webs burst from her fingertips. Weaving her hands back and forth, she sealed the tunnel's entrance. Then she loped away into the abandoned mine.

Q'arlynd let out a long, slow breath. When he was certain the demon-thing was out of earshot, he drifted down to the rockfall. He studied the web a moment: it was haphazard and asymmetrical, something Lolth herself might have created. He pulled a pinch of brimstone-impregnated tallow from a pocket and tossed it at the ground. A quick evocation caused the marble-sized ball of tallow to expand into a fist-sized ball of flame as it rolled toward the base of the web. The magical fire consumed a corner of the web, leaving a space big enough for a drow to pass through.

Q'arlynd was just about to crawl through this when he heard a splash. Not out on the lake, this time, but at the base of the rockfall. He whirled and saw two figures emerging from the water. He sighed in relief as he recognized them as priestesses of Eilistraee.

One was Chizra, the priestess who had taken the dead Protector back to the Promenade. The other was even more familiar to Q'arlynd. It had been nearly two years since he'd seen her last, but he remembered every detail of her lean, muscular body and ice-white hair.

"Leliana," Q'arlynd said as she approached. Belatedly, he remembered to bow. "I hadn't expected to see you—"

"Chizra, watch the lake," Leliana ordered.

Only after the other priestess had turned in that direction, sword in hand, did Leliana acknowledge Q'arlynd. Rather than greet him, she asked a brisk question. "Any sign of the svirfneblin?"

"None at all."

Leliana strode past him to inspect the web. Over her shoulder, she asked, "What kind of spider spun this?"

So it was going to be like that, was it? Q'arlynd opened his mouth to protest to Leliana that he'd done everything he could to protect her daughter's soul. Then he remembered Leliana's skill with truth-compelling prayers. He answered her question, instead.

"It wasn't a spider that spun it, but something demonic. It looked a little like a female draegloth. She came out of the Moondeep and disappeared down the tunnel."

Leliana turned. "Describe her."

Q'arlynd did. When he was done, Leliana looked as though she wanted to spit. She glanced back at the other priestess, who was still keeping an eye on the Moondeep. "That explains the delay in opening the portal. And the water's brackish taste."

Chizra called up from below. "I *thought* it tasted tainted."

Q'arlynd glanced at the web. "Was it one of Lolth's minions who . . ."

He didn't bother finishing his question; Leliana wasn't listening. She stared into the distance and spoke Qilué's name. A moment later, she cocked her head, as if listening, then repeated, swiftly and in an urgent tone, what Q'arlynd had just told her, describing the demon-thing.

That done, Leliana listened again. She blinked rapidly, as if surprised by what she heard.

"What is it?" Q'arlynd asked. "Bad news?"

Leliana gave him the strangest look, an odd mix of reluctance and pity. There was something she wanted to tell him—something important. Had the demon-thing somehow marked or tainted him? He resisted the urge to inspect his body, to see if there were visible signs of corruption. "What? Tell me."

Leliana pressed her lips together. "I can't," she said at last. "Qilué's orders. She said it's better if you don't know."

Q'arlynd's eyes narrowed. "It's my body, my soul. If either has been corrupted, then I have a right to—"

"It's nothing like that," Leliana said. "It's something that happened long ago, to someone else. But that's enough said.

Let's just leave it at that."

Q'arlynd stared at her. Leliana was trying to tell him something, in an oblique way. He wondered what it might be.

Whatever it was, no hints were forthcoming. Leliana, obviously the senior priestess there, turned to Chizra. "Wait here. Conceal yourself well, and warn me if anything else comes through the portal. The wizard and I will try to catch up with the others."

Q'arlynd took a deep breath. "The wizard" was he? Well so be it. "As you command, Lady," he said, giving Leliana an exaggerated bow. Then he followed her into the tunnel.

"What's wrong, Qilué?"

Laeral touched her sister's arm. A moment ago, they had been conversing together on the balcony of the tower. Then Qilué had abruptly broken off in mid-sentence with a far-away look in her eye—a look Laeral knew well. Her sister had been called by someone. An urgent summons, judging by the crease of Qilué's brow.

Qilué didn't answer. Her lips pursed together as she composed a mental reply. She spoke a name aloud: "Cavatina." More silent communication followed.

The summons must have been urgent, indeed.

Laeral waited patiently for her sister to finish. As she waited, she stared at the buildings below. The City of Hope had been raised nearly three years ago by the same high magic that had scoured away ancient Miyeritar. The walled city was laid out like a wheel within a circular wall. Nine roads led from its central plaza to sentinel towers that stood watch over the High Moor. The tower on whose balcony they stood—an exact replica of Blackstaff Tower in Waterdeep—was one of several wizard's towers that had been raised on the night the city was forged. It was one of the most distinctive. Utterly black, forbiddingly stark, it had neither window nor door. Those who knew the passwords could slip through its walls like ghosts; all others were barred by its powerful wards.

Qilué had come to speak to Laeral about something that was troubling her: some fell magic that was originating from the area of Kiaransalee's chief temple. Laeral was no expert in the Dark Seldarine. She was only part-elf, "sister" to Qilué through the grace of Mystra alone, whereas Qilué was wholly drow. They were as different, each from the other, as day and night, Laeral with fair skin and emerald-green eyes, clad in an elegant gown, Qilué head and shoulders taller, with ankle-length white hair and skin the color of midnight, protected by a warrior-priestess's armor. Yet both were Chosen of Mystra, bound from their birth to serve the goddess of magic.

At last, Qilué turned. "One of our priestesses, missing these past two years, has been found."

Laeral smiled brightly. "Certainly that's good news?"

"I'm not sure," Qilué answered slowly. "I thought that coin had landed, but it seems it has been tossed in the air a second time and is spinning still. Whether it will be aid or betrayal this time is unclear."

Laeral frowned. Qilué could be annoyingly cryptic at times. "I'm not sure I follow you, sister."

"The priestess I spoke of was reclaimed by Lolth. Made unclean. The Spider Queen's webs cling to Halisstra still, causing her to stumble. There were deaths in the Shilmista—deaths that may have been by her hand."

"By 'her,' do you mean Lolth . . . or this priestess?"

Qilué sighed. "Both. Or perhaps neither—it is too soon to tell. Eilistraee permitted Halisstra to use one of the Moonspring's portals, after all. In any case, Cavatina has been warned."

"I see," Laeral said, even though she didn't. She steered the conversation back to its original course. "You said you wanted my help with that problem of yours—something to do with the *Faerzress?*"

Qilué nodded. "*Faerzress* are being augmented throughout the Underdark. Each day, the effect spreads farther and grows stronger. Just this morning, we saw the first glimmerings of it in the Promenade. Eilistraee willing, my priestesses will confirm the cause of it soon—and by sword and song, eliminate it. But should they fail, there will be dire consequences for the drow."

"How so?"

"The drow—alone of all of Toril's many races—will be prevented from casting divinations. Nor will they be able to utilize any spell or prayer to magically convey themselves from place to place. For now, this is impossible only in the Dark Wastes, and simply more difficult the farther afield one ventures from the effect's point of origin. But if the augmentation of *Faerzress* continues, such magic will be impossible for drow throughout the Underdark."

"Surely that bodes well for your crusade. Won't it be one more reason for your people to come up to the surface?"

"It would—except for one thing," Qilué said, a grim look in her eye. "Hand in hand with the augmentation of the *Faerzress* comes a second, unforeseen effect. We've noticed it at our settlements on the surface. In recent days, the drow who came up into the light have begun retreating from the World Above, finding excuses to make their way back to the Underdark. I've felt it myself—a subtle, lingering longing that makes me loath to leave the Promenade. These past few days I visited our shrines that lie closer to the source of the effect. The call I felt there to go below was strong. Curious to know more, I allowed it to guide my footsteps and followed it down into the Underdark. I found myself drawn to a cavern filled with *Faerzress*. Once there, I pressed myself against its walls, heedless of danger. I was a moth, drawn to a *Faerzress* flame."

Qilué shivered, despite the sunlight that warmed the tower's dark stone. "If this isn't stopped, we'll all be drawn below. Everything I've worked a lifetime for will be undone."

"Oh, sister," Laeral sighed. "That's terrible. But you said you've sent scouts to snoop around Kiaransalee's temple—the best warriors the Promenade has. Surely they'll put an end to this before it's . . ." She stopped, not wanting to say the words.

Qilué finished the sentence for her. "Too late?" Her jaw clenched. "Sister, that is my most fervent prayer."

"Tell me how I can help," Laeral said. "What would you have me do? Just name it, and it shall be done."

"I wish I knew," Qilué said. She stared out across the city—not at the city itself, but at the horizon. The High Moor was still flat and featureless, but some color had returned. Here and there were splotches of green and fall-red: young trees that had grown these past three years. That's what she loved about the surface. Its beauty was ever-changing, not frozen like the cold stone of the Underdark.

"I asked Eilistraee the same question myself," Qilué continued. "What would she have me do? The goddess's answer, however, puzzled me. 'It will end where it began,' Eilistraee replied. 'The High Moor.'" She turned to Laeral. "What that prophecy means, I cannot say. I thought you might have some idea, sister."

Laeral stood for several moments, lost in thought. Endings. Beginnings. "The City of Hope is an obvious 'beginning,'" she said. "As for an 'ending,' Faertlemiir, Miyeritar's City of High Magic, once stood here millennia ago, until it was laid waste by the killing storm. But that's surely something you've already thought of."

Qilué nodded.

"I'm sorry, sister. I have no answer for you. But I will think long and hard on it. I'll contact you at once if anything occurs to me."

"Thank you."

"In the meantime," Laeral said, "I'm curious. Is that the

Crescent Blade at your hip? Did it really slay a demigod, as the ballads say?"

Instead of smiling, as Laeral had hoped, Qilué's expression grew closed and hard. Her right hand strayed to the hilt. She turned slightly away from Laeral, as if protective of the weapon. As if she half-expected Laeral to take the sword from her.

Then, like clouds rolling away from the sun, Qilué's expression cleared. "It is, indeed." She drew the sword and laid the flat of the blade across her palm, offering it up for Laeral to see.

Laeral noted the break in the blade. "It's been broken. And . . . mended."

"Yes, praise Eilistraee." Qilué's eyes glittered. "In Lolth's domain, no less. One day, it will slay the Spider Queen."

Laeral nodded. As Qilué slid the sword back into its scabbard, she noticed something. "Your wrist: there's a cut there."

Once again, the guarded look returned to Qilué's eye. "A scratch, sister. Nothing more."

"Why didn't it heal?"

Irritation flared in Qilué's eyes. "It's just a scratch."

Had it been anyone else, Laeral wouldn't have worried. But this was Qilué. Such a tiny wound should have healed in less than the blink of an eye.

But it might not be the best time to pursue the question, she thought.

Qilué was proud—perhaps the proudest of the Seven Sisters—and had chosen a difficult path. And it looked as though the work of bringing the drow 'up into the light' was going to increase in difficulty by a thousandfold, perhaps even become impossible. She had every right to be on edge, to grow irritated when "trivial" matters like the scratch on her wrist were pointed out to her.

Except that a wound that Mystra's silver fire couldn't heal was anything but trivial.

"I'll keep an eye on the High Moor for you, sister," Laeral promised. "Let you know if anything unusual happens here. Any more 'endings' or 'beginnings.' I'll consult my scrying fonts. If I learn anything, I'll let you know immediately." She slipped a hand into the crook of Qilué's arm. "In the meantime, can I offer you food? Or wine?"

"No, thank you, sister. I must return to the Promenade as soon as possible."

Laeral gave her sister's arm a comforting squeeze. "The *Faerzress?*"

Qilué nodded. "The *Faerzress.*" She plucked Laeral's hand from her arm. "Farewell." Then she teleported away.

Laeral stared for several moments at the spot Qilué had just occupied. Like all drow, Qilué was reluctant to show her emotions. Laeral could tell, however, that her sister was deeply troubled—and not just by the undoing of a lifetime's work. There was more going on; Laeral was certain of it.

But until Qilué confided in her, Laerel could do little to help.

CHAPTER 9

Mazeer lifted the bottle to her lips, inhaled, and swam forward a few more strokes. Her exhaled bubbles flattened against the roof just above her head. A Nightshadow swam immediately ahead of her, his feet fluttering the water. Ahead of him, the passage they were following narrowed to a crack that looked barely wide enough for a drow to squeeze into. The cleric paused there, sculling in place, and stared into the fissure, his face illuminated by the blue-green *Faerzress* that permeated the nearby stone. Mazeer took another suck on the bottle that trailed by a cord from her wrist, and swam up next to him.

Another dead end? she signed.

The Nightshadow shook his head and his mask fluttered back and forth like wave-lapped seaweed. *It leads down.* His chest rose and fell as he breathed water.

Mazeer sucked another breath from her bottle. Bubbles continued to stream out of it as she lowered it, tickling her arm. *This is pointless. We should go back. This place is a labyrinth.*

It looks as though the crack widens, about a hundred paces below. What if it's the passage that leads to the Acropolis?

Mazeer peered down the narrow crack. She'd been uneasy about closed-in places ever since the time, as a novice wizard, she'd miscast a teleportation spell and wound up wedged inside one of the college's chimneys. Unable to climb out, unable to refresh her teleportation spell because her spellbook was inside her pack, mashed tight against her back, she'd remained stuck inside the chimney until she was faint with hunger and thirst and her clothes were soiled. Eventually, someone conjuring darkfire in the fireplace below had at last heard her hoarse screams for help.

She'd made a point, after that, of learning a spell that would reduce the size of her body. It helped, a little, to know she could use it to free herself if she did get stuck. Yet as she stared down into that long, narrow fissure the old fear made her shudder. She didn't want the Nightshadow above her, blocking the way out.

You go first, she signed. *I'll follow.*

The cleric nodded and edged sideways into the gap. He nodded at the wands sheathed at her wrists. *Just don't be too long in following. If this leads to a monster's lair, I don't want to be fighting alone.*

Mazeer laughed out the breath she'd just drawn from the bottle. 'Monsters' didn't scare her. Back at the college, she'd slain everything the teachers had summoned and thrown at her. Hordes of undead, however, were another matter entirely. Given a choice, she hoped the fissure *would* deadend in a monster's lair, and that one of the other search teams would have the dubious honor of finding the route to the Acropolis. Daffir had predicted that one of the pairs of searchers would find it, though he'd been woefully short on details. Nor had Khorl been much help in predicting what they might face along the way, despite his haughty pride. So much for the "best" the College of Divination could provide. Eilistraee's priestess had been right, Kiaransalee's followers weren't so crazy that they couldn't cast wards.

The cleric pushed away from the ceiling, forcing his body down the fissure. Mazeer waited until he was about a dozen paces below. She pinched the tiny pouch that hung at her throat, whispered a word that shrank her to half her normal size, and followed. To keep the panic at bay, she kept her head tilted back, her eyes on the opening above. Bubbles streamed up toward it each time she exhaled. Up toward freedom. Each push of her hands sent her farther away from it. Even though she had lots of elbow room and plenty of space between her diminished body and the walls of rock on either side, her heart was pounding by the time her foot touched the bottom of the shaft. Loose rock shifted underfoot with a dull clunk.

She tore her eyes away from the exit above and stared ahead. The Nightshadow hovered a few paces away, sculling water. He glared back at her. *Quiet!*

He'd been right, the passage did widen. The cavern at the bottom of the fissure was at least a dozen paces across. About fifty paces beyond the Nightshadow, the ceiling curved up and out of a flat spot on the water: the exit to an air-filled chamber. A rhythmic noise came from that direction, muffled by the intervening water. It sounded like sticks clattering on stone.

The Nightshadow's eyes glittered. *Hear that?* He drew a "breath" of water, held it a moment then exhaled. *I think we've found it. The water here smells of death. Let's take a look.*

Mazeer nodded. The sooner they confirmed it as the passage leading to the Acropolis, the better. Then they could return to the rest of the group.

Mazeer hadn't been keen on setting out to search the maze of water-filled passages with only a Nightshadow as backup. She would have felt better with other conjurers flanking her and the priestesses in the lead, their magical swords between Mazeer and whatever dangers lay ahead. Yet she'd done as Gilkriz ordered.

The Nightshadow touched the phylactery on his arm and motioned for her to follow. Dagger in hand, he swam up toward the surface. Mazeer restored herself to her usual size, and pushed off from her crouched position. Halfway through the cavern, she noticed a spot where the *Faerzress* was dimmer, as though screened by a gauzy curtain. A kick of her legs sent her in that direction. As she swam closer to it, breathing from her bottle, she saw that the "curtain" was a loose tangle of thick strands of colorless thread, nearly invisible in the water, that made up a loosely woven bag with several large tears in it. She touched it, and the strands felt slightly sticky. Below it, she noticed what looked like a knobby white wand wedged in a crack in the floor. She swam down for a look. It turned out to be a femur, small enough to have come from a child.

Or from a svirfneblin.

Spit me like a lizard, she thought. *The svirfneblin who found this passage didn't drown, he got eaten by a water spider.*

She twisted around to warn the Nightshadow. Ripples marked the spot where he'd just climbed out of the water. A heartbeat later, he plunged into the water in a dive. He was only waist-deep when his body abruptly halted and his eyes flared open in alarm. Then something yanked him out of the water, and he vanished from sight.

Mazeer took a breath from her bottle and shouted a spell. Her words exploded in a flurry of bubbles. She swept her free hand in a circle, fist clenched, then opened it. The water shimmered as magical energy infused it. At her command, the water elemental she'd summoned bulged toward the surface just as an enormous spider plunged into the water, dragging the web-bound Nightshadow behind it. The elemental crashed into the monster, snapping two of the spider's legs. Then the battle raged.

The water in the cavern churned into a whirlpool that slammed Mazeer into a wall. Over the tumult of rushing water, she heard a faint crack. Pain lanced through her hand as shards of glass drove into her palm. Her bottle—broken! She fought her way to the surface. She barely had time to draw breath before she was sucked under again by the maelstrom. It slammed her into another wall and one of her ribs cracked. Dizzy with pain, she tried to push off the wall, but couldn't. The force of the water held her fast.

"Help . . . me . . . surface . . ." The words cost her the last of the air in her lungs, but they were enough. A surge of water—one of the elemental's wide "arms"—hurled her toward the surface. She burst into the air like a leaping fish and slammed down onto stone.

She rose, shaking, in a room-sized cavern. A hole in one wall led to a larger cavern beyond. At the far side of the pool—the spot where the Nightshadow had climbed out of the water—strands of web draped the rock. Great gouts of water erupted from the pool, spraying the walls and ceiling. The Nightshadow's web-wrapped body momentarily bobbed to the surface next to a broken spider leg, then got sucked under again.

Mazeer drew a wand woven from green willow twigs and held it ready, in case the spider won the fight. When pieces of spider floated to the surface in a dark slick of blood, she knew that battle was at an end. She snapped her fingers and pointed at a dark shape in the water: the body of the Nightshadow. The elemental bulged, lifting it to the surface. Mazeer bent down and grasped him by his shirt. She hauled him out of the water, grunting at the pain that lanced through her side. Then she passed a hand over the surface of the pool, releasing the elemental.

She rolled the web-shrouded Nightshadow onto his side to drain the water from his lungs. His head flopped and came to rest at an unnatural angle. A crunching noise came from inside his neck: broken bones grinding together.

Mazeer sighed. She had no magic that could revive him. She was on her own. And she wouldn't be able to get back, she thought as she looked ruefully down at the broken chunk of bottle that dangled from the thong around her wrist.

She held her side and breathed shallowly against the pain of her broken rib. The water had stilled, and she could hear the staccato of clicking bone coming from the larger cavern beyond. It sounded like an entire army of skeletons on the march. She peered through the hole and saw distant white dots on the ceiling: the skulls the Darksong Knight had described.

She crept closer to the opening for a better look. The cavern beyond was filled with a vast lake, its depths illuminated from below by the *Faerzress*. At its center stood an island, capped with a forest of stalagmites that made up the buildings of the ruined city. The stalagmites crackled with blue-green light, as if it were a living city decorated with faerie fire, but that was only the glow of the *Faerzress*.

At the center of the island was a massive spire of flat-topped stone. It, too, pulsed with *Faerzress* energy, but the building that stood atop it was black as a starless sky. Mazeer could guess what it was: the Acropolis of Thanatos, temple of Kiaransalee, Queen of the Undead. Above the temple drifted the pale shapes of restless ghosts. Their wails echoed faintly across the lake. Even at a distance, the sound made Mazeer shiver.

Her teleportation spells were useless, thanks to the *Faerzress*. She couldn't escape. And it was unlikely that Daffir or Khorl would be able to use their divinations to find her. The protections that had prevented them from scrying the main cavern likely extended as far as the smaller cavern.

One avenue of communication remained open, however: Eilistraee's high priestess. Mazeer might be stuck, just like that time in the chimney, but this time when she called for help someone would hear her.

"Qilué," she whispered. Despite the cacophony of clattering bone from the cavern beyond, she was wary of raising her voice. "It is Mazeer, of the College of Conjuration and Summoning. One of those traveling in Cavatina's band. Qilué, can you hear me? I've something urgent to report."

The reply came a moment later: a female voice that seemed to sing, rather than speak. *I'm listening.*

"Tell Cavatina I've found the way to Kiaransalee's temple. It's a narrow fissure that leads down to . . ."

The words faded on her lips as a skull leered in through the hole in the wall. Mazeer could see right through it, and the *Faerzress* gave it an eerie, blue-green glow. The body was a trailing wisp of bone-white, with hands whose fingers tapered to dagger-sharp points. Its jaw creaked open. A ghastly din erupted from the blackness within—the sound of hundreds of phlegm-choked voices, groaning in agony.

Waves of despair poured from the apparition and enveloped Mazeer like a cold, moldy blanket. Trembling, with a stomach that felt hollow and sick, she remembered the wand in her hand. Somehow, she forced her arm to rise. She pointed the wand and sobbed out a word. A sickly green ray shot from it, striking the skull.

The apparition never even slowed. It loomed into the cave and clutched at Mazeer with skeletal hands that raked her body, passing through her chest. For a moment, she couldn't breathe. Her legs buckled, sending her to her knees. Then the hands retracted, yanking something from her. Mazeer felt a hollow open as all vestiges of hope and joy were torn from her.

Only bitterness remained.

It was enough. She clutched the emotion like an icy seed, using it to draw herself back to the here and now. Dropping the willow wand, she clawed a second wand from her bracer. This one had a pea-sized sphere of hollow glass at its tip. The creature screamed at her, a soul-numbing wail that slammed against Mazeer's eardrums. She felt her right eardrum rupture. Intense pain flared through that side of her head. Even as the skull's wail drove her past the edge of madness, she shouted the wand's command word. Ripples of energy shot from it. They slammed into the skull and expanded outward from it, encasing it in a bubble of silence.

The apparition raged impotently, mouth open. It clawed at the bubble that surrounded its head, but without effect. The silence ate at it like acid. A portion of the skull dimpled, then crumbled away, leaving a black hole. Hollow eyesockets glared at Mazeer. Then, still raging in utter silence, the creature turned and fled.

Mazeer? Can you hear me? Are you still there?

Mazeer whirled. Her heart pounded even faster than the staccato clacking in the cavern beyond. Thousands of skulls! What was that voice? It was inside her head. A skull! Thousands of them, pressing in on her from every side. She slapped her palms against her ears, and one hand became sticky with blood. The skulls were consuming her from within!

"Get out!" she shrieked. "Get out of my head!"

Mazeer, it's Qilué. You called me.

"The skull is stuck!" Mazeer wailed, beating her forehead with her fists. "Stuck inside the chimney. Light a fire. Get it out!"

It's Qilué, Mazeer, High Priestess of Eilistraee. Listen to me. Let me help you.

"No!" The skulls surrounded her like invisible walls. Mazeer could feel them digging into her back, her arms, her chest. Bones and teeth. Laughing at her. "Stupid girl, getting stuck in a chimney."

Her eyes widened. Had she just said that? Or had it been the voice inside her head? What was that clacking noise?

Like spears, rattling. Spears stabbing her chest, the palm of her hand, the right side of her head. Throbbing. Pain. Her chest was tight. She couldn't breathe. She clawed out a wand, hurled it at the blue-green glow. The fire. It was all around her. Fire and smoke. Making her cough. Too tight, stuck in a chimney . . .

"Get out. Out of here. Must get . . ."

She fell backward. Splashing water choked off her scream. She was cold and wet. Sinking. The water hugged her close, extinguishing the fire. Something brushed against her: a sticky net. She remembered it had caught another drow. He was the one trapped. She laughed, and watched languidly as bubbles danced above her face. There was something she should be doing. Oh yes, the bottle. She raised it to her lips and inhaled deeply. Water slid into her lungs, smooth as a wand into a sheath. She didn't notice the coughing, or the hot flare of pain in her chest.

The skull was gone. At last.

She was free.

Cavatina waited impatiently as Khorl cast his spell. A mirror of polished silver hung on one wall, enlarged by magic from a brooch the wizard had unpinned from his *piwafwi*. Khorl peered into it intently, oblivious to the harsh glare of the reflected *Faerzress*. The blue glow was painfully bright. Cavatina squinted, yet it still hurt her eyes. Backlit by its glare, Khorl's head and shoulders were a dark silhouette.

"Can you see anything?" she asked. "Mazeer told Qilué she'd found the way to the Acropolis. She mentioned a fissure in the rock."

"And a skull," Eldrinn added. "You said she mentioned a skull." He stood next to Daffir, fiddling nervously with a vial he held. If the boy wasn't careful, he was going to drop his potion.

Kâras pushed past him. "What about Telmyz? Is there any sign of him?"

"Patience, all of you," Khorl said. His fingers flicked in front of the mirror as if turning pages. "A scrying cannot be rushed."

Gilkriz stood to one side, arms folded and fingers drumming restlessly. One of his wizards had gone missing. Perhaps he'd already accepted the worst. According to Qilué, Mazeer had been incoherent when her message abruptly cut off. That—and the silence that followed—didn't bode well.

All the other search teams had returned safely, if unsuccessfully. Despite more than a day's worth of searching, none had found the way to the Acropolis.

Khorl's hand dropped. "The mirror reveals nothing." A wave of his hand shrank the polished oval of silver back down to brooch size.

"Conjure up the eyes again," Cavatina ordered. "We need to find Mazeer and Telmyz."

Khorl shook his head firmly. "A second application of that spell will only produce the same result."

Cavatina turned to the human wizard. "Daffir?"

He inclined his head. "I will try, Madam."

As Daffir cast his spell, Cavatina brooded. The message about Mazeer and Telmyz hadn't been the only sending from Qilué. There had been two other sendings from the high priestess a short time after that. The first had contained surprising news: Halisstra lived! She'd somehow escaped the Demonweb Pits, and had been spotted in the Shilmista Forest. Priestesses and Nightshadows had died there, at the hands of Lolth's minions. Halisstra, however had managed to escape through the shrine's portal.

She'd portaled to the Moondeep, where Q'arlynd had spotted her. Not surprisingly, he hadn't recognized his own sister. Halisstra wandered the mine tunnels, somewhere between the Moondeep and the spot where the party rested.

Cavatina would have ordered a search for Halisstra, but Qilué had forbidden it. Eilistraee herself had warned the high priestess that Halisstra had some part to play in the attack on the temple—a role that might be disrupted if too many knew she was there. Cavatina had to trust in the goddess, to let Halisstra find her own path in the dance.

It rankled Cavatina, but an order was an order. A Darksong Knight always did her duty.

One thing was certain. The longer Cavatina and the others lingered there, the better the chance Halisstra would blunder into them. Knowing that, Cavatina had ordered the two priestesses guarding the shaft that was this tunnel's only access point to contact her with a sending *at once* if they spotted anything resembling a demon, and not to engage it in combat themselves—to let her, the party's only Darksong Knight, deal with any demons.

Cavatina turned to the human mage. "Daffir. Anything yet?"

Daffir leaned on his staff, eyes closed. "Mazeer and Telmyz are in a cavern."

"The Acropolis?"

"No," Daffir opened his eyes. "That much, at least, I am certain of. Had they reached it, the name Thanatos would have rung through my mind like a tolling bell."

"Are they still underwater?" Kâras asked.

Daffir shook his head. "That, I cannot tell."

Cavatina struggled to keep her frustration in check. "Keep trying," she told the wizards. She turned to walk back to the spot at the bottom of the shaft, where the others had set up a fortified position, but Kâras caught her arm. "Telmyz is dead," he told her. "This was the wrong way to go."

Cavatina rounded on him. "We don't know that."

"Yes we do. The prayer that allowed him to breathe water would have elapsed long ago. If he's still submerged, he's dead."

"Then we'll recover his body. Return him to the Promenade, where he can be resurrected."

Kâras made a dismissive gesture. "That's not worth the cost."

Cavatina was inclined to agree, for different reasons. Yet her duty was clear. "Our numbers are small. We can't afford the loss of even one of Eilistraee's faithful."

"Precisely," Kâras said. "Which is why we should abandon this route and go another way. You heard the reports of the search teams. There's a veritable labyrinth of passages down there. Trying to figure out which one leads to the Acropolis—if any even do—might take days. We should take a route that we *know* leads to the Acropolis. One that won't cost us any more lives."

"This is our way in," Cavatina said. "The Crones will be watching the other entrances."

"You said Mazeer mentioned a skull. Even if she did find the 'back door' the deep gnomes told you about, it may not be such a secret any more."

"He's right," Gilkriz said, stepping closer. "And the longer we sit here, the more likely we'll be discovered. What if your svirfneblin 'allies' were lying entirely, and this is nothing but a dead-end? I don't want to be trapped down here."

Cavatina stared down at him. "You'd abandon Mazeer?"

Gilkriz unfolded his arms and tugged at his gold sleeves, straightening them. Despite immersion in the Moondeep, his clothes were impeccable. "If she's dead, yes." He nodded at the *Faerzress*. "Solving our problem as quickly as possible is what's most important."

Cavatina glared at him. But she had to admit that Gilkriz was right. So was Kâras.

"I've made up my mind," she told them. "We'll go in another way. One of those other entrances Kâras is so fond of."

His mask hid the smirk she knew was there.

"But we stay together."

The smirk disappeared from his eyes.

"Gilkriz, Eldrinn, assemble your wizards. Get them ready to move. Kâras, do the same for your Nightshadows."

"As you command, Lady," Kâras replied.

Cavatina gave him a tight smile. She knew that Kâras's obedience was the calm before the storm. When he found out *how* she planned on entering that "side door," he wasn't going to like it. She'd had it with this skulking about. It was time for something bolder.

She was just about to pass the word to the two priestesses who guarded the top of the shaft when one of them contacted her with a sending. *Lady Cavatina, the demon you antici-pated! Zindira just spotted it!*

Fall back to the bottom of the shaft, Cavatina ordered, praying they would obey quickly. If they made the mistake of attacking Halisstra, they likely wouldn't survive. *I'm on my way.*

She turned and spoke swiftly. "Kâras, keep the others together. Don't let them follow me up the shaft."

His eyes narrowed in suspicion. "Lady?"

"Our guards have spotted something—possibly a demon." She slapped the flask at her hip. "I'm going to deal with it. You're in charge until I get back."

She sprinted away down the tunnel.

Leliana set a brisk pace through the abandoned mine. Q'arlynd hurried along beside her, glad to be moving again. The sooner he had Eldrinn back in his sight again, the better. The boy might be talented, but he was little more than a novice. There were all sorts of things down there that could kill him. Gigantic undead heads, demonic drow-things . . . why, even something so mundane as a cave-in, Q'arlynd thought as he ducked under a fungus-dotted shoring timber that stank of rot. If Q'arlynd were ever going to unlock Kraanfhaor's Door and plunder the riches that lay behind it, he'd need the secrets locked away in Eldrinn's mind.

In the meantime, he thought, glancing at the bluish glow that infused the tunnel, there was a job to be done: discovering what had augmented the *Faerzress*, and negating it before the College of Divination collapsed.

They walked in silence for some time. Then Leliana spoke. "Aren't you going to ask how Rowaan is, Q'arlynd?"

Q'arlynd took a deep breath. *Here it comes*, he thought. "I intended to, Lady, once there was time."

She halted abruptly. "No time like the present."

Q'arlynd slowly turned. "Lady, they enslaved me with magic that proved even stronger than Qilué's geas. I was forced to speak the words that—"

"What are you talking about?"

"The . . . the gate," Q'arlynd faltered. "Didn't Qilué tell you . . . ?" Belatedly, he realized he'd just said too much.

"She did. She said you were the one who opened the gate that allowed Eilistraee to enter Vhaeraun's domain."

Q'arlynd raised his hands. "Not by choice, I assure you." Then he realized what she'd just said. "*Vhaeraun's domain?*"

"Of course. That was a clever ruse you pulled."

She didn't look angry, so Q'arlynd did his best to recover. "Qilué . . . told you about . . . that?"

Leliana smiled. "She also swore me to secrecy. But now that we're alone . . ." She glanced back the way they'd just come. "I can thank you. For saving Rowaan."

To Q'arlynd's utter surprise, she stepped forward and clasped his arms. She was strong; her hands pinched as they squeezed. Then she stepped abruptly back, as if embarrassed by the show of emotion. That figured; she'd been raised in the Underdark, after all.

"I'm surprised Qilué confided in you," Q'arlynd said, relaxing at last. "But I welcome the opportunity to boast. That switch I pulled was rather clever, wasn't it?"

Leliana's eyes glittered. "How did you ever trick them into reversing the spell? They were *Nightshadows*—didn't they see it coming?"

"Apparently not," said Q'arlynd. Nor had he seen this coming.

"I still can't quite believe they're part of our faith now, that they chose redemption," Leliana continued. "I thought them too steeped in lies and deceit to stick with it. But some did, amazingly enough." She paused. "I'm glad to see you still serve Eilistraee, as well."

"Of course." Q'arlynd waved a hand. "That's why I'm here." It was a conversation he didn't want to get any deeper into than he had to. "But you haven't answered my question. How *is* Rowaan?"

Leliana smiled. "She's well. After I was promoted to the ranks of the Protectors, she took charge of the Misty Forest shrine." Her voice deepened with pride. "There were other, more senior priestesses who could have been named its head priestess, but Qilué chose Rowaan."

Of course she did, Q'arlynd thought. The appointment would have ensured that Rowaan kept her mouth shut about what had really happened, that night in the dark-stone cavern.

He realized why Cavatina had failed to point him out during the briefing at the Promenade. She didn't want to run the risk of him contradicting the official version of what had happened. She wanted her priestesses to believe that Eilistraee was stronger than Vhaeraun—that she had defeated the Masked Lord on his home turf.

Q'arlynd wondered how closely held the true story was. Qilué knew it, of course, and Cavatina—as well as the priest-esses whose souls, together with Rowaan's, had been drawn to Eilistraee when the gate opened. Q'arlynd supposed those priestesses had been bought off, too. And that Valdar, the only Nightshadow to have survived the casting of the gate, had been tracked down and killed to ensure his silence.

The ranks of Eilistraee's faithful had come to include more than one assassin, after all.

"We should get moving, if we want to catch up to the others," he reminded Leliana.

"Yes." She touched a hand to the *Faerzress*. "Too bad we can't teleport. You'd have us there like that." She started to snap her fingers, then touched the *Faerzress* again, as if caressing it.

The gesture disturbed Q'arlynd. He'd felt a similar urge himself. The soft hum of the bluish glow called to him. The *Faerzress* was beautiful, just like faerie fire, but what he felt went deeper than that. It drew him like . . .

He realized he was touching the wall. He jerked his fingers back.

Leliana's eyes met his. She looked as uneasy as he felt. "You're right," she said. "We should get moving."

Out of the corner of his eye, Q'arlynd saw a slight motion farther down the tunnel. A patch of wall dimmed and brightened again, as if the *Faerzress* had momentarily been blocked. Something was slowly creeping away from the spot where Q'arlynd and Leliana stood—something with an outline so blurred it was almost impossible to make out. It was the size and shape of a child.

We're being watched, Q'arlynd warned. He raised his chin slightly, indicating the tunnel behind Leliana. *By a svirfneblin.*

Our guide?

I'm not sure.

Leliana turned and spoke aloud. "There's no need to fear us. We're the ones you came to meet. If we'd meant you harm, we'd already have—"

She suddenly reeled back and groped for the wall. "Mother's blood," she cursed, her voice overly loud. "What did you do *that* for?"

Q'arlynd understood at once what had happened. He too knew magic that could render someone blind and deaf. He shouted a word and flicked his fingers, triggering a ripple of energy that radiated from him, dispelling the effect. His spell revealed two svirfneblin standing only a pace or two away. One cradled a strongbox; the second held a hooked hammer in one hand, an egg-sized, blood-red gemstone in the other. The instant this fellow was revealed, he hurled the stone. It thudded into Q'arlynd's chest. Q'arlynd jumped back and tried to raise a hand, but couldn't. His arms felt weak, soft. He watched, horrified, as the skin shriveled on his hands and his fingers curled like dead leaves. He tried to cast a spell, but his fingers wouldn't move. His arms hung limp and lifeless at his sides.

He felt his eyes widen. Death magic! How in all that was unholy had the svirfneblin gotten hold of that?

He could think of only one answer.

Leliana, able to see again thanks to Q'arlynd's dispelling, touched the holy symbol that hung against her chest and sang out a word. The svirfneblin who'd thrown the gemstone froze in place, held fast by her prayer. She whirled and began singing a second prayer—still not drawing her sword.

"Leliana!" Q'arlynd shouted. "These aren't the—"

Though he spoke the word "guides," he never heard it. Suddenly blinded and deafened, he stumbled about, desperately trying to cast a spell—one that didn't require gestures, a touch, or the tossing of spell components. That left precious little.

He felt someone jostle him—Leliana, at last come to her senses and skewering the deep gnomes with her sword? He hoped so. If it weren't for the damned *Faerzress*, he might have conjured an arcane eye to see what was going on. Instead he did the only thing he could that would put him in the clear. He shouted the word that activated his House insignia, still not hearing his own voice, and felt himself rise.

A hand yanked him down again. The instant it touched him, he shouted out a spell. Whichever of the deep gnomes had just grabbed him would be blind and deaf, too. That should even the odds a little.

Suddenly he could see and hear again. Leliana lay on the floor, unconscious or dead from a wound that had bloodied her scalp. Her sword lay nearby. The deep gnome she'd immobilized a moment ago stood over her, his hammer dark with blood. A second deep gnome stood just behind him, glaring at Q'arlynd.

Q'arlynd tried to draw his ice wand from the sheath on his belt—if his useless hands could just lift it, he might be able to blast the svirfneblin—but his limbs wouldn't cooperate. Out of the corner of his eye, he saw a blur to his right and behind him: the third svirfneblin moving in. Q'arlynd at last fumbled the wand out of its sheath and turned. He struggled to point it at the blurred gnome.

The two svirfneblin behind Q'arlynd moved right and left, flanking him. Backing him against a wall. Q'arlynd shifted his arms, trying to menace them with his wand. It fell from his withered hands and clattered to the floor. The svirfneblin who'd felled Leliana raised his hooked hammer, but the blurred gnome raised a hand.

"Hold," he told them.

Q'arlynd stared at the blurred gnome but could make out no details. He was like every other svirfneblin Q'arlynd had ever seen: mottled gray skin, bald head, just over half Q'arlynd's height, and wearing clothes the color of stone. Why had he just called off the attack?

"Flinderspeld? Is that you?"

The svirfneblin dropped his blur, revealing himself. It *wasn't* Flinderspeld. He had a wider forehead, one ear that cocked at an odd angle, and his hands were more heavily mottled than those of Q'arlynd's former slave. The deep gnome glanced at his two companions and said something in the svirfneblin tongue. They nodded and visibly relaxed.

"I not Flinderspeld," he told Q'arlynd, speaking in the

pidgin language the races of the Underdark shared. "But I know him."

"Who are you?"

"Name's Durth."

"How do you know Flinderspeld?"

"Do business with him."

"Gems?" Q'arlynd guessed. Flinderspeld must have re-entered the gem business after settling in Silverymoon. Q'arlynd wondered if the gem that had withered his arms had been destined for him. He shook his head, not quite believing the odds against this most unlikely of meetings. It made him wonder if Eilistraee really did watch over him. Or maybe she was just watching over her priestesses, he thought, glancing down at Leliana. Either way, Q'arlynd was thankful for Eilistraee's mercies. He shrugged his arms and nodded down at them for Durth's benefit. "Can you heal these?"

"No." Durth shrugged. "Maybe priestess can, if she wakes up. But she be mad at you for blinding her, I think."

The other svirfneblin laughed.

Q'arlynd silently cursed as he realized it had been Leliana who had yanked him down after he levitated. He added a silent prayer that Leliana *would* wake up—and not just because he needed healing. To his surprise, he found he actually cared whether she lived or died.

Durth turned to his companions and motioned for them to get the strongbox, which lay on the floor not far from Leliana. The lid hung from a single hinge and was split nearly in two—probably the result of one of Leliana's sword blows. Inside the box, Q'arlynd could see a fist-sized lump of utter blackness that made his eyes ache whenever he looked directly at it. The thing hovered at the exact center of the strongbox, not touching any of its interior surfaces.

Q'arlynd had seen something similar years before the fall of Ched Nasad. It had been housed in the Arcane Conservatory in a room with walls several paces thick. Great care had been taken so that, like the object in the strongbox, it touched neither walls, nor ceiling, nor floor: a levitation spell, made permanent and backed up by contingencies.

One of the svirfneblin picked up the strongbox and tried to force the lid shut. Q'arlynd took an involuntary step back.

"What?" Durth asked.

"That's voidstone," Q'arlynd croaked.

Even without eyebrows, Durth could still frown. "So?"

Q'arlynd was horrified. The deep gnomes obviously had no idea what they were carrying. "It's a solidified chunk of the negative energy plane," he told them, trying to quiet the inner voice that demanded he run screaming from the deep gnome who so casually held the box. "Anything that touches voidstone is instantly destroyed. If that 'rock' falls out of the box, it won't be pretty."

The deep gnome holding the strong box looked uncomfortable. He stopped fiddling with the lid.

Durth glared at his companion. "We not afraid to die," he told Q'arlynd. "Callarduran Smoothhands will—"

"No he won't," Q'arlynd interrupted. "Voidstone destroys both matter *and* spirit. If that chunk spills from the box, there won't be any souls left for your god to claim."

The deep gnome holding the box turned a lighter shade of gray.

Durth glared at him. "We are paid for the risk."

"By Flinderspeld?" Q'arlynd asked. His former slave should have had more sense than to handle the stuff. "I hope, for your sake, it's some serious coin he's promised you."

Durth's smirk confirmed it.

Q'arlynd nodded at the box. "Is Flinderspeld buying or selling the stuff?"

Durth's eyes narrowed. "What business is that of yours?"

"None," Q'arlynd said. "I just . . . hope he knows what he's dealing with, that's all."

Durth scratched behind his cocked ear. He glanced down at Leliana. "She mean anything to you?"

Q'arlynd kept his voice completely neutral. "She *is* the only one who can heal my arms."

Durth said something in his own language to the deep gnome who was holding the hooked hammer. The other gnome grunted. Leliana had just been granted a reprieve.

Durth glanced furtively around and crooked a finger at Q'arlynd, inviting him to bend down to ear level. Q'arlynd did, and the deep gnome whispered in his ear. "When you get close to Acropolis, hang back a little." He raised a hairless eyebrow. "Got it?"

Q'arlynd did. "The Crones," he whispered back. "You warned them Eilistraee's priestesses were coming."

Durth nodded. "Drow against drow. Seemed fitting then, but I regret it now. The priestesses don't know we play both sides, right?"

The other two gnomes shifted restlessly, as if bored with the conversation and ready to move on. The one who wasn't holding the box twirled his hammer back and forth on the cord that bound it to his wrist.

Q'arlynd suddenly realized what was going on. That last question had been the key—the reason he was still alive. He played dumb by answering it. "That's right."

"Too bad. But a friend of Flinderspeld . . ." Durth shrugged.

Had Q'arlynd been a surface elf, he might have been caught off guard. But Q'arlynd was a drow, born and raised in Ched Nasad. Treachery had been in the very air he breathed. The hammer twirling had been intended as a distraction; Q'arlynd had seen the svirfneblin's other hand slide stealthily into a pocket. When the deep gnome flicked a gemstone at him, Q'arlynd was ready. His cantrip required only the most basic of gestures; the caster had only to point. Q'arlynd flopped one withered arm in Durth's direction, guiding the gemstone to the deep gnome's chest. Durth's eyes widened as it struck him. Then he collapsed.

Q'arlynd lashed out with a foot. It sank into the throat of the deep gnome who'd just tossed the gemstone. The svirfneblin gasped and staggered backward. Q'arlynd twirled, causing his useless arms to windmill. He shouted out a spell as his left hand slapped the head of the deep gnome holding the box. Suddenly both blind and deaf, the deep gnome jerked in surprise. He backed away and halted. He carefully lowered the strongbox to the floor.

Q'arlynd, meanwhile, snapped a second kick at the other gnome—one that slammed the little male's skull into the wall, cracking his head against stone. The deep gnome slumped to the floor, unconscious. Meanwhile, the blinded svirfneblin blurred himself. He backed up the tunnel, trying to escape, but Q'arlynd's foot swept out, tripping him. A kick rendered him unconscious, as well.

Q'arlynd stood, panting. Durth lay on the floor a short distance away, snoring. The second gemstone, Q'arlynd realized, had contained nothing more lethal than a sleep spell. Harmless enough, but Q'arlynd was certain they'd intended to slit his throat the moment he was down.

He didn't have much time; magical sleep didn't last very long. He fell to his knees beside Leliana to listen to her breathing. It was regular enough, but she showed no signs of regaining consciousness.

"Leliana," he said, nudging her with his shoulder. "Can you hear me? Leliana, wake up!"

She didn't stir.

Q'arlynd stood. The strongbox had been knocked over in the scuffle. Fortunately, the voidstone hadn't spilled out; magic held it in place. Gingerly, he touched his foot to the box and rocked it upright. Then he noticed something. The spot where the box had just lain glowed slightly brighter than the rest of the floor. Curious, he used his foot to ease the box to a different spot and tilted it until the open top was close to the floor. Once again, the *Faerzress* brightened to an eye-hurting hue.

He rocked the box upright again. With a thought, he summoned up faerie fire, clothing his body in a sparkling violet radiance. He lowered one of his withered hands to the box—taking great care not to actually touch its contents—and saw the violet glow intensify.

He straightened and nodded to himself. Qilué had been right about who was behind the augmentation of the *Faerzress*, as well as the involuntary manifestations of faerie fire by Sshamath's mages. Whatever the Crones were doing with the voidstone that the deep gnomes were supplying was causing both effects.

He stared down at the strongbox. The chunk of voidstone it held would be the expedition's way in. They could disguise themselves as deep gnomes, carry the voidstone to the Acropolis, and learn what the Crones were up to. Put a stop to it. End the crisis and ensure that the College of Divination would not fall.

Q'arlynd smiled. "Thanks, Eilistraee," he said, only half-jokingly. He nudged Leliana again with his foot, glancing warily at the prone bodies of the deep gnomes. "Now if I could just ask one more favor of you . . ."

Leliana, however, remained unconscious.

Durth snorted in his sleep and rolled over.

Q'arlynd grimaced. Then he remembered what Cavatina had told him, during the briefing. Perhaps Qilué would know what to do.

He whispered her name. A heartbeat later, her voice filled his mind. *Q'arlynd? What is it?*

"The svirfneblin," he said aloud. "They betrayed us. They're trading with the Crones. Supplying them with voidstone." Swiftly, he summed up what he'd just learned, capping it with the fact that he and Leliana were alone—and in trouble.

I will tell the others.

"They're too far away to get here in time! And these svirfneblin may wake up at any moment. Leliana's unconscious, and my arms are withered. I can't very well drag her away. We need your help. Is there anything you can do?"

No. But there's something you can do. Pray.

With that, the communication ended.

Q'arlynd raged at the high priestess's sudden dismissal, even though it was to be expected. He was expendable. Despite his vital discovery of the voidstone.

He stared down at Leliana, then at the slumbering and unconscious svirfneblin. The answer was simple, of course. He could just walk away and leave her there. It was the logical thing to do. The only *sane* thing to do.

Instead he fell to his knees. Pray, Qilué had said. He snorted. As if Eilistraee had time to listen to him. But he was willing to give it a try. If it didn't work, he'd go. At least then, if the deep gnomes killed Leliana, it would be Eilistraee's fault.

He flopped one arm toward the unconscious priestess, moving it until his hand touched her holy symbol. Resting his useless fingers on it, he mumbled a prayer. "Eilistraee, it's uh, Q'arlynd. I pledged myself to you a couple of years ago. I need your help. Leliana needs your help. Heal her."

Durth stirred again. Still asleep, but starting to wake up.

Leliana remained unconscious. Q'arlynd's prayer hadn't worked.

He stood. That was it. He was out of there.

Leliana's eyes fluttered. "Q'arlynd?" She winced, as if speaking had hurt. One of her hands lifted slightly from the floor, grasping weakly.

Q'arlynd fell to his knees beside her and gripped her sleeve with his teeth. He lifted her arm, positioning her hand over her chest, above her holy symbol. He released his grip, and her hand fell on the miniature sword.

"Leliana, you need to heal yourself. If you don't, we're in big trouble."

Leliana nodded weakly. Her lips began to move. Her prayer came in whispered snatches, but a melody was there. Slowly, her voice strengthened. The song's final note burst from her lips with a joyous peal, and her head wound vanished. She sat up, looked around at the svirfneblin, and immediately grasped her sword. She climbed to her feet, murder in her eye.

"Wait!" Q'arlynd said. "We need them. They're our way into the Acropolis. Heal me, and I'll deal with them."

Leliana gave him a suspicious look but eventually nodded. Touching her holy symbol a second time, she sang out a prayer. Q'arlynd sighed in relief as a tingling rushed through his arms. A moment more, and they were functional again. He flexed his fingers and grinned.

"Remember that trick I pulled on the lamia, back when we first met?" he asked.

Leliana nodded.

Q'arlynd grabbed one of the deep gnomes and dragged him over to where Durth lay. "Haul that other one over here. Once I've trapped them, you can use that truth-compelling prayer of yours. These three were on their way to the Acropolis to deliver the contents of that strongbox to the Crones. They're about to tell us everything we need to know in order to do the same."

Leliana raised her eyebrows. "You missed your calling," she said as she grabbed the other unconscious deep gnome and dragged him across the floor. "You should have been a Nightshadow."

"Perhaps I should have," Q'arlynd whispered to himself. Then he cast his spell.

CHAPTER 10

Cavatina levitated up the mineshaft, fully on alert. The description the Protectors had given of the "demon" matched Halisstra, but Cavatina was still cautious. As she rose, she pulled the stopper from her iron flask. If this turned out to be a demon after all, she'd trap it.

She landed softly at the lip of the shaft and looked around. The cavern was wide and filled with ancient debris. Tunnels led off from it in three directions. The glow of the *Faerzress* contrasted with the dark shadows of fallen timbers, winches, tangles of wire, and other abandoned equipment. Halisstra might have been hiding anywhere.

So might any number of undead.

"Halisstra?" Cavatina called softly. The

sword in her hand hummed softly, a precaution against enchantments.

She heard a scuffling in the tunnel to her left. "Halisstra?" she called again, slightly louder. She walked in the direction of the noise.

Something scurried up a support beam beside her. Cavatina turned. A rat stared down at her from a sagging roof timber, eyes gleaming. It regarded her a moment, then scuttled away.

Cavatina stood in silence, wondering if Zindira might have been seeing things—shadows turned into demons by an overactive imagination. Zindira was a Protector, and well trained, yet the encounter with the undead head might have left her jumpy.

Something touched Cavatina's shoulder. She whirled and brought her sword into play. At the last moment, she halted her thrust.

Halisstra stared down at the sword point that touched her midriff, just below the lowest of the eight spider legs protruding from her chest. Her bestial face twisted in a pout. "Is this how you greet a friend?"

Cavatina took a step back, sword still at the ready. If the creature *was* a demon, somehow impersonating Halisstra, it was doing a fine job of it. "Is that really you, Halisstra?"

"You want proof?" The fangs protruding from her cheeks twitched. She pointed at Cavatina's breastplate. "Those dents: they're from Selvetarm's teeth. You were in his jaws—*helpless*—when I passed you the Crescent Blade." She cocked her head. "That's something I'll bet the ballads don't tell."

Cavatina nodded. Indeed it wasn't. She lowered her sword. "Halisstra."

Halisstra bent in a self-deprecating bow. "In the flesh."

"What happened to you after Selvetarm died? I went back to the Demonweb Pits to search for you but couldn't find you. Where have you been?"

Halisstra's shoulders slumped. She was still twice

Cavatina's height. "Lolth captured me. She imprisoned me in her fortress."

"You escaped?"

Halisstra shook her head. Her matted hair was stuck to her shoulders and didn't move. "Lolth bored of me. She threw me out. She said I'd served my purpose."

"Which was . . . ?" Cavatina prompted.

Halisstra's eyes gleamed maliciously. "To help you slay Selvetarm."

Cavatina's lips parted in surprise. "Lolth *wanted* him dead?"

"Of course," Halisstra hung her head. *"He'd* outlived his usefulness, too."

Cavatina tightened her grip on her sword. It was unlike Lolth to simply cast a tool aside. The Spider Queen delighted in destruction and would shred a soul after only the slightest of provocations. Halisstra was probably wrong in saying that Lolth had no further use for her. Was she back under the Spider Queen's thrall? Had she ever *not* been?

"Did Lolth order you to help me kill Selvetarm?"

"No. I did that of my own accord. Because . . ." Halisstra's head lifted. "Because you offered me redemption." She raised a hand and held it out imploringly. "I'm ready to accept it. To atone for all I've done."

Cavatina stared at the proffered hand. The claws that tipped Halisstra's fingers were filthy, jagged as broken glass. The hand itself was misshapen, bestial, its palm scarred.

The gesture seemed sincere, but Cavatina was no fool. Decades of hunting demons had taught her caution. Had the *Faerzress* not prevented her from singing a divination, she might have found out if Halisstra was telling the truth—to find out if it *was* Halisstra, and not just some demon who had been told, by Lolth, the details of her champion's death. As it was, Cavatina would have to resort to other methods.

"Quarthz'ress," she whispered.

Silver light flashed out of the flask, striking Halisstra in the chest. Instead of recoiling, she glanced down dispassionately as the rays ricocheted off her glossy black skin. Slowly, the glow of the flask faded until only the bluish flicker of *Faerzress* remained.

"You think I'm a demon," Halisstra said. She gave an odd, strangled laugh and spread her arms wide. "Go on. Kill me, then."

"If you really are Halisstra, I can't."

"Exactly." Halisstra's hand whipped out and caught the sword, midway down the blade. She yanked—hard—driving it into her own chest.

Cavatina, horrified, yanked it out again. The sword keened as she danced away from the wounded Halisstra. She watched, horrified, as Halisstra doubled over, grunting against the pain. Halisstra braced one hand against the floor and shuddered, breathing in short, shallow gasps. Her other hand clutched her wound. Slowly her flesh closed. At last she rose.

"You see?" she said. "It's me. Lolth still won't let me die." Anguished eyes bored into Cavatina's. "Please. Help me." The hand lifted imploringly again. "Rip Lolth's webs from my soul. Redeem me."

"Halisstra," Cavatina said. "It really *is* you."

She lowered her sword and reached out with her free hand.

Halisstra took it.

A low chuckle escaped from Halisstra's throat like a burble of blood. Then she threw back her head and howled, "Wendonai!"

Suddenly, Cavatina and Halisstra were somewhere . . . else.

Halisstra released Cavatina's hand and leaped backward, laughing. Cavatina whirled. All around her was a flat, featureless plain whose sun-bleached ground glittered as if it had been seeded with salt. A hot wind howled past her, and grit stung her skin. A few paces away stood a pile of flaming skulls. A figure reclined lazily on them, basking in their heat: a demon with horns, folded bat wings and brick-red skin. A balor. He smiled at her, lazily scratching his groin.

Cavatina ripped the iron flask from her belt and held it in front of her. *"Quarthz'ress!"*

The demon disappeared even before silver streaked from the flask. A heartbeat later, the metal grew too hot to hold. It seared Cavatina's palm, forcing her to drop the red-hot flask. She backed slowly away, searching for the vanished demon. The runes of silver embossed on the sides of the flask turned molten, blackened, rearranged themselves in a new pattern, then the flask exploded.

Cavatina ducked as a near-molten shard of it whizzed past her face.

The balor, fully twice her height, appeared next to Cavatina and leered down at her. "Such trinkets will not hold me," he whispered in a breath that stank of sulfur.

Cavatina danced back, menacing the demon with her weapon. The sword's song was high and shrill, a reflection of the tension she felt. Had Demonbane not been destroyed, Cavatina might have been holding a sword that would make even the balor flinch. Instead she had to rely on bravado alone. "You don't scare me, demon."

As she spoke, she touched the silver dagger that hung against her chest and sang a question. Knowledge hummed into her mind. Poison would not harm a balor, nor would fire or cold, lightning or acid. Nor would any of the tricks she might have used against a lesser demon.

Wendonai had no known vulnerabilities.

She let the spell dissipate.

The balor reached over his back to draw his own weapon. The flame-shaped blade of the long sword glowed white. Even from several paces away, Cavatina could feel its heat. A second weapon—a flaming whip—was coiled around the demon's waist like a belt. The hair under him was scorched black.

Cavatina risked a glance to the side. Halisstra crouched just behind the balor, her posture completely submissive. She stared up at the demon, a sly smile on her face. He reached down with his free hand and stroked her head. Idly, as one would stroke a cat. Halisstra both flinched and leaned into the caress at the same time.

Cavatina's lips curled in disgust. "Halisstra. You betrayed me."

Halisstra's glance slid to Cavatina. "Of course." Her lips twisted in a rueful smile. "I am the Lady Penitent. Lolth's battle-captive. What else did you expect?"

"Something more," Cavatina said. "As did Eilistraee. She reached out to you, through me. You spurned her."

"You lie!" Halisstra shouted. She reared to her feet. Standing, she was nearly as tall as the balor. "Eilistraee abandoned me."

"Silence, both of you!" the demon roared.

Halisstra fell back into her crouch. "Yes, Master." One of her hands pawed at his knee. She pointed at Cavatina. "There. You have what you wanted. Return me to—"

"You *dare* make demands of me?" The balor's eyes blazed.

Halisstra cringed. "No, Master, I—"

The balor flicked a finger. With a hollow crunch, Halisstra's chest caved in. The skin of chest and back met, and like a doll from which the stuffing had been yanked, her body folded in two. Halisstra toppled to the ground, blood trickling from mouth and nostrils.

When the demon glanced down at his handiwork, Cavatina lunged. Her sword sang with glee as it slashed the balor's stomach, slicing deep into his flesh.

The demon staggered back, his stomach dribbling gobs of smoking black blood. His whip, sliced in two by Cavatina's sword, fell to the ground behind him, its flames flickering.

"Mortal!" he roared. "Your insolence will cost you dearly." One hand shot up, clawing at the sky.

"Eilistraee!" Cavatina cried. She grasped her holy symbol as the demon's hand swept down, a roaring gout of fire streaming in its wake. "Protect me!"

Fire blazed all around her in a storm of light, heat, and noise. Her clothing and boots burst into flame and were instantly reduced to ash. The straps that held her breastplate charred and parted, and the two halves of metal fell away. The heat was intense, and each indrawn breath filled her lungs with pain. The singing sword grew so hot she was forced to let it fall. It tumbled to the ground with a mournful wail. Blisters erupted on her skin, and the bitter tang of singed hair filled her nostrils. White flame blinded her and smoke boiled in the sky above her head. Yet she did not burn. By Eilistraee's mercy, she did not burn.

The firestorm ended as suddenly as it had begun, leaving her blinking. The singing sword lay silent at her feet, its blade dark with soot.

Cavatina yanked her holy symbol from around her neck. Its silver still gleamed, unblemished by the balor's foul magic. Wendonai might have no natural vulnerabilities, but Halisstra had inadvertently handed Cavatina a weapon she might use.

"Eilistraee!" she cried. "My enemy stands before me: the demon Wendonai. Smite him!"

A note pealed from the holy symbol, pure as thrice-blessed water. The balor, unable to fend off an attack that utilized his name, staggered backward. He threw down his sword and howled in agony, hands clasping his ears.

Cavatina bore down on him, holding the miniature sword before her. A shaft of moonlight split the flat, empty sky, its light eclipsing that of the pale yellow sun. The balor staggered back, his cloven feet punching holes in the ground that welled up with blood.

"Mortal," he panted, black smoke puffing from his nostrils. "You vex me."

He droned a word, low and terrible. It rasped against the pure note of the holy symbol, which trembled in Cavatina's hand, then was parried. The note droned into Cavatina's very core, rattling her bones. Suddenly weak, her body hot and feverish, she trembled. The holy symbol vibrated out of her hand and fell at her feet. The shaft of moonlight disappeared.

All was still for a moment. Then the howling wind returned. On it came Wendonai's triumphant cry. "You think you can best me, mortal," he chortled. "Think again!"

He barked out a word that hit Cavatina like the blast from a furnace, instantly stunning her. Dizzy, she toppled. She landed on her back next to Halisstra's body. Already, the corpse was mending itself, the concavity that was her chest slowly filling, her eyelids fluttering. Halisstra would live. Such was Lolth's infinite torment.

Wendonai loomed over Cavatina, a length of his severed whip in either hand. Bending down, he used them to bind her ankles and wrists. He licked her cheek, leaving a smear of tar on her skin. Hot, sulfuric breath panted in her face.

"Now our fun begins."

Kâras plunged his dagger into the weeping svirfneblin's chest, held it there a moment while the gnome died, then yanked it free. He turned, wiping the blood from his blade. "There," he told the others. "I've given him the 'mercy' you pleaded for. No more arguments."

The others stared at him with a range of expressions. The priestesses had shown open disgust as he'd questioned the third svirfneblin. They were angry that he'd ignored their protests that the other two had told them all they needed to know. One of the Nightshadows looked as though he shared their sentiments, but the other three males nodded in agreement with what Kâras had just done, as did the mages.

Kâras stepped over the mutilated body of the dead svirf-neblin. All three lay on the floor of the tunnel at odd angles, their feet still encased in the re-hardened stone. He nodded at Q'arlynd, and the wizard repeated his spell. The stone softened beneath them, and with a push of his foot, Kâras forced them down into the mud, one by one.

As the wizard made the floor solid again, Kâras turned to the others. "Before Cavatina ran off to chase demons, she named me leader of this expedition," he reminded them. "I'm in charge—you all just heard Qilué confirm this. The Masked Lady herself condones what I just did. There were no signs of her displeasure when I was questioning the svirfneblin. Eilistraee, at least, acknowledges what must be done if our mission is to succeed."

No one seemed ready to argue with that.

"The plan has changed," he told them. He gestured down at the strongbox. "We've learned what's augmenting the *Faerzress:* voidstone. Now we need to find out exactly how the Crones are doing this, so we can put a stop to it. That requires a lighter touch—something a little more subtle than simply charging in and fighting our way to the Acropolis."

The Nightshadows nodded. So did the mages.

"Three of us will disguise ourselves as deep gnomes and infiltrate the Acropolis. We'll learn what we can, and pass the information along to Qilué. The rest of you—"

"Who's going to pose as the three svirfneblin?" Leliana interrupted.

Kâras turned to her. With Cavatina gone, Leliana had assumed command of the other Protectors. She wasn't like the Darksong Knight; she was less prone to erupt when prodded. She had the air of someone who'd been raised in the Underdark, who knew how to keep herself alive by swim-ming with the ever-shifting tide.

"I will," Kâras answered. "I was in Maerimydra when the Crones overran it. I know how they're likely to react."

Leliana nodded. She glanced at her Protectors, obviously trying to decide which of them had the best chance of surviving.

Kâras spoke before she had a chance to announce her choice. "Gindrol and Talzir will come with me. They have the ability to alter their forms, as well." He didn't add the real reason he'd just named those two: that they were the only ones he could come close to trusting. Like him, they'd embraced Eilistraee's faith out of expediency. They kept their old skills well honed.

Leliana held his eyes a moment but made no protest. "All right," she agreed. Unlike Cavatina, she recognized the merits of using the best tools for the job. "The rest of us will circle around to the other side of the Acropolis and move in if you run into trouble."

"Not as one group," Kâras amended. "The Nightshadows' stealth will be wasted in any attack in force. They should go a different way."

"Agreed." Leliana turned to the wizards. "You six have a choice. Come with us or tag along with the Nightshadows."

Gilkriz nodded at his underling. "Jyzrill will accompany one of the Nightshadows."

The shorter male's scowl deepened, but he nodded.

"Khorl will go with the other Nightshadow," Eldrinn said quickly. "And Daffir will join the Protectors. As for Q'arlynd and I—"

"We'll join the Protectors," Q'arlynd interrupted. "My spells are better suited to battle than to stealth. As are Eldrinn's."

A flicker of irritation crossed the younger male's face.

Kâras nodded. "Let's go, then. The water clock's trickling, no time to waste."

The others shouldered their packs and secured their weapons. Leliana, however, drew Kâras aside. "What if Cavatina returns?" she asked. "Someone should wait for her, tell her what's happening."

Kâras gave her a level stare. "Didn't you hear what the moonrat said? The demon took Cavatina. Wherever she's vanished to, not even Qilué can contact her."

"She's a Darksong Knight. She can take care of herself. And that *wasn't* a demon."

"Oh? What was it, then?"

"It was—" Leliana halted abruptly. There was something she didn't want the others to know.

"Your devotion to your superiors is commendable," Kâras said. He pretended to give her request serious consideration. "Very well, then. If you think it's that important, send one of your priestesses back to the spot where Cavatina disappeared."

Leliana turned to the wizard who stood next to her—an odd choice, Kâras thought. "Q'arlynd, I think you should go."

The wizard gave a start. "Me?" He glanced at the young wizard who was nominally in charge of the diviners. "I can't. Eldrinn may need me to—"

Before he could finish, Gilkriz chuckled. "To what? Hold his hand in case he stumbles into a mine shaft and falls?"

The other conjurer added a bark of laughter.

Eldrinn stiffened. "I can take care of myself, Q'arlynd. And you'd do well to remember that Master Seldszar placed *me* in charge of our college's contingent." He folded his arms across his chest. His expression, however, wasn't angry at all. Instead the boy looked . . . desperate, Kâras thought.

Q'arlynd pretended to applaud. "Well done, Eldrinn! You'll convince them you're a mere apprentice, yet." He winked at Gilkriz while pointing at Eldrinn. "A word to the wise: don't turn your back on this one. He's already fooled you once."

This time, it was the diviners who laughed.

Kâras followed the exchange out of habit; one never knew when a tidbit of information could become useful. However amusing the interplay between the mages, it was irrelevant. What mattered was that Kâras accomplish the task the Masked Lord had set for them: putting a stop to whatever the Crones were doing. Not because the effects it had on divination—as far as the Nightshadows were concerned, anything that prevented others from spying on them was a good thing. No, it had to be stopped because the augmented *Faerzress* was luring the drow below. That was where, ultimately, they belonged—in the Underdark—but in order for the Masked Lord's plans to be fulfilled, the Nightshadows needed more time on the surface. They weren't yet strong enough to overthrow Lolth's matriarchies.

"Enough banter." He nodded down at the strongbox. "Let's get moving, before the Crones start to wonder where their voidstone is."

Cavatina expected to die. That didn't bother her. She had served Eilistraee long and well, and her soul would certainly join the goddess's dance for all eternity. But for the first time in decades as a Darksong Knight, she had failed. She, a slayer of a *demigod*, lay at the mercies of a demon. She was trussed up and helpless as a newborn babe, her holy symbol well out of arm's reach, lying in the dust where Wendonai had kicked it. That burned at her pride like a hot coal, impossible to ignore.

She stared up at the balor with a glare fierce enough that it should have withered him where he stood. "Go on," she gritted. "Get it over with. Kill me."

Wendonai chuckled. "You'd like that, wouldn't you?" he taunted, oily black smoke puffing from his mouth as he spoke. He slid his sword into the sheath on his back, extinguishing its flame. Then he squatted beside her, arms resting on his knees, wings folded. The slash in his midriff still gaped; that it had not healed told Cavatina she was within the Abyss—the only plane where a demon could be permanently destroyed. Wendonai didn't seem to be bothered by the entrails dangling from his wound, however, or the black blood that soaked the tangle of hair at his groin and dribbled onto the hard-packed earth below. He was too busy gloating.

Cavatina resolved to do one thing before the demon killed her. At the very least, she would alert the high priestess to Halisstra's treachery. She pretended to cough. It hid the name she urgently whispered: "Qilué."

"She can't hear you," the demon hissed. "Not unless I will it."

"Qilué!" Cavatina shouted. Her voice sounded strange. As if it were echoing back at her.

Qilué didn't answer.

Wendonai laughed.

Despite the residual heat of the whip that bound her, Cavatina felt a shiver slide down her spine. Qilué *should* have heard her name, even from the depths of the Abyss.

The high priestess's silence was more frightening than any demon.

Behind Wendonai, Halisstra groaned and flopped over onto her stomach. Unlike the demon, she was healing. Slowly, she drew her knees up under herself and used her arms to lever herself into a kneeling position. Turning her head slightly, she glanced sidelong at Cavatina through her tangle of hair. One hand twitched out words. *I thought you would kill him. That's why I brought you here.*

Cavatina didn't believe a word of it. Had Halisstra intended that Wendonai be slain, she would have warned Cavatina in advance—or at least hinted at it. No, Halisstra was truly in Lolth's thrall. The Lady Penitent had thrown away her final chance at redemption.

Halisstra was still signing: a single word that ended with the curved finger that turned it into a question. *Attack?* Her glance flicked to the demon.

Cavatina almost laughed. A little late for that. She was bound with magical rope whose heat was agony against her skin, a constant reminder of her humiliating plight. Even so, Cavatina nodded, disguising the gesture as a simple lifting of the head to glance down at her bound wrists. If Halisstra did attack the demon, it just might give Cavatina the moment she needed to roll across the ground to her holy symbol and grab it. Halisstra slowly rose . . .

The demon turned in her direction. "Down," he thundered.

Halisstra collapsed, whimpering.

Cavatina threw herself into a roll, but the demon grabbed her shoulder, halting her. He slammed her onto her back. The weight of his hand on her chest was like a boulder.

"For a Darksong Knight, you're not very smart," he told her.

Cavatina's eyes widened. She hadn't told him she was a Darksong Knight.

The balor smiled. "Oh yes, I can hear your thoughts. Both yours—and Halisstra's."

Was that so? Cavatina envisioned carving the demon into pieces. Slowly.

The balor laughed. "Halisstra bores me. You, on the other hand, I find amusing." He ran a lazy claw down Cavatina's naked body.

Cavatina knew he expected her to shudder under his touch. She kept her eyes on his, steeling herself, not allowing her flesh to so much as twitch.

"You don't frighten me," she said.

"I can see that." The demon lowered his blunt muzzle to her chest and sniffed. When he rose again, he was smiling. "Halisstra betrayed you. She delivered you into my hands. Tell me, priestess of Eilistraee, what will you do to her if you survive this?"

"The Lady of the Dance is infinitely merciful," Cavatina answered. "If Halisstra is truly repentant—"

"But she's not," Wendonai said. "You and I both know it. Remember, I can hear your thoughts. A moment ago, you hoped to reach your holy symbol. Just before that, you fantasized about spitting Halisstra with your sword. You would strangle her with your own two hands and commit her soul to the Abyss forever—if only she could be killed."

Halisstra, still cringing behind the demon, whimpered.

Cavatina said nothing. It was true. In its essence, if not in the exact details.

"Yes," the demon hissed through a jagged row of fangs. "It is, isn't it? There's a dark side to you, Cavatina, lurking just below the surface. One you work hard to suppress. A hardness. An inflexibility, born of pride."

Cavatina said nothing. She had every reason to be proud. Except, she thought ruefully, at this moment.

The demon leaned closer. "You cleave to the rules of your faith, but it's difficult for you, at times. Your temper sometimes . . . slips out. You enjoy the hunt, the kill. A little too much."

"I do as Eilistraee bids."

"Yes, but I can sense something that underlies this. The thing that drove you into demon hunting in the first place. An anger." The demon cocked his head. "Born of jealousy, perhaps? What could you, a Darksong Knight—the oh-so-proud slayer of Selvetarm—possibly be jealous of?"

Cavatina said nothing. She focused on her hatred of demons, of this demon in particular. She pushed everything else out of her mind. Shoved it into a dark corner, where Wendonai couldn't possibly find it.

"Oh, is *that* it?" Wendonai exclaimed, the mock surprise out of place on his bestial, leering face. "All this . . . just because you weren't redeemed?"

Behind him, Halisstra sat up. She leaned forward expectantly, staring at Cavatina.

"I am a priestess of Eilistraee," Cavatina said slowly. "I took the sword oath, just like any other priestess—"

"Not just like them," Wendonai said smoothly. "They were *redeemed*. You . . . merely took the oath."

Cavatina bristled. The demon was playing with her, yanking out her deepest fears and tossing them at her feet. She didn't have to take this. "I had no other patron deity before taking up Eilistraee's sword. I was *born* into the faith. Unlike the others, I didn't need to be redeemed. I had nothing to atone for."

"Luckily for you," Wendonai purred. "For, unlike the other priestesses, you could never, ever, have been redeemed." He leaned closer, the wound in his abdomen dribbling blood. "And do you know why?"

Cavatina said nothing.

"You're different from the other priestesses—in a way that's much more fundamental than where you were born and what deities they were taught to praise before they turned to Eilistraee's faith." He sniffed. "I can smell it on you."

Behind him, Halisstra's eyes widened.

Cavatina could see that what the demon had just said meant something to Halisstra. But Cavatina couldn't allow herself to become distracted by that. Not just then.

She glared up at Wendonai. "Your tricks won't work on me, demon."

"Tricks?" He chuckled, puffing the stench of sulfur into her face. "No trick, this. You . . ." he took a long, slow sniff of her body, moving his blunted muzzle from ankles to neck, lingering here and there, ". . . bear my taint."

Cavatina laughed. "Of course I do." She lifted a shoulder and used it to rub at the smear of tar Wendonai had left on her face earlier, with his tongue. "But a little holy water will take care of that."

"Very amusing," the demon replied. "But that wasn't what I was referring to." He rocked back on his heels. A fresh gout of blood slurped from his wound, and the bulging entrails shifted. With grimy fingers, he prodded them back inside the wound. Absently, as if it were a mere inconvenience. "How familiar are you with the history of your race?"

That took Cavatina by surprise. "What are you talking about?"

"The dark elves. Do you know how it was that they became *dhaerow?*"

He'd used the old word for it. The one that meant "traitor" in the language of the surface elves.

"You mean the Descent?"

Wendonai nodded.

"High magic, worked by the mages and clerics of the elves of Keltormir, Aryvandaar, and other elven enclaves, against the dark elves of ancient Ilythiir and their allies."

"Yes, but why?"

Cavatina knew her history well. She'd taught it to novices many times when explaining why the drow were meant to return to the surface realms. "It was in retaliation for the destruction of Shantel Othreier—which the Ilythiiri attacked only because the empire had laid waste to Miyeritar. The Dark Disaster was brutal, and it had to be answered in kind."

Wendonai's eyes gleamed. "Spoken like a true drow!" he exclaimed. "But there is a portion of the story you don't know, the reason Corellon Larethian consented to driving the dark elves below. The Ilythiiri, you see, were becoming a little too powerful. They had a divine ally. Lolth."

Cavatina snorted. "The Ilythiiri's worship of the Spider Queen is well documented, demon. Tell me something I don't already know."

Wendonai gave her a sly smile. "I was hoping you'd ask me to do that. Let me tell you this, then, priestess. Did you know who Lolth sent among the Ilythiiri to corrupt them?"

Cavatina didn't, but she could guess.

"You are correct. Me. Slowly, over millennia, both before and after the Descent, I had my way with the Ilythiiri. It was . . ." he ran a black, sore-crusted tongue over his lips. ". . . delicious. And with each succeeding generation, with each new squalling *dhaerow* babe born in the thirteen millennia between then and now, my taint spread."

Cavatina could see where the demon was headed. Wendonai was trying to convince her that she bore his taint, that it was the source of all of her faults. But it wasn't. The odd angry outburst and a little—inflexibility, as he'd called it—didn't add up to demonic taint.

"Oh, doesn't it?" Wendonai said. "In your case, unfortunately for you, it does. I can smell it on you, remember?"

Halisstra had been listening intently the whole time, and as if she'd forgotten whom she was addressing, she said. "But you couldn't smell it on me."

"No," Wendonai said flatly over his shoulder. "I couldn't. You're Miyeritari. Not a drop of Ilythiiri blood in you. Do you know what that makes you?"

Hope flickered tentatively to life in Halisstra's eyes. Wendonai crushed it with a word: "Weak."

He laughed—great, gobbling fits of mirth. Halisstra visibly crumpled under the onslaught.

Cavatina, for her part, had to agree with the demon. Halisstra *was* weak. If she hadn't—

"Yes," Wendonai breathed, his attention suddenly riveted on Cavatina. "That's right. If she hadn't been so weak, it wouldn't have come to . . . this." He plucked at the bonds around her wrists, lifting her hands slightly, then letting them fall. "But you're *not* weak, Cavatina. You're strong. Demonic blood flows in your veins. Embrace it."

Cavatina shook her head, refusing to believe. The demon was lying. Twisting things around and trying to trick her.

"Eilistraee," she whispered. "Help me to see the light."

Wendonai shook his massive, horned head. "You just don't give up, do you?" He feigned a sigh. "But think about this. Why is it that only some *dhaerow* can be redeemed? You've seen as much, with your own two eyes."

He paused, and Cavatina could feel filthy mental fingers sifting through her mind. She tried to shove them out, but couldn't.

"That Nightshadow in Cormanthor, for example," Wendonai continued. "The one Halisstra cocooned in her web. You offered him a chance at redemption, and he just wouldn't take it."

No, he wouldn't, Cavatina thought. *And no matter what you say, I won't apologize for sending him to his god.*

"And there's the irony," Wendonai continued as if she'd spoken aloud. "Had you let him live, the pair of you might have been worshiping side by side today." He tapped a claw against his chin, as if thinking. "Then again, perhaps not. Perhaps that male was a descendant of the Ilythiiri, after all. That would explain his reluctance to convert. My taint has spread far and wide, after all. There were so few Miyeritari, after the Dark Disaster, and so very many Ilythiiri." He smiled. "Which explains all of the difficulties Eilistraee has faced in acquiring converts, these past few millennia. Why so few petitioners have come forward, despite the long and tireless efforts of her priestesses. It's so hard, these days, to find someone who can truly repent. To find a *dhaerow* who doesn't bear my taint."

"Lies," Cavatina gritted.

"Are they?" Wendonai breathed. "Look deep into your own soul, Cavatina. Can you honestly say you are without malice, without anger? Where does your unquenchable thirst for vengeance come from? You sublimate it by hunting demons. But if there were no demons to slay, would you turn your anger on your fellow drow? Can you truthfully say you haven't done so already? That fellow in the forest of Cormanthor, for one. The other Nightshadows—the ones who are now part of the faith. You hate them because they've *truly* embraced Eilistraee. Because they're something you can never be. Redeemed. Pure. Without taint."

Cavatina squeezed her fists so tight that fingernails dug into her palms. Her body was knotted tighter than the whip ends that bound her. *It isn't true,* she thought. *None of it.* She was a priestess of Eilistraee. A Darksong Knight. As good, as loyal, as *pure* as any one of them.

"Then why," Wendonai breathed into her ear, "has your goddess turned her face from you? Where is the miracle you were just praying for?"

Cavatina squeezed her eyes shut to hold back the tears. A miracle would come. It *had* to. Eilistraee would answer. Yet a tiny voice, deep within, whimpered that she wouldn't. That Wendonai was right. That a seed of taint lay deep in Cavatina's core, waiting to spread its tendrils through her like a weed. She'd succumbed to it, that time in the Darkwatch, when she'd hacked the dog to pieces. She'd shoved the evil back, forced it back into dormancy, but it lingered there still. Waiting to sprout up anew. And because of it, Eilistraee had abandoned her, just as she'd abandoned Halisstra. For all Cavatina's attempts to conform to the tenets of her faith, she would never be worthy of Eilistraee.

"That's right," the demon panted, his breath hot in her ear. "You can never be redeemed. *Never.*"

Tears squeezed from Cavatina's closed eyes and trickled down her salt-encrusted cheeks. "I can never be—"

Suddenly, she realized the flaw in the demon's logic. If descendants of the Miyeritari were free of demonic taint, they didn't need to be redeemed. Yet redemption existed. The ritual had to have been created for a reason, and the ritual itself gave the answer. Redemption required the penitent to look deep into herself, to confront the evil that lay within her very soul. To pry that evil—that taint—out of the darkness that enshrouded it and expose it to Eilistraee's merciful light and—

Yes, daughter. Yes!

Cavatina couldn't have said, in that moment, if it was the single voice of Eilistraee herself speaking or a chorus of voices. Thousands of souls, speaking with one heart. Priestess and lay worshiper, female and male, Dark Maiden and . . .

Nightshadow.

Cavatina blinked. If a *Nightshadow* could be among the redeemed, why couldn't she?

Yes, the voice said again.

Cavatina could hear the deeper tones that underlay the word. Bass, baritone, soprano, and alto, all blended into the single voice that was the Masked Lady.

Cavatina wept openly. Relief flooded her. She no longer feared Wendonai's taunting, or any physical cruelties he might inflict. In that moment, nothing but one simple fact mattered.

"I am redeemed!" she cried.

The demon reared back, his eyes blazing with fury. Then he threw back his head and howled.

In that instant, Halisstra lunged.

Q'arlynd, Eldrinn, Daffir, and Gilkriz followed the priestesses along the abandoned mineshaft. Leliana had ordered one priestess to wait at the spot where Cavatina had last been seen. Q'arlynd was thankful she'd stopped insisting that *he* go. That left four priestesses under her command. Each took a turn at scouting, ranging ahead of the others and returning to report their findings to Leliana with quick, concise hand signals. Leliana replied with the briefest of gestures, constantly cautioning silence. Each faint grunt, scuff of a foot, or creak of a leather pack brought a warning glare. The *Faerzress* probably wasn't helping. Its sparkling blue glow threw everyone into silhouette.

Gilkriz walked just ahead of Q'arlynd and Eldrinn; Daffir trailed behind. Every few hundred paces, the diviner paused to close his eyes. Whenever he did, he leaned on his staff, bending forward until the wood touched his forehead.

What's he doing? Q'arlynd signed.

Eldrinn glanced ahead at Gilkriz, making sure the conjurer wasn't "listening" in. *Making sure we don't encounter any surprises, I guess.*

Q'arlynd nodded. He'd made discreet enquiries about the staff after returning the feebleminded Eldrinn to Sshamath. He knew everything a staff of divination could do. If there were secret passageways, concealed by magic or mundane means, Daffir would spot them. He'd also be able to see, even with those weak human eyes of his, anything that was invisible or otherwise hidden by magic.

Q'arlynd might have been using his crystal to do the same, had he not been drow. *Have you noticed?* he signed to Eldrinn. *Daffir keeps looking up at the ceiling.*

I noticed. Eldrinn clambered over a fallen beam and waited while Q'arlynd did the same. The boy nodded down at the rotten timber. *Maybe he expects another of these to fall. Let's hope, when it does, it lands on Gilkriz.* He shrugged. *Though Daffir was wrong about the direction the threat came from, last time. Remember he said it was going to rise out of the lake?*

The boy had that wrong, Q'arlynd thought. Daffir had said no such thing. The human had warned that something was approaching. Something big. And it had. He'd predicted not where it had come from, but where it would end up: in the lake. Dissolved to a slurry and washed away.

He'd seen into the future. A common enough accomplishment for a wizard who specialized in divination, but Q'arlynd was starting to wonder if it had been a spell that had been used. Daffir, he recalled, had pressed the staff's diamond to his forehead in just the same way before making his prediction.

They ducked under a sagging beam. Q'arlynd brushed away the cobweb that snagged his hair and flicked a hand to get Eldrinn's attention again. *Your father's staff. Does it hold magic that will reveal the future?*

That wouldn't surprise me. It would explain why the diamond is shaped like an hourglass.

Q'arlynd thought back to when he'd first met Eldrinn, out on the High Moor. Even feeblewitted, the boy had held on to the staff, rather than dropping it in the dust. Part of his spell-blasted mind had recognized it as valuable. As being important to his quest.

Q'arlynd caught the boy's eye. *Could the staff also reveal the past?*

I . . . An odd expression contorted Eldrinn's face—as if he had been about speak aloud but had suddenly forgotten what he was going to say. *I suppose so*, he signed at last.

Q'arlynd laughed aloud. Could the answer to the riddle of Kraanfhaor's Door *really* be that simple?

Gilkriz glanced back at them.

So did the priestess just ahead of them, who flicked a warning. *Quiet!*

Q'arlynd signed a quick apology. Its insincerity was betrayed by his grin, but he didn't care. Hundreds of *kiira* shimmered in his imagination. Thousands of them. He knew how Eldrinn had opened Kraanfhaor's Door: by using his father's staff to look back thousands of years to the time of ancient Miyeritar. The boy had watched one of the original dark elves open it.

Q'arlynd could do the same—all he needed was that staff.

What is it? Eldrinn asked.

Q'arlynd forced the grin from his face. *I'll tell you later.*

A few moments later, he sneaked a glance behind him. The dark lenses that hid Daffir's eyes made it almost impossible to read the human's expression. What's more, Daffir seemed as capable as any drow of hiding his thoughts. If he used his divinations to foresee Q'arlynd's treachery and decided to pre-empt it, there would be little warning.

Q'arlynd would have to be careful when he made his move.

Very careful indeed.

CHAPTER 11

Halisstra watched as the demon worked its torments.
Cavatina lay on her back, helpless and weeping,
the antithesis of the proud Darksong Knight she'd
once been. Wendonai was deep inside her mind,
teasing out jagged scraps of shame and loathing.
Flaying her, body and soul, until she lay weak and
trembling before him.

Halisstra knew just how that felt.

The massive wound the demon had inflicted
upon Halisstra earlier had healed itself, bones
knitting and organs and flesh growing back until
only a shadow of pain remained. She could breathe
without the sharp lance of agony that had blotted
out all else. Even the callus was gone from her
hand; only a faint pucker remained.

She stared at Wendonai's broad back, her eyes

spitting hatred. She'd given him what he wanted: a plaything. She hadn't been stupid enough to expect the demon to keep his promise—freedom would be denied her—but she *had* expected him to return her to Lolth. Wendonai had no further use for Halisstra, after all. Now that she had delivered the Darksong Knight to him, she was insignificant, a creature to be ignored.

That burned.

Still, it might be to her advantage. With Wendonai's attention wholly focused on Cavatina, Halisstra might escape. She would use her *bae'qeshel* magic to render herself invisible and . . .

As soon as she thought that, she cringed. The demon would hear her thoughts!

She waited, wincing in anticipation of his blow. He couldn't kill her. Not without Lolth's complicity. But he could hurt her. Hurt her badly.

Wendonai did nothing. Still bending over the prostrate Cavatina, he continued to torment her, savoring her anguish.

Halisstra straightened from her crouch. It took her several moments to work up her courage, but at last she dared try something. A song, whispered so faintly it was nearly lost amid the wind that eternally scoured this vast, empty plain. She didn't expect her charm to work—Wendonai was a powerful demon, his mind strong as a fortress wall—but she did expect a reaction. Rage, that she would even dare try. Retribution, for her insolence.

Wendonai ignored her.

Or . . . did he?

He'd told Cavatina he could hear her thoughts. Halisstra had assumed the same held true for her. But if that was so, the demon must have known, when Halisstra first suggested Cavatina as a substitute, that the Darksong Knight had killed a demigod. Either Wendonai had been arrogant enough not to care or . . .

He'd lied.

Halisstra smiled. He *couldn't* hear her thoughts, and stupidly, he'd told her why. Her ancestors had been Miyeritari. She didn't bear his taint. That didn't make her weak. It made her strong.

Strong enough to resist him.

Tingling with hope, she glanced around, looking for a way out. The pile of skulls Wendonai used as his throne had burned down to blackened lumps. The wind blew past the skulls, teasing a wisp of ash from the pile.

No, not ash. The streamer of black was coming out of a single eye socket.

Keeping a wary eye on Wendonai, Halisstra eased toward the twisting spiral of ash and touched it with a fingertip. Her flesh paled to gray. The fingertip felt not just cold, but drained of all sensation, all life. The part that was within the tendril of black seemed to shrink, as if Halisstra was viewing it through the wrong side of a lens. The blackness pulled at it, stretching it thinner and thinner and . . .

Halisstra yanked her finger out. Had she not, the darkness would have drawn her irrevocably into itself. Into the void that was the skull's empty eye socket. She knew what the tendril of darkness was: raw negative energy. Seeping out of . . . nowhere. Drawing everything it touched into oblivion.

What bliss that would be.

The wind shifted. In order to reach the tendril of ash, Halisstra would have to move to a spot where Wendonai might see her. At the moment, his attention was wholly focused on Cavatina. He crouched over her, his quivering nostrils savoring her weakness. Demons, however, weren't stupid. Not always. The moment he spotted movement behind him, Halisstra's chance at escape would be extinguished.

She'd have to make sure he didn't spot her, then.

Softly, she began to sing. When her song ended, she was as invisible as the wind. Then she began a second song, one that would provide a distraction.

Before she could complete it, a voice pealed out. It was Cavatina, her voice raised in joyous song, "I . . . am . . . redeemed!"

Wendonai rocked back, astonished. An anguished howl tore itself from his throat.

Snarling out the final word of her song, Halisstra conjured up an image of herself and sent it hurtling toward Wendonai. The illusionary attack would buy her only an instant, but an instant was all she needed. As the false image hurled itself at Wendonai, claws raking and teeth bared, Halisstra dived for the stream of black and plunged both hands into it. The darkness seized them in its icy grip and wrenched her body inside.

Utter cold gripped Halisstra. Her body felt thin and fragile as paper as the negative energy teased it into an impossible length. Thinner, thinner, until it was a ragged flutter. Nothingness loomed, a vacant eye socket that led down into still, cold darkness.

Then oblivion claimed her.

Cavatina's eyes widened in surprise as Halisstra hurled herself at Wendonai. The demon snarled, but made no move to battle Halisstra. Instead he twisted around, staring intently at the pile of skulls.

Halisstra struck him—and disappeared.

An illusion!

Something odd was happening to Cavatina. A brilliant white light poured from her body, illuminating the demon from below and throwing a harsh shadow across the ground behind him. White as the moon, the light sang from Cavatina's pores. A crackling square of darkness drifted down through this light, settling upon Cavatina's face with a velvet-soft touch, then disappearing. The demon, inside her mind a moment ago, was shut out. Peace filled Cavatina's mind, gentle as a mother's lullaby, even as the searing white moonlight poured from her skin with the rage of a mother's wrath.

"Eilistraee!" Cavatina cried.

Wendonai reared to his feet, his leathery wings flapping. He staggered backward, wincing, as if pummeled by invisible blows. He shot Cavatina a look of anguished rage.

"No!" he howled. He shook a blood-red fist at the sky. "I will *not* be denied her!"

Flames erupted on his crimson skin and crawled across it in white-hot waves, licking at the wound in his abdomen. He forced himself, stomp by stomp, toward Cavatina. Bulling his way in through the protective shield that Eilistraee had thrown up around her.

Cavatina threw herself to the side. She rolled onto her stomach, her bound hands scrabbling against the gritty soil. An instant later, her holy symbol was in her hands. Clutching it, she forced herself to her knees. She sang out an urgent note, and the blackened singing sword rose into the air behind Wendonai. Soot exploded from the blade, revealing gleaming steel. Then the sword began to sing.

Wendonai whirled to face it.

Too late. Cavatina yanked her bound hands toward her .chest, urging the sword forward. Its point plunged into the demon's chest, finding his heart. The sword's peal of triumph drowned out the demon's anguished roar and the angry howl of the rising wind. Wendonai staggered, clutching the hilt that was rammed tight against his chest. A bloodied length of steel protruded from his back, quivering in its victory dance.

Before the demon could heal himself, Cavatina sang out another prayer. This time, her voice was funereal and low. The dirge she sang resonated through the blade in the balor's chest and vibrated through his blood with each pulse of his massive heart. He staggered, his cloven feet scuffing furrows in the salt-crusted earth. His wings snapped erect and fluttered stiffly, and his eyes blazed. Even as the dirge forced him to his knees, Wendonai shook his massive horned head.

"This . . . is not finished," he gasped. "You cannot . . . kill me."

Another lie. Wendonai had made one terrible, fatal mistake. Had this battle taken place anywhere else, Cavatina would have been unable to kill him. The demon's essence would have fallen back into the raw chaos of the Abyss, there to be reborn. But in the Abyss, he was as mortal as she was.

Cavatina braced herself. When Wendonai died, the resulting void would tear at the fabric of the Abyss, rupturing it in a tremendous explosion. She, too, would die.

That didn't matter. Her soul would join Eilistraee's eternal dance, and Cavatina would have her victory.

Cavatina was on her knees, still at bound at ankle and wrist with the smoldering remains of the demon's whip. But Eilstraee's symbol was in her hands. Tiny and dull though the ceremonial blade might be, it would be Wendonai's downfall.

She ended her dirge with two droning words: "Die, Wendonai."

The balor's eyes rolled back in its head. He groaned—long and low as tortured metal twisting apart. Then he began to tilt to one side. The wind howled, tearing at Cavatina's hair and driving sharp granules of salt into her bare skin. The demon's hands clawed at the air, as if he were desperately trying to prop himself upright, but to no avail.

With a crash that rattled the ground on which Cavatina knelt, Wendonai fell.

For several heartbeats, the air was utterly still.

Wendonai was dead, even though his body had not been consumed.

And Cavatina was still alive.

A miracle.

The glow that enveloped Cavatina abruptly ended. She let out a shuddering sigh. "Praise be to you, Eilistraee. In my time of need . . ." Realizing something, she amended her prayer of thanksgiving. "Masked Lady," she corrected. "My heartfelt thanks, for . . . everything."

She moistened her wind-chapped lips. They were crusted with salt, but she tasted something far sweeter.

Redemption.

She shuffled on her knees to where the demon lay. Using the length of blade that protruded from his back, she sliced apart the tight binding of leather around her wrists. Then she sat, raised her bound legs, and sawed the bindings off her ankles. She nicked herself in several places but didn't care. It was all part of the dance.

Leaping to her feet, she gave in to it. Whirling, clapping, spinning in place. A victory dance. Not just for herself, but for the Masked Lady. Embracing all that they both had become.

Only in the middle of it did she suddenly remember Halisstra. She whirled in place, but the salt-encrusted plain was as bare as it had always been. Empty and flat, stretching as far as the eye could see.

"Where *is* she?" Cavatina wondered aloud.

She'd asked herself the same question, nearly two years ago, after slaying Selvetarm. Just as she had then, she vowed to search for Halisstra. Only when Cavatina found her again, Halisstra would pay for her treachery.

With a grunt, Cavatina flopped the dead demon onto his side. His lips were pulled back, his fangs exposed in what looked like a grin.

"Go ahead and smile," Cavatina told him. "It's Eilistraee who has the last laugh." She planted a foot on his chest and yanked out the singing sword. She whirled it around her head, letting the dark blood slide from it. The sword pealed its joy.

What now? Cavatina thought as she glanced around. This is the Abyss, and I still need to escape.

Her eye fell on the pile of blackened skulls. A thin tendril of black seeped from the eye socket of one of them. She crouched and peered at its source.

The void she stared into left her mind spinning. For an instant, she felt nothing—not even the beating of her own heart. Her very soul teetered on a blade's edge: on one side, life; on the other . . . nothing. Just a terrifying emptiness.

Cavatina reeled back, sickened. The eye socket was indeed a portal. A portal to death itself.

There had to be another way out of there. Halisstra must have gone somewhere. And if she could escape, then so could Cavatina. She was a Darksong Knight. A slayer of demons. No, a slayer of *demigods*. She . . .

She smiled. There is was again. Pride. It had nearly been her downfall, more than once.

Still, she *would* find a way out of there. When she'd trained as a Darksong Knight, her instructors had foreseen just such an eventuality. More than one of them had followed a demon onto its home ground, slain it, and returned to tell the tale. They'd told her how it was done. The prayer was one Cavatina had never attempted before, but she was certain she could master it.

Anything was possible, with Eilistraee's grace.

Holding her sword in both hands, Cavatina raised it until the blade was horizontal with the ground. Then she spun and sang. Her blade tried to dip toward the skull portal, but she would not allow it. Muscles straining, she kept it level. Then suddenly the point plunged down, driving itself deep into the salt. A shaft of twined moonlight and shadow shot out from that point, a hair's breadth above the ground and thin as a sword blade. A path that only a devotee of the Masked Lady could see. A path to the next nearest portal.

Cavatina yanked her sword from the ground. With the softly humming blade balanced across one bare shoulder, she set out upon the path.

❖ ❖ ❖ ❖ ❖

Kâras stepped down into the boat, taking care that his too-short legs didn't stumble. Getting used to being half his usual size was the easy part. Coping with having his face bare was harder. His mask— a bright red handkerchief— peeped out of the pocket of the leather vest his *piwafwi* had transformed into. He resisted the urge to touch it.

Gindrol and Talzir followed him, each seamless in his magically altered form. Their disguises were perfect to the last detail: bare scalps, mottled gray skin, wiry muscles, and pebble-black eyes. They even wore a deep gnome's suspicious glower. They might have been born svirfneblin, for all anyone could tell.

The rowboat was narrow and black, with blunted ends. The three disguised Nightshadows settled onto its bare wooden seats, Kâras in the front with the strongbox resting on his knees. Gindrol, just behind him, took the oars in hand. Each was a length of fused armbone, ending in a cupped hand.

The splashes of the oars were drowned out by the clattering of bone on bone. The lake-filled cavern was vast, but its entire ceiling was studded with skulls, giving it a bumpy, off-white appearance. The lake itself was utterly flat—the slight wake the rowboat produced immediately stilled. A chill emanated from the water, up through the wooden plank on which Kâras sat. He found himself shivering and tried to force his muscles to relax. He didn't want the others to think he was afraid.

The lake was deep, but the *Faerzress* that permeated the stone there shone up from below, lending the water a faint bluish glow. Silhouettes flitted through its depths: water spiders, hunting their prey.

At the center of the lake lay an island, on which stood the ruined city of V'elddrinnsshar. The island itself was a slumped mass of off-white limestone whose top had been leveled. Streets wound between empty stalagmite buildings that rose like tapering fingers questing for the ceiling. At the center of the island stood a larger spire of stone, its top sheared off. Kiaransalee's temple capped it, a brooding block of black marble. Ghosts flitted above it like demented swallows, their anguished moans filling the air in an eerie chorus.

As the boat drew closer to the island, Kâras could make out huddled shapes choking the streets of the abandoned city: the bodies of the dead. Several lay on the dock, arms or legs draped loosely over the edges where they had fallen. A dozen rose to their feet in silence as the boat scraped against the stone steps that led up to the dock. All were drow, their skin paled to dull gray. Each had flesh pocked with enormous, long-since ruptured blisters: the puffball-like hallmark of the ascomid plague. Had those blisters been fresh, the slightest touch would have ruptured them, releasing a cloud of deadly spores that would propagate the disease. But it had been a century since the plague had swept through there, killing everyone in the city.

Kâras twisted around on his seat and saw that Talzir's eyes were wide, his lips tight. Gindrol, who was rowing, still had his back to the dock.

"Steady," Kâras told them, his svirfneblin voice strange in his ears. "Remember, they need our voidstone. They're not going to kill us . . . yet."

The svirfneblin that was Talzir cracked a grim smile.

One of the undead drow—a female whose finery hung in tatters on her blistered body—staggered down the steps and reached down for the strongbox Kâras held. Shaking his head, he drew it out of her reach.

"This isn't for you, Mistress," he told her. "It's for your Reaper."

A chuckle sounded from one of the doorways at the rear of the dock. From it stepped a drow female wearing the loose black robe and gray skullcap that marked her as a Crone.

Silver rings decorated each finger. An hourglass, filled with white sand, hung against her chest, and a dagger with a bone handle was sheathed at her hip. Her skin was smudged with gray: ashes, taken from a pyre and mixed with rancid fat. Kâras steeled himself against the smell as she approached. Back in Maerimydra, it had always made him gag.

He clambered up the steps, gripping the strongbox. Talzir and Gindrol followed. All three bowed at the Crone's approach. Barely acknowledging them, she tossed the sack she was holding at their feet. It landed with a clatter: the sound of gemstones clicking together.

When she reached out for the strongbox, Kâras feigned reluctance. He shifted the box in his hands, making sure to draw her attention to it. The wood appeared gouged, as if it had been chewed on

"Is there a problem?" she asked. Her voice was as cold as a corpse.

"We were attacked." Kâras said. "A bulette mistook the strongbox for its lunch."

"Good thing it didn't swallow the contents," Talzir piped up from behind him, "or it would have gotten a terrible stomach ache." He gave a nervous-sounding laugh.

The Crone's eyes narrowed. "Give it to me."

Kâras shifted his feet. "But—"

"Give it to me!"

Kâras obliged, lifting the strongbox. Just as the Crone's hand was about to touch it, he moved the box upward. Her hand passed through the illusionary lid and touched the voidstone. For the briefest of instants, her eyes widened in alarm and her mouth parted in a scream.

Then she was gone.

With a thought, Kâras altered his form. His body doubled in size, changed gender, assumed the face he'd just been staring up at. His vest became a robe, his mask a skullcap, and the dragon-skin ring on his finger multiplied itself by eight and turned silver.

He stared disdainfully down at the other two Night-shadows and shouted in a cold female voice, "Where did he go? Speak!"

The undead drow glanced back and forth between the transformed Kâras and the spot where the real Crone had just been standing. One of them pawed at Kâras's sleeve, and he warned it off with a glare.

Gindrol and Talzir, meanwhile, played their parts to perfection. Shuffling, nervous, they refused to meet the "Crone's" eyes. On cue, the boat rocked, as if an invisible person were stepping into it. Kâras stared in that direction. "Ah. Lost his nerve, did he?"

Gindrol bent to scoop up the sack, but Kâras stamped a foot down on it. He pretended to open the strongbox. The illusionary lid sprang open, and he looked inside. The void-stone was a dark, fist-sized hollow at the center of the box. With a satisfied nod, he pretended to close the missing lid.

He removed his foot from the sack. "Go," he ordered the other two.

Cringing, they retrieved the sack and scrambled back to the boat.

All part of the act.

It was lost on the undead, of course. The animated corpses that surrounded Kâras hadn't the intelligence to understand the subtle scene the three Nightshadows had just played out. But the quth-maren that stepped out of a nearby doorway did. Tall and gaunt, made up of nothing more than oozing muscle stitched rudely over bone, it stared at Kâras with eyes that wept blood. As Kâras met its stare, panic welled inside him. He felt if he were drowning, thrashing about in panic, going under in a sea of blood.

Masked Lord, he pleaded fiercely, *strengthen me*.

The panic dissipated, leaving only a nervous bead of sweat that trickled down the small of Kâras's back. He glared at the animated dead who clustered around him, fawning for his attention. "Clear a path for me," he ordered.

The quth-maren nodded. It waved a hand, and the plague-killed drow standing on the dock folded to the ground, lifeless once more. Then it gave a hacking cough, deep in its chest. A wad of blood-tinged mucous shot from its mouth and landed on the stomach of a corpse that had lain down immediately in front of Kâras. The acidic spit sizzled, burning clean through the body, down to the stone beneath.

The quth-maren gave a gurgling chuckle and padded up the dock, leaving bloody footprints in its wake.

Behind Kâras, Gindrol and Talzir pulled away from the dock. The splashes of their oars were rapidly lost amid the clattering of the skulls overhead and the wails of the ghosts that flitted above.

Kâras forced his shoulders erect and followed the quth-maren with a haughty, confident step. They walked through the ruined city. Everywhere Kâras looked lay plague victims, preserved by fell magic. They rose at his approach, bowing in subservience to the Crone he appeared to be. Some plucked at his cloak with blistered fingers; he shrugged them away imperiously.

Movement down a side street caught his eye. He glanced in that direction and saw a monstrous hound nearly four times his height, made up of a seething mass of bodies, with teeth made from broken femurs. It sniffed at the dead, selected one, and closed its teeth around it. Lifting the corpse into the air, the monstrous hound shook its head, scattering chunks of flesh left and right. It paused in this gruesome task to stare back at Kâras, blood dribbling from its mouth like drool.

Kâras averted his eyes and walked on. All around him, however, were equally horrific sights. Ghouls scuttled like crabs across the corpses, snapping off choice pieces and sucking on them. Specters drifted in and out of walls, leaving a rime of frost in their wake. Finger-sized gravecrawlers wriggled into the nostrils and ears of the bodies that lay on the ground, gradually calcifying the dead.

Kâras had seen it all before. Just as they had then, his guts churned in horror. He'd thought himself ready. It had been five years since the fall of Maerimydra, after all. Five years since he'd escaped from the horror of a city conquered both from without, by the army of Kurgoth Hellspawn, and from within, by the traitorous priestesses of House T'sarran.

You survived then, he told himself sternly. You'll survive now.

But his thoughts kept turning traitorously back to that time. To all the near misses, the almost-fatal mistakes. Becoming the consort of one of Kiaransalee's priestesses, for example. How badly that had gone! Later, he'd thrown in his lot with a group of survivors hiding in the ruins. All had gone well until they decided to take on the Crones, a suicidal task. Kâras had taken his leave of them, fleeing Maerimydra with the sackful of the treasures he'd been able to scavenge.

Later, he'd heard they'd actually done it: thrown down Kiaransalee's high priestess with the help of adventurers from beyond the city. That thought should have bolstered him, given him the confidence he so desperately needed . But he was haunted still by the memories of the long months he'd spent constantly on the run from the undead. The moans of the ghosts above reminded him of the shrieks that had cut down the other members of his House like invisible scythes. The clattering that filled the air reminded him of the bony touch of a skeletal hand on his shoulder.

Stop thinking about it, he told himself sternly. He forced down the gorge that rose in his throat. He would do as his god commanded. Discover what the Crones were doing with the voidstone, learn how to stop it, then get out. The Masked Lord would protect him, just as he had in Maerimydra. And if Kâras died . . . well, then the fear that roiled in his guts would end. He'd be taken up into the Masked Lord's shadowy embrace.

He knew where he had to go: into the temple atop that central spire. The Acropolis of Thanatos was the only logical place for the voidstone to be delivered to. The blue-green glow that suffused the column it stood on confirmed it. The *Faerzress* was brightest at the top of the spire, just underneath the temple. It pulsed with an eye-stinging glow.

The quth-maren led Kâras to the base of a staircase that spiraled up to the temple. On each side of the stair stood a boneclaw: a skeletal humanoid twice Kâras's height with fingers that ended in scything claws. One of the boneclaws lashed out as Kâras approached, its claws extending until they were several paces long. Their tips plunged into the rock in front, back and to either side of Kâras, forming the bars of a razor-sharp cage.

Kâras jerked to a halt. "Release me," he ordered. He flipped up his hood, using it as an excuse to touch the skullcap he wore—his disguised holy symbol. Silently, he prayed to the Masked Lord, *Drive him back. Make him obey.*

The boneclaw twisted its wrist, snapping off its claws near their tips. Fresh points sprouted immediately from the stubs as it returned its hand to its side. "Pass," it hissed through clenched teeth.

Kâras stepped over the broken claw stubs. Then he climbed the stairs. The quth-maren didn't follow. It remained at the base of the stalagmite, craning its neck up to watch him, its lipless mouth twisted in a mocking smile.

Did it know something Kâras didn't?

Kâras shook off his apprehension. He needed to watch where he was going. The stairs were covered with trickles of what smelled like dribbling, rancid fat. He had to concentrate on each step to keep from slipping.

At last he reached the level stop of the spire. Here, for the first time since setting foot on the island, he saw other Crones. All were dressed as he was, in loose black robes, some with their hoods pulled up. The silver rings they wore on every finger glinted blue, reflecting the light of the *Faerzress*. Most of the Crones hurried past on errands of their own, but others stood rocking in place, arms clasped tight around their bodies, tittering with mad laughter. One squatted over a corpse, yarding out its withered entrails and carefully coiling them around a spool.

Kâras walked steadily toward the temple. Built of black marble veined with red, it was a chaotic jumble of angles, misshapen windows and gaping doorways. The closer he got, the greater his urge to cringe and cower. His feet felt heavy as stone. Each dragging step forward was an effort that caused his heart to pound wildly in his ears. A part of his mind gibbered in terror at what he was about to do. This is the Acropolis, it shrieked. Kiaransalee's temple. You don't dare enter it. They'll know you, see you for what you are. Turn back!

A whimper struggled to escape his throat. With a savage effort, he swallowed it down. He shifted the strongbox into the crook of one arm and adjusted his hood, using the motion to once again brush his fingers against the skullcap-mask. *Masked Lord*, he silently prayed, *give me strength*.

Confidence stirred like a whisper in the darkness, then flooded him like a shaft of moonlight. His shoulders squared, his heart lightened, his step grew more confident. I can do it, he told himself. Just a few steps more.

Then he was inside.

He halted as abruptly as he'd entered. If he hadn't, it all would have ended right there. He stood on the edge of a precipice; the interior of the Acropolis of Thanatos was nothing more than an empty hole. Walls, floors, ceiling beams—all ended abruptly, as if the stone building were a squash that had been scraped empty by a spoon. At the center of this hollow hung a sphere of utter blackness. Kâras could feel it tugging at him, and he found himself leaning toward it. When he flinched back, a tiny fragment of marble broke off from the edge where his foot had been. The chip of stone flew toward the sphere at the center of the hollow space, spiraling in toward it, then was gone.

"Voidstone," he whispered.

The sphere sucked hungrily at his essence, chilling him until his bones ached. He tried to take the measure of the thing but couldn't. It was enormous, as large as a small building. The Crones must have been working at it for years, building it up one tiny chunk at a time.

Seeing the immensity of it, his heart sank. Destroying it would take dozens of priests, working in concert to channel positive energy into it. Before there was even a hope of attempting this, the army of undead that filled the streets below would have to be defeated.

Cavatina had been right. They *would* have to mount an attack on the Acropolis.

The sphere of darkness wasn't entirely featureless. If Kâras turned his head slightly, he could see shapes and movement out of the corner of his eye. Wild images filled the voidstone's depths: the towers of a city, rows of skeletal undead lined up like soldiers, a plaza filled with capering ghouls, a minotaur seated on a bone throne. The latter twisted around to stare at Kâras. A bestial muzzle pressed against the surface of the voidstone sphere from within. Lips twitched in a grimace, revealing elongated fangs.

Free me, the minotaur hissed. *And my legions will serve you.*

"Soon, Lord Casus," a soft voice answered. "Soon."

Kâras started, nearly dropping the strongbox. Slowly he turned.

Standing just behind him was a female he recognized: Cabrath, of House Nelinderra. Her face was clean of the death's head paint she habitually wore, but she looked no better for it. Her lips were a narrow slash, her nose a second, vertical slash, and her eyes mere slits. She wore black robes trimmed with purple. She toyed with a bone-handled dagger whose blade was a tapering glimmer of blue energy. The harsh light glinted off the silver rings on her fingers.

Kâras was surprised to see her there. He'd assumed she'd

died with the rest of the Crones when Kiaransalee's cult in Maerimydra was overthrown.

A bone-white aura wavered around her, chill as mist in a graveyard. It brushed against Kâras—he didn't dare flinch, lest Cabrath realize something was wrong. Its brief touch left him feeling sick and weak. In another moment, he thought, he would faint. Tumble and slide down the slope in front of him into the voidstone and be consumed.

Staring at the orb was better than looking into Cabrath's terrible amber eyes. Kâras tore his gaze away from her. The voidstone was black again, unmarked by visions.

Cabrath drifted around in front of Kâras, her hair streaming back toward the voidstone. Her body was translucent; Kâras could see the voidstone right through her. She *was* dead.

She tilted her head at the voidstone. "Feed him."

Kâras hesitated, even though he knew there was little he could do. In death, Cabrath had become something more than the mere priestess she had been. As a spirit, she could slay him with a touch, with a word, between one heartbeat and the next. Any spell he tried would die on his lips before he could complete it.

He tossed the strongbox at the voidstone sphere. Cabrath moved to intercept it. As the box passed through her ghostly body, she threw out her arms and shrieked with wild laughter. For just an instant, she seemed solid again, corporeal, except for her aura. She spun in place and watched the box strike the larger sphere and disappear, releasing the chunk of voidstone it held. Her gaunt face held a look of first eager anticipation, then disappointment.

"Go!" she shrieked over her shoulder at Kâras, not deigning to look at him. "Find more!"

Kâras bowed. As he started to back away, a section of the voidstone bulged outward. Horror filled Kâras as he realized the chunk of voidstone he'd just added might tip the balance. Were the armies of the undead minotaur about to be released?

The bulge in the voidstone erupted. A figure tumbled out, screaming like a thing damned. She was a massive female drow, twice as large as Q'arlynd, with a bestial face, matted hair, and spiderlike legs protruding from her chest. Cabrath whirled, barely dodging the tumbling form. The newcomer sailed past her and crashed into a wall. Cabrath glanced between the bestial female and the voidstone, a shocked look on her face.

The demonic drow scrambled to her feet. She stared wildly around—at the hollowed-out temple, at Kâras, at the voidstone, at Cabrath. Then she threw back her head and shrieked with laughter, a sound as brittle as breaking glass.

"Lolth!" she cried. "I'm your plaything no longer. I've won! I'm dead!"

Kâras stared at the voidstone. It was smooth and spherical once more. The skeletal legions were *not* issuing forth from it. Not yet. And Cabrath seemed just as surprised by what had just happened as Kâras was. The spirit stared at the demonic drow, a puzzled frown on her face.

Slowly Kâras backed out of the temple. He'd find a quiet place, report to Qilué—and let her decide what to do next.

CHAPTER 12

Leliana halted the group when she spotted Brindell running back through the tunnel. The halfling's eyes were wide with terror. Unlike a drow, she wore her emotions where everyone could see them.

Brindell skidded to a halt in front of Leliana, her copper-colored hair damp with sweat. "A wave," she gasped, fear making her forget to use the silent speech, "of putrid flesh. It's headed this way, dissolving everything in its path."

"Mother's blood," Leliana whispered. She could hear it, even then. A bubbling, gurgling sound, overlaid with a faint, sizzling hiss. She turned to the mages, several paces behind her, and signaled for them to turn back.

But we're almost there, Gilkriz protested.

According to the map . . . His hands fluttered to a halt as he stared at something behind Leliana.

Leliana spun. The thing Brindell had spotted was in view. It looked like a waist-deep puddle of bruised fat, wide enough to fill the tunnel from side to side. Veins as thick as legs bulged as it oozed forward—one broke, spraying the tunnel walls with red. Boils rose on the surface of the thing and erupted with wet pops. The monstrosity was still a hundred paces away, but even at that distance Leliana could smell the stench of corruption.

"Join my prayer!" she shouted. "Drive it back."

The priestesses burst into song, lifting the miniature swords that were the symbols of their faith. "By sword and by song, we command thee. By moonlight be driven back . . ."

The monstrosity surged on, unaffected by the priestess's prayers.

Leliana lowered her holy symbol. If they couldn't stop this thing, they'd be forced to retreat through the shaft they'd just climbed to reach this tunnel. A shaft that led only down. A *deep* shaft. Before they reached bottom, the monstrosity would be spilling down on top of them.

A streak of frost shot past Leliana's shoulder: one of the wizards, casting a spell. Ice crystals blossomed across the leading edge of the putrid wave, freezing it. An instant later, however, the ice cracked and the monstrosity surged forward again. As it came on, a rat burst from a crack in the tunnel wall just ahead of the oozing mass and scurried up a timber, trying to escape. The putrid mass flowed after it, climbing the wall. The rat shrieked as it was enveloped and dissolved. The timber it had tried to climb fell to pieces and was also consumed.

"Out of the way!" Gilkriz yelled, shoving past her. *"Kulg!"* he cried, slamming his stiff-fingered hands in front of him as if they were a gate closing.

With a rumble and a thud, the tunnel ahead slammed

shut. A wall of solid stone stood where an open passage had been a moment before, blocking the monster's path.

Brindell let out a whooping cheer. "Praise be to Eilistraee! We're safe."

The others were more restrained; they merely murmured their relief.

"That's it, then," Leliana said. She turned her back on the wall. "We'll have to go another . . ."

She paused. What was that sound?

There it was again. A faint noise, coming from the shaft they'd just climbed.

Tash'kla ran to it and peered down. *Another one!* she signed—as if maintaining silence would save them. *Coming up the shaft!*

"Gilkriz!" Leliana barked.

The conjurer nodded. He ran over to where Tash'kla stood and repeated his spell, bringing his hands together. Rock groaned, bulged. The top of the shaft slammed shut.

Brindell glanced back and forth between the blocked tunnel and the plugged shaft. "Now what?"

Leliana looked around. What indeed?

She noticed the human wizard standing slightly apart from the group, intently studying a portion of the tunnel wall. "What is it, Daffir? Have you spotted something?"

He turned, leaning on his staff. "A doorway, hidden by magic." He pointed. "Here."

The dark lenses hovering in front of his eyes hid his expression, but his voice had a strained sound Leliana didn't like. "Where does it lead?"

"To death. And . . . freedom."

"Whose death?" Gilkriz asked, striding forward. He peered at the wall, his face illuminated by the *Faerzress* glow.

Daffir shrugged.

"We certainly can't stay here," Tash'kla said. "We'll run out of air." She raised her sword in both hands in front of her; the blade hummed softly. "I'm ready to face death, if it means finding a way past those monsters."

"So am I," Brindell said. She fingered her holy symbol with a pudgy hand.

"Perhaps the divination wasn't a literal one," Eldrinn said. " 'Death' could mean the Crones, and the door may be another route to the Acropolis, hence 'freedom.' " He turned to the wizard beside him. "What do you think, Q'arlynd?"

"Why don't you try opening it, Daffir?" Q'arlynd suggested, moving closer to the other wizard. "Let's see what's behind the door, and decide."

Q'arlynd's eyes, Leliana noted, kept straying to the staff Daffir held.

"Just be ready," she told the others. "Anything could come through that door." She readied her sword. "Go ahead, Daffir."

Daffir balled his hand into a fist, raised it to his lips, and barked a word into it.

Nothing happened. The wall looked as solid as ever.

"I need assistance," he said. "Gilkriz, Q'arlynd, can you aid me?"

The conjurer nodded. So did Q'arlynd, but less eagerly.

"On the count of three, then," Daffir said. "One . . ."

Gilkriz raised his fist to his lips. Q'arlynd motioned for Eldrinn to step back, then did the same.

"Two . . ."

The priestesses also heeded the warning. All took a step back.

"Three!"

All three mages spat out a word in unison. As it left their lips, a black iron door became visible. It had no handle, but a knocker shaped like a goat's head hung dead-center on its pitted metal surface. The knocker reared up and thudded its horns against metal with a hollow boom. The door creaked open, away from them, releasing a puff of dust-scented air.

Leliana stepped forward. The top of the door was level with her chest, so she had to bend slightly to peer inside. Even without a prayer of divination, she could feel the tainted chill that spilled from the room. When her eye fell on the statue that stood against the far wall, between two arched exits, she understood why. Like the door knocker, it had a goat's head. Blood-red gems glinted in the eye sockets, reflecting the light from the *Faerzress* that glimmered from every surface, including the statue itself. The statue had a duergar's squat proportions but stood fully twice Leliana's height, its curving horns nearly scraping the ceiling of the room. Arms folded against its chest, it stared down at a pool of silver that shimmered at its cloven feet: quicksilver.

The priestesses and wizards crowded behind her, curiosity overcoming their apprehension. "What is that?" Tash'kla breathed. "A golem?"

"There's a rune on its chest," Gilkriz said. "A duergar rune. It's faded, but I can still make it out: 'Orcus.' "

Leliana immediately sang a prayer. Behind her, she heard the other priestesses do the same.

"That means something to you?" the conjurer asked.

Leliana nodded. "Orcus is a demon. Prince of the dead. Kiaransalee killed him."

Q'arlynd squatted beside her. "You said he 'is' a demon. Did he rise from the dead?"

"Yes, despite Kiaransalee's best efforts. She not only killed him but conquered his realm—that layer of the Abyss known as Thanatos. Her priestesses marked the victory by naming her chief temple after it. But the demon lord eventually returned to reclaim his realm."

"Did the duergar of these parts worship Orcus?" Gilkriz asked.

"The ones who dug this mine obviously did," Leliana answered. "It's odd, though, that this shrine remains intact. Kiaransalee's followers made it their mission to eradicate all vestiges of the demon prince. Legend has it the goddess worked magic that erased Orcus's name, wherever and however it had been written."

"And yet this rune remains," Gilkriz said.

"Maybe we should close the door," Eldrinn blurted.

Q'arlynd stared at the room's far wall. "I'm wondering where those corridors go, myself. I don't know if any of you has noticed, but they're not glowing. The *Faerzress* ends at the wall on each side of those arches. I think they're portals."

"Go ahead and try one, then," Gilkriz suggested, his voice silky. "We've got diviners to spare."

Q'arlynd bristled. His fingers twitched.

"Enough," Leliana reprimanded. "I've made my decision: we're going to seal this room and take our chances with the putrid ooze. As Gilkriz pointed out earlier, we were almost at the Crone's cavern when—"

"Madam," Daffir said, his soft voice interrupting her. "Please stand aside."

Leliana turned. "What is it, Daffir? Do you see something?"

"Yes. My destiny."

He moved closer to the door and peered inside. His head tilted, as if he were glancing at something the others couldn't see. Then he nodded. He straightened and handed his staff to Eldrinn, startling the boy, then ducked down low and entered the room.

"Stop!" Leliana cried. She grabbed for his robe, but missed. "We need you. You're the only one who . . ."

Daffir crossed the room with swift, purposeful strides.

"Protectors," Leliana barked. "Stand ready."

The priestesses lifted their swords and touched holy symbols.

Without so much as a backward glance, Daffir entered the corridor to the left of the statue and vanished.

Several moments passed.

Gilkriz broke the silence with a snort. "Diviners," he muttered. He waggled his fingers beside his temple. *Crazy.*

Leliana expected a retort from Eldrinn or Q'arlynd, but the pair had drawn apart from the others. She could see Q'arlynd's arms moving—he was saying something to the younger wizard in rapid, silent gestures—but his back was to her and she couldn't see his hands. The boy's eyes widened. Then he nodded. He clutched the staff with both hands and drew it to his chest protectively.

Leliana caught Gilkriz's eye. "Seal that door," she ordered. She was just about to find out what Q'arlynd and Eldrinn were up to when Qilué's voice sang out in her head.

Leliana, I have news. Kâras has penetrated the Acropolis. He's discovered what the Crones are up to.

Gilkriz was casting the spell that sealed the door, his chanting a distraction. Leliana clapped her hands against her ears to block it out. She listened as Qilué described what Kâras had discovered: a massive orb of voidstone at the heart of the Acropolis, guarded by a ghostly Crone. And that wasn't the worst of it.

Judging by what Kâras described, the Crones are attempting to open a gate to the negative energy plane, just as they did in Maerimydra, Qilué told her. *And I fear I know what they're trying to bring through it. An army of undead, commanded by a vampire minotaur. The legions of the Death Heart.*

"The Death Heart," Leliana repeated, her voice tight.

We must stop them. This time, we won't have the help of the Guardians. And Cavatina . . .

The voice stopped.

"Qilué?" Leliana asked. "Are you still there?"

The others had fallen silent. They stared tensely at Leliana.

Cavatina is beyond my reach. I fear the worst.

Leliana felt, rather than heard, Qilué's anguished sigh.

It's up to you, Leliana. You have to find a way to take the Acropolis. To halt what's happening before the Crones spill an unholy blight upon this world.

"The Nightshadows aren't with us," Leliana said. "They went another way. And we—"

So Kâras told me. You'll need reinforcements. I'll be sending others through the portal, but I want those of you who are already there to move on the Acropolis at once. Kâras said he could already see shapes moving inside the voidstone. It already spat out one monster. It won't be long, now, before the gate cracks open.

Leliana wet her lips nervously. "Lady," she ventured. "Will you be leading the reinforcements?"

I . . . can't. There are . . . matters here I have to deal with.

"So be it, Lady," Leliana said. "We'll do what we can."

May Eilistraee lend strength to your sword and harmony to your song. Farewell.

Farewell? The word carved a hollow in Leliana's gut. Did Qilué have so little faith in her that she was already counting Leliana as lost? For the space of a heartbeat, Leliana regretted ever volunteering for this mission. Then anger eclipsed fear. She would prove Qilué wrong. She would do it. Take the Acropolis and destroy the voidstone. Without reinforcements.

And if she failed, well, dying wouldn't be anything new. She'd already given her life for the Lady once before. She smiled grimly, remembering the battle in the Misty Forest.

The others were waiting. Leliana steeled herself. Swiftly, she relayed what Qilué had just told her. "Lady Qilué has ordered us to attack the Acropolis and destroy the voidstone. She'll send reinforcements, but they probably won't make it in time. Which means it's up to us." She stared at the wall Gilkriz had plugged the tunnel with. "We're going to have to fight our way past that monster."

The other Protectors nodded grimly, their expressions matching her own.

Gilkriz took a deep breath and stared at the wall he'd conjured. "Let me know when you're ready." He raised his hands.

"Wait!" Q'arlynd said. "There may be another way to reach the Acropolis."

Leliana turned. "What way is that, Q'arlynd? Spit it out."

"I have an idea, Lady, inspired by the combined magic we three wizards just utilized to open the door." He gestured at the wall. The door, closed, was once again cloaked by illusion.

"Go on," Leliana said.

"You'll be utilizing positive energy to destroy the void-stone, correct?"

"That's the general plan. With Eilistraee's blessing, enough of us will get close enough to it to do just that."

Q'arlynd actually smiled. "What if I told you I could get *all* of us to the Acropolis?" He snapped his fingers. "Like that."

"I'm listening."

Q'arlynd slapped a hand against the wall. "The only thing preventing me from teleporting us into the cavern that holds the Acropolis is the *Faerzress*. There may be a way to counter it, however."

Gilkriz's eyebrows rose. "Suddenly you're an expert on *Faerzress?*"

Q'arlynd smiled. "When I lingered behind at the Moondeep, I conducted an experiment. I attempted a teleport. Faerie fire didn't erupt from my body, as it did back in Sshamath, but from the cavern wall that I . . . inadvertently touched. From within the *Faerzress*. The touch of my body somehow drew it to the surface of the rock. I think the problem lies within us—some unique link we drow have to *Faerzress* energy, which in turn is fed by negative energy. We draw the *Faerzress* in, somehow, and release it as faerie fire. It would therefore follow that, if we can fill our bodies with positive energy, we can force the *Faerzress* out. Then I can—"

All at once, Leliana saw what he was getting at. "Teleport us all to the Acropolis," she said, finishing his thought for him.

"Exactly."

"All very well, in theory," Gilkriz said in a dry voice. "But Q'arlynd's never even seen the Acropolis."

"I studied the map and heard a detailed description of the temple. For me, that's enough."

Leliana nodded. "I think it's worth a try."

The others nodded. All except Gilkriz, who stood with his arms folded, fingers drumming restlessly against his sleeves.

"All right then." Q'arlynd shrugged back his *piwafwi* and flexed his fingers. "Eldrinn, stand next to me; I may need your assistance with the spell. The rest of you, form a circle around me and link hands. As I finish my casting, I'll touch one of you, and we'll all go together."

"Eldrinn's a novice," Gilkriz protested. "What help will he be?"

"That's where you're wrong," Q'arlynd said. "Eldrinn's assisted my teleports before. He knows exactly what to do, and when. Just join hands with the others, Gilkriz, and you'll come along. Unless . . ." Q'arlynd arched an eyebrow. "Unless you'd rather remain here, snug and secure behind these lovely walls you just conjured, until it's all over and we can send someone back to fetch you."

The conjurer's nostrils flared, but he joined the circle. "I *still* don't believe this will work," he muttered.

"You haven't seen me teleport." The wizard nodded in Leliana's direction. "She has."

Gilkriz said nothing.

"Just be sure," Q'arlynd instructed the priestesses, "to maintain the flow of positive energy even after we reach the Acropolis. Hold it for at least a moment or two. Otherwise, we may miss our mark. If we land off target, we could wind up in solid stone. And that would be, well . . . unfortunate."

"Define 'unfortunate,' " Leliana said.

Q'arlynd grimaced. "Missing a few pounds of flesh, at best. At worst, you'll be meeting Eilistraee a lot sooner than anticipated."

Leliana turned to the priestesses. "Make your preparations. If this works, in another moment or two we'll be facing not just Crones and their undead minions, but a ghost."

The Protectors readied their weapons.

Leliana glanced at the halfling. "Brindell?"

The halfling tucked a silence stone into the pocket of her sling. "I'll be ready."

The priestesses formed a circle facing inward. Each stood with her sword in her right hand, her left hand on the shoulder of the person next to her. Their swords hummed softly. Gilkriz stood next to Brindell, who had to stand on tiptoe to reach his shoulder.

"Right," Leliana said. "Let's begin."

They sang, each keeping her attention focused inward, on the energy they were summoning into themselves and channeling to the center of their circle, where Q'arlynd and Eldrinn stood. On the song's second verse, a glimmer of moonlight blossomed around each priestess. Slowly, the circles of light expanded into the center of the circle. Each left a patch of shadow in its wake: shadow that obscured the glow of the *Faerzress*.

"It's working!" Eldrinn cried. "I can feel it!"

Q'arlynd grasped the boy's wrist. He raised his free hand; it hovered just over Leliana's shoulder. She felt the positive energy fill her, a sense of warmth and well-being as soothing as a soft hymn. She nodded at Q'arlynd: the signal. He snapped out an incantation and slapped his hand down on her shoulder.

Her stomach did a flipflop as the floor lurched sideways under her feet. Suddenly, she was standing with the others next to a building that loomed darkly beside them. The temple atop the Acropolis! Startled Crones whirled to face them, shrieking in anger. The Protectors' swords replied with a gleeful peal.

Just as Q'arlynd had instructed them, the Protectors held the final note of their song a moment longer. Q'arlynd's hand lifted from Leliana's shoulder. His eyes met hers, and his expression seemed strangely apologetic. Then he and Eldrinn disappeared.

Leliana blinked in surprise. Had something gone wrong with his spell?

"Cowards!" Gilkriz shouted at the empty space within their circle.

The Crones surged forward, hands raised. Fell magic crackled from their fingertips. At Leliana's shouted order the Protectors whirled to face outward, raised swords pealing as the priestesses cried out their battle hymns. Then the Crones were upon them.

As the Protectors fought with song and sword, Brindell slipped between the combatants and ran toward the temple, her sling whirling. She must have spotted something within the building. A moment later, a monstrous figure, twice the height of a drow and with spider legs protruding from her chest, burst from the doorway.

"Halisstra?" Leliana gasped. "But how . . . ?"

Brindell hurled her stone. It struck Halisstra's chest dead center, between the scrabbling spider legs. Halisstra skidded to a halt and shouted something, but her voice was swallowed by the silence that clung to her.

A hand raked Leliana's side, tearing open an bloody wound—a Crone, taking advantage of the distraction. Leliana slashed, her sword severing the Crone's arm. The Crone reeled away, howling.

Leliana chanced another glance and felt the blood drain from her face. A ghostly form had risen out of solid stone directly behind Brindell—the translucent image of a Crone. The spirit they'd been warned about! The halfling had her back to the thing; she'd never see it in time.

Leliana dodged between two Crones and rushed the spirit, singing a battle prayer that made her sword shimmer. But even as her weapon swept down, the spirit threw back her head and wailed.

The sound stabbed into Leliana like an icy finger, breaking her stride. Her sword connected with something—a glancing blow, struck a heartbeat too late. Leliana staggered past the spirit, her heart fluttering in her chest. All around her, she saw her companions turn an ashen gray as they sagged to the ground. Leliana and Tash'kla remained on their feet, but only barely. Tash'kla was bent over nearly double, arms clutching her chest, her sword limp in her hand.

The spirit gave a ghostly laugh. "Finish them," she whispered.

The Crones closed in.

Cavatina stared at the spiderlike figure up ahead. Large as an ox, it stood at the end of the thread-thin path of moonlight she'd been following. She'd seen its kind before: retrievers often ventured into the prime material plane to hunt down those who had drawn the ire of a demon lord. She wasn't surprised to find one guarding the portal.

What was surprising was that the retriever hadn't moved. She'd observed it for some time, and it hadn't so much as shifted a leg. It stood, rigid as a statue. It might have been poised there for a day, or for a millennium, waiting for someone to approach the portal.

Cavatina took a deep breath, mentally preparing herself. The battle with Wendonai had left her drained. She was naked, armed only with her singing sword. She would have to be careful.

She approached the retriever warily, sword in hand. The portal was a hole in the ground a pace or two from it, a round pucker in the hard, cracked soil. Next to this opening lay a huddled body. As she drew nearer, she recognized him by his robe: Daffir, the human diviner.

Even from several paces away, she could see that the human was dead. Fire had burned away his hair and crisped much of his scalp, revealing charred bone. The lenses that once hovered in front of his eyes lay on the ground nearby. His robe was a shredded mess, soaked with blood. He lay with one arm thrust stiffly forward, the fingers of that hand curled tight around a small silver disk. Sunlight glinted from it.

Cavatina crept closer. The retriever remained motionless.

She stepped around Daffir's body, close enough to have touched the demon. She leaned forward and prodded one of its legs with the point of her sword.

The blade clinked against solid stone.

She glanced back at Daffir. "So you managed to turn one of its rays back at it, did you?" She raised her sword in salute to the dead male. "Well done." She sang a prayer, asking Eilistraee to claim Daffir's soul, should it not already be spoken for by some other deity.

Her feet were sore from her long walk across the hard, salty plain and she was tired of having to constantly carry her sword. Daffir had boots and belt. She took both. She hacked off the bottom of the leather sheath that held his dagger, modifying it to accommodate her sword. Then she cinched the belt around her waist. The wizard's clothes were a ruined, bloody mess, so she left them on his body. She picked up his eye lenses and mirror and tied them into a piece of cloth, then knotted this around his wrist. If the priestesses back at the Promenade succeeded in reviving Daffir, he would need them.

These preparations made, she seized Daffir by the ankles and dragged him over to the portal. Rolling him into it wouldn't be a very dignified way to get him back, but she couldn't very well carry him. If there were hostile creatures on the other side of the portal, she'd need both hands free to fight.

With a grunt, she rolled Daffir into the hole.

His body vanished.

Cavatina drew her sword and held it in both hands. "Watch over me, Eilistraee," she whispered. "Guide my steps."

She leaped into the portal.

"Down" was suddenly behind her. She landed flat on her back on a cold stone floor, knocking the wind from her lungs. She scrambled to her feet and whirled, her sword humming a deadly warning. She was in a room, next to a quicksilver pool—a room dominated by a goat-headed statue twice her height.

A statue of the demon prince Orcus.

"Eilistraee!" she cried. "Shield me!"

Moonlight streaked with shadow erupted from her skin, washing out the fainter light of the *Faerzress*-impregnated walls, ceiling and floor.

The statue didn't move. It was, it would seem, mere stone. But appearances could be deceiving.

She stood directly in front of an arch that led into darkness, and a second arch stood on the other side of the statue. Across the room was a slab of studded iron that looked like a door. She backed away from the statue, half turned to the door, and searched for a handle with one hand.

There wasn't one.

"Looks like there's only one way out of here," she whispered, speaking to Daffir's corpse as much as to herself. "That other portal. I just wish you were still alive to tell me where it leads."

She dragged his body in front of the second arch. She lay her sword on the floor, tucked her hands under his body, and started to roll him into the portal. Before she could finish, she felt something tug on Daffir. Alarmed, she yanked the body back—hard enough to reveal hands clutching Daffir's robe. Each of the dark fingers was adorned with a silver ring.

A Crone!

Cavatina snatched up her sword. As the silver-ringed hands yanked Daffir back through the portal, she thrust through it, aiming for the spot where the Crone would be. The sweet peal of her sword was muffled as it passed into what lay beyond. She felt the weapon strike home. She yanked it back; the blade was bright with blood.

"Eilistraee!" she cried.

Sword singing, she charged into the portal.

Q'arlynd landed on a stone floor with an ankle-jolting thud. Thick, hot smoke surrounded him, blown by a roaring wind. Beside him, Eldrinn staggered sideways, his hand tearing out of Q'arlynd's grasp. Q'arlynd heard the clatter of the staff falling and rolling away. He could see nothing, however. The smoke was too thick, and it stabbed into his throat and lungs each time he breathed. Tears streamed from his eyes.

"Eldrinn!" he coughed. "The staff!"

He heard more rattling.

"Got it," the boy wheezed back.

Through the smoke, Q'arlynd saw a blue-green glow that shone brightly from the floor and walls. *Faerzress*? Worry flooded him. Had he landed off target? Or had the *Faerzress* there simply grown that strong?

"Someone's in the corridor," a husky female voice cried from somewhere to Q'arlynd's left. "Inside the smoke!"

"Alexa?" Eldrinn shouted back. "Is that you?"

"It's Eldrinn! He's back!"

More voices were talking, but not loud enough for Q'arlynd to make out the words.

"And Q'arlynd—I'm here, too!" he shouted. He didn't want anyone blasting him with a spell. When no one did, he let out a sigh of relief—which quickly turned into a rattling cough.

Eldrinn bumped into him from behind, and Q'arlynd grabbed the boy's *piwafwi*. Dragging Eldrinn in his wake, he fought his way toward the voices, forcing himself sideways through the howling wind.

They were out of the smoke. Kraanfhaor's Door was just ahead, and so were Alexa, Baltak, Piri, and Zarifar. Q'arlynd's teleport had been precisely on target, after all.

"What in the Nine Hells . . ." he coughed, ". . . are you apprentices . . ." he coughed again, ". . . *doing?*"

Piri crouched, holding a rod that extended into a hole he was busy burning in the stone beside the door. Heat waves danced above the rod. But for his demon-skinned hands, Piri's skin would have blistered away. Smoke billowed past him, out of the blackened hole.

Zarifar stood next to him, twiddling his index fingers, directing the smoke away down the corridor Q'arlynd had just teleported to. He stared dreamily at the fierce horizontal tornados his spell had turned the smoke into.

Baltak and Alexa stood next to a pile of gear. Bedrolls had been spread out on the floor. Alexa hurried forward to help Eldrinn, who'd doubled over in a coughing fit. Baltak remained where he was, hands on his hips. He'd abandoned his owlbear accoutrements for something new. His muscular body bore a layer of coin-sized, ice-white scales. The dragons carved into the door's surface had probably inspired his latest shapeshift.

"About time you two got back," he bellowed, his voice reverberating in his chest. "We're almost through."

"Let's see if you're right." Piri eased the rod out of the hole, hand over hand. Metal scraped against stone. A spent stonefire bomb pot was attached to the end of the rod, and the metal just below it was white-hot. The light of it lent a garish sheen to Piri's oily, green-tinted skin.

"How was Sschindylryn?" Alexa asked.

Eldrinn straightened. "Huh?"

"Knee-deep in travelers, as usual," Q'arlynd quickly answered.

"And the trade mission?" Baltak asked.

"It's drawing to a successful conclusion, even as we speak," Q'arlynd said, catching Eldrinn's eye.

"That's right," Eldrinn said. "Successful. No need for us there, any more. The negotiations were going so well we were able to leave early."

Q'arlynd hid his wince behind a nod and a smile. The boy's fumbling words sounded suspicious. But at least Eldrinn had stopped protesting. The boy had taken some convincing, but he'd eventually come around to Q'arlynd's way of thinking.

Neither of them, Q'arlynd had explained to Eldrinn before they'd teleported, knew a spell that would channel positive energy. They would be unable to help destroy the voidstone. Once Q'arlynd teleported the priestesses to the Acropolis, their part in the expedition would be at an end.

In the meantime, there was Kraanfhaor's Door to worry about. The staff had to be used before the *Faerzress* grew so intense that it blocked divinations altogether. Had Q'arlynd and Eldrinn remained at the Acropolis and waited for the priestesses to finish their work, it might have been days before they could return to Kraanfhaor's Door. By then, it might have been too late.

Thanks to Q'arlynd's teleport, the priestesses had sprung a surprise attack on the Acropolis. Even then, those singing swords of theirs would be making short work of the Crones. And Leliana and her priestesses would deal with the voidstone. All according to plan.

Q'arlynd had no reason to feel guilty.

None at all.

Piri let the rod clatter to the floor and waved his hands back and forth, cooling them. He could feel heat, even if it didn't harm him. "I hear Sschindylryn is having problems with their *Faerzress*." He nodded at the walls. "It's getting worse here, too."

Q'arlynd gave a noncommittal grunt and walked over to the door. Smoke curled from the hole beside it, though not in the dark billows it had before. Zarifar was still playing with the wind he'd conjured up, so it was hard to hear what anyone said above its roaring.

Q'arlynd caught his arm. "Stop that."

Zarifar lowered his hands and blinked. "Oh, hello, Q'arlynd. Where did you come from?"

Q'arlynd crouched and peered into the hole. Though the stonefire bomb had blackened and melted the stone next to it, the door itself was unblemished. Not so much as a streak of soot marked it. The hole was about ten paces deep, the length of the rod Piri had just hauled out of it. Kraanfhaor's Door, Q'arlynd saw, was just as thick.

He touched the front of the door. The stone under his fingers was cooler by far than the hot air that filled the corridor.

Q'arlynd nodded down at the stonefire bomb. "That isn't going to work."

"That's what I told them," Baltak boomed.

"We've proved one thing, at least," Piri said. "The stone that makes up that door exists in some sort of extradimensional space. Each time the stonefire started to reveal the far side of the door, it extended farther."

Alexa picked up a wooden tray and began sorting through the glass vials it held. "I tried several different acids on the door itself, but none made even the slightest mark."

"Frost won't crack it, either," Baltak boomed. He slapped a hand against the door. His fingers ended in claws, clear and glistening as ice. They scritched against the door as he drew them across it. "The stone can't even be scratched."

"There are patterns," Zarifar said. "I tried to identify them, but I can't quite . . ." His fingers traced lines in the air. "They seem so familiar, and yet . . ." he shrugged and let his hand fall, "they elude me."

"Excellent!" Q'arlynd announced.

The others stared at him blankly.

"Listen to you—you're working together. Well done."

His students glanced sidelong at one another when he said that—wary that he'd been talking between the lines. Had they let down their guard, shown some vulnerability, done something wrong?

Q'arlynd chuckled. "Well done," he repeated. "And I mean just what I say."

It was the truth. Leaving his apprentices on their own had been the best move he could have made. Had he remained there, he would have directed their experiments, led them along by the nose like rothé. Instead they'd tried to come up with solutions on their own. Fruitless attempts, but attempts just the same. Their initial decision to work together might have been motivated by a desire to keep an eye on each other, but that didn't matter. They'd become a team.

And since Q'arlynd knew how to open the door, they'd reap the rewards.

The anticipation nearly made Q'arlynd giddy.

He realized he was smiling. He set his face in a more serious expression. A smile could be an unnerving thing, to a drow. It usually preceded some sort of painful punishment.

"Eldrinn," Q'arlynd said, "your staff. It's time to open this door."

"You really think the staff is the solution?"

"We'll know that soon enough."

"I can't believe it!" Baltak shouted. "Q'arlynd knew how to open it, all along."

"Why didn't you tell us?" Piri asked, his voice thick with suspicion.

"It was a test," Q'arlynd answered, "of your willingness to work together. You passed."

He took the staff from Eldrinn. As the others crowded around, he closed his eyes. It took a moment to block out the rustles of their clothing, and their rapid, anxious breaths, but soon he achieved full concentration. He drew the staff toward himself and touched his forehead to the crystal at the center of it, just as Daffir had done.

"Show me the past," he whispered. "Show me how the Miyeritari opened this door."

Despite Q'arlynd's concentration, he heard Alexa's surprised murmur, "It can do that?"

Q'arlynd waited several moments, but nothing happened. No visions popped into his mind, no voices whispered in his ear. He tried for several moments more, with his eyes open. Nothing.

Heat prickled his cheeks. Daffir had never uttered a word when using the staff, but perhaps there was some silent mental command that was required. Eldrinn had assured Q'arlynd there wasn't, but knowledge of the command may have been stripped from the boy's mind by the feeblewit spell.

Q'arlynd felt a mind tickle his—probably Baltak. Q'arlynd pushed whoever it was out. "Don't distract me," he growled. "I'll show you how it's done in just a moment."

He decided to test the staff. Silently, he implored it to show him a vision, from just a short time ago, of the arrival of himself and Eldrinn. A vision instantly coalesced in his mind: the pair of them, stumbling out of a thick pall of smoke. Elated, Q'arlynd banished that vision and concentrated harder, trying to force his mind back to the distant past. Centuries ago. Millennia. He caught a fleeting glimpse of a brown-skinned elf, standing in front of the door, hand raised. Then the *Faerzress* crackled across the vision, obscuring it in a blaze of blue-green light.

"Spit me on a lance," Q'arlynd whispered fiercely.

He glared at the nearest wall. The *Faerzress* wasn't strong enough—yet—to block divinations entirely. But it wasn't allowing him to maintain the concentration he needed to reach so far back into the past.

Q'arlynd's palms were damp with sweat. The voidstone, obviously, had not yet been destroyed. Had his decision to part ways with the priestesses been a terrible mistake? Were Leliana and the others lying dead atop the Acropolis, even then? If so, the *Faerzress* there would continue to brighten, eventually rendering all divination impossible. If Q'arlynd had remained at the Acropolis and blasted a few of the Crones with his spells, might the priestesses have prevailed?

"What's wrong, Q'arlynd?" Eldrinn asked.

"Nothing," Q'arlynd said tersely. Irritation flared inside him at the fact that Eldrinn, a mere boy—an apprentice—had been able to pluck the necessary vision from the past when Q'arlynd couldn't. But that had been nearly two years ago, prior to the *Faerzress*. He . . .

Just a moment. Q'arlynd didn't need to look back to the time of ancient Miyeritar. Kraanfhaor's Door had been opened much more recently than that. Eldrinn had opened it less than two years ago. And Q'arlynd himself had opened it even more recently than that.

He closed his eyes again and concentrated. Show me myself, opening the door, he silently commanded the staff. Show me how I did it.

The *Faerzress* still impeded the divination, but it didn't obscure it entirely. Q'arlynd watched, fascinated, as an image of himself appeared. The vision-Q'arlynd had a *kiira* on his forehead, and was walking toward the door. It was odd, observing himself—and a little unnerving, to see the glassy look in his own eyes. The *kiira* had been utterly controlling him. He watched intently as the vision-Q'arlynd stepped up to the door, raised a hand, touched a finger to the massive block of stone and . . .

The vision-Q'arlynd bent forward and cupped a hand over his moving fingers, blocking Q'arlynd's view of his hand.

The *kiira* had anticipated that someone might be watching.

Q'arlynd took a deep breath, steadying himself. It didn't matter. He could still solve the riddle by observing Eldrinn. There had been no *kiira* on Eldrinn's forehead, the first time *he'd* opened the door.

He tried again. Show me Eldrinn, he silently commanded the staff. Show me the first time he opened Kraanfhaor's Door.

In his mind's eye, Eldrinn appeared, standing in front of Kraanfhaor's Door. The boy was wearing different clothes, and was holding the staff. Another male—the soldier Q'arlynd had found dead on the High Moor—stood next to Eldrinn. The fellow was going to die soon but didn't know it, poor wretch.

Q'arlynd shoved the useless sentiment aside and concentrated on Eldrinn. He watched as the boy held the staff to his forehead, just as Q'arlynd was doing. After a moment, Eldrinn laughed. His hand moved up to the door, his finger traced a sign.

Q'arlynd leaned forward expectantly but could see only a portion of the sign, the same sequence they'd glimpsed during their experiment with the chitine. The rest was hidden when the soldier stepped up next to Eldrinn, blocking Q'arlynd's view.

The vision faded.

"Well?" Baltak boomed.

"I'm making progress," Q'arlynd snapped.

He stood, thinking. If he shifted position, to the opposite side of the vision-Eldrinn, he might be able to see the entire sign. He strode to that side of the door and summoned up the vision again. He peered intently through the obscuring blur of faerie fire as the vision-Eldrinn went through the same motions, walking up to the door, touching the staff to his forehead, and tracing his finger along the door.

Then the same thing happened, someone blocked the view. And yet Q'arlynd could see the soldier clearly, standing just behind Eldrinn. Had a *third* person been there when Eldrinn opened the door?

Whoever it had been, Q'arlynd couldn't make out details. The form was vague, indistinct. It was there, but somehow . . . not there.

Q'arlynd's jaw was clenched. Realizing that would betray his frustration, he pretended to stretch sore neck muscles. He didn't want the others thinking the door had defeated him. Calm down, he told himself, and try again.

He moved to the other side of the door and summoned up the vision again. Once again, someone blocked his view. Q'arlynd concentrated on this person, trying to bring him into focus. The staff fought him. It felt as if the diamond and his forehead were two lodestones, pushing each other apart.

Q'arlynd persevered, concentrating until sweat beaded on his temple.

At last he saw that the third person clearly. The person's back was to him, but Q'arlynd recognized him at once by his distinctive hairclip. It was *Eldrinn* blocking the view.

For a moment, Q'arlynd thought the real Eldrinn had stepped in front of him. Then he remembered that his eyes were closed. The duplicate Eldrinn was also holding the staff. The two Eldrinns were identical in every way, except that one held the staff to the side as he traced the sign on the door, while the other held the staff to his forehead, eyes closed. And no matter what Q'arlynd did, the second Eldrinn blocked his view.

Q'arlynd tried to force the second Eldrinn out of the vision, so that he could see how the first was opening the door, but the staff wouldn't let him. He drew the staff closer, until the diamond was a painful dent against his forehead, and gritted out through clenched teeth, "Show . . . me . . ."

The staff flew from Q'arlynd's fingers and clattered to the floor.

Q'arlynd swore, barely suppressing the urge to kick it.

"What's wrong?" Piri asked, backing away in alarm.

Alexa shrugged. "Maybe it doesn't want to show him the past."

"Maybe he's got it wrong," Baltak rumbled. "Maybe the staff doesn't show the past, but the future."

"It shows both," Eldrinn said. "I'm certain of—"

"Of course it does!" Q'arlynd cried. He threw back his head and laughed. That was it! *That* was why there had been a double Eldrinn in the vision, because the staff was showing Q'arlynd two pasts at the same time—pasts that were separated by mere moments. Eldrinn hadn't used the staff to reveal how the ancient Miyeritari had opened the door. The boy had looked into the future, instead. His own future. He'd watched *himself* open the door, then duplicated what was about to happen.

Q'arlynd reached out and gently punched Eldrinn on the shoulder. "*Very* clever. Very clever indeed."

The boy blinked, uncomprehending. "Huh?"

The other apprentices mirrored his blank stare.

Q'arlynd scooped up the staff. "All right," he told his students. "I'm going to try it again. As before, please maintain silence. And . . ." he tapped his temple, "keep your distance." He closed his eyes and touched his forehead to the diamond.

Show me the future, he silently commanded. Show me myself, a few moments from now, opening the door.

The moment he thought the words, the push-pull sensation came back. He tightened his grip on the staff, refusing to let it tear from his hands. Then the vision came, as commanded. Q'arlynd watched, barely breathing, as his hand lifted to trace a sign on the door. A *different* sign from the one the vision-Eldrinn had traced.

Then, just as the *kiira*-dominated Q'arlynd from the past had done, the Q'arlynd of the future deliberately hid the sign he was tracing from sight.

"Why did you do that?" he exploded.

The vision ended.

His apprentices stared at him, waiting expectantly. For once, even Baltak said nothing.

Q'arlynd was still trying to make sense of what he'd just seen. Like the *kiira*, his future self didn't want anyone to see how he opened the door. But that meant that Q'arlynd himself couldn't see how it was done. Yet *someone* had to observe how it was done, or the door couldn't be opened.

Q'arlynd stroked his chin, thinking. An idea occurred to him—one that he almost instinctively rejected. Grudgingly, however, he realized it was the only course of action that might work. If he invited the others into his mind, let them watch the vision-Q'arlynd from the future open the door, perhaps one of them might able to recognize the sign from its first, preliminary motions.

He glanced around at his apprentices. At Baltak, his broad chest puffed with his own self-importance. Piri, slinking about in his demon skin. Eldrinn, chewing his lip, no doubt nervous about what his father was going to say about their having abandoned the expedition to the Acropolis. Alexa, standing next to the boy, taller than him by a head. And Zarifar, who stared dreamily at the door, not paying the slightest bit of attention to the others.

"I need your help," Q'arlynd said, each word a stone he had to force out. "Use your rings to join minds with me, everyone. Observe the vision I'm seeing. You're about to see me, in the immediate future, opening Kraanfhaor's Door. Pay close attention to my hand, we need to know what arcane sign is being made."

Eldrinn's eyebrows rose. "So *that's* how I did it."

"Yes."

The others glanced at the boy, a new respect in their eyes.

"Let's begin," Q'arlynd told them.

A moment later, he felt them slip into his mind, one by one. Thrusting their way in or stealing in on velvet slippers, as was their wont. Baltak had to elbow Zarifar to get the latter's attention, but at last the geometer mage was inside, too—for all the good that would do.

Q'arlynd drew the staff toward himself. "Show me," he commanded it. "Show me the future. Show me myself, opening the door."

As it had before, the vision unfolded. When it finished, Q'arlynd lowered the staff. "Well?"

His apprentices glanced sidelong at one another, stared at the ceiling, or scowled, thinking—all but Zarifar, who swayed back and forth, humming. Then Zarifar struck a pose. He pirouetted on one foot, one hand raised above his head.

Piri eased away, as if afraid Zarifar's madness might be contagious.

Q'arlynd grabbed Zarifar's wrist. "What are you doing?"

Zarifar tugged against the restraining hand as if he couldn't understand why he'd suddenly stopped twirling. "The pattern," he said. His raised fingers twitched. "I'm the *pattern*."

Alexa signed something to Eldrinn. Q'arlynd caught only the last word and the finger flick that made it a question: . . . *feeblewit?*

Q'arlynd sighed and let go of Zarifar's arm. Maybe Alexa was right. Something had stripped both his own and Eldrinn's minds of memories. It was possible that merely observing that last vision might have done the same to Zarifar.

Zarifar stopped dancing and grabbed Q'arlynd's left arm in both hands. "The *pattern*," he said again, his eyes bright and intense, all trace of their former dreaminess gone. He yanked Q'arlynd's hand up in front of his face and waved it back and forth. "The pattern!"

Q'arlynd scoffed. All he was looking at was his own raised hand and the leather wristband below it, which bore his House insignia.

"Yes," Zarifar breathed. "*That* pattern."

Belatedly, Q'arlynd realized the apprentice's mind was still touching his own.

Zarifar at last let go of his arm.

Q'arlynd realized his mouth was hanging open. He didn't care. He couldn't believe what he'd just heard. "*That's* what opened Kraanfhaor's Door?" He waggled his fingers, pretending to practice a gesture. Silently, he asked Zarifar a question: *Have I got it right? The pattern is the glyph for House Melarn?*

Zarifar nodded.

Q'arlynd had to fight hard to hide his smile.

The others might, in time, figure out the truth. Q'arlynd doubted it would matter. In his vision of Eldrinn opening the door—the vision he *hadn't* shared with them—Eldrinn had traced a different symbol on the door. A different House glyph, Q'arlynd surmised. Likely that of his own House.

Kraanfhaor's Door, he suspected, would open only to someone who knew how to use his own, very personal, knock.

Q'arlynd understood why he had hidden his hand from view. Why he *would* hide his hand from view.

"Right," he said. "Time to get this thing open."

He handed the staff to Eldrinn then turned, faced the door, and raised his hand.

CHAPTER 13

Halisstra stared at the ghost that floated a few paces away. The spirit stared back at her with hollow, haunted eyes. Behind the ghost, a drow female in gray robes and skullcap slipped quietly out through the door, exiting the ruined building.

The spirit's voice was a chill whisper. "You serve Lolth?"

Halisstra gave a feral grin. "I *was* the Lady Penitent. But no more. I'm dead."

"Dead?" The spirit laughed softly. "No. You live."

Halisstra blinked in surprise. She was alive? She glanced down at herself and saw her bruises fading, the slow knitting of the flesh she'd scraped in her tumble from the portal. The sight sent a chill through her. She *hadn't* died on the Negative Energy Plane. Lolth, once again, had forced her to live.

"No," she snarled in dismay.

The spirit drifted closer. "You wish to die?"

Halisstra took a step back. "Where am I?" She glanced around. "What is this place?"

"The Acropolis of Thanatos."

Halisstra noted the rings on those ghostly fingers. "You serve Kiaransalee."

"Yes."

Through the ghost's translucent body, Halisstra spotted a tiny spider on the wall behind the spirit. Her eyes widened. Lolth's sign—in Kiaransalee's stronghold. Halisstra hadn't arrived by chance. The Spider Queen had sent her.

A test!

Halisstra flexed her claws. Her eyes locked on the spirit. Before she could spring, however, a commotion erupted outside. Halisstra heard several female voices, singing a hymn, and a male voice, shouting an insult. The ghost started, let out a whispered curse, then slipped through a wall, disappearing.

Halisstra hurried to the doorway and peered out.

Five priestesses of Eilistraee stood in a circle, swords in hand. With them was a male wearing cloth-of-gold and a skullcap. They were surrounded by more than a dozen of Kiaransalee's priestesses. Gray-robed Crones bore down on them, cackling and chanting.

Halisstra hesitated. What did Lolth expect her to do? Slay the living? The dead? Both?

One of Eilistraee's priestesses—a halfling—burst from the circle, whirling a sling over her head. Halisstra had been spotted! That decided it. She leaped from the ruined building. She, too, could fight with song—with her *bae'qeshel* magic. But even as she began to sing, the halfling's stone thudded into her chest and smashed to pieces against her hardened skin. Silence enveloped her.

The halfling halted and fitted another stone to her sling. She didn't see the spirit-Crone rising out of the stone

behind her. Another of Eilistraee's priestesses spotted it and
rushed the spirit, sword raised. Before she could get close,
the ghostly Crone opened her mouth in a wail Halisstra
couldn't hear. Like stalks of scythed wheat, the priestesses
of Eilistraee fell.

Halisstra snarled, envying them.

Now only the Crones remained. No matter. Halisstra
would still do her best to prove herself. She lashed out with
a fist, snapping the neck of a nearby Crone. She tore a second
to pieces with her claws.

The ghost-Crone turned, her pale face a study in rage.
Her features stretched, thinned, became even more ghastly.
When the priestess shrieked, Halisstra could feel waves of
magical fear billowing toward her. Her body, however, was a
rock that parted this chill current. The magical fear skewed
off to each side, leaving her unscathed.

Halisstra taunted the spirit in silent speech. *Kill me.
Lolth dares you to try.*

Mention of the goddess's name maddened the spirit. She
howled loud enough to send a tremble through the stone on
which Halisstra stood. Something hit the ground next to
Halisstra's foot in utter silence, exploding into white fragments: a skull. Halisstra glanced up. The building she'd
just exited stood in an enormous cavern with a knobby
white ceiling. Loosened by the ghost's wailing, other skulls
tumbled from it. Through this ghastly rain, the ghost
drifted forward.

Halisstra threw open her arms in invitation.

Out of the corner of her eye, she saw one of the gray-robed
females pounce on a body that had just rolled into view out
of nowhere. As the female bent, a sword blade skewered
her eye and exploded out of the back of her skull. The blade
yanked back, disappearing. A drow leaped into view through
an invisible gate—a female who was naked, bruised, and
holding a singing sword.

Cavatina. She had escaped the Abyss!

The Darksong Knight's eyes locked accusingly on Halisstra, who made out the word without hearing it: "You!"

Halisstra whirled and sprinted back to the hollowed-out building. The ghostly Crone flew after her—moving faster than Halisstra had anticipated. Just as Halisstra reached the doorway, the ghost struck her back and flowed through her, boiling out of her chest in a chill white cloud.

Emptiness rushed into Halisstra in an icy wave, draining her of all sensation. She stumbled and fell. As she tumbled through the air toward the black sphere, she saw Cavatina bearing down on the ghost from behind, sword in one hand, holy symbol in the other, her body and weapon wreathed in twined auras of radiance and shadow. Then the Darksong Knight thrust her sword into the ghost's back. The ghost whirled, Cavatina's blade still within her spinning torso, and plunged her dagger into Cavatina's throat.

For the space of a heartbeat, the two glared at one another, eye to eye. Then the ghost exploded into a thousand fragments of mist. Cavatina slumped to the ground, blood pumping from her throat. And Halisstra was sucked into the void.

Q'arlynd traced the House Melarn glyph on the door with a forefinger. Just as Zarifar had observed, it resembled a dancing drow: triangle head; two strokes down for arms, one hand turned down, the other up; two angled strokes that were bent legs, each ending in a crescent representing a foot.

Q'arlynd lowered his hands. He waited for the door to open, barely daring to breathe. This was it, the moment he'd been striving toward for so long. A moment more, and wealth unheard of would fall into his hands.

He kept watch on his five apprentices. He'd ushered them all to his right, to a spot where he could watch for sudden moves. Each looked tense, expectant. Even Zarifar leaned forward, eyes on the door.

For several painfully long moments, there was only silence.

"Huh," Baltak grunted. "It didn't work."

Q'arlynd wet his lips. He could see that. He'd try again. He raised his hand and touched the door . . .

And felt a bulge rise under his fingertip. A bulge with a sharp point.

A *kiira!* Expelled from the door.

With trembling fingers, he eased it out of the block of carved stone. Gleaming crimson against his dark fingers, hexagonal in cross section, it was half the length of his little finger and tapered to a point at each end.

Eldrinn's hand twitched in a silent gesture: the betrayal Q'arlynd had been fearing, but from an unexpected source. With a thought, Q'arlynd activated his ring, rendering all of his apprentices rigid. Then he shook his head. "Eldrinn. I never thought you'd be the one to—"

"Cahal!" Piri cried. He lunged forward and slapped a hand against Q'arlynd's cheek—a bare-fingered hand.

Q'arlynd leaped away from Piri, but too late. The left side of his face was already numb. A cold, prickling sensation spread down his neck, toward his heart. Poison! It didn't fell him, however. As a boy, Q'arlynd had been deliberately exposed to several common poisons to inoculate him against the worst of their sting.

Piri's surprise at seeing Q'arlynd still on his feet gave Q'arlynd the instant he needed. He scrabbled at his pocket, found the fur-wrapped sliver of glass. He thrust it at Piri and shouted an evocation. Lightning burst from his hand, striking the other wizard in the chest.

Piri reeled back, clutching at the spot where his demon skin had been blasted away to expose raw red flesh. He raised his hand to cast a spell, but Q'arlynd's second lightning bolt slammed into him before he could complete it. Piri crashed into the wall, then slumped at the feet of the other apprentices, dead. Still frozen by the enchantment, they stared past him at the spot where Q'arlynd stood.

Q'arlynd glared at them, silently daring the rest of them to attempt what Piri just had. The poison had spread to his left arm; the fingers of that hand felt thick and unresponsive. But the poison had halted its spread after numbing that one arm. It wasn't strong enough to kill him.

The remaining four apprentices could see and hear him, even if they couldn't move or respond. Q'arlynd glanced down at Piri. Wisps of smoke rose from Piri's chest, filling the air with a burned-meat smell. Q'arlynd patted down the apprentice's pockets and found his ring.

"What he just did," he told the others in a flat voice as he tucked Piri's ring into a pocket, "was stupid." With his good hand, he lifted the *kiira* up where they could see it. "I promised to share the secrets of this lorestone with you. I'll keep that promise, but only if I can trust you. Your actions, when the enchantment I just cast on you wears off, will determine whether I keep that promise. In the meantime, please reflect on the fact that I'm the master of this school, and you four who remain are mere apprentices. Conduct yourselves accordingly."

Q'arlynd stared into the depths of the *kiira* and took a deep breath. Did he dare touch it to his forehead? Would the lorestone feeblemind him or rip all memory of what had just transpired from his mind?

He could feel an awareness pressing against his. Eldinn's. The boy's mind was filled with anger and outrage. A single thought forced its way through: *I tried to warn you about Piri. I saw him remove his ring.*

Q'arlynd's eyebrow rose. "Did you?" He'd been wrong about the boy; Eldrinn *hadn't* been about to cast a spell. He stood, stroking his chin, debating whether to release Eldrinn. The enchantment that rooted his apprentices to the spot would keep them out of mischief, but if anything went wrong in the meantime, the boy just might be able to help.

Q'arlynd touched Eldrinn's forehead, releasing him. "Stand over there," he instructed. "Keep silent and observe."

Eldrinn nodded. He did exactly as he was told.

Q'arlynd took a deep breath. Then he touched the *kiira* to his forehead.

A presence exploded into his mind, filling it. His own awareness became a small, slippery thing. A tiny minnow, swimming blindly up the vast current of time. The other awareness swept toward him: an enormous entity, swollen with knowledge. Powerful and ancient. Thousands upon thousands of memories, twined into a single sentience. Q'alrynd's intellect—the acquired knowledge of a century— was but a dim candle compared to the fierce red blaze of its combined wisdom. It blinded him, shrank his own paltry thoughts to insignificant shadows.

But at the same time, it welcomed him and made him warm.

Q'arlynd Melarn?

Q'arlynd's lips formed the required word of their own accord. "Yes."

Welcome, grandson.

The second word reverberated with deeper meaning. "Grandson" was inadequate to the task. Whoever was speaking through the *kiira* was much farther removed from Q'arlynd's time than that. Not mere centuries, but millennia.

Yes.

Q'arlynd no longer saw the corridor he stood in, the door in front of him, or his apprentices. All faded to distant shadows. His mind's eye filled instead with the figure the *kiira* shaped for it. A female with long white hair and a face that reminded Q'arlynd of his mother—but without the harsh lines and pinched, suspicious eyes. Instead, this female's expression conveyed both serenity and sorrow. On her forehead was a *kiira*. He was startled to see how dark it was against her skin. Her face wasn't an ebon hue, but something several shades lighter. A faded brown.

Understanding filled him. "You're a dark elf," he said. "Not a drow."

I am what we were.

The figure suddenly changed. A male stood where she'd been a moment ago, his skin as black as Q'arlynd's own. *And I am what we became.*

"I am honored to meet you, ancestors," Q'arlynd said, bowing low. Excitement surged through him. At last! Dark elves, from the time of the Descent! He couldn't even begin to guess what secrets their minds might hold.

High magic?

Q'arlynd nodded carefully. He'd have to keep a tighter rein on his thoughts. The *kiira* was able to hear his every word, even those that remained unspoken. "Yes. If you'll teach it to me."

The male ancestor's eyes blazed. *High magic is what condemned us! We were uncorrupted, still clean. Not like them.* Q'arlynd's head wrenched to the side, directed by a mind that was not his own. It forced him to look at the dim shadows that were his apprentices. *And yet we were condemned to share the same fate as these Ilythiiri.*

The sentience released Q'arlynd. Relief flooded him. Losing control of his body, even for a moment, had felt uncomfortably close to the time he'd been forced to wear his slave ring.

It wasn't enough for Aryvandaar to wipe Miyeritar from the face of Faerûn with their killing storm, the presence continued. *They could have left those few who survived to eke out their lives, but even that small mercy was beyond them. They and their allies had to alter our very bodies and drive us from the surface with their dominating magic, forever imprisoning us in the Dark Realms Below, together with those whose alliance we never sought.*

Q'arlynd drew in a sharp breath at what his ancestor had just said. Those two words. *Z'ress*—to hold dominance or to remain in force. And *faer*—magic. Q'arlynd had heard these words for a lifetime, but always the other way around. As *Faerzress*: "magic that remained." *Faerzress*, he'd been taught during his days as a novice at the Arcane Conservatory, was native to the Underdark. A form of raw magic that was similar to a volcano, or a rushing river, in its ability to build or carve away stone. Something that had always been around, from the moment of the world's creation.

With the words reversed, the resulting term took on an entirely different layer of meaning. "Dominating magic." Magic that compelled.

"You mean to tell me that *Faerzress* was a creation of high magic?" Q'arlynd asked. "That it was linked to the Descent?"

It created much of the Dark Realms Below. It lured us into that prison and locked us inside. The male frowned. *Did it never occur to you to question why the drow chose to found their cities in regions that were permeated with Faerzress?*

Q'arlynd understood. "Because we were drawn to it? That would make sense. It would ensure we couldn't teleport out. Or use divination to view the World Above."

Thus we were "contained." That was the word the mages of Aryvandaar coined for our imprisonment. We could, through manual effort, return to the surface—climb up through those few tunnels the Faerzress *had created that touched upon the World Above—but each time we emerged, the warriors of Aryvandaar beat us down again.* The male shook his head sadly. *And now we learn, through your thoughts, that it has become possible for us to escape this prison and reclaim the daylit sky—but that this freedom may once again be denied us. That the* Faerzress *ebbed, but is rising again.*

"I played my part. I teleported the Protectors to the Acropolis. Whatever the Crones are creating with the voidstone will be destroyed."

And if it isn't?

The male was replaced by the female who had spoken when Q'arlynd first placed the *kiira* on his forehead. *I am disappointed in you, grandson,* she intoned. *I would have expected more of someone who had sworn himself to the Lady.*

Q'arlynd glanced down at his wrist—at the House insignia that adorned his bracer. The glyph it bore was no mere stick figure. It was, just as Zarifar had observed, the figure of a dancing female.

Eilistraee.

Q'arlynd swore softly, "Mother's blood."

The male returned. *Indeed, grandson. It flows in your veins—and in the veins of all who can trace their ancestry back through bloodlines that are of pure Miyeritari descent. I suspect there are few of us, now—fewer with each generation. The Ilythiiri will have mixed their bloodlines with ours, producing yet more offspring who bear the demon's taint. But I am glad to hear that some of us continue to serve the goddess. Some of us remember her and keep the faith.*

Both voices spoke together. Male and female, backed up by a chorus of dozens more. *That is why this lorestone, and others like it, were placed here. Because we knew that, some day, the goddess might guide the footsteps of someone who would be able to hear us.*

"Me," Q'arlynd whispered.

Yes.

He touched a finger to his forehead. "But why did you strip me of my memories, the first time I wore you?"

That was a different selu'kiira. *Because you were not of its House, its embodied sentiences stripped you of all memory of it and forced you to return it to this place. They did the same to the boy. He was of the correct House but not wholly worthy of wearing that selu'kiira. He is fortunate that some dark elf blood, at least, flows in his veins. Else he would have died the instant it touched his mind.*

"Just as the chitines did?"

He felt their disapproval and overheard a snatch of conversation.

. . . certain he is Miyeritari?

He is.

"So . . ." Q'arlynd glanced at Kraanfhaor's Door. By concentrating, he could just make it out. "There are more *kiira* in there?"

Dozens. One from each House whose patriarch or matriarch survived the Killing Storm.

He touched his forehead. "And since I'm a Melarn—a pure descendant of your House—you'll teach me high magic?"

When you're ready to wield arselu'tel'quess, *then yes.*

"What must I do to prepare?"

Learn to trust.

"Done." Q'arlynd waved a hand in the direction of his apprentices. "You can see the proof. I brought them along to share in whatever knowledge I might glean."

Is that why three of them still stand bound by your magic?

"I had to. Piri—"

You placed that enchantment into the rings long before that.

"Yes, but the point remains that Piri—"

What did you expect of someone who bonded with a demon? the male chided.

You cannot fault Q'arlynd for trying, the female interjected. *The yearning for companionship, for family, comes instinctively to him. It was only the cruelties he suffered as a child that beat it into dormancy. There is a kindness in him still.*

Q'arlynd bristled. They seemed to be implying that he was the equivalent of a surface elf, soft and weak. Not a true drow at all.

Your skin may be black, but you're no dhaerow, the female said. She gave the word its original meaning: traitor. *A spark of moonlight flickers within your heart. The* dhaerow *did their best to extinguish it, but it dances there still.*

That sounded just like something Qilué had once said.

"Enough about me," Q'arlynd said. "Now, about those spells . . ."

When you're ready. After a century or two of study, perhaps.

"Surely I don't need to wait so long! Aren't you forgetting something? I already cast high magic, once before."

When Eilistraee willed it, yes.

Q'arlynd clutched at that straw. "Well, doesn't she will it again? If Kiaransalee's Crones aren't defeated, *Faerzress* throughout the Underdark will become as potent as it was at the time of the Descent. Your descendants are going to be trapped, just as you were. Aryvandaar will *win*."

Righteous anger hit him like a physical blow. He reeled. Then a wordless song eclipsed the angry voices. So beautiful was it that Q'arlynd's eyes welled with tears. A memory flooded his mind: Halisstra, singing to him, healing him, that time he lay unconscious after the riding accident.

Halisstra had used *bae'qeshel* magic, rather than Eilistraee's hymn, but she had saved him just the same. Maybe the goddess had been watching over him even then, using Halisstra as a conduit to . . .

"That's it!" he gasped. He turned his attention to the spot where the chorus had come from. By concentrating intently, he could see a crowd. Dozens of people.

"Are you all mages?" he asked.

Mages, priestesses, warriors—for nearly three millennia the matrons and patrons of our House wore this lorestone.

"And the other *kiira* you spoke of—do they all contain the combined wisdom of mages and clerics as well?"

Of course.

"And each *kiira* is capable of casting the spell that stripped my memories when I wore the wrong lorestone?"

Yes.

Q'arlynd laughed with delight. "Then we still have a chance. Listen."

Swiftly, he outlined his idea.

That may be possible, the lorestone said when he was done. *With Eilistraee's blessing. I know that it is possible to hand you the sword you seek. As to whether you can wield it . . .*

"We have to at least try."

Yes.

As the voices of his ancestors faded, Q'arlynd became aware of his surroundings once more. Eldrinn was watching him intently, his eyes gleaming.

"We've got work ahead," Q'arlynd told him with a grim smile. "Kiaransalee is about to get a taste of her own poison."

Cavatina gasped as her awareness returned to her body. A moment ago, she'd been drifting toward Eilistraee's sacred grove, weaving her way through the moonstone-hung boughs, her spirit dancing in time with a song whose beauty made her weep. Now she lay on her back on a cold stone floor, her throat tight and sore. Eilistraee's song had vanished, replaced by a ghastly wailing and the muffled rattle of bones.

A male bent over her, one hand resting lightly just above her left breast.

And she was naked.

"Kâras," she growled. She was halfway to her feet, fists raised to fend him off, when she realized what he must have done. She lowered her hands and turned her motion into a bow. A little less gracefully than she would have liked, but a bow nonetheless. "You healed me?"

He nodded.

"Thank you."

Cavatina glanced around. They were in a small, cell-like chamber with stone walls and a single exit. The door was closed and barred with what looked like a femur. The walls bore ghastly murals, painted with what looked like dried blood. Shifting shadows screened the worst of it—Kâras's doing, no doubt.

There was no point in asking what had happened. Cavatina remembered all too well the feel of the ghost's dagger plunging into her neck. "Where are we?" she asked, rubbing her throat.

"A distant corner of the Acropolis," Kâras said in a low, cautious voice. "A chamber, now hallowed by the Masked Lady. But my prayer won't hold the Crones at bay for long. Even Cabrath—the spirit you slew—will rejuvenate eventually."

Cavatina's eyebrows rose. "You *knew* her?"

"I knew *of* her, when she was still alive. She was one of Kiaransalee's priestesses, back in Maerimydra. A mortal, then."

Cavatina let that go. She glanced around but didn't see her singing sword. "What about Leliana and the other Protectors?"

"Dead. I'm the only one who still lives. Even disguised, I could drag only one of you away." He pulled a small, silvered sword, hanging from a broken chain, out of his pocket. Her holy symbol. "I managed to retrieve this."

Cavatina took it. She held it to her chest and whispered a heartfelt prayer of thanks. "I'm surprised that . . ." She stopped herself just in time. She'd been about to question why he hadn't just skulked away from the Acropolis and saved himself—that would have been more in keeping for a Nightshadow, after all—then realized there was no point in stirring up old arguments.

He guessed her intent, despite her silence. "The Masked Lady commands, I obey."

Cavatina nodded her approval. He had a sense of duty. Perhaps she'd been wrong about the Nightshadows, after all. She'd learned a lot, in recent days.

"What do you suggest we do now?"

Kâras seemed surprised she'd asked his advice. His eyes narrowed, as though he expected a trick. Then he shrugged. "We're outnumbered, probably a hundred to one. And that's just counting the Crones, all of whom will rise as revenants shortly after we kill them, if we don't take the time to permanently lay them to rest."

Cavatina tightened her grip on her holy symbol. "Then we'll make sure we do just that."

Kâras shook his head. "There isn't time. The Crones are doing something with a voidstone. Something terrible."

From somewhere outside the room came a series of sharp cracks, followed by the sound of falling rubble. The ground trembled under Cavatina's feet. She heard a hail of thuds on the roof. White dust drifted down from the rafters, gritty as powdered bone.

Cavatina shook it from her hair. "Have you contacted Qilué?"

"She's not answering."

If it were true, it didn't bode well. Cavatina concentrated on the high priestess's face and said in an urgent voice, "Qilué?"

No reply came.

Kâras gave her a flat, I-told-you-so stare.

"All right, then," Cavatina pushed that worry aside. It helped that she'd had a taste of what lay ahead. She wasn't afraid to die. Not anymore. "We'll carry the battle forward on our own. Do what we can to stop . . . whatever it is the Crones are up to."

She wound the chain of her holy symbol around her wrist and secured it. Then she glanced down at Kâras. "Before we begin, I'll need you to disguise me." She smiled grimly. "Let's just hope I do as good a job of impersonating a Crone as you did at feigning paralysis, that time the revenant attacked us."

The corners of Kâras's eyes slowly crinkled. He touched fingers to his mask and cast his spell.

As a gray robe cloaked her body and silver rings appeared on her fingers, Cavatina shuddered. She could feel her holy symbol against her wrist but couldn't see it. "Masked Lady," she whispered. "Forgive me this blasphemy."

She sensed Eilistraee's approval. Or, at least, her recognition that this was necessary.

Kâras, also disguised as a Crone, eased open the door. Together, they crept outside.

The main part of the temple lay just around the corner. As soon as they rounded it, Cavatina's hopes sank. The flat space ahead was packed with Crones. They stood, side by side, chanting and waving ring-bedecked hands. In front of them was what remained of Kiaransalee's chief temple, reduced to rubble. Hovering above was a sphere of utter darkness: the voidstone Kâras had spoken of earlier. Drifting above it, leading the Crones in prayer, was the spirit Cavatina thought she had slain.

Cavatina was shocked. It should have taken days for the ghost to rejuvenate. The voidstone must have accelerated the process.

Even as Cavatina and Kâras watched, the sphere of blackness expanded. Within the voidstone, Cavatina saw shapes: a vast army of undead, jostling one another and prodding at the sphere from within. At the front of their ranks stood an enormous, undead minotaur, eyes blazing with unholy fire.

Fire that matched the *Faerzress* pulsing through the stone below.

Cavatina glanced at Kâras. His illusionary face betrayed the grimness he felt. Cavatina could see the lack of hope in his eyes.

She feigned an optimism she didn't fee. "The spirit," she breathed. "We need to destroy her. What could permanently lay Cabrath to rest?"

"Only one thing," Kâras whispered back.

Hope sparked to life in Cavatina. "What's that?"

"Killing Kiaransalee."

Cavatina laughed bitterly. With the Crescent Blade in hand, she might have been able to do just that. But that weapon was back at the Promenade, in Qilué's keeping. Cavatina was unarmed.

"Let's do what we can."

Kâras nodded.

Side by side, they shouldered their way into the chanting throng.

Q'arlynd handed a *kiira* to each of his apprentices. Baltak, eyes glittering greedily, clenched his fist around the stone. Alexa peered into the depths of her gemstone as if trying to assess its worth—or perhaps its mineral content. Zarifar closed his eyes and rolled his back and forth between his palms in a series of short jerks, turning the hexagonal crystal one facet at a time, his lips silently counting.

Eldrinn stared warily at the *kiira* he'd been handed. "Is it going to feeblemind me?"

"It might," Q'arlynd answered truthfully. The boy was only a half-drow, after all.

Alexa and Baltak glanced up sharply.

Q'arlynd raised a hand. "This isn't a time for lies. Too much is at stake. None of you belong to a House that matches what you hold. Yet the lorestones have agreed to impart the ability to work *arselu'tel'quess*. When our casting is done, they'll erase all knowledge of the spell from your minds. That might feeblemind you—or it might not. But even if it does," he said as he touched the *kiira* on his own forehead, "I've mastered this lorestone. I'll still have my wits about me, and will see to it that yours are restored."

Baltak stared a challenge at him. "I can see what Eldrinn gets out of it, saving his college from ruin, but what about the rest of us?"

Q'arlynd raised an eyebrow. "Casting high magic doesn't appeal to you?"

"Not if I can't remember how to do it afterward," Baltak snorted. His eyes strayed to Piri's corpse. "How do we know you won't kill us, too, once we're feebleminded?"

Alexa snorted. "Don't be stupid, Baltak. If he'd wanted to do that, he would have blasted us while we were still held by his spell."

The transmogrifist continued to stare at Q'arlynd. "No he wouldn't. If he had, we wouldn't have been around to cast his spell for him."

"Enough!" Q'arlynd snapped. "Can't you see what's happening?" He waved a hand at the walls. The *Faerzress* that infused them had brightened noticeably even in the short time it had taken to explain to his apprentices what he'd planned. It glowed with a steady, blue-green light.

"The *Faerzress* is increasing in power by leaps and bounds. We have no idea what other ill effects that may cause. Divination and teleportation may only be the first of several strains of magic to be denied the drow. I know it's difficult, but you've got to trust in the *kiira*—and in me. And in the school we're going to build together. You've come with me this far. Trusted me. Why stop now?"

He strode over to the dead wizard and touched a lorestone to Piri's forehead. It instantly adhered. As Q'arlynd's *kiira* had promised, Piri was restored to life. The demon-skinned apprentice sat up slowly, his eyes staring straight ahead.

Q'arlynd turned to the others, rubbing his left arm. It still tingled from the poison. "It was a struggle, convincing my ancestors that we needed Piri, but they saw the wisdom in letting him participate. For our spell, we need a sixth caster."

"A sixth body, you mean," Baltak grumbled. "Look at him; he's no better than a walking corpse. The *kiira*'s in control."

"Piri will be restored to full awareness once we're done," Q'arlynd said. He bent down and returned the ring to Piri's finger. "The *kiira* promised it."

"What if it's lying?" Baltak countered. "What if *you're* lying?"

Q'arlynd returned Baltak's stare. "Join minds with me. Look deep into my thoughts. Search for hidden motivations, hidden treachery. All of you, take a good, long look. And once you're satisfied, perhaps we'll get this done."

The instant Q'arlynd dropped his mental defenses, Baltak barged in. Alexa and Eldrinn joined their minds with Q'arlynd's more tentatively. Zarifar drifted in last, his mind busy tracing the pattern their respective bodies formed. A hexagon, made up of Q'arlynd, the four apprentices who were not yet wearing *kiira*, and Piri, who was.

For several moments, Q'arlynd felt his four apprentices rummaging through his secrets. Allowing this was difficult, the equivalent of permitting a hunting lizard to slowly run its tongue along one's exposed flesh. When they discovered the memories of the additional spells he'd ensorcelled their rings with, he sensed their blunt anger. He also heard their mental nods as they learned that the "trade mission" he and Eldrinn had been on was a ruse—being drow, they'd anticipated the lie—as well as their surprise when they learned of the priestesses' mission to the Acropolis of Thanatos. He could all but feel their eyebrows rising as they learned of Q'arlynd's admission into the ranks of Eilistraee's faithful, and their glee at learning some of the secrets of that forbidden faith. He also felt their sharp indignation at the revelation that the *kiira* were going to use their bodies—that the five apprentices would, at best, be conduits for the high magic they were about to cast.

But they also, as they probed even deeper into Q'arlynd's thoughts and memories, saw the dreams his mind contained. Dreams of founding something that was truly a unity of purpose, of will. Not the resurrection of a noble drow House, but the creation of something new. A union that would transcend the colleges and Houses from which they had each come.

"Well?" Q'arlynd breathed. He asked the question both with his voice and with his heart.

Eldrinn lifted his *kiira*. "I'm convinced."

"As am I," Alexa said quickly.

Zarifar opened his eyes and silently nodded.

"Right," Baltak said. He tried to step in front of the other apprentices, to take charge, but Q'arlynd placed a hand on his shoulder, restraining him. Baltak, for once, relented.

"On my three-count," Q'arlynd said. "And be sure to keep your minds linked with mine. One . . . two . . . three!"

As the others pressed their lorestones against their foreheads, Q'arlynd felt the awarenesses that were the other five *kiira* join them. Each of the apprentices reacted as he'd expected: Baltak with a mental grapple, Alexa with tentative experimentation, Zarifar with a dreamy acceptance, and Eldrinn with cautious curiosity. An instant later, each succumbed as the *kiira* took hold. The lorestones spoke to one another through the linkage of the rings the six of them wore.

The combined awarenesses of Q'arlynd and the *kiira* he wore answered them.

It is time. Begin.

Together, they wove a spell. Guided by the *kiira*, the six drow in unison spoke the words to an enchantment. As the spell waxed, the *Faerzress* brightened. Through Q'arlynd had to squint against its glare, he forced himself to keep staring at it. The *Faerzress* was their link to Kiaransalee's minions, to the undead that drew their power from its negative energy, to the Crones who venerated and created those abominations—to the Goddess of Death herself.

From each and every one of those minds, something was about to be erased. Not a memory, but a single word.

In a roundabout way, the inspiration for the enchantment had come from Kiaransalee herself. When Q'arlynd had heard Leliana's story about Kiaransalee erasing Orcus's name from shrines and temples the length and breadth of

Faerûn, he'd accepted the story at face value. The goddess must have acted out of simple vanity, he surmised. Ever the conquering queen, she wanted to obliterate all evidence of one who had ruled before her.

Q'arlynd had come to realize the deeper implications. All deities needed worshipers to survive. Without a steady stream of the faithful praying to them on Toril and later entering their domains after death, the gods and goddesses would slowly fade away.

What better way to end Kiaransalee's worship than by erasing her name from every worshiper's mind? Even from the mind of the very goddess herself.

Q'arlynd slapped a hand against the wall. "Kiaransalee!" he cried.

His spell rippled outward through the *Faerzress*. Like fire through dry kindling, it burned the minds of Kiaransalee's faithful. It arced through the Negative Energy Plane, streaking like a bolt of lightning through that vast void and exploding out into the corner of the Demonweb Pits that was Kiaransalee's domain.

Q'arlynd heard a tumultuous cry—thousands of voices, shrieking. Abruptly, they choked off into silence.

The silence of the grave.

It is done.

He bowed in thanks. When he rose, he saw that the *Faerzress* which filled the corridor was muted. Yet it was still there.

His eyes widened in alarm. "Did we fail?"

We succeeded. We halted the progression of the Faerzress. But even high magic can't turn back time.

Q'arlynd nodded, exhausted. He wondered how Sshamath fared. Was divination magic still possible there? Would the College of Divination teeter and eventually fall? If it did, Q'arlynd would be right back where he'd started, without a master to nominate his school.

At least he still had the *kiira*.

His apprentices stood next to him, glassy-eyed. In unison, they began to move. Stiff as golems, they removed the lorestones from their foreheads, traced the House glyph of their *kiira* on Kraanfhaor's Door, and pressed the lorestone against it. The door drew them into itself and its stone smoothed over, leaving no trace of their entry.

Like humans suddenly awakened from sleep, Q'arlynd's apprentices shook their heads and stared wonderingly around. For several moments, each wore an expression as vacant as Zarifar's.

Then Baltak put his hands on his hips. "Where in the Abyss are we? And what's that thing on your forehead?"

Q'arlynd smiled wearily. "That's a long story. When we return to Sshamath, I'll tell it to you."

CHAPTER 14

Close enough, Cavatina signed.

They halted near the front of the crowd. The Crones pressed tightly on all sides. The sphere of voidstone hung only a few paces ahead of them, looming as large as the temple had once been. Waves of negative energy crackled from it, chilling the air. The *Faezress* underfoot brightened with each pulse. The spirit floated above the voidstone, hands raised, leading the chanting in a mournful moan.

Beside Cavatina, the disguised Kâras raised his arms and mouthed in time with the chant. Cavatina did the same. Odd, that it was a Nightshadow she'd wind up making her final stand with. And yet, somehow, appropriate.

She caught Kâras's eye and flicked a hand. *Now.*

"Eilistraee!" Cavatina sang out, letting her disguise fall away.

The nearest Crones spun to face her, their faces twisted with rage.

Beside her, Kâras plunged his dagger into a Crone and touched Cavatina's arm. Energy flowed into her, augmenting her prayer.

"By my song, lay these foul abominations forever to rest!" Cavatina sang, even as the Crones leaped at her, their curved fingers raking wounds into her flesh that instantly festered. Beside her, Kâras slashed desperately with his dagger, trying to take down as many as he could.

In answer to her prayer, moonlight streaked with shadow erupted from the holy symbol clenched in Cavatina's fist. It spread through the ranks of the Crones in a flood. Several of the closest Crones collapsed as it washed clean the death magic that had animated them. Others—those who hadn't yet embraced undeath—continued their attack. Cavatina went down under their scrabbling hands and lost sight of Kâras. But she caught a glimpse of the spirit as the pool of moonlight and shadow she'd summoned struck it. The ghost twisted, wailing, as Eilistraee's holy song tore at its substance.

Then the spell ended.

The spirit remained.

The ghost threw back its head. Its chest swelled. As it exhaled, a ghastly keening began.

"Eilistraee!" Cavatina cried. "Lend me your—"

The keening struck Cavatina like a clapper hitting a bell, sending her body into violent convulsions that choked off her prayer. The Crones, meanwhile, bore down on Cavatina. Their hooked fingers tore open her hand, and her holy symbol fell to the ground. The Crones nearest it reeled away from it, wailing, but others leaped onto Cavatina, knocking her down. Her chin cracked against stone and she tasted blood. Each new laceration was a sharp slash of pain. She struggled to rise but could not. She glanced left, and saw Kâras a pace or two away, no longer disguised as a Crone. He lay in a pool of blood, his flesh scored by dozens of wounds. He wasn't moving.

Cavatina felt cold—the chill of the grave. Barely conscious, she strove to choke out her goddess's name through chattering teeth. "Eil . . . is . . . tr—"

The ghost loomed before her. "You have lost," she hissed, her whisper somehow carrying clearly above the enraged cries of the Crones. "When we are done with you, not a scrap of your soul will remain." She drew back, cackling. A sweeping gesture took in both Cavatina and Kâras—and sphere of voidstone. "Throw them into it."

Echoing their head priestess's laughter, the Crones hoisted Cavatina and Kâras into the air. Twice, they nearly dropped Cavatina. She was awash in her own blood, her body almost too slippery to hold. With the last of her strength, Cavatina fought to lift her head, to face her doom bravely. There was no use commending her soul to Eilistraee; in another moment it would all be over. As the Crones bore her to the crumbling lip of stone surrounding the voidstone sphere, Cavatina uttered one final, whispered prayer.

"Eilistraee. Don't let it end like this. Please."

"Now!" the spirit cried.

The Crones swung Cavatina backward, preparing to toss her toward the voidstone sphere. But half of them collapsed, going from undeath to death in a blink. Those who remained—the living—struggled to hold Cavatina aloft, but weren't strong enough. They dropped her and stumbled away, as if they'd given up on killing her.

A skull smashed down into the stone a couple of paces away from Cavatina. Then another. She twisted around and spotted Kâras, also lying on the ground. Skulls tumbled from the ceiling above, smashing to pieces all around him.

With the last of her flagging strength, Cavatina forced herself off the ground, one arm raised above her head to fend off the falling skulls. Something had just happened—but what? She looked wearily around, blinking the blood from her eyes.

The spirit was gone.

The Crones milled about, not paying the slightest attention to Cavatina and Kâras. A moment earlier, they had been purposeful and grim, but they grew confused confused. They stared at each other, at the corpses of the undead Crones who had fallen, at the silver rings on their own fingers, perplexed looks on their faces. One of them—a Crone who had been holding Cavatina aloft just moments ago—glanced down at Cavatina with a frown, as if trying to remember who she was.

Cavatina struggled to her feet. The possibility occurred to her that whatever had just happened might be the work of Qilué. Had the Crescent Blade claimed a second deity? Was *that* why the high priestess hadn't answered her summons a short time ago—because she'd been preparing to slay . . .

She paused, uncertain. What was the name of that goddess again?

Cavatina glanced around at the milling, gray-robed females. She remembered what they called themselves—Crones—and that they served a goddess of death. But try as she might, Cavatina couldn't remember that goddess's name.

A skull slammed into Cavatina's shoulder, nearly knocking her to the ground. She staggered to her holy symbol and fell to her knees beside it. One hand pressing against the miniature sword, she prayed.

"Eilistraee," she said through thickened lips. "Heal me."

Eilistraee's grace flowed into Cavatina. Her wounds closed. She was not as strong as she might be, but at least she could stand. She dragged Kâras into the lee of a nearby wall, out of the rain of skulls. Then she swung around to face the voidstone.

The sphere still hung above the ruined temple, but it was no longer expanding. The skulls that struck it vanished, instantly obliterated. The undead legions inside the sphere shouted and pounded against its walls, but could not escape. All the while, the Crones milled about between the fallen undead like club-stunned rothé. Shuffling. Uncertain. A handful of those that still lived were down, knocked to the ground by the rain of falling skulls. For several moments more, the ghastly rain continued. When it at last ended, a dirgelike moan filled the air. The Crones, mourning.

The crowd had thinned enough so that Cavatina could see the bodies of the fallen Protectors, and the wizards Daffir and Gilkriz. Leliana lay among them, too, her singing sword beside her.

Cavatina walked to it and picked it up.

As she raised it, the weapon sang out a strident peal. To Eilistraee. To victory.

"Qilué!" she called.

A moment later, the high priestesses's mind touched hers. *Cavatina! Where are you?*

Swiftly, Cavatina described what had just happened. "Lady Qilué, was it your doing?"

No. I wasn't the one who killed . . . her.

Cavatina noted the hesitation in Qilué's mental voice. "What happened, then?"

I can't answer that. But now is the moment to strike. We need to deal with the surviving Crones—swiftly—before the effect is undone.

Cavatina glanced around at the milling Crones. Their faces, no longer contorted with the madness of their faith, looked lost, tired, and sad. One of them touched Cavatina's arm and looked pleadingly into her eyes, as if seeking an answer to a question she didn't know how to ask.

Cavatina shrugged her off. "Should we offer them redemption?" she asked Qilué. "There may be some who—"

Qilué's mental voice lashed out like a whip. *No. Kill them.*

"But—"

Eilistraee demands their deaths. They cannot be redeemed. Kill them.

Cavatina lifted her weapon. That had been an order. And a Darksong Knight did as her high priestess commanded. Cavatina told herself that the Crones had sown the seeds of their own destruction by choosing to worship . . . whatever evil goddess had just been slain. Cavatina was merely the scythe that fulfilled that grim harvest.

Lips pressed together in a grim line, she swung her weapon. Right, left, cutting down Crones. Easy as reaping wheat.

The remaining Crones didn't even put up a fight. Sword blow by sword blow, they fell.

Cavatina led fully three dozen priestesses—reinforcements from the Promenade—in song. They stood in a wide circle around the shattered ruin that had been Kiaransalee's temple, swords pointed at the voidstone. As they sang, healing energy flowed up their blades and across the space between their metal and the sphere. Brighter even than a full moon, the raw positive energy spun the voidstone around, grinding it down like a pebble in a stream.

Eight Nightshadows worked with the priestesses. They were less skilled in summoning the healing energies of the Prime Material Plane, but they had a role nonetheless. Their chant—whispered from behind their masks—would ensure that after the voidstone had been destroyed, any link with the Negative Energy Plane would be sealed.

Elsewhere on the island, other Protectors chased down the few undead that had survived Kiaransalee's fall. As for those priestesses and Nightshadows who had fallen in the earlier battles, their bodies were even then being carried back to the Moondeep Sea. They would be returned to the

Promenade and resurrected, Eilistraee willing. So too would Daffir and Gilkriz, if possible. If not, their bodies would be returned to Sshamath for burial. The same would hold true for Mazeer, once her body was found.

Kâras was healed. He stood to Cavatina's immediate right. It no longer galled her to see a Nightshadow participating in one of Eilistraee's sacred rituals. Since her redemption, that anger had dissipated. She understood, then, how a Nightshadow might feel after carrying out an assassination: exactly as Cavatina had felt after Qilué ordered her to kill the remaining Crones.

The voidstone shrank to the size of a boulder, a melon, a fist, a pea. Then, with a boom that was swallowed the instant it sounded, it disappeared. The priestesses lowered their swords and fell silent, and the Nightshadows dropped their hands.

"Lady Qilué," Cavatina called. "It is done. The voidstone is destroyed. But . . ." She glanced down at her feet and saw that the stone still glowed as brightly as before. "But the *Faerzress* hasn't diminished."

I can see that.

"It's reached the Promenade?"

It has.

"Lady, should we try to—?"

Nothing more can be done. Return to the Promenade.

And that was it. The entirety of the high priestess's message. No praise for what Cavatina and her expedition had accomplished, no further comment. Just that curt order.

"Is something wrong?" Kâras asked.

Cavatina realized she was letting her worry show. "I don't know. Lady Qilué didn't seem . . ." She closed her mouth, declining to say more. Kâras had proven himself, but confiding her fears to him didn't feel appropriate, even though he shared her command. "We're done here. We're to return to the Promenade—promptly. Qilué probably has another mission for us."

"The Masked Lady's will be done," Kâras murmured. His eyes, however, didn't match his tone. There was a gleam to them that made Cavatina wary.

He started to turn away, but Cavatina planted herself in his path. "What is it, Kâras?" she demanded. "What are you thinking?"

He hesitated. Then shrugged. "Only that Lady Qilué is growing more like a Nightshadow each day. She's playing her *sava* pieces very close to her chest. I find that . . . amusing."

Cavatina took a deep breath. Kâras was up to his old tricks again. Trying to provoke her into an argument. "I don't," she answered flatly. "But it's the way things are now. We're all going to have to get used to it. Make the best of our new partners and continue the dance as best we can."

Kâras's eyebrows rose slightly. "Out of the light, into the shadows—back and forth, as the Masked Lady wills it."

"Yes."

Their eyes met, locked, then, as if at some unspoken command, both turned away.

Q'arlynd strode into the dining hall, surprised that Seldszar had agreed to meet with him at a time that would interrupt the master's supper. Judging by the extra place that had been laid at the table, Seldszar was expecting someone else to join him. Q'arlynd would have to come quickly to the point before that person arrived.

The elder wizard set down his fork and stared up at Q'arlynd through the crystal spheres that orbited his head. If he noted the invisible *kiira* affixed to Q'arlynd's forehead, he gave no sign. "You wanted to speak to me?"

Q'arlynd bowed. "I wanted to compliment you, Master Seldszar, on solving the problem of the faerie fire."

Master Seldszar frowned. "There is work yet to be done. The *Faerzress* that has sprung up outside our city presents new challenges."

"Indeed. But at least the effect is no longer increasing. The 'scouting expedition' put an end to that."

"So it did." The frown deepened. "Unfortunately, not before the College of Divination was greatly weakened."

Q'arlynd carefully hid his flinch. He did his best not to think about having abandoned the mission. "Ours wasn't the only college to suffer," he pointed out. "The College of Conjuration and Summoning also faces challenges. Its master is being held responsible for the fact that teleportation in and out of the city is no longer possible."

"That's true. But you didn't come here to tell me what I already know."

Q'arlynd bowed his head in agreement. "I understand you and Master Urlryn are working together on your mutual problem? Trying to find a way to break the link between drow and *Faerzress?*"

Master Seldszar's eyebrows rose. "You've been making enquiries. Either that or your scrying skills have improved."

"The former," Q'arlynd said. "A source within the College of Conjuration and Summoning."

"My son's consort?"

Q'arlynd smiled.

"You didn't come here to tell me that, either. Please come to the point."

Q'arlynd glanced at the bottle of fungus wine that stood on the massive dining table, wishing he could wet his lips with it. He took a deep breath, instead. "What if I were to tell you I've been speaking with dark elves from the distant past—from the time of ancient Miyeritar? With those who have first-hand knowledge of how the link between dark elves and *Faerzress* was forged, and who want to see it undone?"

Master Seldszar was no longer even glancing at his spheres. "I'd listen. Very carefully." He gestured at the seat across the table from him. "Sit. Pour yourself some wine."

Q'arlynd did as instructed. He took a polite sip of the wine, then set his goblet down. "You've noted the *kiira* on my forehead?"

"The moment you walked into the dining hall." Seldszar's eyes glittered. He leaned forward and spoke in a low voice. "I thank you for recovering it."

Q'arlynd refused to be intimidated.

"It can be worn only by a descendant of House Melarn," he warned Seldszar. "Since the fall of Ched Nasad, there is only one surviving member of that House. Me. If anyone else were to wear this *kiira*, they'd wind up as Eldrinn did, that time I fetched him home from the High Moor. A drooling idiot." Q'arlynd cocked his head. "Hardly a fit state for the master of a college, wouldn't you say?"

Master Seldszar leaned back in his chair, his eyes locked on Q'arlynd's. "What do you want?"

"I've founded a school. I want it recognized as a college. I want a seat on the Conclave. To achieve that, I'm going to need a nomination from a master. From you."

"And if I refuse?"

Q'arlynd shrugged. "Then I'll speak to Master Urlryn instead."

Seldszar laughed, startling Q'arlynd.

"You wonder what I find so amusing," Seldszar said. "What if I were to tell *you* I'd already heard this conversation, once before?" He flicked a finger at his spheres. "That it was a little obscured by the sizzle of faerie fire, but that I'd gotten the gist of it, just the same. That I gave my staff of divination to Daffir not because I thought he might need it, but because I knew *you'd* need it. That I knew there was a *selu'kiira* waiting within Kraanfhaor's Door that I might claim, myself, once you've shown me how. What would you say then?"

Q'arlynd raised his eyebrows. "I'd say the alliance between our respective colleges appears to be a foregone conclusion."

Master Seldszar smiled and raised his goblet. "Are you still planning on calling yours the College of Ancient Arcana?"

"How did you know that? Did Eldrinn . . ." Q'arlynd realized what a foolish question that was, and laughed. He clinked his goblet against Seldszar's. "To alliances."

CODA

Kiaransalee's dust-dry face creaked as she grimaced. She glared down at the masked Priestess piece Eilistraee had just moved. "You think you can flank me?" she cackled. "Think again."

With a shove of a bony hand, she pushed one of her own Priestess pieces forward to block the move. The piece wavered as she released it, twisting like a wisp of smoke. It looked as though a breath might blow it apart. And yet Eilistraee could sense, even from a distance, that it contained a will as solid and unshakeable as stone.

Swiftly, Kiaransalee moved a second piece—a smaller Priestess, sculpted from putrid gray flesh—into a flanking position. Then she sat back on the marble tombstone that served as her chair, her bony, ring-bedecked fingers resting on her knees. She stared smugly at Lolth, gesturing at the piece she'd just blocked. "Your move. If your demon-Warrior attacks her other Priestess, she won't be able to counter it without losing this one."

Lolth made no comment. She waved a hand above the *sava* board, using the webs that trailed from it to brush away the mold that had fallen from Kiaransalee's tattered robe. As Lolth's hand moved toward her demonic Warrior piece, Kiaransalee cackled in anticipation. When Lolth instead picked up the Priestess piece with the spider legs protruding from its chest, and moved it to flank the pieces Kiaransalee had moved, the lichlike goddess's yellowed teeth snapped shut.

"What are you doing?" Kiaransalee cried. A withered finger stabbed at Eilistraee's Priestess piece, rocking it slightly. "You've just given that piece an escape!"

"How cunning of you, Kiaransalee, to point out the perfectly obvious," Lolth said. One white eyebrow arched. "And how stupid of you to think I would play on your side."

Eilistraee too was startled by Lolth's move. She searched for a trap in it, but saw none. Her Priestess piece could easily take Lolth's Warrior piece. Was this what Lolth had intended? Did the Spider Queen mean to deliberately sacrifice it, just as she had done with Selvetarm?

"Your move, daughter," Lolth said, leaning forward on her black iron throne. "We're waiting."

Eilistraee refused to be hurried. She scanned the board carefully, trying to decide if Lolth's move had been a feint. It didn't appear to be—and the opportunity it opened up was too good to ignore. She picked up her Priestess piece and moved it into the space the bat-winged piece occupied. "Priestess takes Warrior."

She lifted Lolth's piece from the board—and gasped as the heat of it seared her fingers. She dropped it. The Warrior piece tumbled toward the *sava* board, bat wings fluttering raggedly. An instant before it struck the board it erupted into a ball of flame. Consumed. Gone. Not so much as a speck of ash remained.

Eilistraee stared, astonished. The Warrior piece had not *allowed* her to set it to the side of the board, but had instead removed itself from the game. She'd underestimated its power. It was nearly equal to that of Lolth's Mother piece.

Was that why Lolth had sacrificed it?

Lolth toyed with a strand of web-tangled hair and watched Eilistraee, waiting for a reaction. Kiaransalee merely stared, her empty eyesockets revealing nothing. Eilistraee's fingertips still burned from the Warrior piece's touch, but the mask she wore hid the worried pinch of her lips. She placed her burned hand on one of the trees next to her, as if casually leaning upon it. A surreptitious brush of her fingertips against one of its moonstone fruits healed her fingertips. A slight red mark remained, however, on her wrist, where the base of the Warrior piece had touched it.

That was troubling. But there was still a game to be played.

A series of moves followed. Kiaransalee shoved her two Priestess pieces toward the piece Lolth had just moved, forcing it to retreat across the board. Eilistraee moved a Priestess piece forward, saw it taken by those Kiaransalee wielded. Lolth played a waiting game while Kiaransalee advanced. Eilistraee was forced to the defensive. Back and forth, the pieces moved across the *sava* board. Several of Eilistraee's Priestess pieces fell.

At long last, Kiaransalee made the move Eilistraee had been waiting for. The undead goddess moved a lesser Priestess piece out of the way, then pushed her Mother piece forward. From its new position, the Mother piece was poised to capture either the Priestess that had taken Lolth's demonic Warrior earlier, or the masked Priestess that had been the first of Eilistraee's pieces to move into Kiaransalee's House. If either of these pieces fell, it would open a path to the heart of Eilistraee's House.

The Goddess of Death gave a low chuckle, dry as dust. Her bones creaked as she sat smugly back on her tombstone. "Your move, Eilistraee," she said gloatingly. "Your *last* move."

Lolth nodded approvingly. "What a cunning web you've woven, Kiaransalee," she said in a voice as dry as Kiaransalee's own. "I can't see a single thing Eilistraee can do to counter it."

Kiaransalee missed the sarcasm. Eilistraee didn't. She saw the rise of her mother's eyebrow, the slight nod of her head.

"I make my own choices," Eilistraee told her coldly.

"That may be," Lolth smirked. "But you follow my lead. You always have, ever since Arvandor."

"Sacrifices are necessary, if the drow are to be saved."

During this exchange, Kiaransalee's expression sharpened. She leaned forward, her wrinkled forehead creasing in a tight frown. She turned her head back and forth, hollow eyesockets searching the board.

Eilistraee had to make her move. Now. Before the Goddess of Death spotted what was coming and found some new way to cheat.

Eilistraee scooped up the Wizard piece that had been standing at the very edge of the board and moved it. Swiftly, to the very heart of Kiaransalee's House. "Wizard takes Mother!" she sang, her voice a victory peal.

"No!" Kiaransalee rocked forward, her bony hands scrabbling at the board. She grabbed a Priestess piece, but it turned to mist that drifted away through her hands. She snatched at another piece, which likewise vanished. She tried desperately to move one piece after another, but they would no longer obey her commands.

"No!" she cried again, a long, fading wail. Her body began to crumple in on itself, curling and flaking apart like a rotting leaf.

"Yes," Eilistraee said firmly. She leaned forward and scooped Kiaransalee's Mother piece from the board. As the

Goddess of Death shrank to a tiny, forlorn pile of tattered skin flakes, the Mother piece turned to ash in Eilistraee's hand. Eilistraee turned her hand palm-up, lifted her mask, and blew the ash away.

Kiaransalee was gone. Her domain lingered a moment longer. Then its tombstones cracked and crumbled, its graves sagged in and became empty hollows. As it disappeared, the domains of Eilistraee and Lolth came together to fill the gap. A single silver ring that had fallen from Kiaransalee's fingers rolled across the *sava* board, grew increasingly tarnished, then fell onto its side. Lolth leaned forward and touched it, and it crumbled to dust.

Once again, there were only two players. Mother and daughter, malice and mercy, darkness and moonlight— shadow-streaked moonlight from a moon half-waned, but moonlight, just the same.

Eilistraee stared at Lolth across the *sava* board.

"Your move."

DRAMATIS PERSONAE

Eilistraee's Faithful

Q'ilué Veladorn (KIE-loo-ay VEL-a-dorn), one of the Seven Sisters, chosen of Eilistraee and Mystra, drow high priestess of the Promenade

Cavatina Xarann (cav-a-TEEN-a zar-ANN), Darksong Knight, drow priestess of Eilistraee

Leliana Vrinn (lell-lee-AH-nuh VRIN), drow priestess of Eilistraee, Protector of the Promenade, mother of Rowaan

Miverra (miv-AIR-uh), drow priestess of Eilistraee

Rowaan Vrinn (roe-WAHN VRIN), drow priestess of Eilistraee, head priestess of the Misty Forest shrine, daughter of Leliana

Brindell (BRIN-dell), halfling priestess of Eilistraee, Protector of the Promenade

Halav (hah-LAHV), drow priestess of Eilistraee, Protector of the Promenade

Tash'kla (TASH-kluh), drow priestess of Eilistraee, Protector of the Promenade

Chizra (CHIZ-ruh), drow priestess of Eilistraee, Protector of the Promenade

Zindira (zin-DEE-ruh), drow priestess of Eilistraee, Protector of the Promenade

Shoshara (show-SHAH-ruh), drow priestess of Eilistraee in the Shilmista Forest, aka the Forest of Shadows

Nightshadows

Valdar Jaerle (VAL-dar JARE-lay), drow cleric of Vhaeraun, one of four who opened the portal between the domains of Eilistraee and Vhaeraun

Kâras (kah-RASS), drow rogue and Black Moon cleric of the "Masked Lady," formerly of Maerimydra

Nar'bith (nar-BITH), drow cleric of the "Masked Lady"

Gindrol (JIN-drawl), drow cleric of the "Masked Lady"

Telmyz (tell-MEEZ), drow cleric of the "Masked Lady"

Talzir (tal-ZEER), drow cleric of the "Masked Lady"

Glorst, drow cleric of the "Masked Lady" in the Shilmista Forest, aka the Forest of Shadows

Kiaransalee's Cultists

Cabrath Nelinderra (ka-BRATH nel-in-DAIR-uh), keening spirit, priestess of Kiaransalee, head priestess of the Acropolis of Thanatos

Lolth's Minions

Halisstra Melarn (HAL-is-truh mel-ARN), sister of Q'arlynd Melarn, formerly a drow priestess of Lolth in Ched Nasad, later a priestess of Eilistraee, now Lolth's "Lady Penitent"

Wendonai (WEN-doe-nie), balor demon, corruptor of the Illythiri dark elves

Residents of Sshamath

Q'arlynd Melarn (KAR-lind mel-ARN), brother of Halisstra Melarn, battle wizard, formerly of Ched Nasad

Eldrinn Elpragh (EL-drin el-PRAG), drow wizard specializing in divination, son of Seldszar Elpragh

Piri (PEE-ree), drow wizard acolyte of the skin, apprentice of Q'arlynd Melarn

Baltak (BALL-tak), drow wizard, transmogrifist, apprentice of Q'arlynd Melarn

Zarifar (ZAR-ee-far), drow wizard, geometer, apprentice of Q'arlynd Melarn

Alexa (al-ECKS-uh), drow wizard specializing in conjuration, apprentice of Q'arlynd Melarn

Seldszar Elpragh (SELDS-zar el-PRAG), drow wizard, Master of the College of Divination, member of Sshamath's ruling Conclave, father of Eldrinn Elpragh

Khorl Krissellian (KORL kris-SELL-ee-un), sun elf sorcerer of the College of Divination

Daffir the Prescient (da-FEER), human wizard of the College of Divination

Urlryn Khalazza (URL-rinn ka-LAZ-zuh), drow wizard, Master of the College of Conjuration and Summoning, member of Sshamath's ruling Conclave

Gilkriz (GILL-kriz), drow wizard of the College of Conjuration and Summoning

Jyzrill (JIEZ-rill), drow wizard of the College of Conjuration and Summoning

Mazeer (mah-ZEER), drow wizard of the College of Conjuration and Summoning

Darbleth (DAR-bleth), duergar metal crafter

Klizik (KLIZ-ik), drow merchant, slave house proprietor

Other Folk

Laeral Silverhand (LARE-all), one of the Seven Sisters, chosen of Eilistraee and Mystra

Flinderspeld (flin-der-SPELLED), svirfneblin gem merchant, formerly Q'arlynd Melarn's slave

PHILIP ATHANS

The *New York Times* best-selling author of *Annihilation* and *Baldur's Gate* tells an epic tale of vision and heartbreak, of madness and ambition, that could change the map of Faerûn forever.

THE WATERCOURSE TRILOGY

BOOK I
WHISPER OF WAVES
The city-state of Innarlith sits on one edge of the Lake of Steam, just waiting for someone to drag it forward from obscurity. Will that someone be a Red Wizard of Thay, a street urchin who grew up to be the richest man in Innarlith, or a strange outsider who cares nothing for power but has grand ambitions all his own?

BOOK II
LIES OF LIGHT
A beautiful girl is haunted by spirits with dark intentions, an ambitious senator sells more than just his votes, and all the while construction proceeds on a canal that will alter the flow of trade in Faerûn.

BOOK III
SCREAM OF STONE
As the canal nears completion, scores will be settled, power will be bought and stolen, souls will be crushed and redeemed, and the power of one man's vision will be the only constant in a city-state gone mad.

"Once again it is Philip Athans moving the FORGOTTEN REALMS to new ground and new vibrancy."
—R.A. Salvatore

You cannot escape them, you cannot conquer them,
you can only hope to survive . . .

THE DUNGEONS

DEPTHS OF MADNESS
Erik Scott de Bie
Twilight awakes in the dungeon of a deranged wizard surrounded by strangers as
lost as she is. Twisted magic and deadly traps stand between her and escape, and
threaten to drive Twilight mad—if she lives long enough. . . .

THE HOWLING DELVE
Jaleigh Johnson
Meisha returns to find her former master insane, and sealed in his dungeon home
by Shadow Thieves. She must escape, but her survival isn't enough: she must also
rescue the mentor she left behind.

STARDEEP
Bruce R. Cordell
The seals that imprison an eldritch wizard within his prison are breaking
down, and the elves scramble to find the reason before the wizard's
nightmarish revolution begins.
November 2007

CRYPT OF THE MOANING DIAMOND
Rosemary Jones
When an avalanche of stone traps siegebreakers undermining the walls of a
captured city, their only hope lies deep within the tunnels. With water rising around
them, and an occupying army waiting above them, will they be able to escape alive?
December 2007